FOREWORD

I would just like to first say THANK YOU to everyone who has been patiently waiting for this book to come out. It feels like it's been a long time coming, and I'm so glad to finally get it out into all of my wonderful fans' hands!

The Witch Within is kind of like the "season finale" of the Witch Squad's first year at the Paranormal Institute for Witches. I think you're going to like the fact that it wraps up a lot of the ongoing storylines from season one, so that in "season two" we can start delving into some new storylines.

With that said, I do have one fun, shorter book planned. It's going to be about the girls on a little summer getaway. The lead in for that, you'll see, is at the end of this book. But after that, the next "season" starts with the girls as second year witches at the Institute!! So if you don't already get emails when my new books come out and you'd like to, you can sign up for my newsletter by clicking here. If you're already signed up, no need to do so again.

Once again, I'd just like to thank all of my AMAZING readers! Thank you to everyone who's left feedback on social media or who's left reviews. All of your positive energy and feedback has pushed me harder to keep moving and keep writing stories about these girls!! I appreciate each and every one of you!

XOXO
    M.Z.

THE WITCH WITHIN

A WITCH SQUAD COZY MYSTERY

M.Z. ANDREWS

MⱭA

The Witch Within
The Witch Squad Cozy Mystery Series: Book #8

by
M.Z. Andrews

Copyright © 2018 by M.Z. Andrews

ISBN-13: 978-1721068968
ISBN-10: 1721068961

"*B*ut, Mom!"

"I've made myself perfectly clear, Jaclyn-Rose. And you know how I feel about begging."

JaclynRose Stone, known to her friends as simply Jax, plumped out her bottom lip and stomped one striped witchy foot on the floor with her hands fisted by her sides. "But that's not fair!"

"This discussion is over. You may see yourself to the door."

With her brows lifted and her mouth agape, Jax plopped down into the chair in front of her mother's desk. "Uh! But, Mom, I don't want to go to normal college! It's not *my fault* Gran cursed me and our family!"

Sorceress SaraLynn Stone's frosty blue eyes snapped up off the papers she'd been grading, and she turned her glare onto her daughter. "Phyllis Habernackle is *not* your grandmother, JaclynRose, and I refuse to hear you call her as such."

Jax shrank in her seat. "Well, she's Mercy and Reign's

grandmother, and they're my cousins, so she's kind of like my grandmother." Jax's voice was small now, intimidated by the veracity with which her mother spoke.

"That woman cursed our family. How you could think of her as family…" Sorceress Stone swallowed hard before shaking her head haughtily. "It's just beyond me. I've already allowed you to live with her daughter. Isn't that enough?"

Jax splayed her thin fingers out in front of herself. Looking down at them, she responded quietly. "I mean, I appreciate you letting me live with Aunt Linda and Mercy and Reign and all my friends for the rest of the semester. I just don't understand why you want me to go to a normal college in the fall."

Sorceress Stone furrowed her brow. "Well, obviously it's because you're not a witch and you'll never *be* a witch. It's ridiculous to maintain hope after what we've learned about the curse put upon you and our family. College is supposed to prepare you for a life past high school. How will you support yourself as an adult if you don't have any kind of real-world skills or an education?"

"But you let me go to witch school this year."

"I had hoped that perhaps by your eighteenth birthday you might have been granted your powers, which is why I've allowed this charade to go on for as long as it has. But now that we know the truth—it's simply pointless."

"Pointless! But, Mom…"

Sorceress Stone closed her eyes and shook her head. She inhaled a deep breath through her long, thin nose. Exhaling slowly, she opened her eyes and glared at her only child. "Now it's time for you to go to a trade school or a secular college where you can learn a *real skill*. Perhaps nursing. That's a noble profession. I believe you possess the proper acumen for a career such as that."

"Nursing? But, Mom, I wanna be a *witch!*"

"JaclynRose, stop being obtuse. You'll never *be* a witch. You're a mere human and *that* is *that*."

Jax's bottom lip quivered. She'd never heard her mother speak with such finality regarding her witch status. In the back of her mind, Jax knew that her mother had been holding out hope for all those years, just as Jax had. But now that it had come to light that Phyllis Habernackle had cursed her family as retribution for something that Jax's *own* grandmother had done to Phyllis years ago, Jax knew her mother had finally given up any hope that Jax might someday get her powers. "But, Mom..."

Sorceress Stone planted both of her palms on her desk and pushed herself into a standing position. Her long white hair rippled down over her shoulders and back. "This conversation is over. You may see yourself out."

Jax bit her bottom lip and tried to keep from crying even as her eyes became glossy. She hung her head and turned towards the door. Reaching out to take the knob in her hand, she turned to look back at her mother one last time. There was so much more that she wanted to say. Her mouth opened, but no words came out. With her head lowered, she opened the door and quietly left the room.

The second she was out the door, Holly Rockwell, who was seated in a chair in the secretary's office, lurched up and out of her seat to rush to Jax's side. "Well, what did she want?"

Jax took one look at Holly's expectant face and burst into tears.

Holly wrapped her arms around Jax's tiny shoulders. "Oh! Jaxie! What did she say? It can't have been *that* bad!"

Seated behind her desk, Brittany Hobbs, Sorceress Stone's secretary, grabbed a tissue and walked it over to Jax. "Here, sweetie."

Still clinging to Holly, Jax took the tissue and sniffled. "Thank you." Her shoulders shook as Holly squeezed her tightly. Finally, she disengaged from Holly and stood up straighter, blotting the tears that continued to fall.

"Gosh, Jax. What in the world did she say?"

Jax could barely get the words out. "Sh-she said I-I have to go to noooormal college next yeeeeearrrrrr," she bawled. "Because I'm not a *witchhhhhh*."

2

*S*eated in a group on the bleachers later that afternoon, Alba leaned over and whispered loudly to our little group. "What's Shorty's problem?"

Jax sat two rows below us with her arms crossed and her chin tucked down against her chest. Her eyes were glued to her mother as she entered from the other side of the auditorium.

Holly put a hand in front of her mouth to muffle her words so Jax wouldn't hear. "Sorceress Stone called her into her office this morning and told her she has to go to normal college next year."

I sucked in my breath sharply. "What?!" Holly's words came as a shock to me. Jax hadn't said a word to me about it. I couldn't believe Sorceress Stone would really be *that* evil that she'd kick her own daughter out of witch college. "Why?"

Holly rolled her eyes. "Well, obvs, because she's not a witch."

With my feet up on the seat of the row in front of me,

I flipped my long auburn braid over my shoulder and leaned forward until my chest rested on my knees. I looked sideways at Holly. "So? I told her we'd work on figuring out how to get the curse reversed."

Holly shrugged. "I guess Sorceress Stone thinks she's a lost cause."

Sorceress Stone infuriated me. She treated her daughter like a cast-off piece of jewelry. Something to have worn once and then tossed out when it didn't fit her style anymore. "So she just throws her out on her butt? Some mother."

Alba puffed air out her nose. "Stone was born without an empathy card. The woman's a disaster as far as mothers go."

"Alba," I hissed, glancing down at Jax and hoping she hadn't heard Alba. Despite the horrible way Jax's mother treated her, I knew how she felt about us bad-mouthing Sorceress Stone. No matter what happened between the two women, Jax had always found reasons to continue loving her mother.

Alba shrugged and leaned backwards against the wooden bleacher behind her, letting her butt fall into the gap between seats. "Hey, listen. I call 'em like I see 'em. We all know the truth about Stone. It's not like it's some big secret."

"Yeah, well, you don't have to make her feel worse about it than she already does," I muttered.

"Hello, girls."

Alba, Holly, and I looked up to see Libby and Cinder Hafström, second-year witches at the Paranormal Institute for Witches, standing at the end of our row of seats. Cinder's fiery-red hair flared out around her shoulders as she looked down at us. Between her hair, her fire-starting abilities, and her fiery demeanor, most girls called her the Fire Queen and her frosty-haired, ice-shooting twin sister, Libby, the Ice Princess.

The girls and I had befriended the twins, who hailed from Sweden, during our first week of classes and they'd helped us when we'd had to save Jax from a particularly harrowing hostage situation during the first week of school. Because of our fairly close friendship, we just called the girls by their first names.

"Hey, Cin," I said with a grin, pulling my Converse sneakers off the row in front of me and sitting up straighter. "Hey, Lib."

Libby stuck her head around her sister's shoulder. "Mind if we join you?"

I slid closer to Holly, and Alba sat up and scooted closer to me. "Nope, there's plenty of room."

The duo passed us, filling the two empty spots on the other side of Alba. As the rest of the auditorium filled and the noise level steadily increased, I looked around curiously. A small wooden stage had been erected in the center of the auditorium with a podium sitting center stage. Off to the right of the podium was a row of chairs with five older women I didn't recognize seated in them. Brittany Hobbs rushed around the platform like a little worker bee, while Sorceress Stone greeted each of the women in the chairs with a perfunctory handshake.

"So, anyone know what this assembly is about?" I asked.

"Cinder and I do," said Libby in her pronounced Swedish accent. "We went to the same assembly last year."

"So what's it about?" asked Holly. "And what's up with all those old ladies sitting down there?"

Libby was just about to respond when Sorceress Stone tapped a finger on the microphone, sending a crackling noise skittering across the gymnasium and making much of the chatter quiet down.

"You'll see," whispered Cinder.

"Good morning, witches!" shouted Sorceress Stone into the microphone as if she were suddenly a Hunger Games announcer or something. The three words came out with more enthusiasm than I'd heard her muster up in the entire nine months that I'd gone to her school. I curled my lip and wondered if her sudden enthusiasm wasn't for the benefit of the panel of women behind her, making me that much more curious as to who they were.

Several voices from the bleachers shouted back at her. "Good morning, Sorceress Stone!"

Alba glanced over at me. Rolling her eyes, she whispered out of the side of her mouth, "Brownnosers."

Holly laughed.

"Today is a very special day here at the Paranormal Institute for Witches. With only one week remaining of the current school year, the time has come to discuss finals week and declaration requirements for the first-year students as well as graduation requirements for the second-year students."

Several of the older girls around the room applauded. I doubted the applause was for Sorceress Stone. It was more likely for themselves, as they were excited to finally graduate and be rid of the Paranormal Institute for Witches and Sorceress Stone once and for all. I knew I couldn't wait for that day to come.

"But before we begin the business for the week," continued Sorceress Stone, holding up one long, skinny finger, "it is my very great honor to introduce to you a group of very special witches. The women you see behind me are the newly appointed members of the Great Witches Council!"

Cheers went up around the room. When they died down, Sorceress Stone continued.

"The members of the Great Witches Council are Institute alumni. Each of these members has experienced great success in her life since walking our hallowed halls. New members are appointed to their positions by the departing Council members. These witches have come to us from all around the United States and from many different walks of life, and I'm very honored to bring them all here to you today! And now I'd like to introduce the Council to you. Beginning on the left, we have Stella Blackwood!"

The woman on the end pulled herself to her feet with the aid of a gnarled red cedar cane as thunderous applause lit up the audience. Stella was a short, round woman with shoulder-length flaxen hair that swept across one eye. She wore a loose, flowing black tunic with color-fully patterned leggings underneath. She smiled out at the audience and straightened her back, giving a sweeping wave.

"Sorceress Blackwood has come to us all the way from Alaska. She was an herbalism major during her time at the Institute, and she's spent the last few decades of her life researching new, plant-based potion ingredients. In addition, she's consulted for some major pharmaceutical companies in providing plant-based remedies for medical conditions and diseases."

Stella gave one more perfunctory wave to the crowd before sitting back down.

"Next we have Poppy Ellabee. Poppy is not only a former student of the Institute, but she's a former instructor as well. During her time as a student, she double-majored in animal science and animal spirits, and she went on to teach those subjects for years. Now that she's retired, Poppy volunteers for pet shelters in her home state of Nevada and has created a foundation that matches witches with their spirit animals."

Legends of Poppy Ellabee abounded. She'd been a popular instructor back in her day, and both animal sciences and animal spirits were popular subjects at the Institute, so most of the students had heard of her. The Animal Powers Club in the upper left corner of the bleachers went wild, cheering and whistling for Poppy. Likely because she was a regular financial donor to the organization. She was so philanthropic that she'd even had a scholarship named after her: the Ellabee Animal Spirits Scholarship.

The woman stood. She was taller and nimbler than Stella Blackwood. Her brown hair was cut fashionably to the bottoms of her earlobes, and she wore brown pants and loafers with a cream blouse and a paisley silk scarf tied around her neck. As Poppy shot the crowd a wide, friendly smile, her eyes crinkled in the corners. She waved animatedly before sitting down.

"Third up is Elodie Goodwitch. Elodie hails from a small town in Iowa. She was a potions major in her day at the Institute, and now she owns a very popular magical apothecary in her hometown."

Elodie waved excitedly. She was a tiny woman with narrow shoulders, big, bright green eyes, and curly brown hair that seemed to form a glowing halo around her head.

"Next up is Daphne Fletcher!"

Daphne waited for Elodie to sit before standing herself. She grinned at the crowd. Daphne was a silver-haired woman with the lines of age marring her otherwise pretty face. By far, Daphne was the oldest of the group, and yet she looked spry in the army fatigues she wore as she stood at attention.

"Daphne was a general magic studies major, and after her time at the Institute, she ended up going on to work in the public sector. She took a consultant position with the Texas Army National Guard and assists with statewide emergencies, such as fire control, disaster relief, and other very commendable service activities."

After the cheers for Daphne died down, Sorceress Stone turned her gaze on the last of the group. The final woman's lips were puckered into a small protruding circle as she looked out at the crowd. She had sunflower-blond hair and green eyes, a small nose and ears, and high cheekbones, and she was tall and thin. On paper, one might regard all of her features as attractive. But when everything was totaled up, her face looked pained and uptight. And instead of pretty, her face came off as contrived, as if she'd seen the inside of one too many plastic surgeons' offices.

"This is Gemma Overbrook. Gemma was also a general studies major at the Institute. Sorceress Overbrook has since gone on to found the first online institution for our craft, the Overbrook School of Witchcraft. Not only does she provide classes for those just learning their craft, but she also offers continuing education courses for those witches requiring refresher courses and for those who would like to acquire additional magical skills."

Sorceress Stone paused then and looked back at the group she'd just introduced. She leaned into the microphone. "Please help me in welcoming these five Institute alums, and thank them for taking time out of their very busy schedules to be here today and for the rest of this week!" She clapped.

The crowd cheered, excited to have well-known alums in our midst. When the cheering had settled down, Sorceress Stone continued. "Now it's time to get down to business. Before we discuss graduation requirements, I'd like to take a few moments to address our first-year students. For you, the end of this week will be spent on finals. Each of your classes will host both final written and practical application examinations. In order to move on to the second year, you must pass all of your examinations. Students receiving an average grade of lower than a C in any class will be required to retake that class before moving on to the second semester."

My mouth widened slightly. *A C*?! Nothing lower than a C? I bit on the inside of my lip. I wasn't doing particularly well in my Advanced Kinetic Energy class, and I'd already decided that I'd be satisfied to get a D in the class. And now I had to pull my average up to a C? *Ugh*.

Alba turned to look at me, one eyebrow peaked. "Don't worry," she whispered. Whether she'd sensed a change in my body language or she'd read my mind, which she did on occasion, I wasn't sure. "I'll practice with you this week."

I nodded at her and whispered back, "Thanks."

After the chatter around the room died down, Sorceress Stone continued. "Now, as you all know, graduation is *this* Sunday! Not only will second-year witches be on stage receiving their Powers Unleashed certificates, but first-year witches will also be on stage making their major declarations!"

With a heavy heart, I glanced down at Jax. I knew what I'd be majoring in. Alba and Holly knew what they were majoring in. Sweets had dropped out of school because she'd gotten a job in her area of expertise already. But poor Jax not only didn't have the powers of a witch, but now her mother wasn't going to let her go on to her second year of witch school. There would be no major declaration for her.

Trying to be inconspicuous, Jax tugged the sleeve of her shirt down over her fingers and used the cuff to blot at her eyes. She was crying and trying very hard not to let us see her.

Holly rubbed Jax's back, and Alba reached down and tousled Jax's soft, spiky green hair. Holly had colored and cut it for St. Patrick's Day, and Jax had liked the green so much, she'd decided to keep it until her birthday. Despite their attempts at making her feel better, Jax didn't move.

Knowing that this was once again all Sorceress Stone's fault, I felt a surge of anger welling up inside of me. I wanted to corner the woman and let her have it. I wanted to tell her what a horrible mother she'd been for all of Jax's life and force her to see what a great person Jax had grown up to be despite the neglect she'd suffered for the last eighteen years. But mostly I just wanted her to show love to her daughter.

As her voice poured through the speakers once again, I groaned in disgust. Just hearing her speak grated on my nerves.

"Now that we have gotten that out of the way, we must discuss graduation. I must remind our graduating witches that instead of final testing as done when moving from first year to second year, there will only be a final project. In order to graduate, candidates must demonstrate the knowledge, skills, and abilities they have gained throughout the last two years at the Institute by the manipulation of the four elements: fire, water, earth, and air. The project, which will be judged by the members of the Great Witches Council, will be presented throughout the week. It's a simple pass-or-fail system. Results will be announced at the graduation ceremony. Those who fail must repeat second year before receiving their Powers Unleashed certificates."

Excited squeals went up around the room.

"I think the main thing to note here is that in order to graduate, you must impress our judges. Fail to impress, and—well…" She lifted her brows as she shook her head gently. "You just may fail to graduate."

3

*T*hat afternoon, my mother lifted a stack of books and some trash off one of the tables in the dining room of Habernackle's Bed, Breakfast, and Beyond. Her red hair, streaked with random strands of white, was piled in a bun on top of her head and she wore a green apron over her clothes. She frowned when she saw me come into the restaurant.

"Mercy, it would really be nice if your friends picked up after themselves and maybe helped out a little around here." She strode over to the staircase that led up to the bedrooms and dropped the books and the garbage on the bottom step.

I rolled my eyes. "Ugh, those are Holly's. You don't have to tell me. I already know she's a total slob. Alba tells her to pick up after herself in their room all the time too. She never listens."

"Well, can you take those things up to her room, please? I'm trying to prepare for the dinner rush."

My shoulders crumpled inward. "But, Mom! I just got

home from class. I'm starving! I was headed to the kitchen to have a snack. I have a ton of homework. Finals are this week, you know."

"Really, Mercy? How old are you? You can't help out a little around here? Run the books upstairs, and then you can have a snack."

I looked at the stack of Holly's books at the bottom of the stairs and the empty coffee cup emblazoned with the Paranormally Delicious logo on it and found myself wanting to wring Holly's neck. To look at the girl, she was completely put together. Probably one of the most put together people I knew, honestly. She rarely left her room without full hair and makeup. She agonized over her clothing selection like she was picking her wedding dress, and she lived for her accessories.

But at home, she couldn't be more different. Her makeup and hair products covered the counter of our shared bathroom. The agonizing over her clothing meant she tried on a dozen outfits every morning before school, just to discard her non-selections onto the floor. It drove Alba crazy. The two of them had gotten into it on more than one occasion, which annoyed me even more because then Sweets would get involved. She always had to defuse the situation, which meant we had to listen to her go on and on about the importance of a witch's coven and how important it was that we all got along. I wasn't particularly fond of those long lectures. Sweets was, after all, a friend, not my mother.

"Fine," I finally grumbled. After all, I did appreciate the fact that my mother had given the girls and me a place to stay after we'd moved out of the dorms. Granted, it was a temporary arrangement, but I still appreciated not living under Sorceress Stone's watchful eye anymore. I reached down and scooped up Holly's books and her empty coffee cup. "Where's Reign?"

"In the kitchen."

"Can't I just go say hi first and grab a couple cookies?"

My mother stopped setting tables and looked at me sharply.

I knew that look all too well. I lifted my brows. "Fine. Fine. I'm going." I stomped up the stairs and burst into the room that Holly and Alba shared. Inside, I found Holly at her vanity debating between earrings and Alba sitting on their shared bed with her legs crossed at the ankles and a textbook in her lap.

"Ugh," I groaned. "Holly!"

Holly swiveled around with a bright smile on her face, holding two pairs of earrings up to her ears. "Which ones, Mercy, the blue ones or the silver ones?"

"Like I care?" I snapped.

Alba chuckled silently to herself.

Holly wrinkled her nose. "Uh! Rude?" Shooting us both the stink eye, she turned back around to face the mirror. "Personally, I prefer the silver ones, but I like that the blue ones match my eyes."

"Holly, you need to start picking up after yourself. My mom's getting annoyed." I held out the stack of books and the empty coffee cup she'd left downstairs.

Holly shrugged. "Sorry," she said noncommittally. "Is Reign down there?"

"Yeah, he's in the kitchen," I grumbled. "What do you want me to do with these books?"

Holly didn't even turn around. "Just toss 'em on the bed."

Alba looked up at Holly sharply. "No, don't just toss 'em on the bed. Put 'em on her nightstand." She pointed at Holly's side of their shared queen-sized bed. "Cosmo, I'm sick of your messes. I can't live like this anymore. It was never this bad in the dorms."

"That's because Sorceress Stone did random room checks," said Holly. She smiled happily. "Isn't it nice not to have to do those anymore?"

"No, it's not nice!" said Alba through gritted teeth. "I'm sick of your piles of clothes everywhere. You get makeup on all of my stuff. The room constantly smells like fingernail polish remover, and this morning I stepped on one of your earrings on the way to the shower."

Holly's eyes brightened as she turned to look at Alba. "You found my earring? Was it the pink spiky one? I've been looking for that one all week!"

Alba's face curled into a snarl. "Yes, as a matter of fact, it *was* the pink spiky one. And it spiked me right in the middle of my foot."

Holly looked around. "Well, what did you do with it? Maybe I'll change into my new pink shirt and wear those."

"I threw it away. That's what I did with it."

"Threw it away! Why would you do that?"

Alba leaned her head back against the headboard and palmed her forehead. "Red. You need to get her out of here before I blow a gasket."

I rolled my eyes and held the door open wider. "Come on, Holl. Let's go. You can hang out in my room until Alba cools down."

Holly wrinkled her nose. "I don't know what *she's* got to cool down about. She threw away *my* earring."

"Cosmo... I'm warning you. You're on my last nerve!"

"Let's go, Holl." I reached out and grabbed Holly by the wrist and dragged her out of the room. I was tired. I'd had a long day at school and had a ton of studying to do. I really didn't need to be cleaning bits of Alba off the walls after she exploded.

Holly dragged her feet as I pulled her out of the room, but out in the hallway, she perked up almost immediately. "How do I look?"

I gave her a once-over. Her blue off-the-shoulder crop top matched her eyes, but she showed almost as much skin on top as she did on the bottom with her short white shorts and wedge sandals. "I don't know. You're missing the top part of your shirt," I said, pointing at the tops of her exposed breasts.

Holly giggled while rolling her eyes. "Okay, *Alba*." She flipped her wavy blond hair over her shoulders and did a little wriggle in front of me, making her boobs bounce like a pair of overinflated beach balls. "No, I'm serious. Do you like this top? It's from Dixie Carlton's new line. It came in the mail today while we were in class."

I wrinkled my nose. "Dixie Carlton has a clothing line? I thought she was an actress."

"Well, duh, she's an actress, but she's also Insta-Famous and she just launched her own clothing line. This is from her spring collection. She models almost everything in her line, and I'm not trying to toot my own horn or anything, but I think I look better in this top than she does!"

I shrugged. "I mean, of course you look good, but…"

That was all Holly wanted to hear. She squealed before I could finish my sentence, then rushed towards the stairs. "Thanks, Merc! I'm going downstairs to get a snack."

"Oh, hey! Bring me a couple of my mom's chocolate chip cookies, would you?" I asked, heading towards the room I shared with Jax and Sweets.

A frown passed over Holly's face, but only for a second. "Okay, fine." She disappeared, flouncing down the stairs with a big smile on her face.

I knew where she was going. To flirt with my brother. She'd flirted with him since the day she'd met him, but it had picked up considerably since we'd moved into the B&B. Of course, as usual, Reign wanted nothing to do with Holly, so her attempts weren't very concerning.

I pushed open my bedroom door to find the lights on and Jax curled up on her side of our bed. "Hey, Jax." I dumped my backpack down on the floor and then flopped backwards onto the bed.

"Hi, Mercy," she said in a tiny voice.

"Did I wake you up?"

"No, I was just laying here."

"Why? You sick?"

"No. I'm not sick."

"Then what's the matter?"

Jax sniffled and rolled onto her other side, giving me her back. "Nothing."

"Oh, come on, Jax. Are you still riled up about your mom wanting you to go to regular college next year?"

Jax was quiet, but I noticed her shoulders shaking. "No." The voice came out in a high-pitched tiny squeal, which was the sound her voice made right before she started bawling.

I sighed and rolled out of bed, then walked around to the other side of the bed so I could face her. "Oh, come on, Jax. You don't have to try and hide it. I know that's what's the matter. I just don't understand why you're so worried about it. I told you we'd try and get Gran to reverse the curse she put on you."

"But, Mercy," said Jax, sitting up in bed and grinding her fists into her eyes, "what if she won't do it? Then I won't be able to go to college with you and the girls next fall. And there's no regular colleges in Aspen Falls either, so I won't even get to live with you."

Sitting on the edge of the bed, I patted her leg. "Have a little faith, Jax. We'll figure something out."

Her brows drew together. "You promise?"

"Yeah, of course. I wouldn't leave you hanging. You're family."

Jax lurched forward in bed and wrapped her scrawny arms around my shoulders. "Thanks, Mercy, you're the best!"

Just then Alba threw open the door. "I've had it with her, Red. I'm not even kidding. Shorty, switch rooms with me."

"What?" squealed Jax, her eyes widening.

"Switch rooms with me. You and Cosmo get along good. You two should stay together."

Jax's head shook rapidly from side to side. "Noooo!"

"Oh, come on," begged Alba.

"But Mercy and I are cousins. I can't leave her."

"First of all, you're not *real* cousins. And second of all, graduation is in a week and then I'll be moving out for the summer. You and Red can room up then if you want."

"You're moving out for the summer?" I asked, surprised. It was the first I'd heard Alba mention her plans for the summer.

"Duh? I'm married. You thought I was gonna live at the B&B all summer with you losers?"

I rolled my eyes. Alba really had a way with words. "Thanks."

"Use your brain, Red. People at college go home for the summers."

"I didn't say I thought you were staying, Alba. I just hadn't heard you say a word about it, so I didn't know what your plans were."

"Yeah, well, my plan is to move home. I'll be back in the fall."

Jax's face fell. "But I might not be here in the fall."

"Shut it, Shorty. You'll be here in the fall. We'll figure something out."

"That's what I told her."

Suddenly Holly was back in the room with a pouty bottom lip and droopy eyes. We all looked down at her as she crumpled onto the bed.

Alba stared at her. "Who crapped in *your* cornflakes?"

"Reign just left to go on a date."

"So?"

"So?! Didn't you hear me? He left to go on *a date!*"

Alba didn't seem to get it. "And?"

Holly wrinkled her nose in Alba's direction and her face reddened. "And I don't like it! He didn't even *look* at me."

"You know he's not into you, right? It's high time you got over it."

Alba had taken the words right out of my mouth. I was thankful I didn't have to be the blunt one.

"Sucking on a lemon first thing every morning really isn't a very good idea. It makes you sour. You know that, Alba?" snapped Holly. Then she looked at Jax. "Jaxie, you wanna room together until graduation? I really can't take Alba's bad attitude anymore. It's bringing me down, and I'm barely going to pass this semester, so I don't need my sour roommate dragging me into the briar patch with her."

As Alba's eyes brightened, Jax's jaw dropped. "But I'm *Mercy's* and Sweets' roommate. I can't leave them."

"Sure ya can, Shorty. It's easy. I'll even move your clothes for you."

"I'd have to move my clothes?!"

"Well, obviously," said Alba.

"Mercy…" Jax looked at me, her eyes pleading for help. I didn't know what to say. We'd spent the last nine months listening to Holly and Alba bickering like sisters, and I, for one, was over it. I wasn't sure that I wanted to switch Jax for Alba, but it was only for a week. I didn't have any good reason why they shouldn't switch.

"It's only a week, Jax. We'll be rooming together all summer, or until we find our new place."

Jax looked from me to Holly to Alba. I could tell she really didn't want to switch, but she felt like she was being ganged up on. While I felt bad, I was exhausted and just didn't have the energy to argue with the girls anymore. "Fine," she whined with her brow furrowed.

Alba smiled widely. "Sweet. I'll go pack my stuff."

Before Alba could leave the room, Sweets appeared in the doorway. "Hey, girls."

"Hey, Sweets," said Alba, pushing past her and disappearing into the hallway. "How was work?"

"It was okay," said Sweets, looking over her shoulder at Alba disappearing into her room down the hall. "Where's she going?"

I sighed. "To get her stuff. Alba and Jax are switching rooms for the rest of the school year."

Sweets looked at Jax curiously. "They are? Why?"

Jax crossed her arms over her barely-there breasts and looked like she was fighting back tears.

"Because Alba's a royal pain in my ass," said Holly bluntly.

"Holly!" chastised Sweets.

Holly held up her flattened palm to Sweets. "Bup," she snapped. "I don't want to hear it. We all agreed. It's just for the last week of school. No big deal."

"You okay with it, Jax?" asked Sweets.

"I guess. I don't really have a choice." Jax sighed. "Today's been a really bad day. First my mom tells me I can't go to witch college in the fall, and now I have to move out of my room."

Sweets' eyes widened. "Sorceress Stone told you you can't go to the Institute in the fall?!"

"Yeah."

"But that's crazy! You're her daughter!"

"I know," breathed Jax, her bottom lip trembling.

"I certainly wouldn't get her a Mother's Day present, that's for sure," said Holly under her breath as Alba reappeared with an armful of clothes she'd pulled out of one of one of her drawers.

"Get who a Mother's Day present?"

"Sorceress Stone," said Sweets.

"Oh, yeah. Hell no, I wouldn't get that woman a present. I don't care if she *is* Shorty's mother. That woman doesn't deserve the title of mother, let alone an entire day *devoted* to her."

I nodded. "Especially since your birthday's the same day as Mother's Day, Jax. The day should be all about you."

That did the trick. A smile spilled across Jax's face, brightening her eyes. She loved to talk about her birthday. Besides talking about any topic related to witches, her next favorite topic was her birthday. "So what are we going to do for my birthday?"

"Well, it's the same day as graduation," I said. "So unfortunately, we've got a lot going on. Mother's Day, Libby and Cinder's graduation, major declaration day, *and* your birthday. Plus, I'm pretty sure Libby and Cinder mentioned their class is throwing a big graduation party that night."

"A party?!" Jax's eyes lit up as if she hadn't heard anything else I'd said.

"Yeah, for Libby and Cinder's graduation."

"I don't care. We could pretend it's my birthday party," said Jax with a brilliant smile.

"I mean, if you want. Maybe we could go out to dinner before the party," I suggested, looking at the rest of the girls.

Sweets nodded. "Yeah, that would be fun."

Jax sucked in her breath excitedly. "All of us going out to eat together for my birthday *and* a party?!"

We all nodded.

"Oh, you girls are the best!" She leapt up and took turns hugging each of us.

When she got to Alba, Alba held her hand out, palm facing Jax. "Hug me and I'm not going."

Jax stopped short of her. "Okay," she said in a small voice.

"Now listen, before we go getting all hot and bothered about your birthday and the graduation party, we still have to figure out how to lift the curse so you can get your powers," said Alba, rocking her weight onto her other leg.

"I was just thinking the same thing," I said. "I have a *ton* of studying to do to get ready for finals, but how about after dinner, we run over to see Gran and see what we can do to convince her to lift the curse?"

"Can we?!" asked Jax excitedly, looking around the room.

Sweets fell onto the small futon in our room. It was the same one that Jax had brought to college. We'd gotten Reign to move it to the B&B so Sweets could have a bed. "I'm exhausted and my feet are killing me, but once I eat, I think I'll get my second wind."

"I'm almost done with my homework," said Alba. "Then I got nothing else going on. I'm up for it."

Holly shrugged flippantly. "I don't really feel like studying anyway. Count me in, too."

"Yay!" cheered Jax. "I have the best friends a girl could ever ask for!"

4

*G*ran was having supper at the Baileys' when I called to ask if she minded if the girls and I stopped over for a visit. She sounded surprised, but happy to hear from me, and said we were welcome to stop by Char and Vic's place anytime that evening. So the girls and I all loaded into Sweets' small Ford Taurus and headed over.

"So how's this going to go?" asked Sweets, looking at us in her rearview mirror.

I let my head fall back against the headrest. "I have no idea. I don't expect it to be easy."

"Well, maybe we can convince Char and Vic to help," said Sweets. Charlotte and Victor Bailey were an elderly couple that were not only friends of ours but also Sweets' bosses at Bailey's Bakery and Sweets. Like my grand-mother, Char was also a witch, and before Vic's *accident*, he'd been a wizard. "I mean, they both love Jax. I'm sure they think she deserves her powers, just like we all do."

"Yeah, I mean, we can sure try." I shrugged and then

looked over at Sweets. "Speaking of the Baileys, how are things going over at the bakery? You haven't said much lately."

Sweets turned on her signal, took a left, and drove down a side street. "That's because it's really been busy, and without Louis around, I've been doing everything myself. I need to work on getting someone new hired. Char said I could advertise. I just haven't had time to write up an ad. And to go through interviews?" She leaned her head back against the headrest. "Ugh, I just really don't have that kind of time at the moment."

"Well, all I can say is that I'm glad they fired that scumbag for trying to frame you for Mr. Bailey's murder," said Alba.

Sweets' eyes brightened as she turned to look at Alba. "Oh, definitely! I mean, don't get me wrong. I'm not complaining about having to do Louis's work. I was doing most of it anyway. It's amazing how much lighter the atmosphere is there without him. I actually enjoy going to work. I'm just exhausted by the end of the day."

"So Louis gets fired and Auggie Stone gets off scot-free? That hardly seems fair." Alba shook her head and looked out the window.

Jax piped up next to me. "Mmm. I'm pretty sure I heard she was reported to the Great Witches Council."

I nodded. "I heard the same thing. Mom said that since the intent to harm wasn't there, she pretty much got off with just a slap on the wrist and a warning to be more careful with who she gives potions to."

"Who reported her? Sorceress Stone?" asked Holly.

"Puh!" I spat. "You really think Sorceress Stone would report her own mother?"

Holly shrugged.

"No, I heard Char and Gran reported her," said Jax, referring to my grandmother, not hers. Jax was my half-brother Reign's first cousin. By roundabout means, she thought that made her and me cousins, and therefore she considered my grandmother and Reign's grandmother to be *her* grandmother too. Which I personally thought was nuts, because my grandmother was the one who had cursed the Stone family all those years ago and the reason that Jax had never gotten her powers. Why would Jax want to claim Gran as her own?

"Yeah, that doesn't surprise me," said Alba with a nod.

Char had had every right to report Auggie for the role that she'd played in Vic's accident. I would have done the exact same thing. It was only unfortunate that Auggie hadn't gotten into more trouble.

Sweets pulled her car up next to the Baileys' small bungalow-style house, and we all got out of the car. It was May in Aspen Falls, Pennsylvania, and for a spring evening, it was warmer than one would expect. It almost felt like summer. The combination of the warm spring evening mixed with the thought that my first year of witch school was nearing a close had me bounding up the sidewalk with an unusual burst of energy.

"Damn, Red. You got ants in your pants or something?"

I bounced up and down on the pavement, swinging my arms next to me. "No, but this weather makes me feel like jogging or something. Doesn't it make you feel like getting your run on?"

Alba rolled her eyes. "I don't run unless a zombie is

chasing me. Even then, I might just let him catch me if it means I don't have to run."

Sweets and Jax giggled.

I smiled. "Yeah, I hear that. I'm not much of a runner either. But if feels like summer is finally around the corner! Doesn't it feel good to finally shake off the cold weather?"

Jax plumped out her bottom lip. "I only wish that you guys weren't leaving for the summer. It would've been so much fun to hang out together all summer. We could've gone swimming and gone for hikes and taken Chesney on long walks—"

"Yeah, I don't know about all that," I interjected, holding up a hand to stop her from continuing. "But Jax has a point. Do you realize how *boring* it's going to be in Aspen Falls without you girls?"

"Well, *I'm* not going anywhere. I have a job and this is where I live now." Sweets giggled and threw her arms out on either side of herself. "I guess you could say I'm finally all grown up." She giggled at her own little joke.

"Yeah, well, I have a husband, so I'm more grown up than you," said Alba.

Holly flipped her hair over her shoulder and quirked a brow. "I'm pretty sure adults don't argue about who's more adult than the other one. But just having a husband doesn't make you an adult."

"And you think running home to Daddy for the summer makes *you* an adult?"

"I never said it made me an adult, *Alba.*"

"Good, because you're not, *Holly.*"

Standing between Holly and Alba on Char's front porch, I held a hand out on either side of myself. "You two really need to quit arguing. We came to help Jax, and the two of you are going to spoil it. Now shut up so I can knock on the door."

Holly bit her glossed lip.

Alba leaned against the yellow siding. "Knock already, then. Jeez. We don't have all night."

I glared at her while knocking on the door. From outside, we heard a recliner snapping into place, and seconds later, Char's puffy white head appeared in the doorway.

"Hey, Char."

"Well, hello, girls! Welcome!" Char opened the door, and swiped the air in front of her grandly as she stepped back for us to enter. "Come in, come in. So excited to have you all join us. We just made some popcorn and popped in a movie. Would you like to join us?"

"Thanks, Char, but no, we just came to visit Gran."

A small tan Chihuahua was seated on the arm of Char's recliner.

I gave him a small wave. "Hi, Mr. Bailey."

"It's so good to see you, Mercy!" boomed Mr. Bailey's big voice out of the frail body.

One by one, each of the girls said their hellos and filed into the house behind me.

Gran was seated on the sofa with a blanket covering her lap and a bowl of popcorn lying on the side table. "Hey, Gran."

"Mercy! It's about time you came to see your old gran. Come over here and give me a hug!" She held her arms out wide but didn't get up.

I leaned over, and Gran tugged me down onto her

lap. Her arms squeezed tightly around my neck so I couldn't get back up. "Jeez, Gran."

"What?" she squawked in my ear. "I never get hugs from my favorite granddaughter anymore. You used to give me hugs all the time."

I tried to wiggle out of her viselike grip. "I'm your *only* granddaughter, and *yeah*, maybe when I was *five!*" Gran, Mom, and I had been a very close-knit group of witches at one time in my life. But as I'd come to find out about Gran's past—feuding with the Stone family, how she'd treated my mother when she was younger, and what she'd done to my brother—I'd sort of grown apart from her. Recently, however, after finding out what had really happened all those years ago, I'd felt myself relenting and forgiving her a little. After all, Jax's grandmother had done some pretty horrible things to my family, so I could kind of understand where she'd been coming from. And when Reign had stopped hating her for what she'd done to him all those years ago, I'd figured it was time I stopped holding a grudge as well.

"Oh, come on. You got more in you than that," grumped Gran.

"Fine." I squeezed her a little harder, until I felt her let loose a little. "Good to see you."

"Good to see you too," she agreed, finally letting me stand up. Gran looked over the rest of my friends. "I see you brought the whole squad."

"Yup."

"Hi, Gran," chirped Jax, rushing my grandmother to give her a hug.

"Hello, Jax." Gran patted Jax's back while she attacked her neck with a pair of scrawny arms.

"Well, come on in, sit, sit," instructed Char, taking her place next to Vic.

Jax let go of Gran and then perched herself up on the armrest right next to her while Alba, Sweets, and Holly took spots on the sofa on the other side of Gran. I stood, watching them all.

"So," said Char. "To what do we owe the honor of this visit?"

All the girls looked at me, the only one standing. I lifted a shoulder noncommittally. I wasn't entirely sure where to begin. "Oh, you know, I just figured I hadn't seen Gran in a while."

"Isn't that sweet," said Gran, with one eyebrow lifted. "I can't say I remember the last time my granddaughter came to visit me just because she hadn't seen me in a while. Seems a little sketchy if you ask me."

Char nodded. "Sketchy sounds like the appropriate word. Don't you agree, Vic?"

"Oh, now can't a granddaughter just drop in from time to time to see her grandmother? Why does there have to be an ulterior motive?"

Gran sat forward in her seat. "Oh, there doesn't. Just usually in the case of my granddaughter, there is."

"Gran!" I breathed.

"Knock off the act, dearie. Just tell me what you and your friends are up to, so we can get on with watching our show."

"Up to?" I scratched the back of my neck and looked innocently at my friends.

Before I could say anything else, Jax leapt off the arm of the couch and spun to face Gran. "Gran, we came to beg you to take the curse off of my family."

Gran lifted her brows and gave a tip of the head before crossing her arms over her heavy chest. "Ahh. I wondered as much. I've been waiting for this day."

Jax smiled brilliantly. "You have?! So you'll do it? You'll take the curse off?"

Gran frowned and lifted her chin, sticking her nose in the air. "Nope. Not gonna happen."

"Gran!" I said.

She wagged a finger in my direction. "I don't want to hear it, Mercy Mae Habernackle. Jax's grandmother *killed* your grandfather. I don't care if it *was* accidental! Her family deserves everything it gets!"

"But it's *Jax*! You can hardly think *Jax* deserves to be punished for her grandmother's actions?!"

Gran closed her eyes and stubbornly lifted her nose into the air once again.

"Char, can't you help us?" begged Sweets from the sofa.

Char swished her lips sideways. "You girls know how much I love you all. Especially Jax. But Auggie Stone is responsible for what happened to my poor Vic, too."

Vic jumped down to the floor. "But, Sugar Pop, I'm still here! What's done is done. I don't want Jax to pay for what happened to me! It wasn't her fault in any way, shape, or form! We can't punish her for Auggie's actions."

Char clucked her tongue and tipped her head sideways. "I'm sorry, Vic. I can't go against Phil. She's been through too much as it is. I will *not* side with Augusta Stone on this one, even if that means not helping Jax become a witch." She looked at Jax. "I'm sorry, sweetheart. I want to see you come into your powers, but I understand why Phil doesn't want to give in to your grandmother."

"But it wouldn't be giving in to Jax's grandmother," said Alba. "She's not the one asking. She could care less about her granddaughter. They don't even *know* each other."

Jax nodded. "Alba's right. I only met my grandma once, when I was a little girl. She's never bothered to call or write me over the years. Not even a single birthday card!"

"Come on, Gran. Jax's birthday is on Sunday. I promised I'd help her get her powers before her birthday."

Gran pointed a finger at me. "What have I told you about making promises you can't keep?" Then she turned to look Jax up and down. She lifted a brow. "Ah, a birthday. You'll be how old?"

"Eighteen," said Jax.

Gran pursed her lips. "Eighteen. Is that right?"

Jax nodded.

Gran's head lifted before turning away from Jax.

Something about that tiny movement made me suspicious. Like there was something that Gran wasn't saying. I looked at my grandmother with narrowed eyes. "Why?"

Gran swatted the air. "Oh, nothing."

"No, not nothing. What?"

Gran lifted a shoulder. "You won't like what I have to say."

"I probably won't, but I'd at least like to hear it."

Grant let out a puff of air. "Well, it's just that Jax is what they call a legacy. She comes from a very long line of witches. You're a legacy too, Mercy. By all rights, had nature taken its course, Jax *should* have been born a witch just like you were."

My mouth gaped. "Uh! See, Gran! This *is* your fault!" I glanced over at Jax. She looked like she was about to cry.

Her big blue eyes were wide as she said in a small voice, "I was definitely going to be a witch?"

Gran nodded. "Oh yes. No question in my mind."

I shook my head. "Gran, this is wrong!"

Alba looked at Gran intently. "I don't understand. What does Jax being a legacy have to do with her turning eighteen?"

Gran sighed and then leaned back. "Simple. If for some reason a legacy doesn't become a witch by her eighteenth birthday, she'll never get her powers."

"What?!" squealed Jax, looking around the room and then staring at Char for confirmation.

With a small sigh, Char nodded. "Phil's right. I'm sorry, Jax."

"But my birthday's in less than a *week*! If Gran won't lift the curse, how am I supposed to get my powers within a *week*?! That's not enough time to figure out how to reverse the curse."

"The curse wasn't meant to be reversed," said Gran, her tone more than a little callous.

I'd just about had enough of my grandmother. "Gran, I can't believe you. You want your family to come around more often, and yet you refuse to give in, even a little! How am I supposed to want to be a part of your life if you won't help out my friend, who's done *nothing* wrong?!"

Gran pointed a finger at me and stared me down with a completely serious face. "Because we're a family. And family sticks together. Especially witch families. Covens are everything to a witch."

I wasn't about to let her intimidate me. "Gran, you can wag that witchy finger at me all you want, but Jax is my family too. All these girls are. And we stick together. If you don't lift the curse off of Jax I will be forced to do it myself."

Gran smiled at me and then leaned back in her seat with her arms crossed over her chest. "Fine. Do it. I dare you. In fact, I double dog dare you. There's only one way to lift a curse the size of the one I put on the Stone family. If you think you can do it, then by all means, *do it.*"

5

*L*eaving the Baileys' that night, the five of us drove away solemnly. No one wanted to talk about the challenge we now faced. Not only did we have to figure out *how* to lift the curse, but we also had to get it done in the short week's time before Jax's eighteenth birthday. No one wanted to say out loud how impossible that all sounded, so instead of talking about it, we all just went quietly to our rooms.

The jingle of the door opening brought Chesney, my small chestnut-colored Cavapoo, barreling towards me. I scooped him up and cuddled him against my chest. "Hey, buddy."

On the other side of the dining room, my mom leaned on the counter with Detective Mark Whitman seated across from her in one of the barstools. "Hi, Mercy."

"Hi, Mom. Oh, hey, Detective Whitman." I sat down at the counter, holding Chesney over one shoulder. He licked my earlobe, forcing me to finally break out a smile. "Quit, Ches, that tickles."

Leaning across the counter, my mom rested her head in the palm of her hand. "Where were all of you girls?"

"We went to go see Gran. She was over at Char's place."

Mom looked surprised. "You went to see your grandmother? Really?"

I rested Chesney's butt on the counter. "Yes, really. Why is that such a surprise to everyone? She's my *grandmother*, isn't she?"

"Well, yes, but I thought you were kind of upset with her because of…" She trailed off and glanced at her boyfriend and then back at me. "Well, you know. *Everything*."

I lifted a shoulder and nuzzled Chesney against my cheek. "Yeah, well, forgive and forget, isn't that what you've always taught me?"

"Yes, I suppose, but you've never actually *listened*."

"I listen, Mom. You just don't realize it."

Detective Whitman lifted his dark eyebrows. "Well, Linda. I better get going. I've got a lot of work to do back at the office." He pushed himself up and grabbed the paper bag and the Styrofoam cup of coffee off the counter. "Thanks for supper. I really appreciate it. It should make the night go a little smoother."

My mom smiled at him as she walked around the counter. "Anytime, Mark."

They exchanged hugs, and before they could lock lips, I gave them my back. I didn't need to see that. Seconds later, I felt Detective Whitman's oversized hand tousling my hair.

"See ya, Mercy."

"Bye."

He waved as he walked away. "Bye, Linda. I'll call you tomorrow."

Mom walked him to the door. I waited for her, and when she came back, she took her spot behind the counter again.

"Do you seriously have to do that in front of me?"

Mom looked clueless. "Do what?"

I wrinkled my nose. "You know, make out with your boyfriend?"

"I wasn't making out with Mark. I gave him a hug and a kiss goodbye. What's wrong with that? You were the one that wanted us together so badly."

"Well, yeah. But you just don't have to do it in *front* of me. I mean, I'm not a kid. I assumed that mushy stuff is happening, but I'd rather it be off camera than on, if you catch my drift."

Mom rolled her eyes. "Fine. I'll do my best to keep it *off* camera. Just for you, sweetheart. Does that make you feel better?"

"Much."

"So things are going good between you two?"

Mom smiled dreamily. "Couldn't be better."

"And Merrick's taking it well that you picked Detective Whitman over him?"

Mom swished her lips to the side and stood up straight, adjusting her apron. "Let's just say he's doing his best to get over it."

"Yeah? What's that mean?"

"Well, he's sulking a bit."

"You've seen him?!"

Mom nodded. "Mm-hmm. He came in earlier for dinner."

My eyes widened. The nerve! "No he didn't!"

Mom sighed and pulled her apron off. "Yeah, while you girls were gone. Mark got here just as he was leaving. Needless to say, neither was very happy to see the other."

"What did he want?"

"I guess just to talk, and say hello to Reign. He told me he was going out of town for a few days to clear his head. He said he understood I'd made my decision, but he admitted he was pretty lonely in Aspen Falls. I guess he and his sisters don't really visit that much, and it gets lonely over at their place."

"Then he should get a girlfriend, not come sniffing around my mother!"

"Mercy, you're not being very empathetic. Reign is his son, and they're trying to bond right now, so as long as Merrick and Reign both live in Aspen Falls, we're bound to see each other."

My nostrils flared as I pushed my chair back and stood up. "It's hard to be empathetic where Merrick Stone is concerned. Sorry, Mom. Listen, I gotta go. I should probably do a little studying for finals before I go to bed. I'm a little worried about not passing my Advanced Kinetic Energy final."

After hanging up her apron, Mom came around the counter and took Chesney out of my arms. "Only one more week, Mercy Bear. You've got this. I have faith in you."

"Thanks, Mom. I'm glad one of us has faith in me."

6

*L*ater that evening, Sweets sat quietly on her futon, flipping through a cooking magazine she'd gotten in the mail while Alba sat next to me on the bed, channel surfing. I had a textbook open in my lap but found I was having a hard time concentrating on magic studies. My mind kept rolling back to Jax and everything that Gran had told us about legacies and the ridiculously short amount of time that we had left to reverse the curse. We had until *Sunday*. It was *Monday night*!

With a heavy heart, I pictured Jax sitting in Holly's room, crying over the news. She had to be upset about Gran not being willing to help us, and about the new information we'd learned. I silently wondered if Holly would be too self-absorbed to make Jax feel better. Mom's words replayed in my ear. *Mercy, you're not being very empathetic.* I sighed quietly. *Maybe I oughta suggest we invite Jax over.*

Before I could say anything, Sweets looked up from her magazine. "Guys, I feel like Jax shouldn't be over there without us tonight. She can't be in a very good place right now."

I looked over at her, bright-eyed. "Yeah, I was just thinking the same thing."

Sweets closed her magazine. "Why don't you text Jax and see if she and Holly want to come over here?"

Next to me, Alba groaned and flicked off the TV. "Shorty only. I just switched rooms to get *away* from Cosmo."

"Oh, come on, Alba. Now's not the time to be petty."

"Petty!" breathed Alba. "I'm not being petty. All that girl does is primp and take selfies. I'm over it."

"Alba! That's glam shaming," said Sweets with a knowing nod. "And that's not okay."

Alba looked at Sweets like she was off her rocker. "Glam shaming? That's a thing? I mean, who invents stuff like that?"

I rolled my eyes. "She got that off *The Bachelor.*"

Sweets giggled.

"Anyway, Alba, Sweets is right. Now's not the time to be petty. I'm going to invite Jax and Holly over. We need to make Jax feel better." Before Alba could object, I fired off a text message to Jax. *Hey, Jax. You and Holl wanna come hang out with us for a while?*

I'd no sooner hit Send than my bedroom door flew open and Jax burst inside, followed by Holly. Smiling from ear to ear, Jax wore her long-sleeved black cat onesie, the one with the cat ears on the hood. Her face was covered in a green mud mask and she carried a stuffed unicorn in her arms. "I got your text!" chirped Jax.

Alba snuffed air out her nose. "Well, that was fast."

Holly followed Jax inside, her face covered in a layer of green glop just like Jax's. Instead of a cat onesie, Holy wore a white unicorn onesie with a twisted purple horn and pink-and-white ears on the hood, an iridescent layer of pink and purple glitter covering the whole thing. The two girls sat down on my bed.

I wrinkled my nose at them. "What in the world are you *wearing*?!"

Holly lowered her brows. "Don't make fun," she said glumly. "Jax was sad about all that stuff your grandmother said, so I told her we could have a pajama party and do facials. She wanted us to wear onesies, and I didn't have one, so she made me wear one of hers." When we all wouldn't stop staring at her, she wrinkled her nose. "I was *trying* to cheer her up."

"By looking like an idiot?" said Alba.

"Alba!" shouted Jax, Sweets, and Holly in unison.

I crawled between them on the bed and held a hand up in both of their faces. "Okay, okay. This is a fighting-free zone and a fighting-free night. We're supposed to be trying to cheer Jax up, and fighting is only going to make her feel worse."

Jax smiled at me. "Thanks, Mercy. I already know what would cheer me up."

"What, Jax?" asked Sweets from the futon.

"If we figured out how to lift the curse!"

"Jaaax," I sighed. "I'd love to figure that out, but it's going to require some research. We'll have to hit the books in the Great Witch's Library tomorrow."

Alba nodded. "That's exactly what I was thinking too."

Jax clapped her hands together. "Yay!"

I winced. Gran had seemed pretty confident when I'd said I would have to lift the curse if she didn't. It was almost as if she knew it was going to be impossible to do. The thought worried me. What if we couldn't figure it out by the deadline? "Just, don't get your hopes up, Jax. Alright?"

"Oh, I won't," she chirped.

I could tell by the sound of her voice that it was pretty much too late. She'd already gotten her hopes up. I needed to change the subject, I couldn't talk about it anymore. Between curse reversing and finals, I was too stressed out. I reached over and plucked the remote control out of Alba's hand. "So, what are we watching tonight? A movie?" I asked, looking around.

Holly bounced up and grabbed a DVD off of her dresser. She flashed it at the group. "Yes! I just got Dixie Carlton's new movie. Let's watch this!"

Jax wrinkled her nose. "That's a horror movie, Holly."

"I'd watch it," said Alba with a nod. "You know, I heard Dixie Carlton's a witch."

Holly shook her head. "No, I'm pretty sure that's just a rumor. I heard that one of her ex-boyfriends was salty about their breakup, so he started telling people that."

"You know I hate scary movies, Holly." Jax frowned and then promptly sucked in her breath. "Oh! I know, how about we start the next season of *Glee*!"

Alba and Jax lurched for the remote control I held in my hand at the same time. Alba nearly laid Jax out grabbing it first. "No! I am not watching that crap anymore, Shorty. I don't care if it's your birthday week or you're depressed or whatever. That show is annoying. All they do is sing."

Jax plumped out her bottom lip. "But, Alba! I love Glee!"

"Of course you do," said Alba, flicking on the television. "How about a little *Walking Dead?*"

"Ugh, no," said Holly. "How about we start *Grey's Anatomy* over again? I miss McDreamy."

"We all miss McDreamy," sighed Sweets.

"I don't wanna watch *Grey's* all over again," I said, wrinkling my nose. "We binged way too hard the first time we watched it. I literally didn't get out of bed for an entire weekend after the plane crash."

The room went silent for several long seconds. I was pretty sure Sweets, Holly, and Jax were considering it a moment of silence for Lexie Grey and Mark Sloan. But all I could think about was the fact that I probably wouldn't be in danger of failing Advanced Kinetic Energy if I'd practiced more instead of watching the countless episodes of *Grey's Anatomy* well into the early morning hours.

Finally, Holly broke the silence. "Okay, well, if we're not going to watch *Grey's*, how about *Gossip Girl?*"

Alba frowned. "Eww. Don't make me lose my supper."

I pulled the remote out of Alba's hand and began scrolling through Netflix. "Anyone seen *Vampire Diaries?*"

Everyone's heads shook, but no one said anything encouraging.

I shrugged. "Sounds better than *Glee*, don't you think, Alba?"

"Slightly," she grumbled.

"Diaries—sounds very *Gossip Girl*–like, right, Holly?"

Holly lifted a shoulder. "I guess."

I pointed at one of the characters on the screen. "Look, Sweets. That's Boone from *Lost*. You loved him in that show."

Sweets' eyes lit up as she sucked in her breath. "Ohhh, you're right! I'm in."

"And, Jax, we all know how much you love vampires. What do you say?"

Jax nodded excitedly. "I'm in too. But can we make popcorn first?"

"Duh," I said.

Holly and Jax leapt off the bed, threw open the door, and ran down the hallway.

Following them to the door, I looked back at Sweets and Alba, who hadn't moved. "You two coming?"

Alba curled her lip. "How many idiots does it take to make a couple bags of popcorn?"

I could hear Holly and Jax bounding down the stairs, giggling. "Apparently it takes three of us, alright? So shut it. You coming, Sweets?"

Sweets shook her head. "No, my feet are killing me. Bring me a bowl, though, would you?"

I nodded. "Sure thing."

By the time I got downstairs, Jax and Holly already had the box of microwave popcorn out and were singing a Meghan Trainor song, Jax's new favorite, and doing a little dance to it. I always knew when Jax had a new favorite song because she'd belt it out on repeat in the shower for weeks at a time and then, just as soon as it had appeared, it would be gone, to be replaced by her next new "favorite song." It was an annoying, yet weirdly lovable, quality of my undeniably quirky roommate.

I pulled a bag of popcorn out of the box and unwrapped it as they danced around the kitchen, singing wildly. "No worries, guys. I got it." I was thankful my mother was done prepping for breakfast and had gone to bed. Otherwise, she'd surely ask me to ask them to turn it down a notch.

After inserting a bag into the microwave and turning it on, I turned around to find Jax and Holly singing into a pair of spatulas that had been left to dry by the sink.

I hopped up on the counter, waiting for the microwave to beep watching them while they danced.

"You must have confused me, confused me with…" they sang, sticking their butts out at me while simultaneously spinning the tails sewn to the back of their onesies. "You must have confused me, confused me with…"

I couldn't help laughing at them as they sang. And then suddenly, my brother Reign was in the kitchen. I held a finger up to my lips, keeping him from interrupting the little show they were putting on for me. In his army boots, he tiptoed past the microwave to jump up on the counter and sit next to me. The girls kept singing. They hadn't even noticed his entrance. I glanced over at him. Fresh from his date, he wore dark denim jeans and a long-sleeved button-down flannel shirt over a black V-neck, and his dark hair had been recently cut. I had to admit, my brother was looking his best.

The girls' voices hit a crescendo. "Your momma raised you better than that, *huh!*" The duo spun around with emphasis when they hit the *huh*.

Holly's blue eyes widened the second she saw Reign in

the kitchen, watching her and Jax. In horror, her fingers climbed to the green facial mask on her face.

Jax had the opposite reaction. She flew forward and threw her arms around him as he slid off the counter. "Reign!"

"Hey, cuz." He chuckled as he gave her a squeeze. Looking over Jax's head, he stared at Holly, who for once appeared speechless around my brother. "Lookin' good, ladies."

"Thanks," chirped Jax. Letting go of him, she scooted back to stand next to Holly. "We did facials."

"I see that." He pointed at Holly. "Nice unicorn costume, Holl."

Holly's hands flew up to her hood. "I-it's Jax's. She was sad. I-I was just trying to cheer her up." She looked as if she wanted to crawl into a hole.

Reign almost looked surprised as he smiled at Holly. "Oh yeah? Well, that was nice of you." Then he looked at Jax. "So you were sad? Why's that? Whose ass do I have to kick?"

"Gran's," I said, as if that answered it all.

His eyes swung up towards the ceiling. "Go figure. What'd she do now?"

"She won't undo the curse she put on Jax," I said. "The girls and I have decided we're going to have to do it ourselves."

"Well, if I can help in any way…"

"Oh, don't worry," I said with a smile. "I know where you live."

"Yeah, you do."

I glanced over at Holly. It was as if her feet were bolted to the floor. I could tell she wasn't sure what to do.

Flee the scene, or stay and talk to my brother and pretend she *wasn't* wearing a ridiculous unicorn onesie with her face painted green. I looked down at my Batman watch. "So what are you doing home so early? Kind of an early date. Strike out?"

"Meh," he said, pulling the bag of popcorn out of the microwave for me when it dinged. "She wasn't my type."

I frowned. "Then why'd you go out with her?"

"It was a setup. Mom's friend's sister's cousin or something. Supposedly Char set it all up." He waved a hand in the air. "Anyway, it didn't work out."

I plumped out a lip and raised my brows at him as I put a new bag of popcorn into the microwave. "Aww, poor Reigny."

"Shut up," he said, slugging me playfully. "There are about a million more fish in the sea."

"But you *are* dating," confirmed Jax.

Reign smiled. "Yeah. I finally feel at home in this town, but it's too boring not to at least go on a date once in a while."

"I know some girls at school that might be willing to go out with you," said Jax excitedly.

Holly shot Jax an evil glare, which bounced off Jax like a tennis ball against a brick wall.

"That *might* go out with me?" Reign repeated with a dumb expression on his face. He chuckled. "Not to toot my own horn, but I haven't exactly had to twist anyone's arm to go out with me as of yet. And I think I'd rather go out with a girl that *wants* to go out with me. Not one that's doing my kid cousin a favor or something."

I glanced over at Holly. I knew exactly what she was

thinking. *She'd* go out with him without having her arm twisted, but Reign had never given her a second glance.

Jax shrugged. "Well, if you change your mind, I know a lot of girls."

Reign ran a hand over Jax's cat ears and gave her hoodie a tousle. "Thanks, Nugget, but I'm good on finding my own dates. I'm not exactly a troll, you know."

"So you say," I said with a grin.

Reign held a fist up to me and pretended like he was going to hit me with a right cross while I ducked behind Jax. Then he gave us all a once-over. "Well, I can see the three of you have big plans for tonight. Yoda convention, right?"

Holly's mask hid the crimson blush that I was sure had flooded her face.

Jax wrapped an arm around my waist. "We're going to watch *Vampire Diaries* and eat popcorn in Mercy's room."

"Mercy's room? Wait, I thought Mercy's room was *your* room? Am I missing something?"

Jax frowned. "Yeah, Alba didn't want to room with Holly anymore, so she made me trade rooms with her."

"Alba didn't want to room with Holly?" He looked over at Holly. "Why not?"

Holly's eyes widened again after having been suddenly put on the spot. "Sh-she just… I mean, she didn't…"

"She said she's tired of Holly being such a slob," I blurted. Holly's wide eyes and balled fists told me she probably wanted to deck me for saying that, but I didn't really care. It wasn't like I wanted Holly and my brother to get together anyway.

"Holly's a *slob?*" said Reign incredulously. "I hardly see Holly as a slob!"

"Thank you, Reign," she said sweetly, through her hardening mask.

"Yeah, you don't know Holly like we do," said Jax. "She's kind of a mess."

"Jax! I'm not a mess!"

"Well, *you* might not be a mess, but your room's a mess," clarified Jax.

"Oh my God," she murmured, ducking her head and looking like she wanted to crawl under a rock. I actually felt bad for her for a split second.

I threw an arm over Holly's shoulder. "Eh, she's not *that* bad."

Reign gave Holly a crooked little smile. "I guess I have to agree with you. Anyone who dresses like Yoda wearing a unicorn costume just to cheer up my cousin can't be *that* bad."

Slowly Holly's eyes lifted to look at Reign excitedly. I knew then—his small compliment had just made her entire week. "Really?"

He nodded. "I hate that Gran won't hook Jax up with her powers. I bet Jax was pretty destroyed about getting denied. So you trying to cheer her up is a pretty big deal in my book." He looked at her seriously then, his dark onyx eyes shining with sincerity. "So thank you, Holly. I really appreciate it."

Despite her facial mask, Holly grinned. "You're welcome, Reign. Thanks."

7

*T*he next day it was only Alba and I that met between classes to start our research. Jax had stayed home sick that morning, complaining of, in her words, a "tummy ache." I was positive it was just anxiety and stress, but we'd all thought it was a good idea that she stay and let us handle her predicament. Not being a witch, there wasn't much she'd be able to do to help anyway. Sweets had to work, and Holly had to turn in some late assignments to one of her teachers.

Seated at a table in the Great Witch's Library, we found Cinder and Libby brainstorming final graduation project ideas. We'd quickly discovered that they'd yet to come up with any good ideas, and were open to any suggestions we had.

Alba slid into one of the chairs across from the girls. "What if you made a really big bonfire outside?"

Cinder raised one unimpressed brow. "Lame."

Alba held up her hands defensively. "Bear with me. Right, so it's this *really big* bonfire. Like huge." Her arms rolled up around her in waves, like big flames as she demonstrated her idea.

I rolled my eyes. It was obvious that Alba was making it up as she went along.

"A-and then you make it rain, right?" Her fingers now wiggled in front of her as her arms moved up and down. "And then you whip up the wind and the wind blows and then there's smoke, obviously, because you know when the rain puts out the bonfire—"

"Lame."

"I'm not finished!"

Cinder folded her arms across her chest and leaned back in her chair, shaking her head. She was already tired of listening.

Alba kept going. "Right, so that gets you earth, because, well, the bonfire is *on* the earth. It gets you fire, it gets you water, and the wind is the air." Alba ticked each item off on her fingers. She exploded her fingers out in front of herself. "Boom. Project complete."

Cinder glanced straight-faced over at Libby and then at me. Then she swung her eyes back over to Alba. "Are you finished?"

Alba smiled and nodded. "Yeah. What do you think?"

"I think it's lame."

The smile disappeared off of Alba's face and appeared on mine.

Alba's eyes narrowed into slits as she glared at me. "You think it's funny, Red?"

I shrugged. "Perhaps I find it mildly amusing."

"Then let's hear your brilliant idea."

"I never said I had an idea," I said with a chuckle. I looked at Cinder.

"Listen, Stone said to impress her. That wouldn't impress our mother," said Cinder, shooting Alba a raised eyebrow and nary a smile.

Alba looked unhappy. "Yeah, well. You said you didn't have any ideas. I was just trying to help."

"We said we didn't have any *good* ideas," said Cinder. "We had plenty of bad ones. We didn't need any more of those."

I let out a sigh. "Well, you just have to relax and get creative. You're probably pushing too hard. You know? Like forcing it. You can't force creativity. Creativity just *happens*."

Alba stood up and looked down at Cinder. "Well, the *Fire Queen* can relax and get creative. I'm done trying to be helpful. I'm gonna start researching possible ways to lift the curse."

That made Libby lean forward on her elbows and look up at Alba curiously. "Lift the curse. What curse?"

"The curse on Jax," said Alba plainly.

Libby looked over at me. "What curse on Jax?"

I took a deep breath. The fact that Jax wasn't a witch was not common knowledge. Everyone at school assumed she was a witch, just like we had when we'd first met her. Libby and Cinder, however, knew the truth. What they didn't know about was the Stone and Habernackle family feud. Discovering the truth about the curse between families was a relatively new turn of events, one that Jax hadn't wanted out, so we'd kept it to ourselves. "Well, you know Jax isn't a witch…"

The twins nodded.

"Like, a million years ago, my granny put a curse on Jax's grandmother, Augusta Stone," I said. "Well, really she put it on the whole Stone family. It's a long story, but Gran put the curse on the Stones because Auggie accidentally killed my granddad when my mom was just a little kid."

"Surely you are joking," said Cinder.

I shook my head sadly. "I wish I was. I wish none of it had ever happened, because the mistakes of those that came before us have continued impacting our lives to this very day. Jax hasn't become a witch and won't ever come into her powers if we don't get the curse reversed by her eighteenth birthday."

Libby's eyes widened. "But isn't her birthday on graduation day?"

I nodded my head sadly.

"But that's less than a week away!"

"Yup. We have a lot of work to do," I said with a sad nod.

"And you're over here trying to help us with our project?" said Cinder. "Why aren't you working on reversing the curse your grandmother put on Jax?"

I shrugged. I happened to be the queen of procrastination. And while I wanted nothing more than for Jax to get her powers before her birthday, I had absolutely no idea where to start. "We'll get to it."

"You'll get to it!" Libby and Cinder said in unison.

Libby shook her head. "Mercy, you have got to get started now! Before you run out of time!"

I pushed myself up to a standing position and looked around. Alba was already off, combing through the card catalog for ideas, I assumed. "Alright, I'll look. It's just that I really don't know where to start."

Libby looked at her sister. "Cinder, could we spare some time to help the girls out?"

"Lib, no! I wish we did, but we have to work on our graduation project."

"We'll think of something," said Libby. "I'm really not too worried. But if we're supposed to relax and get creative, this might help us free our minds. Besides, after graduation we may never see these girls again. Wouldn't it be fun to get to work on this with them for a little while at least?"

Cinder looked at me and then across the room at Alba. "You have no idea what you're doing, do you?"

I shook my head. "Absolutely clueless."

Cinder's shoulders slumped forward and a sigh escaped her. "Oh, fine. My sister and I will help you."

Libby clapped her hands. "This is exciting!"

"Can you guys keep it down? You're gonna wake the ghosts in here!" shouted Alba from across the room.

I waved Alba over. "Alba, come here. I've got great news."

Groaning, Alba slammed the card catalog drawer shut and sauntered over to me. "What do ya want, Red? We got work to do."

"Libby and Cinder are going to help us reverse the curse on Jax."

"Yeah? You two know how to do it?"

Libby and Cinder exchanged looks.

"Well, no, not exactly, but we can figure it out," said Libby.

"Yeah, well, Red and I can figure it out too."

"But if we help you, maybe it'll help us think of a graduation project," said Libby.

I smiled. "I agree. I think it's just the distraction you need." For the first time that day, I finally felt like we could possibly make Jax's dream come true.

"Alright, then, it's settled. We're doing this together," said Libby. Then she held her hands out across the table. "But nobody can tell Jax."

My eyes widened. "What?!"

Alba lowered her brows. "Yeah, what Red said. What?!"

"It should be a surprise!" said Libby.

"For her birthday," agreed Cinder.

I glanced up at Alba skeptically.

She shrugged as she met my eyes. "That's actually not a bad idea. Then we don't have to get Shorty a present. You know how much I hate shopping."

"But Jax will literally flip out if she thinks we aren't helping her," I said.

"We'll make something up," Alba assured me. "I think it's a great idea. Just think how excited and happy she'll be when she gets her powers."

I wondered how I'd be able to keep it from Jax. "Well, if you think it's a good idea…"

Alba nodded confidently. "I think it's a great idea. And we can't tell the other girls. Sweets's got the biggest mouth in the world, and I ain't workin' with Cosmo. She's a nitwit. She'll spill the beans for sure. Plus I get enough of her at home."

I waved a hand. I was just anxious to get started. "Whatever. We'll keep this to ourselves. It's won't be that long anyway. Alright. When can we start?"

Alba looked around the room. "I mean, I got nothin' goin' on right now. Can't we start now?"

We both looked at Libby and Cinder.

Cinder looked at her sister. "We're already here."

"Yes, for sure, now's good," she agreed.

"Alright, then, spread out and let's see what we can find!"

$\mathcal{O}$ver an hour later, I found myself buried between dusty stacks of centuries-old books. Even though I'd skipped my Advanced Spells class to do research, I hadn't found myself any closer to finding a way to reverse the curse. I'd been staring at books so long my eyes burned.

Libby's voice called out over the stacks of books. "Girls, come here."

Glad for the distraction, I shut the book I'd been flipping through and stood up. My back was sore from leaning over the table, and it felt good to give it a stretch. I arched my back and felt a cool breeze zip past me. As I rubbed the gooseflesh off my arms, I glanced behind me, looking for an air vent or a moving fan. When I didn't see anything, I headed towards Libby.

"Find something?" asked Alba as the three of us approached Libby's table.

"Maybe," she said slowly. She pointed a long ice-blue fingernail at a page in a book she had open in front of her. "This book is about curses. There are two important things that I've learned."

"Two things?" I asked.

She nodded.

"Why do I not like the sound of this?"

"Yeah, me either," agreed Alba.

Libby pointed at the page she'd been reading. "The first thing I discovered is that when a witch puts a curse on multiple people at the same time, it makes it much harder to reverse."

I curled my lip. "So because Gran put the curse on basically the whole Stone family, we aren't going to be able to do anything about it?"

Libby lifted a shoulder. "Well, not exactly. You see, it only says that it's more difficult to reverse group curses as opposed to curses placed on an individual. It doesn't say it's impossible. I feel like if it were impossible, it would say that. Don't you?"

Alba nodded. "Yeah, it definitely would say impossible." She smiled. "That means there's a way to do it. I feel good about that. We just have to figure out what that way is."

I looked at Libby as my stomach rolled with unease. "You said you found out two things. What's the other thing?"

Libby wrinkled her nose. "The other thing is the length of time since the curse was invoked. Curses invoked more recently are a lot easier to reverse. Curses that happened long ago are much more difficult, and according to the book, doing so may result in unforeseen consequences."

"Great," I groaned.

Cinder plopped down into a chair across from her sister. "We've been looking for hours. I don't see this as good news. It just means that this is going to be even more difficult than we first thought."

"Yeah, I think you're right. This isn't going to be as

simple as muttering a chant, lighting a few candles, and mixing together some ingredients into a magical potion."

I pulled up the chair next to Cinder and let my head fall forward into my hands. Why did everything have to be so difficult? It seemed like forever since I'd started witch school, and it had been one problem after the next. When would our problems end?

Suddenly, the sound of a wailing siren filled the empty spaces of the room.

Alba and I looked at each other. There had only been a few instances during the past nine months when I'd heard that siren, and none of those instances had resulted in good news.

"What in the…?"

Brittany Hobbs's voice crackled over the loudspeaker. "All students, please report to the gymnasium. All students, please report to the gymnasium."

The four of us exchanged glances.

"This can't be good," said Alba.

I rubbed my bumpy arms again, and when I felt my teeth began to chatter, I realized it hadn't been a cold breeze I'd been feeling after all. "No. Definitely not good."

8

I sat in the gym, sandwiched between Libby and Alba, with Cinder sitting in the row behind us, all of us quietly watching the rest of the witches file in. Their deafening chatter echoed off the walls and made the auditorium feel fuller than it was. Starting to feel more than slightly claustrophobic, I couldn't help but wonder what in the world was going on.

And then, much to all of our surprise, in marched the whiz kids! They came pouring in from the rarely used back entrance. My mind reeled. Since I'd been to campus, *none* of our assemblies had *ever* included the men from the Paranormal Institute for Wizards next door. In fact, besides occasionally sharing the common quad area, or seeing an occasional boy visiting the girls' dorm lobby in the evenings, I couldn't think of a single time I'd seen the whiz kids on our side of the campus! The looks on their faces told me that they were just as confused as we were.

And then I saw Hugh. He was one of the last men to

enter. I hadn't seen him since we'd broken up. And despite it being my choice to end the relationship, I still felt that familiar butterfly feeling in the pit of my stomach when I saw him. His eyes scanned the crowd. I knew he was looking for me. It took him about ten seconds to spot me. He gave a little tip of his cowboy hat when we finally locked eyes.

I sighed. *Oh man, he's hot.* I gave him a little wave as he followed the men up into the far side of the bleachers. Our eyes only parted when he took his seat.

I rubbed my arms. My chills were stronger now. Something very, very bad was about to be announced. I just knew it.

By the time that Holly appeared at the bottom of the bleachers, the place was packed. Literally wall-to-wall witches and wizards. From the floor, she looked up to find us in our normal spot. I stuck my hand up and gave a wave through the crowd. She climbed up to squeeze in between me and Libby and leaned over to me. "Did you see the whiz kids are here?"

"Yeah, I saw them."

"I've never seen them on our side of campus before. What's all this about?"

"Your guess is as good as mine. Have you heard from Jax at all today?"

Holly pulled her phone out of her back pocket and looked down at it. "Nope. No texts. Why?"

"I don't know. It just seems unlike Jax not to shoot one of us a text to see how things are going. You know?"

Holly lifted a shoulder. "Oh. She's probably just sleeping."

"Maybe." I tried rubbing the bumps off my arms

again, but then a thought hit me, and it was as if the blood had iced up in my veins. "Oh my God, you don't think something happened to Jax, do you?"

Holly's eyes widened. "I hope not." She flipped her phone over. "I'll text her."

When the room suddenly quieted down, I looked down at the gymnasium floor. Brittany Hobbs had just entered.

"This is weird," I whispered. "Where's Sorceress Stone?"

Alba leaned over to me. "You getting any kind of vibe, Red?"

I showed her my arm. "For sure. This isn't good at all." My heart beat wildly in my chest as I stared at Holly's phone.

Alba's head dipped. "Ah man, this sucks! We don't have time to be dealing with another mystery right now." She turned her attention back to Brittany on the floor in front of us.

I didn't tell her my fears, or that Sorceress Stone's absence made me really worried about Jax. I swallowed hard, took a deep breath, and then closed my eyes and tried to count to ten.

When I'd gotten to eight, Holly elbowed me, showing me her phone. She'd shot off a simple "r u ok?" to Jax.

Jax had texted back. "Yeah, still in bed. Tummy hurts."

The unease that had settled into the pit of my stomach dissipated almost immediately. I smiled at Holly. "Oh, thank God." I slumped forward in relief as Brittany tapped the microphone.

Her usually healthy complexion now appeared pallid,

as if all the blood had drained from her face. Even her usually perky blond hair looked limp and colorless. "Settle down, students. Please, settle down."

As the voices died down completely, I noticed Brittany pull a tissue from her sleeve and dot her eyes. It was obvious she was fighting to keep it together. I knew it. Something really big had happened.

"Ladies, I need to make an announcement. We've had a situation present itself just a few minutes ago, and due to unforeseen circumstances, classes have been canceled for the rest of the week."

The auditorium broke out into stunned gasps.

"But graduation is this weekend!" shouted someone from the crowd.

Brittany nodded. "Yes, details are still being worked out. As far as I know, graduation presentations and the ceremony will proceed as planned."

"What about finals for the first-year students?" asked another voice from the crowd.

"As of right now, those are being postponed until the Monday immediately after graduation."

Gasps filled the room.

"You mean we have to come back after graduation?!" cried someone, stating exactly what I'd been thinking.

"But I have plane tickets for Monday," shouted another.

"I do too," whispered Holly.

"Yeah, me too," agreed Alba loudly.

"Yes, I know, it's an inconvenience, but I have no choice."

"What about the wizards' school?" asked a deep voice from the crowd.

"Because Sorcerer Stone has recently gone out of town, it goes for the wizards' school as well. And that's all I can say. I'm so sorry," mumbled Brittany before skittering out of the room as if demons were hot on her tail.

"What in the world got into her?" breathed Holly.

I shook my head and glanced sideways at Alba. "I have no idea, but we need to find out what's going on."

"Oh yeah. For sure."

Cinder leaned down and whispered in my ear, "We're coming with you."

"Fine, we'll all go," I said. "Come on."

*S*tanding in front of Brittany's desk, Alba looked down at Sorceress Stone's right-hand woman. "Brittany, come on, you've gotta tell us what's going on."

Brittany shook her head. "I'm sorry, girls. I can't say anything."

"Well, there has to be more to the story," said Alba.

"There has to be!" I agreed. I looked around. "Where's Sorceress Stone?"

Alba started towards her office.

"She's not in there," said Brittany.

"Well, where is she?"

Doe-eyed, Brittany dotted at the corners of her eyes with a wadded-up tissue. "I-I can't tell you."

Alba tipped her head sideways. I could tell she was getting heated. "Well, you're gonna have to. We're not leaving until you do. I have plane tickets to fly out on Monday after graduation. They're nonrefundable, and

I'm not sticking around to take finals when I'm supposed to be on my way home."

"I'm really sorry, girls. I don't have any answers for you right now."

"Yeah, Brittany, we get that *you* don't have any answers," seethed Alba.

I held a hand out to stop her from losing her temper. "That's why we wanna talk to Sorceress Stone. We'll take our issues up with *her*. Now please, can't you just tell us where she is?"

"No, I can't." Brittany's face looked pained.

"Something big happened. We already know it."

"Fine," said Cinder, pulling back her shoulders and looking down at Brittany. "If you won't tell us where Sorceress Stone is, then where are the members of the Great Witches Council? We'll air our grievances with them."

Brittany's eyes widened. "The Great Witches Council?"

"Yes," said Libby.

Brittany looked around nervously. "Umm."

We all stared at her as she thought about that request.

"Well, I'm not sure that I should tell you that either."

"Just tell us, Brittany," I said. Our patience was wearing thin. "You know we'll find out with or without you."

"Tell us and then we'll leave you alone," said Cinder.

Brittany looked around like she was worried someone might hear her spill the beans. "Okay, but you can't tell them I told you."

"Fine. We won't tell," assured Alba. "Just tell us where they are."

"They're sequestered in the teachers' lounge." Brittany looked relieved to have finally let out the secret.

"Teachers' lounge?" said Alba. "Anyone know we had a teachers' lounge on campus?"

Libby and Cinder nodded. "It's on the second floor of the Canterbury Building. We know where to go," said Libby.

Cinder waved us out the door. "Come on. Let's go."

"Thank you, Brittany," chirped Holly as the five of us took off.

The Canterbury Building wasn't far away, so it took us only a couple minutes to make our way from Brittany's office to the second floor. On the way, Libby and Cinder explained that they'd had to meet a teacher there during their first year, so they knew exactly where we were going. They led us up the stairs to a wooden door at the end of the long hallway of classrooms.

Standing in front of the teachers' lounge, Alba and Holly flanked me on either side with the twins right behind us. My limbs were heavy with dread and my goose bumps at an all-time high as I lifted my arm to knock on the door. The energy surrounding us felt intense. Like a thick, heavy blanket had covered us all. It didn't feel good. It felt dark. Almost sinister. I wondered if the rest of the girls felt it too as we waited for the door to open.

After what seemed like an eternity, the door finally popped open and Poppy Ellabee stuck her head out. "Oh!" she said, looking surprised to see a group of students looking back at her. "I'm sorry, I thought you were going to be Ms. Hobbs."

"Hello, Sorceress Ellabee," I began. "We're looking for Sorceress Stone. Have you seen her?"

Poppy Ellabee's brows knitted together in surprise. "Why, yes, dear. She's in here. I'm afraid you can't see her right now, though."

Alba shoved me sideways so she could stand face-to-face with Poppy. "Listen, we just got told by the *secretary* that classes are canceled for the week and we all have to come back for finals on Monday. I have plane tickets back to Jersey for Monday. We weren't given a reason. No explanation. Just a sorry, change of plans, I hope you bought travel protection."

Poppy looked at us kindly, though her face looked pale. "Yes, I know you're probably frustrated…"

"Frustrated? I don't think you could classify what I'm feeling right now as frustration. I'd rank it a little higher on the anger scale. Pissed off might be a better way to put it."

I elbowed Alba in the ribs. Swearing at a member of the Great Witches Council wasn't going to get us what we wanted.

"Yes, I'm very sorry about your inconvenience."

"At the very least we deserve an explanation and the right to be able to speak to Sorceress Stone. I wanna air out my grievances about this."

Poppy gave us a tight smile. "Unfortunately there's been an issue that we can't disclose, and it has put a wrench into plans for the final week of school. Now, I can assure you that…"

Alba tipped her head sideways as she stared at Poppy. "Something happened to Stone," she whispered under her breath.

"Excuse me?"

Alba looked at me then. "Red. Something happened to Stone. Your Spidey senses still telling you something?"

My teeth continued to chatter. "Definitely."

Alba looked closely at Poppy again. Alba had spent the last year studying mind reading. I wondered if she wasn't picking up some of Poppy's thoughts.

Poppy shifted uncomfortably in her brown leather loafers.

This time, Alba nodded her head as the words came out more firmly. It wasn't a question. It was a statement. "Something happened to Stone. What happened to her?"

Poppy's hand went to the collar of her shirt. "Well, I…"

Alba didn't wait for an answer. Instead, she pushed her way past Poppy into the teachers' lounge.

"Stop! You can't go in there—"

But Poppy Ellabee's plea fell on deaf ears as the girls and I followed Alba into the lounge. There was a small kitchen to our right and a sofa beneath the window in front of us. In the center of the room was a long conference table which the rest of the members of the Great Witches Council were hovering over. The second they saw us, they rushed towards us.

"They can't be in here," shouted one of them.

I wasn't sure which, because the second she moved away from the table, I was able to see what they were standing over, and my breath caught in my throat.

Sorceress Stone lay unconscious on the table. Her face was paler than usual and her arms were crossed across her chest.

My eyes widened and my heart dropped into my

stomach. She looked... *dead*. "No!" I breathed. It couldn't be! Not Jax's mom!

"Oh my God," whispered Holly, covering her gaping mouth with her hand.

Alba took one look at Sorceress Stone, and then she looked up at the faces of the Council scattered around the room. "Is she dead?"

One of the women, the one who'd been introduced as Gemma Overbrook, the founder of the Overbrook School of Witchcraft, stepped forward. "You girls can't be in here." She glanced over at Poppy Ellabee. "Poppy, why did you let these girls in?"

"I couldn't stop them! They just pushed right past me," she mumbled.

Gemma's arm lifted and her finger flicked towards the door. "You have to leave."

But we weren't leaving. Especially not now. Not until we found out if Sorceress Stone was okay.

"Tell us! Is she dead?" asked Cinder.

"Leave!" Gemma's voice was more commanding.

Alba lifted her chin spitefully. "No. We're not leaving until we know what's going on here. Sorceress Stone is our headmistress. We have a right to know what's going on!"

"They're going to tell the whole school if we let them go," said Elodie Goodwitch, wringing her hands in front of her. "You know that, right? We might as well just fill them in. Otherwise they'll think we've got something to hide." Elodie looked up at us then. "We'll tell them in exchange for their silence, of course."

"For our silence?" I breathed. "Do you really think we'd keep whatever's going on here to ourselves?!" Obviously she didn't know us! We weren't about to just let this rest. This was Jax's mother! We had to find out what was going on!

The woman in the army fatigues, Daphne Fletcher, stepped forward. She gestured towards the sofa that sat beneath a row of window ledges filled with plants. "Girls, have a seat." When we didn't move, she lifted her brows. "Please?"

The five of us, unsure of what else to do, took seats as requested.

Daphne looked back at the rest of the women, and when one of them gave her a nod, she began. "I really hate to have you find out this way, but in answer to your question—yes. Sorceress Stone is dead."

Sorceress Stone dead. I almost couldn't comprehend the words. I couldn't believe it! Jax! She was going to lose it! To lose her mother?! I knew they didn't have a great relationship, but *still*, it was her *mother.* She'd quite literally *lose it*!

"Poor Jax," whispered Holly as tears sprang into her eyes.

Libby and Cinder both held hands to their mouths as I noticed them exchange wide, surprised eyes.

"What happened to her?" Only Alba seemed capable of reining in her emotions. In that moment, I was thankful for her ability to separate emotion from business. We didn't have time to be emotional right now. What we needed was to be strong for Jax and to find out what happened and what we could do about it!

Daphne gave another look over her shoulder at the women huddled behind her. "Unfortunately, we aren't really sure."

"Well, you're gonna have to try and figure it out," said Alba. Her fuse was short now, and rightfully so.

"We were having a discussion about just that, before you burst in uninvited," snapped Gemma Overbrook.

"Gemma," said Daphne quietly. "Please. Let me talk to these girls. Maybe you should sit down too. We've all had an incredibly stressful day and I know tensions are at an all-time high right now."

The tension I'd felt in the hallway was twice as strong in the lounge. When Gemma turned her back to Daphne, I realized what I'd sensed was the tension between the members of the Council. It made me wonder if their *discussion* prior to our arrival had really been more of an argument.

Daphne looked at us again. Her eyes looked to be genuinely filled with concern. "I'll tell you what we know. Sorceress Stone was here with us—we were discussing the judging requirements of the graduation project and the specific things she wanted us to watch out for. Everything was fine. Then all of a sudden, it was as if someone snapped their fingers and the next thing we all knew, she was dead on the table. Just like this."

I made a face. "You're saying she went from being alive and talking to being dead on the table?"

Daphne nodded. "In the blink of an eye."

"Not possible," said Libby, shaking her head.

"Yes," agreed Daphne. "Not possible out in the nonparanormal world."

Cinder cocked her head sideways. "But here it is?"

Daphne nodded. "Of course. Any witch powerful enough could have made time stand still in order to kill Sorceress Stone."

Holly's fingernails hung from her bottom lip. "So you're saying another *witch* did this to her?"

Daphne swallowed hard and looked at the women in the room. "Yes. There's no other explanation. But not just *any* witch, I'm afraid. No one else knew we were here. We believe that one of the witches in this very room did this to her. It had to have been one of us."

9

*A*s the initial shock of the situation began to wear off, I couldn't help but shake my head. Something about the whole thing didn't feel right. Why hadn't the Council called the paramedics or the police? Where was Merrick? And the Black Witch, where was she? Sorceress Stone was *their* sister after all. Was there that much of a disconnect between the siblings that they wouldn't even come when their own sister had died? And not just that, where was Sorceress Stone's ghost? Why hadn't she appeared to me? How did no one in the room know what had happened? And was this really all happening right before graduation? Right after the announcement of a big "graduation project"? It just wasn't adding up.

As Daphne conferred with the rest of the Great Witches Council over what else she was at liberty to reveal, I looked at the group I'd come with and curled my lip. "The wicked witch is dead?"

"Yeah," agreed Alba knowingly. "Seems sketchy."

"Super sketchy," said Cinder.

"Sketchy that they don't know what happened?" asked Holly.

"Or sketchy that Sorceress Stone's really dead?" added Libby.

"Both," I whispered. "If I had to put money on this, I'd guess that Stone isn't really dead. This is a stunt. A graduation project at its finest. They get a few students to think that she's dead and see who reacts, see what do they do, yadda yadda yadda."

Holly didn't look convinced. "That's possible, I guess. But what if she *really is* dead? Jax is gonna be devastated."

I shook my head. "There's no way she's really dead. Where's Merrick Stone? Where's the Black Witch? Where's Detective Whitman?!"

Holly swished her lips to the side. "I don't know, Mercy. She *looks* dead. I really don't think we can take this too lightly."

I threw my hands out on either side of myself, giving a little gesture towards Stone's body lying flat on the table. "Fine, someone go take her pulse."

"Take her pulse?" Holly sounded horrified. "As in *touch* her?"

"Well, we can't take her pulse by looking at her," snapped Alba. "Yeah, as in touch her."

Holly's eyes widened. "I'm not touching her!"

"Me either," I agreed.

"Oh, fine. Cin and I will do it." Libby stood up, handing me her backpack. "Hold my bag."

With the five members of the Great Witches Council huddled in a corner, Libby and Cinder approached

Stone's body unnoticed. I jumped to my feet too. I couldn't let this go down without seeing with my own eyes what they saw. Jax's emotional stability was at stake. Holly and Alba either didn't want to be alone on the chairs or they felt the same way that I did.

The five of us stood around Sorceress Stone's perfectly still body. Her face was relaxed and her skin looked pliable and rubbery, not taut and tense like it usually did. I fully expected her to sit up and yell at us. Perhaps even launch into a rant or send us to the tower as a punishment for being in the same room as her. But she did none of those things. She looked as if she wasn't breathing either. If this was some kind of trick, they'd done a good job at making it look real.

Libby reached a nervous hand out and placed her fingers on the side of Sorceress Stone's neck. When she didn't readily find a pulse, she moved her fingers around, hoping she'd merely not found the right spot. When that didn't work, she took Sorceress Stone's wrist. There had to be a pulse there. But nothing seemed to make a difference. She looked up at us with sad, sincere eyes and shook her head. "I don't know, I think she's really dead," she whispered.

My head swiveled back and forth on my neck. It couldn't be. *Really dead?* Sorceress SaraLynn Stone was *dead?* If she hadn't been one of my best friends' mothers, I might have actually taken the time to think about how I felt about that fact. The wicked witch *was* dead. But she *was* my best friend's mother. And regardless of the multitude of horrible things she'd done to my friends and myself, she was Jax's only parent. Her grandmother could never be a parent to her. Neither her aunt nor her uncle were suitable replacements—not that her own mother had been that great of a mother in the first place, but she'd been *something*. She'd at the very least not made Jax an orphan! But now Jax would truly be alone!

"Girls, this doesn't feel right," I whispered.

Alba eyed the witches in the corner suspiciously. "I'm with Red. They're acting funny."

As if they'd heard us, they broke from their little huddle and strode over to the table.

"We're still working out the next best course of action," said Daphne. "It is my opinion that we should involve the local authorities at this point, but we're split on that decision."

I nodded. "Yes! That's exactly what we need to do!" What I didn't understand was why they hadn't done it already! If Stone actually was dead and this wasn't some sort of sick, twisted game, it was time to get serious and investigate.

"Red, if we call Whitman, word will be all over campus and all over town in two seconds flat," whispered Alba. "We can't let that happen. We have to be the ones to tell Jax." She looked up at the Council. "How long ago did this happen?"

"Not long," said Poppy nervously. "Maybe an hour, hour and a half ago."

"And you're all claiming that none of you know how this happened?"

"Obviously, we think *someone* here knows. We just don't know which one of us knows," said Daphne.

I frowned. "Well, in that case, we can't trust any of you."

"Exactly. We'll have to treat you all like suspects,"

agreed Alba. "We're making the decisions from here on out." Alba looked over her shoulder at us. "Girls, can I have a word?"

The five of us took a step back, so we could talk privately. The minute we did, the five members of the Council got into their own private huddle once again.

"Red's right. None of these people can be trusted. I still don't know that I believe that Stone's truly dead. This could still be some big act," she shook her head. "Or, Stone could really be dead. We just don't know. But the fact of the matter is, if she's really dead, we need to figure out how to save her. We can't just let her die."

Libby stared at Stone's cold, seemingly dead body. "How do you expect to save her?"

Alba shook her head. "I have no idea. We need to put our heads together, do some research, and figure it out."

Cinder frowned. "I don't think we can just focus on saving her. What happens if we save her and the person who killed her freezes time and kills her again?" She shook her head. "It's not enough to just try and save her life. We have to figure out who did this."

Alba nodded agreeably. "You're right. We definitely need to solve the mystery of which of the witches can't be trusted, but we also need to do our best to save Shorty's mom."

"But what about Jax's powers? And the curse?" I said. "We just don't have time to do it all!"

"You think Jax would rather have her powers over her *mother*?"

"Well, no…" I'd feel a lot more confident in that answer if Jax's mother had actually been *nice* to her. But in all reality, I knew Jax. Family meant everything to her. Alba was right. We had to save her mother.

"Can't we do it all?" asked Cinder. "Can't we reverse the curse *and* save her mother *and* find the killer?"

"You think we have enough time to do all of that?" I asked. "Graduation is in five days!"

Libby lifted a shoulder. "There *are* five of us. We could split up."

Holly shook her head. "We can't leave Sweets out of this. She's going to want to help."

"Yeah," I said, nodding. "And we'll have to do all of this without Jax knowing. She just can't know about her mother. So until we've either fixed everything or exhausted our options trying, we don't tell. It'll kill her."

I looked back at Sorceress Stone. "Do you really think we're safe to just leave Stone like this while we try to figure out how to save her?"

Libby's eyes brightened as if a light switch had flipped on inside her mind. "I know exactly what we need to do. We need to preserve the body. She hasn't been gone that long. I'll freeze her body. That way, the guilty witch can't do anything to her without unfreezing her first."

"It won't hurt her?" asked Holly.

Libby shook her head. "Not at all. Trust me. I've used this spell on many a dead animal while I ran to get Mother to save them back home in Sweden. That's why I came to the Institute to study magical cryptopreservation. I know what I'm doing."

Holly wrinkled her nose. "Oh, *that's* what crypto… whatever means? I knew that was your major, but I didn't know what it was."

I looked at Libby curiously. "How long will the spell last?"

"Until I unthaw her," said Libby simply. "A couple of hours, a couple of days, a couple of years. It's up to me."

"Good enough for me. Freeze her. We need to get started on coming up with a plan. The clock is ticking."

Libby nodded and held her hands out on either side of herself to motion us back. "Stand back." She inhaled a deep lungful of air and then began to blow in Sorceress Stone's direction.

It took only a moment for the Great Witches Council to notice what Libby was doing. Gemma Overbrook moved towards Sorceress Stone, furrowing her brows. "What's going on?"

Ignoring her, Libby continued to blow, emitting a frosty white gust of frigid air. It was slow at first, but as it picked up speed, it cooled the air around and behind Sorceress Stone, forcing the rest of the Council to move away from the body. The group of them went around the table to get behind Libby. Standing next to us, they all watched in shock as Libby worked her magic.

"What is she doing?" asked Gemma, her hand on her hip, staring at us.

"She's preserving the body," said Alba.

"Preserving the body?!" snapped Gemma. "Whatever for! This is highly inappropriate, as a member of the Great Witches Council, I cannot let this continue!"

Gemma's hands went up, and a bright orange burst of electrical energy discharged from the palms of her hands. She'd aimed for Libby, but as a younger witch, Alba had faster reflexes. She shot her own charge of electrical energy, deflecting Gemma's shot. Gemma's eyes widened. "How dare you!"

Libby stopped blowing, but Alba didn't back down. She looked at Gemma firmly. "Sorceress Stone is *our* teacher. One of you killed her. Because of that, *we* are taking over. Once we've figured out who is responsible for her murder, we will allow you to resume your authority over us. Until then, *we* are in charge."

Gemma looked stunned. "You think five veteran witches are going to kneel to five *student* witches?!"

"If you don't, you can kneel to the police and the former Great Witches Council, because we will be informing them all of Sorceress Stone's murder. There will be an immediate inquest, and it's highly likely that you'll all be held in contempt for impeding a murder investigation. It won't be long before you're all sentenced to an eternity without your powers, and quite possibly a life behind bars. If that's what you'd prefer, then by all means, do not kneel to five *student* witches." The venom in Alba's voice was commendable. I was proud of her for standing up to the powerful witches before us.

Gemma's face flushed red, but she didn't back down. "You wouldn't dare!"

Daphne took hold of Gemma's elbow. "Gemma, they're trying to help. I don't think we have much of a choice here. This needs to get resolved. They're impartial. They'll figure out the truth."

Gemma let out an exasperated sigh and turned her back to us.

Daphne gave Alba a nod. "Do what you have to do, girls. We'll follow your lead."

With that, Libby finished encapsulating Sorceress

Stone's body into a frosty, steaming block of ice. Through the blue-tinted slab, we could see Sorceress Stone lying still inside.

My eyes widened. "Way to go, Lib!"

Cinder patted her twin on her shoulder. "Now we've got a little breathing room and some time to think."

I looked up at Cinder and Libby. "We don't have any time to spare. Alba, Holly, and I have had a lot of experience with handling an investigation. I think the first thing we need to do is interview the five of these witches and find out what they know."

Alba nodded. "I agree with Red. We find out what they know, what they saw, and their relationships with Stone, and then we go from there."

"But we should be trying to figure out how to save Sorceress Stone," said Libby. "I think that should be our first priority."

Cinder nodded in agreement. "I agree. The murderer can wait. Sorceress Stone cannot."

Alba frowned. "I think this is where we split up. How about you two go see what you can figure out about saving Stone? The three of us will do the interviews."

Cinder nodded. "Yes, I agree. We'll make more progress that way."

"Let's meet in the quad in an hour or so," said Alba.

"I'll text you when we're headed that way," I added.

Libby and Cinder nodded and took off.

I turned around to face the Great Witches Council. Their faces told me they were all in varying levels of shock over both the events of the morning and the fact that we'd taken charge so quickly. "Alright. Let's get started. We're going to interview each of you indepen-

dently. We have to find out what each of you saw. So…
which one of you would like to start?"

Surprisingly, it was Gemma that stepped forward first.
"Me. I'll start. I've got nothing to hide, and I can't wait to
prove it."

10

I nodded at her. "Alright, then. Should we step out into the hallway?"

Gemma held her hand out. "After you."

Alba led the way, carrying a folding chair with her. In the hallway, she placed it beneath a wide corkboard full of posters and announcements that hung on the wall. "Please, Sorceress Overbrook, have a seat."

Gemma's mouth quirked slightly. She put her hands on her hips. "I'll stand, thank you."

I shot Alba a look.

"So. We should get started. What would you like to know?"

She wanted to be direct. I could be direct too. "I'll be blunt. Did you kill Sorceress Stone?"

From the corner of my eye, I saw Holly's eyes widen.

Gemma pursed her lips. "No," she said, her jaw tight. "I didn't. I had no reason to want the woman dead."

"Do you know who killed her?" asked Alba.

"If I did, we wouldn't be going through all of this,

89

now would we?"

I blinked. Perhaps we'd come in a little hot. "How about we start with you telling us your version of the events of today?"

"My version of events? My version of events is just like everyone else's," she said.

Alba tipped her head sideways. "I don't know about that. It can't be like everyone else's, because one of you killed Stone. So if you don't mind, we'd like to get your version of the events straight from you."

Gemma closed her eyes, lifted her brows, and let out a throaty sigh. Whether she intended it to or not, the gestures and her body language came off as arrogant and made me dislike Gemma Overbrook. "Where should I start?"

"How about we start even further back than today? Did you know SaraLynn Stone prior to coming here today?"

Gemma's mouth, which had already begun to open, snapped shut. It was as if she'd thought better of her response to that question. Her eyes skirted each of us, unable to make eye contact now. "Yes, I knew her prior to coming here today."

Alba peered at her through narrowed eyes. "Oh yeah, how's that?"

"We were old comrades."

"Comrades?" asked Cinder, quirking a brow.

I looked at Gemma. Comrades seemed like an odd word choice. "Do you mean old friends?"

"That's the definition of the word, isn't it?" she asked. Her attitude was shockingly blatant. Murdering someone had to take a certain amount of spunk, and if her attitude was any indication, she certainly seemed to have the spunk to do such a thing to Sorceress Stone.

"So you and Stone were old friends. Where did you meet?" asked Alba.

"We met at the Institute. We were classmates."

"Did you keep in touch over the years?" asked Libby.

Gemma shook her head and then kind of looked down at her hands as if she was inspecting her fingernails. "No, we did not keep in touch. After graduation we went our separate ways. Occasionally I'd hear something through the paranormal grapevine about her—what she was up to and all that. But, no, our friendship just sort of fizzled after our days at the Institute."

I glanced over at Holly and Alba. It had occurred to me that that might happen to my own little group of friends after we all graduated. Alba would head to the East Coast to be with her husband, and no doubt Holly would go back to the West Coast, where the sunshine and cute boys were rampant. Sweets would stay in Aspen Falls and run the bakery, at least for a while. Jax and I were the most likely to stay friends, mainly because our families were so closely intertwined, but it still worried me that it wouldn't all be the same after we graduated in another year. Gemma's words seemed to kind of confirm what I'd already worried about. "So was today the first time you'd seen her since you were both students?"

Gemma nodded. "It was. And of course, SaraLynn hadn't changed a bit."

"And did she recognize you?" asked Alba.

"Oh yes. But there wasn't a lot of time for personal chitchat. I came with the Council, and we had important matters to discuss."

"Important matters to discuss? Like what?" asked Cinder.

That was when Gemma looked directly up at us again. "That is confidential information. Great Witches Council matters. Not for the public to know."

"But we're investigating the death of Sorceress Stone. I think we have a right—" I began.

Gemma glared at me then, her nostrils flaring slightly. "You have *no* rights, where Council business is concerned."

"If Sorceress Stone was discussed—"

Gemma crossed her arms over her chest and turned her head slightly. "I have nothing further to say about Council business."

I sighed. "Fine. Sorceress Overbrook, can you remind us again what it is that you do for a living?"

Gemma almost seemed to smile, as if that was a subject she felt good talking about. "Why yes, I am the founder of the Overbrook School of Witchcraft."

"And that's purely an online school?" asked Alba.

"Yes, it is."

"How do you teach magic online?" asked Holly, confused.

Gemma looked at her haughtily. "Oh, I can assure you, it can be done! My school is very successful."

"I'm sure it is," said Alba, fighting an eye roll. "How about we get to the part when Stone came into the Council's meeting? Tell us about that."

"Well, we'd just called her over—"

"To discuss graduation project requirements?" asked Holly.

"More or less. And she'd just begun to go over the

requirements when I blinked, and when I opened my eyes again, she was just… on the table. Just like you saw her in there."

"In the blink of an eye?" I asked.

Gemma nodded. "That's right. Literally in the blink of an eye."

"Did you notice anything different about the room or the rest of the witches at that point?" asked Alba.

Gemma frowned and gave a light shrug. "Not that I recall. I mean, we were all so shocked that we jumped up and ran to the table."

"Did anyone attempt any life-saving measures?" I asked.

"Daphne tried CPR. She had training in that, but SaraLynn didn't respond to it. In addition, it was hard to know what kind of life-saving measures to attempt when you have no knowledge regarding the cause of death. There were no visible wounds on her body. She was just dead. If it was a heart attack, a poisoning, some type of magical means, anything, we really don't know."

"Why didn't you call an ambulance? Perhaps they could have helped her."

Gemma puffed air out her nose. "Listen. SaraLynn was *dead* when we found her. She wasn't *almost* dead. She wasn't *sort of* dead. She was *dead.* Okay? Why would we have called for an ambulance for a woman that's already dead? We discussed it, and we decided that we needed to have some kind of investigation, but that that would take time. We knew we couldn't very well hold classes and finals during that time, so we decided to call SaraLynn's secretary over so we could cancel the rest of the week's classes. Then we'd figure out how to proceed at that point. We'd only begun to discuss things when the group of you barged in and took over. So we really never got that far. Things just happened so fast."

"Why did you all assume that it was one of the witches on the Council that killed Stone?" asked Alba.

"Like we mentioned in there, no one else knew we were even in the lounge. SaraLynn didn't want us interrupted, so she'd given her secretary strict instructions not to tell any of her faculty or any of the students where we were meeting. In addition, I recall seeing SaraLynn lock the door when she entered the room. It's obvious it was someone that has powers that killed her. They were able to put some kind of freezing spell on all of us. I just think it's obvious that it had to be one of the other four women on the Council."

"And do you have any suspicions about any of the other witches on the Council that you'd like to share?"

"Suspicions about any of the other witches?"

"Yeah, you know, like do you know if anyone had a motive to want Sorceress Stone dead?"

Gemma thought about it for several long seconds. Finally, she nodded. "Yes. Perhaps Daphne had a reason to do it."

"Daphne!" I said in surprise. Daphne had seemed like the most helpful of the group, and the *least* likely to have done it. "Why would you say Daphne?"

Gemma lowered her chin. "I know that she comes off as all nicey-nice and everything, but I happen to know that Sorceress Stone knew a secret about Daphne Fletcher. And I can promise you, it was a secret worth killing over."

11

*D*aphne Fletcher joined us in the hallway next. She had no problem accepting the chair we offered her, and looked up at us with what appeared to be genuine concern coloring her green eyes. "I'm really sorry about your teacher, girls."

"Thank you," said Holly. "We actually didn't like her very much, but she was our friend's mom, so we mostly just feel bad for our friend."

I elbowed Holly in the ribs. "Holly!"

Holly rubbed the spot I'd poked and looked at me in surprise. "What? It's true!"

"Yes, but it sounds horrible to say out loud."

Daphne smiled kindly at us. "It's alright. I know Sorceress Stone was known to be a bit... oh, how shall I say it? Temperamental?"

"You knew?" asked Alba.

"Yes, it's fairly common knowledge that Sorceress Stone ruled with an iron fist."

"So you knew her well?" I asked.

Daphne lifted her brows. "Oh, no, no, no. This was actually the first time she and I had ever met."

"The first time? But you seemed to know about her temper—" said Holly.

Daphne held up a hand. "Hearsay, pure hearsay. No firsthand knowledge myself, I can assure you. Being on the Council, I am privy to certain bits of information."

"So, all the members of the Great Witches Council know about her temperament?" I asked.

"Yes," she said quietly. "She'd never taken it *too* far, correct?" She glanced up at our faces.

I wondered if almost turning us into snakes counted as taking it too far. Or repeatedly locking us in the tower. Firing electric blasts of energy at us, perhaps?

When we didn't speak, Daphne looked confused. "Of course, maybe not everything got reported to us?"

"I would assume not everything got reported," agreed Alba.

"Oh, I'm so sorry, girls. If she did anything to any of you—"

I waved a hand at her. That was neither here nor there. Sorceress Stone was dead now, and deliberating about her crimes against us wasn't going to bring her back to life or help us solve the mystery surrounding her death. Gemma Overbrook's suspicions about Daphne Fletcher's secret were at the forefront of my brain, though. I wanted to get to the bottom of that secret. "So, if we're understanding you correctly, today was the first time you've ever been face-to-face with Sorceress Stone?" I asked.

Daphne nodded. "Yes, that's correct. Well, yesterday was the first time. When I got to town."

"You're from Texas? Is that right, Sorceress Fletcher?"

Daphne nodded. "Yes, that's right."

"And you're in the Army or something?" asked Alba.

"I'm not actually *in* the Army. I provide contractual services *to* the Texas Army National Guard."

"What does that mean? What do you actually *do*?"

"Well, for example, if there's a big fire, I use magic to help the team put it out. I've altered the paths of predicted tornadoes and hurricanes, and I reversed flooding near the Gulf. I've also aided in search and rescues. I've done a little bit of everything. But because they contract me, they just use me when they need me."

I was starting to get it. "So, what do you in your spare time?"

Daphne shrugged. "Well, even though I'm contracted, I don't have a *lot* of spare time. I get quite a lot of contracts, and those people are my family, so whenever they call, I come running. It's always great to be taken back into the fold. But I also do what other women my age do. I've got five grown children. Two boys and three girls. I've got eight grandchildren. So I'm a grandma in my free time, mostly. I do a lot of reading. I volunteer in my town. Trust me, I'm never bored."

I believed her, too. Daphne was the oldest woman on the Council by far, but she had the spirit of a much younger witch, and just as much spunk as Gemma Over-brook—if not more!

"Sorceress Fletcher, we have recently come to under-stand that Sorceress Stone knew a secret about you."

"Excuse me?"

I nodded and continued sharing the few details that Gemma Overbrook had shared with us. "Isn't it true that

Sorceress Stone knew a particularly interesting tidbit of information about you, that, if released to the Texas Army National Guard, might have ended your contractual services with them?"

Daphne's eyes widened. Her face turned ashen and her jaw went slack. "A tidbit of information?" she whispered.

"Yes. A rather important secret," I added.

She shook her head. "I-I don't know what you're talking about."

Alba put a hand on the wall just over Daphne's shoulder and leaned down closer to her face. "I think you know *exactly* what we're talking about."

Daphne's eyes moved wildly in their sockets. No doubt she was wondering if she could fib her way out of trouble or if we really did know everything already.

Alba put the brakes on that for her. "No need to lie. We know everything. So how about we just get it out in the open, shall we?"

Daphne swallowed hard. "It's really not that big of a deal."

"Sorceress Overbrook made it sound like it was a fairly big deal."

"She would," said Daphne, rolling her eyes.

"What's that supposed to mean?" asked Holly.

Daphne thought better of whatever she had to say and smiled instead. "Nothing. Listen, girls, as you know, Sorceress Overbrook runs an online witch academy. She provides continuing education classes for older witches, such as myself. I have recently partaken in some of her classes. Is that such a big deal?"

Alba grinned at her. "Taking a few night classes in

and of itself isn't a big deal, no. But the reason *behind* taking those classes is what's a big deal."

Daphne cleared her throat and shook her head. "I don't know what you're insinuating."

Alba shrugged. "I'm not insinuating anything. The fact is, we know *why* you were taking those classes, and so did Sorceress Stone."

When Daphne didn't say anything, Alba continued. "Sorceress Stone knew that you were losing your powers, didn't she? She knew that the real reason you were taking classes at Gemma Overbrook's School of Witchcraft was because you were trying to jump-start your powers into working again."

"I wouldn't phrase it exactly like that…"

"And isn't it true that Sorceress Stone was threatening to tell the Texas Army National Guard the truth about you, that you had lost your powers?"

"No, I—"

"Is that why you killed her?" I asked. "So she wouldn't tell anyone else your secret?"

Alba nodded. "Because if the Texas Army National Guard discovered that you were no longer able to fulfill your contractual services, they'd be forced to cut ties with you. Isn't that right, Sorceress Fletcher?"

"I can't be sure about that, but I certainly didn't—"

"And since you've never been an active member of the National Guard, you wouldn't be offered any retire-ment benefits. Isn't that *also* correct?"

Daphne lifted her brows and shook her head lightly from side to side. "Well, yes. That's true. But I knew that going in. I knew I wouldn't receive retirement benefits as a contractor. What's that supposed to mean?"

"Just that perhaps your income would dry up if they terminated your contract," said Alba.

"I've been fully aware for years that my income from them would dry up when I chose to retire." Daphne looked hurt now. "But you girls don't understand——"

"Just tell us the truth. Did Stone threaten to tell the National Guard about your lack of powers, Sorceress Fletcher?"

"She——"

"Did you get upset with her?"

"I——"

But Alba wouldn't let her get a word in edgewise. "Upset enough to kill her?"

Daphne shot out of her chair. "That is enough, young lady! Yes, Sorceress Stone discovered that my powers were fading, but that did not make me want to *kill her*! I would *never* kill anyone! I'm not that kind of a person! I've taken oaths to protect lives! It's been my life's mission! Yes, it made me upset that she was going to tell, but only because I'd not gotten my full strength back."

"Your full strength?" I asked, lifting a brow.

Daphne nodded and began to pace. "You see, about a year ago, I got sick. It was a really bad bout of influenza, and then I got pneumonia on top of it. As you all may know, when witches get sick, our powers weaken until we're well again. So when I got sick at my advanced age, the virus stripped my powers of their intensity. Magic is like a muscle. You have to exercise magic regularly, just like you have to exercise your muscles daily. If you don't use it, you lose it! So during the time that I was sick, I really lost a lot of my magic muscle. I was only taking classes to flex my muscles once again, so to speak, so I could get my magical strength back. I knew I'd do it eventually. I wasn't worried that I wouldn't get it back. And even if I didn't ever get my powers back, it would have been alright. I've been preparing for retirement for years! I have a large savings account. I have family that will look after me if I need them to. But now I'm in fine condition, and my powers are slowly getting back to their normal strength. So, as much as Sorceress Overbrook would like to point a finger at me, I must really say that I had nothing to do with Sorceress SaraLynn Stone's untimely passing."

We were all silent as we processed her words. It was strange, but my gut was telling me we could trust her. I wasn't sure if it was witchy intuition or something else, but I felt like she was probably telling the truth.

Apparently Alba did too. Her shoulders fell slightly and she took a step backwards. "I'm sorry," she said quietly. "I shouldn't have been so rough on you. It's just that Sorceress Stone is my friend's mom. We have to get this mystery solved."

Daphne nodded. "I understand. I'm sorry I got so worked up too."

"Please, sit back down. I'll contain myself," said Alba, gesturing towards the chair.

When Daphne sat, Alba had to take a walk. She strode away, her arms shaking by her side.

As she paced the width of the hallway, I looked down at Daphne. "Sorceress Fletcher, can you think of any of the other four witches that might want to hurt Sorceress Stone?"

She leaned back in her seat and crossed her arms over her chest. "You know, I've been thinking about that ever since this happened. And I'm not just trying to point the finger back in the direction from which it was pointed at me, but the only one that I truly get a bad read from is Gemma. I don't know if it's because she's got something to hide or if it's because she just sort of assumed this leadership position when everything went down, but something just rubs me the wrong way about her. And usually, I get along with everyone. You know?"

I hadn't wanted to say it, but I was getting the same feeling from Gemma too.

Holly nodded. "I felt it too."

Alba stopped pacing to agree with us. "And I don't like the fact that Overbrook tried to throw you under the bus by telling Stone about your secret. That kind of information should be kept confidential."

I nodded. "Daphne, can you remember anything specific or unusual that happened before or after the time that Sorceress Stone was found dead on the table?"

Daphne grimaced. "Unusual? Aside from the fact that, in what was the flash of an eye, she went from standing and speaking to dead on the table?"

"Yeah, aside from that," said Alba. "Like, what were the rest of the women in the room doing when that happened?"

Daphne lifted both arms in a baffled shrug. "They were just sitting around the room. I don't think anyone changed positions. You know, we all got pretty worked up the minute we saw her. There wasn't a lot of time to look around and see what everyone else was doing."

I nodded. "Yeah, that's kind of what we're hearing. Sorceress Fletcher, thank you for your time. If you think of anything or see anything in there, would you please let us know?"

She nodded. "Of course I will." She began to walk away. "And just so you all know, I think it's very commendable of you all to be taking charge in such a devastating situation. You all have the makings of some very fine witches, and more than just that, some very fine women. Your families should all be very proud of you."

12

*S*tella Blackwood was the third witch we interviewed. In getting to know her a little better, we learned she'd gone to the Institute when she was younger, as had her older siblings. After graduating, she'd met and married a man from Alaska and she'd moved away, never to return to Aspen Falls again, until now.

"Did you go to school with Sorceress Stone?" asked Holly.

"Oh no, SaraLynn was quite a number of years older than me. She'd already graduated years before I came to the Institute."

That answered one question for me. I'd been wondering how old Stella was, and yet I hadn't wanted to be rude and ask. The woman walked with a very pronounced limp and needed a cane to keep her moving, but her face didn't seem that old. Now I wondered if she'd been in an accident or had been born with some kind of physical handicap.

"Had you met Sorceress Stone before coming to campus this week?" I asked.

"No. As a matter of fact, this was the very first time we'd met. I'd always looked forward to meeting her but never had the opportunity."

Holly quirked a brow. "You actually looked forward to meeting Sorceress Stone? Why?"

Stella smiled. "Oh, I've just heard about her a lot over the years. She's a pretty well-known sorceress."

Holly rolled her eyes. "Huh. Meeting Sorceress Stone. Hashtag life-goal," she muttered sarcastically.

"Sorceress Blackwood, what's your version of events before Sorceress Stone was found on the table?" I asked.

"I'm sure the same as everyone else's version of events. It happened very fast. We were all just having a conversation. And then the next thing we knew, we blinked and there she was. On the table. Dead."

"Did you notice anyone acting strangely at that time? See anything odd?"

"Aside from the fact that she was dead? I didn't notice anything else. I was too shocked."

"Sorceress Blackwood, do you know any of the other witches on the Council?" asked Alba.

"Like personally?"

Alba nodded.

"Oh, no. Not at all."

"So you really don't know what might have been the killer's motive?"

"I wouldn't have a clue! I'm shocked over what happened. It's devastating, really, and to be honest, it's a little uncomfortable in there, knowing that one of the other four women is a murderer. I really hope we get this resolved quickly, so I don't have to be sequestered in that room with a killer for long."

"Yes, that would be uncomfortable," agreed Holly. "We'll do our best to hurry this up."

Stella nodded. "Thank you. I appreciate that." She pulled herself to her feet and began to limp heavily on her cane towards the lounge.

"Did you hurt yourself?" I knew it was probably rude to ask, but I my curiosity had gotten the better of me.

Stella stopped walking and looked back at us. "Oh. No, no, dears. I was born this way. It was a birth defect. My father, who was a very powerful wizard, was quite upset about my condition when I was born and attempted to magically manipulate my condition. For the first few years of my life, it worked. But then, when I got a little older, my symptoms returned and one of my legs stopped growing before the other did. As a result I've got this permanent limp, I'm afraid. It's also why I never grew very tall like the rest of my siblings."

I felt awkward now. I'd expected her to say she just had bad knees or had been in a car accident or something. "Oh, I'm sorry for asking."

She smiled kindly. "It's quite alright, dear. Let me know if you have any other questions, I'd be happy to answer them."

Next to come out was Elodie Goodwitch. Of all the witches that had come out to see us thus far, Elodie appeared to either be the most shaken, or the most nervous. The small woman's hands trembled as they rolled over each other, clinging to the hollow space under her rib cage.

"Hello, Sorceress Goodwitch," said Holly with a hint of a smile. "Would you like to take a seat?"

She nodded at us but couldn't seem to take her eyes off Holly. "You look so much better, sweetheart."

Holly furrowed her brows. "Excuse me?"

"Oh, it's just that the last time I saw you, you weren't feeling very well. I'm glad to see you're feeling better."

We all stared at Holly. She'd met Elodie before?

But Holly shook her head. "I'm sorry, I really don't know what you're talking about. I don't think we've ever met."

Elodie looked at the rest of us with curious eyes. "You don't remember me?"

We all shook our heads.

She touched the tips of her fingers to her chest. "I'm Elodie Goodwitch. I own the magical apothecary in Norwalk."

I lifted the corner of my mouth. Was that supposed to ring a bell with us? I mean, I remembered Sorceress Stone saying that during Elodie's introductions, but that's all I'd ever heard of Elodie Goodwitch.

"I don't know about them, but I've never heard of you," said Alba.

All of our heads bobbed in agreement.

She furrowed her brow. "But you're the Witch Squad, right?"

Holly, Alba, and I all exchanged curious glances.

Alba's head tilted slightly to the side. "Yeah?"

Elodie nodded. "I thought so." Then she lowered her voice. "Don't worry, you don't have to say anything. I found out the truth, and I understand completely now."

"The truth?"

Elodie looked up at me expectantly. "So, you have questions for me?"

Well, now I had a *lot* of questions. Like what was she talking about? And how did she know us? And were we supposed to know her? I shook my head. I didn't even know where to start!

Thankfully, Alba took hold of the situation, asking her about her time at the Institute and about her life. Elodie reminded us that she'd been a potions major during her time at the Institute and then she'd met just a regular man from Iowa and moved there to be with him and to start a family. There she'd opened her magical apothecary. Eventually, she'd divorced, but because she had her business and her family, she'd decided to stay there. She swore up and down she'd never gone to school with Sorceress Stone, nor had she gone to school with any of the other witches on the Council.

"I know that you didn't go to school with Sorceress Stone, but had you met her before joining the Council?" asked Alba.

Elodie held her breath. The girls and I exchanged looks when we noticed her tensing up. Did she have something to hide? Slowly, her head began to bob. "I knew of her, but had not met her personally. My daughter attended school here," she explained.

That was interesting. I was suddenly curious if perhaps her daughter disliked Sorceress Stone as much as we did. "Did you have any issues with her as your daughter's teacher?" I asked.

"Issues?" Elodie looked up at me sharply.

"Yeah. You know, did Stone do anything to your daughter?" said Alba bluntly. "Punish her too severely, lock her in a tower, shoot her with electricity—you know, stuff like that?"

Elodie cleared her throat and shook her head. "I really don't have any idea what you're talking about."

Maybe it was just my friends and me that were punished because we were friends of Sorceress Stone's daughter or something. I really wasn't sure. But Elodie not knowing what we were talking about meant that *her* daughter hadn't experienced the wicked witch the way that we had. I sighed. "Sorceress Goodwitch, do you have any idea who might have wanted to harm Sorceress Stone?"

Elodie shook her head. "No, I don't. I've been thinking about it, and I'm really not sure. All the ladies in the room seem friendly enough. I can't imagine any of them doing it."

"And yet you're all sure it was someone in that room?" asked Alba.

Elodie nodded. "Quite sure. The door was locked. No one else even knew we were in there as far as I knew."

With one more person to interview and all of our stomachs rumbling for lunch, we asked Elodie to alert us to any new developments or clues she could think of and then dismissed her.

"One more to go," I said, rubbing my stomach. "And then lunch. I'm starving."

"Me too," agreed Holly. "I can't believe we're going to have to go sit at lunch and not tell *anyone* that Sorceress Stone is dead. It's going to be so hard."

"Yeah, and we're going to have to figure out what to tell Shorty. There's no way she's gonna go the whole day without hearing that classes got canceled for the rest of the week."

I rubbed my forehead with the palm of my hand. Telling Jax was going to be the hardest thing I'd ever done. I loathed the thought.

Poppy Ellabee, the last to be interviewed, entered the hallway. "Where do you want me?" she asked, looking from face to face.

Alba pointed at the chair and Poppy took a seat quietly.

"Sorceress Ellabee, Sorceress Stone mentioned in your introduction yesterday that you were a former teacher at the Institute," I began. "There's a scholarship named after you, is that correct?"

Sorceress Ellabee nodded. "Yes, an animal spirits scholarship."

"When you taught here at the Institute, did you work with Sorceress Stone?" asked Alba.

"Yes, in fact, I did. Years and years ago, Sorceress Stone and I were colleagues here at the Institute," she said sweetly. "That was before she ran the place, though."

"Did the two of you get along?" I asked.

"Oh, you know, for the most part," said Poppy. "I get along with just about everybody."

"But there were times that you didn't get along?" asked Alba.

Poppy considered that for a second. "I wouldn't say there were times that we didn't get *along*. There were just times that we didn't see eye to eye."

"Did you ever get into any fights or anything?" I asked.

Poppy sucked in her breath, covering her mouth with a hand. "Oh, heavens no!"

"Do you know any of the other witches on the Council?"

"Not particularly well. The only one I've ever heard of is Gemma Overbrook. I believe we've attended some educators' conferences together over the years. Perhaps we've spoken on an occasion or two, but I really wouldn't go so far as to say that I *know* her personally."

"And do you think Gemma could have had anything to do with this?" asked Holly.

Poppy shook her head. "Listen, ladies. I *wish* that I could point you in the right direction, but I can't. I don't know who did this any more than you do, but I can assure you I'll do whatever it takes to help you figure it out."

"You'll keep an ear out for anything while you're in there?"

Poppy nodded. "Of course! I've already been keeping my ear to the ground."

"But you haven't heard anything yet?"

"Not yet," she said, hanging her head. "But it just happened. Things are sure to get riled up the longer we sit in there waiting. Do you have a plan for solving this horrendous crime?"

Alba and I exchanged looks. I wished we had a plan. But for now, the only plan was to eat something and have a good long discussion. We could only hope that the answer would come to us.

13

*T*he outdoor quad was mostly empty by the time the five of us sat down together with our lunch trays. It was a warm afternoon in mid-May. The sun shone brightly overhead as if it had no knowledge of the dark fingers of evil that had just grabbed hold of the Paranormal Institute for Witches.

Adjusting my black-rimmed glasses on my nose, I flipped my long braid over my shoulder, pulled my silver-ware packet off my tray and unrolled my napkin. While the cold burger and fries in front of me didn't look even remotely appealing after what we'd just been through, I couldn't help the fact that my stomach growled uncontrollably due to a lack of breakfast.

"Well, what did you girls find out?" I asked, looking up at Libby and Cinder.

Cinder sighed. "Nothing yet, but we'll keep looking after lunch."

"We'll all look after lunch," said Alba. Her somber face mirrored my own and the rest of the girls' faces.

I poked at my food. "Guys, I don't even know what to do next."

Holly shook her head sadly. "Me either. I think I'm still in shock, to be honest. I mean, Sorceress Stone is dead? What is that?"

"Yes, this is horrible," agreed Libby.

I shook my head. It all felt surreal. Like we were going to wake up in the morning and find out that this was all one big joke. And knowing Sorceress Stone, I had a sneaking suspicion the joke was on us. "What if she's really not dead? What if this *is* all part of some weird graduation project?"

Cinder winced. "I don't think so. I watched my friends go through graduation last year. Nothing like this happened."

"It could be new."

"It could be," agreed Cinder.

"But Sorceress Stone didn't know that Jax wasn't going to be at school today," said Holly. "If this was all a test, she had to assume her daughter would see her dead. Would she really do that to Jax?"

"Are you kidding? Stone doesn't care about her daughter. I hate to say it, because, I mean that really sucks, but it's the truth." Alba shook her head. "But I don't think it's a hoax. I think something really happened to her."

"Then why didn't I see her ghost?" I shoved three fries in my mouth as I thought about everything.

"You don't always see the person's ghost," said Holly.

"And knowing how much Stone hates us, we're the last people you'd think she'd want to appear to," said Alba, taking a bite of her hamburger. "And what extra sucks is that we don't even know which one of those witches in there is guilty!"

"Yeah, so if we can actually figure out how to bring Sorceress Stone back to life, the killer's probably just going to kill her all over again," said Holly.

I glanced across the table at Libby. "Do you really think we'll be able to bring her back to life after you've frozen her?"

"It's not about freezing her, Mercy. Freezing her is merely going to keep her body safe from decomposition, losing further brain function, and such. This is about whether or not we can figure out how to bring her back to life. If we can figure that out, unfreezing her is a snap and will not result in any long-term damage."

"But we have to figure out how to bring her back to life." I looked at Alba and Holly who sat across from one another. "We haven't had a lot of luck with that in the past."

"No, we haven't," agreed Alba. "But we've learned a lot of lessons. And isn't that the point? Sorceress Stone is a witch. She's not a mortal. We know there's a *way* to bring a paranormal being back to life. We just have to figure out how. I think we could have done it right with Vic if it had occurred to us to have preserved the body. I mean, he'd been embalmed by the time we got to him. I think that was our problem."

"Maybe," I said with a nod. "But we also have to figure out who did it, and we have to stop them from doing it again. *Plus* we have to reverse the curse on Jax. We have so much to do and hardly any time to do it."

Holly looked around. "So where do we start?"

Libby groaned. "The answer is buried somewhere in the Great Witch's Library. We just have to find it."

---

*W*e made quick work of our lunch and then headed straight to the Great Witch's Library to get back to work. With so much to be done, we agreed to split up. Alba and I were going to concentrate our energies on figuring out how to bring Sorceress Stone back to life, and Holly, Libby, and Cinder were going to work on figuring out how to get the curse lifted from Jax's family.

By late in the day, my neck and back hurt from poring over books all day. An unintentional groan escaped my lips as I leaned back in my seat and rubbed my neck.

Alba looked up at me. "Yeah, my neck hurts too."

"It's literally like trying to find a needle in a haystack. I think I'm ready to go home and call it a day."

Alba's brows sprang up. "Go home? Red! Stone's dead on the table in the teachers' lounge, and there are five witches in there waiting for us to figure out what to do. There is no going home!"

"Alba, you can't be serious. We can't sit here all night! This is ridiculous. We need to go. I think better when I'm comfortable. This place is dusty and cold, and these chairs are so hard that my butt's numb. Plus if we go home, I can talk to Mom. Maybe she'll know what to do about Sorceress Stone."

Alba stared at me. "You can't tell Linda what happened, Red."

"Can't tell Mom? Why not? She won't tell Jax. I'll make her promise."

"Duh. Use your brain, smarty. Because she's dating Detective Whitman. You know if she finds out what happened, she'll feel compelled to tell him exactly what's up. Then, not only do we have a curse to undo, a murder to solve, and a body to bring back to life, but we also have a nosy detective in the way."

"He won't—"

"He will, Red. I guarantee it. He'll make us unfreeze Stone, which makes the chances of her coming back to life slim to none. He'll probably have to throw all those old witches in a holding cell back at his station. Can you imagine? The scandal! The entire Great Witches Council in the slammer?" Alba shook her head. "No. We can't tell Whitman, and you can't tell your mom because that's exactly what she's gonna do."

"Alba, what are we supposed to do without Detective Whitman's help? Without him, we have no forensic evidence! We have no cause of death. We've got nothing!"

"We're witches. We'll figure it out on our own. I'm telling you, for this particular case, he's just gonna be in our way!"

"You girls figure something out?" asked Cinder, strolling over to us, book in hand.

"Hardly," I spat. "I'm exhausted. It's been a very long day, and I think I'm ready to go home."

Alba glared at me. "You find anything about reversing the curse?"

Cinder grimaced. "No. Like Libby said this morning, the fact that this happened so long ago and that there are so many people involved really makes this difficult to remove."

Alba slammed her hand on the table. She looked at me. "The fact of the matter is, there would've never been a curse in the first place if it hadn't been for Auggie Stone poisoning your grandfather. As much as I don't wanna do this, maybe what we need to do is talk to Auggie about helping us reverse the curse. She's pretty powerful. She might even be able to help us bring her daughter back to life."

Suddenly, a lightbulb turned on in my mind. My eyes widened and I sat up straighter in my chair. "Wait. What did you just say?"

"Maybe we need to talk to Auggie about helping us reverse the curse?"

I shook my head and waved my hand backwards excitedly. "No, before that."

Alba looked confused. "None of this would have ever happened if it hadn't been for Auggie Stone poisoning your grandfather?"

"Bingo," I said, pointing at her.

"Bingo? What are you talking about, Red?"

Libby and Cinder looked just as confused as Alba.

"Don't you get it? None of this would have happened if Auggie Stone hadn't poisoned my granddad."

Alba stared at me with her brow furrowed. "Duh."

"If Auggie Stone hadn't poisoned my grandfather, he'd still be alive!" The thought excited me. How cool would it be to have a grandfather in my life?! For years I'd wanted to have a dad in my life, but having my grandfather in my life would've been almost as good.

"Yeah, well, we can't even think of a way to reverse a

silly old curse," said Libby. "Now you want to go off on a wild tangent and try and bring your grandfather back to life? We're in a little bit of a time crunch, I'm afraid."

I shook my head. "No, no, no. You don't get what I'm saying." The ideas were still flooding in. I pushed myself up and shoved my chair under the table. I had to walk around a little and let out some of the nervous energy that was starting to build in my system. "If he hadn't been killed, the curse would've never happened." I smiled at the group wildly. They all stared back at me with blank expressions on their faces. "Don't you get it, girls? It's not about *reversing* the curse. It's about making sure the curse *never* happened!"

Libby and Cinder's eyes both widened simultaneously. "A time reversal spell!" they said in unison.

Alba palmed her forehead. "Red, do you know how dangerous that is? We haven't learned a single thing about messing with time."

I looked at the twins. "Have either of you?"

They both shook their heads.

Libby lifted a shoulder. "Not like a full-fledged travel-back-in-time spell. We've done a five-minute time rewind before. But that's completely different."

"Well, then, we've got a lot of work to do to figure out how to do a full-fledged travel-back-in-time spell," I said excitedly. "Let's check the card catalog. There has to be a book here."

The group of us rushed over to the card catalog, and Alba pulled open the T drawer. She flipped through cards until she got to a card that said "Time travel spells." She'd no sooner glanced at it than she looked up at me and the rest of the girls. "Third floor."

"Looks like we're paying Clara a visit, girls."

_____

*C*lara Mason was the third floor's resident ghost. She'd assisted us in checking out books on a few other occasions, and now, after a year of witch school, I was finally unafraid of paying her a visit. After retrieving the key from its secret hiding spot, we rushed the stairs to find Clara waiting for us at the top with a smile on her face.

"Hello, girls," she said in her usual sweet voice.

"Hi, Clara," said Holly, also braver than she'd been during those first few months of school.

"I haven't seen you in quite a while. How are things going?"

"Not so good, I'm afraid," I said. "Clara, these are two of our friends. This is Libby, and this is Cinder."

"It's so nice to meet you, girls."

Neither Libby nor Cinder had the ghost-seeing abilities of a medium, so seeing Clara was a bit of a shock to them. They both gave her nervous smiles. "Nice to meet you too," they said in unison.

"I'm sorry things aren't going well for you. What can I help you with?"

"We need to find a book—" I began.

Alba cut in. "About time travel. It's by Davis Krasnikov."

"Oh! I know the very book!" Clara turned around and started towards the stacks. "It's called *Traveling into Time*. What an amazing read. Mr. Krasnikov chronicled his journey through time in that book. I've read it several times. It's a very interesting book."

Alba curled her lip. "You mean it's an autobiography?"

"Why, yes," she said, stopping in her tracks and turning around to face us again. "Do you still want it?"

"Do you have any other books on time travel?" asked Alba. "More like an instructional book or a spell book."

Clara tapped a finger on her chin. "No, I'm afraid not. At least not up here. There might be other books on time travel on the second floor. But that's the only book I have." She smiled kindly. "But I think you'll really like it. It's a riveting read."

"Does he tell how he managed to travel back in time?" asked Cinder.

Clara nodded. "He did go into some detail about his early failures and how he ultimately succeeded in time traveling."

"Then we'll take it," said Alba.

Clara handed Alba the book. On the cover was a picture of an old man holding an infant. "That's Davis," she said, pointing at the old man.

"Is that his baby?" asked Holly.

Clara giggled. "Oh no, dear. That's Davis too. He's holding himself as a baby during one of his trips through time."

Alba smiled broadly. "This has gotta work." She pulled the card from the front pocket. "I'll check it out. Three days, right?"

"Yes, dear. Three days," Clara agreed. If the book wasn't returned by sunset on the third day, whoever checked out the book would pay the penalty by taking Clara's place as the third-floor ghost.

Alba nodded as she scribbled her name on the small card and handed it to Clara. "Don't worry. I'll have it back by then."

"Very good, dear. Thank you so much for coming to see me again."

"Thank you for your help, Clara."

At the bottom of the stairs, Alba looked at me curiously. "If this is only an autobiography, I wonder why they're keeping it on the third floor. I thought only books that were potentially dangerous were kept up there."

"That's got to mean that there are directions," I said hopefully. "Come on. Let's take it home and go from there."

14

*A*fter packing up our stuff and leaving the library, we released the members of the Great Witches Council back to their appointed housing for the evening. Then, using Alba's telekinetic abilities, the five of us hid Sorceress Stone's body in the Institute's tower. It was fitting that we took her there, as it had seemed to be her favorite place to put us when she was punishing us. We wanted to ensure that whoever was responsible for her death wouldn't be able to find her while we went home for the evening.

When she'd been properly stowed away, Libby and Cinder went back to their dorm room, and Alba, Holly, and I drove back to Habernackle's to eat supper and pore over the book we'd checked out.

Anxiety ate away at me as I steered my old beater of a car back into town. I didn't know what we'd say to Jax or my mother if they asked. I glanced into the rearview mirror, meeting Holly's eyes. "Maybe we should swing by the bakery to tell Sweets what happened."

"We're gonna see her in like a half hour," said Alba. "We can't tell her then?"

"I mean, we can, but Jax will be around," I said. "I was hoping to avoid Jax as much as I can. I'm scared she'll see right through me the second she lays eyes on me."

With her eyes round, Holly nodded. "I know what you mean. I have no idea how I'm supposed to share a room with her tonight and not spill the beans."

"But you're not going to, right?" snapped Alba.

Holly nodded. "Well, of course I'm not going to tell her! I mean, I'll do my best anyway."

"You better not."

"I said I wouldn't," said Holly, crossing her arms and looking out the window.

I rolled my eyes. I was already feeling lousy. I didn't need their bickering on top of it. "She said she wouldn't, Alba. Chill."

"You chill."

"How about we all chill?" I turned into a parking spot in front of Bailey's Bakery and Sweets. "I realize that this is a very stressful time and we have a lot on our plates— possibly the most we've had on our plates all year. A lot is riding on our shoulders, which is exactly why we can't afford to lose our heads right now."

Neither Alba nor Holly said anything. I gave a nod, shut off the car, and climbed out. I didn't bother to lock it. If someone wanted to steal the hunk of junk, I was quite willing to let them have it. The thing burned more oil than gas, the heater squealed like a stuck pig when I ran the fan on anything higher than two, and it made clunking noises when I made left-hand turns. Reign had been promising since he'd moved to Aspen Falls that he was going to fix it, but then he'd gotten the B&B and had been too busy ever since. With Sweets, the only other member of the Witch Squad to own a car, now a full-time working woman, I'd become the official driver for the rest of us.

The bell chimed as I opened the door to Bailey's Bakery and Sweets. The warm, moist, intoxicating scent of fresh bread enveloped me as I stepped inside. I loved the smell. Sweets even came home smelling like bread most days. I was pretty sure the scent was even better than perfume.

Sweets poked her head out from the kitchen seconds after the bell chimed. "Welcome to Bailey's—" she sang before she realized who it was. "Oh, it's you girls! What in the world are you doing here?"

I buried my hands in my hoodie's wide pocket. "Hey, Sweets. You got a sec? We need to talk to you."

Drying her hands on the front of her apron, she looked down at her watch. "Did you get out of class early?"

"Classes were canceled today," said Holly.

Char Bailey came bounding around the corner next with an empty tray in her hands. "Oh! Well hello, girls! Coming to visit Sweets, or coming to have sweets?" She laughed at her little joke.

"No," I said somberly. "We came to talk to Sweets. Mind if we steal her for a second?"

Char waved a hand at us. "Oh no. Heaven knows this one deserves a break. She's hardly sat down all day." She shooed Sweets along. "Go, go. Sit with your friends."

Sweets followed Alba, Holly, and me to a table in the corner. "Where's Jax?"

"She stayed home from school today," said Holly. "She wasn't feeling well this morning."

"I think it's nerves," I said. "Anxiety about not getting her powers."

Sweets nodded excitedly. "Oh, yes! Is that what you've come to talk about?" Suddenly her eyes widened and she sucked in a little breath. "Oh, I had the *best idea ever* today. I was thinking maybe we could all secretly work on getting Jax her powers as a present for her birthday!"

"Yeah," I said with a half-smile. "We kind of thought the same thing too."

Sweets clapped her hands together excitedly. "Oh, how fun! You have no idea how much I miss doing magic and going on adventures with you girls! This will be just like old times."

I lifted my eyebrows. "More like old times than you realize. We actually aren't here to discuss Jax's powers. At least, not exactly."

Sweets' smile disappeared. "What do you mean?" She glanced around the table, taking in all of our straight faces. "Is Jax alright?"

"Yeah, Jax is fine," Holly assured her. "But her mother isn't."

"Her mother isn't? What are you talking about. Sorceress Stone's her mother."

"Exactly," said Alba.

Sweets shook her short brown hair. "You girls aren't making any sense. Is Sorceress Stone sick?"

Holly shook her head sadly. "No, she's not sick."

"Okay, well, did something happened to her?"

I nodded and put a hand over Sweets'. "Yes. She's dead, Sweets."

"Dead! Who's dead?"

"Sorceress Stone!" snapped Alba.

I shot her an annoyed look. Sometimes the woman just didn't have any patience.

"Wait. Sorceress Stone is dead?" It took a moment for the words to sink into Sweets' mind. "Is this a joke?"

"We wish it was," I said. "But unfortunately, it's not."

Sweets stood up. "Sorceress Stone is dead?!"

Alba tugged on her arm and pulled her back down to the table. "Do you mind keeping your voice down? We don't want Char to hear!"

Sweets' eyes were wide as they flashed back towards the kitchen. "But—if Sorceress Stone's dead, won't Char find out? I'm sure it'll be in the papers—"

"We're keeping it on the down-low for now," explained Alba with a frown.

"We?" Sweets sucked in her breath as the color drained from her face. "Oh my God! Did you three *kill* her?!"

Alba's head lolled back on her shoulders.

"No, Sweets! How could you say that! We would never kill Jax's mom!"

"Well, I don't understand. Why are you keeping it on the down low? How did it even happen?"

I sighed, and then the three of us launched into an explanation of what had happened. We told her about the Great Witches Council and about Libby and Cinder and the graduation projects and how we'd planned to try and reverse the curse and get Jax's powers for her birthday, and on and on we went. Finally, we explained the part about how we were going to go back in time and figure out who'd killed Sorceress Stone and do what we could to bring her back to life and try and stop the curse from ever being put on Jax in the first place.

"But that sounds so hard!" said Sweets emphatically.

"Yeah, ridiculously hard. But we have to do it. We can't let Jax's mom die. Even if it *is* Sorceress Stone," I said. I wasn't sure that we'd be going to all that extra trouble if it had been just *anyone* that treated us as poorly as Sorceress Stone had. She was lucky her daughter was a friend of ours.

Sweets looked back over her shoulder again. "So what am I supposed to say to Char?"

"Say nothing!" said Alba. "She'll have no reason to ask you anything."

"And we aren't telling Jax anything either?"

I shrugged. "We have no choice. Jax would lose it if we told her everything that's gone down today. We don't have time to coddle Jax right now, but hopefully, if we do everything right, we won't have to."

"So… how are you planning to do all of this investigative work without Jax finding out? She might have stayed home from school sick today, but you know she'll want to go to school tomorrow."

Alba and I exchanged looks. We hadn't thought of that. Classes had been canceled for the rest of the week. If Jax found that out, she'd start asking why, and then she'd know something was up. "We need to find someone to keep her occupied for a few days."

Just then, Char Bailey came striding out from the kitchen and opened up the glass case that held all of the delectables that Sweets had labored over all day. One by one, she began to pull out the trays.

"Girls, if I spend the next couple of days helping you, Char's going to need someone to help her out here. She can't do it all alone. Maybe we could convince Jax to fill in for me."

"But Char will want to know why you need the time off," said Holly.

Sweets nodded. "I'm going to have to fill her in if we want her to keep Jax occupied until we sort all of this out."

We all stared at Char. The puffy-haired elderly woman was sweet, but she was most definitely not one of those sweet women that didn't ask any questions. No, Char Bailey was a snoop, through and through. She wasn't going to just believe any old lie we threw her way.

"So can I tell her?"

"What if you just tell her we want to try and get Jax's powers for her for her birthday?" I suggested. "Don't mention anything about Sorceress Stone."

"That might work," said Alba. "Except she's on your grandmother's side when it comes to reversing the curse."

I lifted a shoulder. "We don't have to tell her *how* we're planning to get Jax's powers. And Gran told me to give it my best shot. Char knows we're going to try something. And she likes Jax. I think she'll be willing to help us out, at least by babysitting Jax for a day or two."

"Oh fine, go ahead and ask," grumbled Alba.

Sweets smiled. "Great. She'll be happy to help." Sweets stood up and waved at Char. "Hey, Char, can we talk to you for a second?"

"Sure thing, girlies. Just let me put this tray down."

We waited patiently while Char finished wiping the tray she was working on and then put it on top of the checkout counter. She wiped her hands on her apron and then sauntered over to us with a smile on her face. "What's shakin', ladies?"

"Char, the girls really need my help with a project. I was wondering if you'd consider letting me have the next few days off work," began Sweets slowly.

I could tell she hated asking for time off, but we were going to need all of our magic powers working together if we were going to make a dent in our problems.

Char lifted her penciled-on eyebrows in surprise. "Oh! Well... I suppose you have been working awful hard." She scratched her chin. "I might be able to run the place by myself. Maybe Vic could watch the counter..."

"Actually, that's the other part of my request. I was hoping maybe Jax could take my place while I was gone. I know she can't do the actual recipes because she can't do magic, but she could certainly watch the counter and wait on the customers. She'd be super cheerful and friendly."

Char looked surprised. "Jax!"

"Yes."

"Why Jax? Doesn't she have school?"

"Well, here's the thing," began Sweets. She looked around. "Can you keep a secret?"

Char pointed at herself in surprise. "Me? A secret? Who do I have to keep a secret from?"

"From Gran!" I said pointedly. "Especially from Gran. And from Jax. And from my mom. Well, basically from everyone."

"From everyone!" breathed Char. She shook her

head. "I don't know, girls. You do know who you're talking to, don't you?"

Char was right. I didn't know what we were thinking. She was one of the busiest busybodies in all of Aspen Falls.

Char chuckled. "I mean, I can sure *try*. No promises."

"You don't have to keep the secret for more than a few days," said Sweets. "Just until we get some things figured out."

Char considered that for a moment. "Just a few days, huh? Maybe I can handle that. What's going on?" She looked at us with narrowed eyes—her witchy radar up.

"We're going to try and get Jax's powers for her for her eighteenth birthday," said Sweets.

"We want it to be a surprise, though," I added.

Char wrinkled her nose. "You don't think she'll figure it out?"

"Eh, if she does, she does," said Alba. "But we need her out of our hair while we work on it. Are you in?"

Char's head bobbed backwards. "Ahhh, now I get it. You want me to babysit."

I swished my lips off to the side and nodded. "Essentially, yes. What do you say?"

Char shrugged. "Phil said there's no way you're undoing her curse."

"Well, we gotta try," said Alba.

Holly nodded. "We owe it to Jax to try."

"Whatever," said Char. "I get along with Jax. She's a good kid. She can hang out here and watch the counter until you're done trying. I'll feel really bad for her when you can't deliver, though. I'm afraid it'll break the poor thing's heart."

"We don't intend to fail," I said. The words came out sounding more assured than I felt.

"Whatever. I'll keep an eye on her while you try."

Sweets squealed and jumped up and hugged Char. "Oh, thanks, Char. You're the best boss a girl could ask for!"

15

"*H*i, Mercy," said Jax.

I stopped just inside my bedroom door, my hand frozen on the light switch. Jax was lying on our bed, cuddling her plush unicorn in the dark.

"Jax! What are you doing in here? Why aren't you in your room?" My plan had been to avoid her until I absolutely couldn't anymore. Then I'd make an excuse about why I had to ditch her, and I'd hide in the bathroom for the rest of the evening.

Jax's face crumpled. "Why aren't I in *my* room? *This* used to be my room until yesterday. I napped in here today, because Holly's bed is lumpy, and I'm used to *this* bed. Plus it's really messy in there. I can't sleep around that much mess."

"Oh," I said slowly. "Okay. Sorry, you just surprised me. I'm gonna go downstairs and have a snack." I'd already had a snack, but Jax didn't need to know that.

"Mercy! Wait!"

I paused as my hand touched the doorknob, but I didn't turn around. I couldn't look at her.

"I was hoping you'd tell me all about what happened at school today."

"What happened? Nothing happened. Why? Did someone say something happened?" I wondered if she'd heard from her one of her other friends that classes had been canceled for the rest of the week.

"Oh, no. No one said anything. I'm just lonely. I wanted to hear about school. That's all."

I still couldn't turn around. "Umm, school was fine. Nothing exciting to report. All's well that ends well, you know. How was your day? Are you feeling better?"

"My stomach is feeling a little better. I think I was just worried about getting my powers and all. Did you have any time today to research how to lift the curse off me?" I heard hope lifting her voice.

"Mmm, not yet. We were really busy with classes. Maybe tomorrow."

"Oh," she said in a small voice.

"I'm going to go get a snack now. I'm starving."

"Okay."

I disappeared into the hallway, shutting the door behind me before Jax could ask any more questions.

Alba was coming out of the bathroom as I hit the top of the stairs. "Hey, Red. Where you going?"

"Jax is in my room," I whisper-hissed. "She grilled me about my day. I can't stay in there. There's too much pressure. I'm gonna go downstairs. Why don't you come down there and bring the book? We can hide in the kitchen while we read it."

"Yeah, alright. I'll leave my backpack in my room and change into some comfy clothes and be right down."

I blinked at her. She was wearing sweatpants and a crewneck sweatshirt. I wasn't sure how she planned to get any more comfortable than she already was. "Mmmkay, see you down there, then." I raced down the stairs and into the kitchen, where my brother was busy doing meal prep for the dinner rush that would start any second. "Hey."

Reign looked up from chopping vegetables. "Hey, sis, where's the fire?"

"Fire?"

He chuckled. "I don't know. Just seemed like you were in an awful big hurry."

I relaxed a little. "Oh. No. No hurry. I'm just trying to find a spot to hang out where Jax won't find me."

"Hiding from Jax? She getting on your nerves or something?"

"Oh no, nothing like that. Not today, anyway."

Reign stopped chopping and looked up at me. "Well, then, what happened?"

I tipped my head sideways and looked at the swinging doors. "Where's Mom?"

"In her room taking a nap before the big rush. Why?"

"Can you keep a secret?"

"Depends."

"On what?"

"On whether it's hurting Jax or not."

"Oh, well, it kind of is, but I think you'll agree, I can't tell her what happened."

A deep V formed between Reign's eyes. He pulled his

shoulders back to look down at me. It was very reminiscent of his Stone heritage. "Spill."

I sucked in a deep breath. "Something really really bad happened today at school."

He looked skeptical. "Can't be that bad. I didn't hear a word about it. I run a diner. We hear the scuttlebutt down here first. Sometimes even before things even happen."

"You didn't hear about it because we didn't tell anyone. We didn't want Jax or Detective Whitman to find out."

"Whitman? What's he got to do with this?"

"I'm getting to it. There's something you need to know about Sorceress Stone."

"Red!" barked Alba as she burst through the double swinging doors.

"Alba!" My heart lurched in my chest.

Alba trained her narrowed, suspicious eyes on me. "You weren't about to tell Reign about our day, were you?"

"Well, I…"

Holly and Sweets were behind Alba. They both exchanged looks.

"Because I'm pretty sure we agreed that was between the four of us."

I looked at my brother. "Reign's not going to tell anyone, right, Reign?"

He looked frustrated now. "Okay, what's going on? What kind of trouble did you guys get into?"

Holly, who would usually rush forward to assure my brother that she hadn't gotten into any trouble, stayed still. I think she was still smarting over the embarrassment of being caught dancing around the kitchen with the green face mask on, wearing Jax's unicorn onesie.

"I'm just going to tell him, Alba. He might know how to help."

"It's a bad idea, Red. I'm telling you."

"Alba, if my sister and my cousin are wrapped up in something serious. I think I have a right to know."

Alba stared at him and then swept her hand backwards in front of her, magically sending the veggies in front of Reign skittering across the counter. "You tell a soul and there's gonna be consequences."

Reign put the knife down and tipped his head sideways. "Are you threatening me?" With his palms flat on the counter, he leaned forward to peer at Alba.

"Just know that until we work this problem out, you're gonna have to keep your trap shut. Got it, Slick?"

Reign gritted his teeth. Ignoring Alba, he turned to face me. "Mercy, now I'm getting really worried. What's going on?"

I swallowed hard and then glanced around, almost unable to make eye contact with my brother. "Sorceress Stone is dead."

He shook his head. "I'm sorry. What?"

I nodded. "She's dead, Reign."

"SaraLynn is dead?!"

"We didn't kill her!" spouted Holly, her hand up in front of herself defensively.

"Well, I'd certainly hope not!" He looked up at me. "Surely you're kidding?"

"No. I wish I was."

Reign shook his head, his mouth gaping slightly. "I don't believe it. How'd she die? And why haven't I heard a word about it so far? I mean, this is a really big deal."

"The Great Witches Council, which is the governing body for the Paranormal Institute, is in town this week for graduation stuff. The five witches on the Council and Sorceress Stone were in the teachers' lounge having a meeting about graduation requirements when someone must have done a magical spell on her and the rest of the group and *killed* her. We're pretty sure it's one of the members of the Council, but we're investigating right now, trying to figure out what happened to her."

Reign shook his head. "I can't believe what I'm hearing right now. This is huge. I don't want to call her my aunt, because she's not worth anything as an aunt, but she's my father's sister and my cousin's mom! They're gonna be devastated! Has anyone told Merrick?"

"Reign! No! You're not getting it. We haven't told anyone! And you can't tell either. We haven't even notified Detective Whitman. We're going to try and bring Sorceress Stone back to life."

"Back to life?!" Reign sounded appalled.

"Yeah. We know it can be done. She's not a mortal. She's a witch. We sort of did it with Mr. Bailey, but we didn't think to preserve his body. This time, Libby thought of it."

"Who's Libby?"

"The Ice Princess. She's a second-year," said Sweets from across the room.

"A friend of ours," I added.

"Okay, so, I have a *million* questions I need to have answered before I agree to keep this to myself," he said uneasily.

"Yeah, see, I told ya, Red. Telling Mr. Macho here wasn't a good idea. You shoulda listened to me."

"No, you did the right thing, Mercy. I'll do what I can to help."

"Well, we've already got Char Bailey helping keep Jax entertained for the rest of the week so we can work on solving the murder, bringing Stone back to life, and getting the curse lifted off Jax."

"You're going to try and get the curse lifted?" asked Reign, his eyes wide. "Oh man, Jax will love that."

"Yeah, well, it's not going to mean a thing to her if we can't bring her mother back to life," said Alba.

"So what can I help with?"

"We're going to try and go back in time," revealed Holly. "And undo some of the things that were done."

Reign looked down at me. "Go back in time?! Is that safe?"

"I guess we'll find out," I said with a little shrug.

"When?"

"Hopefully tomorrow. We checked a book out from the Great Witch's Library. Hopefully it's got some good information in it about time travel."

Reign shook his head as if his mind was blown. "Wow. Time travel. I don't know, sis. That sounds dangerous. You girls shouldn't go alone. I wanna come along."

I was shocked to hear Reign's offer.

"You?!" Alba's head shook immediately. "No. Absolutely not. No way. We work alone."

"I'm okay with Reign coming," said Holly, her face red.

"Yeah, me too," agreed Sweets.

Reign looked at me. "Look, I wanna help Jax. And if

that means saving her mother, then I'm in. I'd also like to see Jax become a witch. If anyone deserves good things, it's her."

I knew my brother had magical powers, just like I did, but I'd yet to see him use them. I had no idea what he could bring to the table, but I couldn't imagine him coming could hurt anything. I shrugged. "Fine with me. We have *tons* of work to do."

Alba frowned. "Are you guys kidding me? Should we just take the whole freaking town too?"

"Alba," I breathed. "You can't be serious. It's Reign. He's hardly the whole town. He's Jax's cousin and my brother. This is his dad's sister we're talking about here. Can't you see why it might be reasonable of him to want to go along too? He's not just some guy off the street. He's family."

Alba threw her hands up in the air and strode out of the room. "Whatever. I'm going to bed."

"But what about dinner? What about the book, and making plans?" I hollered after her.

But she was already gone. I dropped my arms next to me. "I guess we'll be making plans upstairs. But, Reign, you can't tell Jax any of this. Or Mom. If you tell Mom, she'll feel required to tell Detective Whitman, and then our plans might as well be shot."

"Yeah, I won't tell. Just keep me in the loop, alright?"

I threw my arms around my brother, thankful that he wanted to help us. It had felt like such a daunting task, but knowing that he was willing to help seemed to take a little of the pressure off. "Thanks, Reign."

*S*urprisingly, I managed to avoid Jax all evening. But it wasn't until later that night that we had a chance to talk about the book Alba had spent the last few hours absorbed in reading. She'd had time to cool off by then.

"This Krasnikov guy really goes through a lot of technical stuff trying to figure out how to make time travel possible," said Alba. "He spends the entire beginning of the book talking about his failures."

"I really don't care about his failures," I said as I channel surfed. "I just want to know he did it."

"He talks a lot about astral planes and astrophysics and wormholes and the theory of relativity. He's a really smart guy." Alba shook her head. "I wish I understood half of this stuff. Time manipulation woulda been a really cool major."

I didn't have the energy to think about astrophysics and other crazy intelligent mumbo-jumbo like that. I was tired, so the cogs in my brain were *barely* turning. I just wanted to know how to go back in time and stop Sorceress Stone from getting killed, and then we could go unwind Jax's curse and be done with it. I didn't need to know the hows and whys, just the solution. "Mmkay, skip to the part where he figured it out, Alba. Can we do it?"

Leaning back against our headboard, Alba nodded wide-eyed, staring at the open book in her lap. "Oh, totally. I think between all of our skills, we've got the capability to make it happen."

Sweets clapped her hands together. "Yay! You have no idea how much I needed this! I've been working nonstop, and getting to practice a little witchcraft again is so exciting."

I yawned before crawling under the covers. "I'd hardly call this exciting, but I can understand not wanting to spend the day cooking for once. I'm lucky other people like to cook, because if it was up to me, I'd eat Pop Tarts and jelly beans twenty-four seven."

Alba looked at me out of the side of her eye. "How old are you again?"

I kicked her under the blankets. "Quit."

"Okay, so anyway, the gist of it is, Krasnikov was finally able to go back in time via a wormhole he created using magic. So we create the wormhole, which I think is going to be harder than it sounds, then we do the spell asking the spirits to send us back to the time of whatever-we-want, and then we travel backwards. We do what we need to do, then we repeat the process all over again, and off we go."

"And it all works out for him in the end?" asks Sweets.

Alba bit her lips between her teeth. "I mean, I'm not *that* fast of a reader. I'm up to about chapter seven. There are..." She flipped through to the end of the book. "Forty-two chapters."

"Well, we don't have time to read forty-two chapters. We need to do this tomorrow."

"I am a little concerned about how fast time in the present moves while we're back in time. Krasnikov makes it sound like time moves much faster in present day than in the past," said Alba, flipping through the pages.

I reached over and clicked off the lamp on my side of the bed. "You know what? We'll deal with that tomorrow.

I need to get some sleep. I'm exhausted. Today was too much for me, and tomorrow is going to be even worse."

"Yeah, I know. I'll just read a few more chapters to see exactly how he made the wormholes, and then I'll shut the light off."

"Alrighty. Night, Sweets."

"Night, Mercy."

"Night, Alba."

"Yeah, yeah. Whatever."

16

The next morning, we all stared down at Sweets as she writhed around on her futon, holding her stomach and whining. "Ohhh, Jax! I think I got whatever it is you had yesterday."

Jax pouted out her bottom lip. "Aww, poor Sweets. Want me to go make you some breakfast? Maybe some toast or a bowl of oatmeal?"

Sweets' eyes widened and she shook her head. "No, thanks. I don't think I can eat."

Jax put her hand on Sweets' forehead. "Wow, you can't eat? You must really be sick. Maybe I should call Char and tell her you won't be in to work today."

"I called Char earlier this morning. She said she'd open up for me. But I can't stay home. There's no way Char can do everything by herself all day. She needs to at least have help watching the counter." Still wearing her pajamas, Sweets attempted to get up off of her futon.

Jax put a hand on either shoulder and pushed her back down. "Sweets. You can't go into work today! You're sick! What if you breathe on all the cupcakes? You'll make everyone in Aspen Falls sick! I'll call Char and tell her you can't make it."

"Jax, you heard her," I said. "Char can't work alone. Sorry, Sweets. I think you're going to have to go in. I can drive you if you want?"

Jax's eyes widened. "Mercy! You really think Sweets can go to work like this? Look at her. She looks terrible! Look at the dark circles under her eyes! And look how pale she is! I think she even looks a little bloated." She turned to Holly. "Doesn't she look a little bloated to you?"

Sweets wrinkled her nose as she looked up at Jax. "Thanks?"

Jax waved at hand at her assuredly. "Oh, it's just the virus. It's not you, Sweets."

I had to stifle a giggle. The four of us knew Sweets wasn't any sicker than I was at that moment, but we needed to invent a reason for Jax to offer to work for Sweets so she wouldn't suspect that anything was up. If it was her idea, then she wouldn't question anything that came up in the next few days.

"Shorty, she can't stay home. She has too much work to do, and Char can't do it all alone. It's too bad there isn't someone else Char could call to fill in for ya, Sweets. I'm sure one of us would do it if we didn't have finals this week."

Jax sat down on the corner of the bed. I could tell the wheels were spinning in her mind.

"Yeah, but finals aren't until tomorrow, and yesterday we literally did *nothing* in class," I said. It was the truth. We hadn't done anything in class because we hadn't *had class.*

"We didn't?" asked Jax.

I shook my head. "Nope. It's pretty much just study time right now. I don't even get why we *have* to go to class this week. I'd watch the bakery for you, Sweets, but I've missed too many classes this year already. Stone threatened to kick me out of school if I missed any more."

"Yeah, well, I'm not working at a *bakery*," said Alba. "I don't do baking, and I don't do customer service. They're not my thing."

"You can say that again," said Holly. "Well, I have to turn a paper in today, so I can't miss class."

"It's okay, girls, it's really not necessary. I can go in to work today."

I tried hard not to look at Jax. I wanted her volunteering to be authentic and not forced. It took her a second of milling it over in her mind for Jax to finally nod. "I'll take your place today, Sweets."

Sweets looked at Jax coyly. "Oh, Jaxie, I can't let you do that."

Jax stood up. "No, I want to. Really." She smiled excitedly. "It'll be a great change of pace. Besides, the fact of the matter is, there's no way I'm passing this year anyway. Without my powers, I can't pass a single finals exam. You girls all have a chance to move on to the next year. You all need to go to class. Plus, I really want you all to find some time to get to the library to figure out how to reverse the curse." She nodded as if she'd made up her mind. "Plus, it's my fault you're sick anyway. I want to do this."

Sweets cocked her head sideways. "That's so sweet of you, Jax. I think maybe I'll let you. I really could use the sleep. Thanks."

"No problem."

I beamed at her. "Okay, well, then, if that's settled, Jax, you should probably be getting off to work. Do you need a ride?"

"It's only a few blocks away. I can walk." Jax pulled on her pointy-toed witch boots over her pink striped leggings. "Are you going to be okay here alone all day, Sweets?"

Sweets nodded. "Linda will keep an eye on me. Mercy, can you hand me my phone? I should call Char and let her know that Jax is going to work for me today."

After tying the laces on her witch boots, she stood up. "Tell her I'm on my way!" Jax leaned over and wrapped her arms around Sweets' neck. "Okay, well, I hope you get to feeling better soon. I guess I'll see you girls later."

I handed Sweets her phone and gave Jax a wave as I finished braiding my hair. "Bye, Jax."

Everyone said their goodbyes, and seconds later the four of us were alone in my room. Alba shut the door. "Jeez, I thought I was gonna have to give her the boot myself."

"It happened exactly like it should have." I looked at Sweets. "Sweets, how long will it take you to get ready?"

Sweets stood up and peeled off her nightgown, revealing that she was fully clothed underneath. "I'm ready." She stopped short of moving and gave herself a once-over in the mirror. "Although maybe I need to do something about these circles under my eyes."

"You're fine, Sweets. Jax was seeing things. Alright, let's go get Reign, and we're outta here."

Holly clapped her hands together excitedly. "This is going to be so fun spending the whole day with Reign. How do I look, girls?" She struck a pose, putting a hand on one hip and tossing her perfect blond waves back over her shoulder with the other hand. She wore a short skirt, wedge sandals, and a sleeveless blush-colored button-down blouse that exposed all of her cleavage.

Alba groaned. "Like a working girl, same as always."

"Alba, you're so mean!" snapped Holly, adjusting the small gold bracelet she wore on her wrist.

"Mean? It's called honesty." Alba pointed at her shirt. "That outfit is completely impractical. We're doing magic today, not going clubbing."

"I know that."

"Maybe if you wore your sneakers or buttoned up your shirt or something."

"I'm certainly not wearing sneakers with this outfit, and…" Holly looked down at her boobs. Her bra had them lifted and smashed together so the sides were touching. "This is how my shirt's supposed to be."

"If that was how it was supposed to be, they wouldn't put the buttons there. But they did put the buttons there, so that means you're supposed to button it up. Hurry up. We don't got all day."

Holly ran her fingers through her hair. "I don't have to listen to you, Alba."

Alba fisted a hand and held it up in front of herself. "Yeah? How about you listen to my—"

I jumped between the two girls before Alba could finish her sentence. "Nope. This is not happening. There is no fighting today." I looked at Alba and then at Holly. "I'm talking to both of you. Got it?"

"We don't have time for this, Red."

"Call a truce. Just for today. Tomorrow, *after* we've saved Sorceress Stone and gotten Jax's powers, then you can do whatever you want. Today we need to work like a well-oiled machine."

"Fine. Whatever. Truce," sighed Alba.

Holly nodded in agreement. "Yeah, truce."

"Now hug it out," said Sweets, pointing at them both.

"Oh, hell no! I ain't hugging her." Alba's head shook disdainfully.

"Yeah, Sweets. That's not happening. We'll be good. You have our word. Come on, let's go get Reign!" said Holly, breezing past me out the door, her shirt still unbuttoned.

Downstairs, Reign had a hiking backpack slung over one shoulder. "It's about time. Jax left five minutes ago," said Reign. "I packed us some food and a few emergency supplies. I wasn't sure how long we'd be gone."

Holly grinned from ear to ear and smoothed her hair down over her shoulders. "You're so smart, Reign. I'm glad you're going with us."

"I'm thankful you all allowed me to go. All I want to do is help my family, especially Jax. She doesn't deserve the hand she was dealt."

I winced. Reign hadn't been dealt a very good hand either. "Neither do you, bro."

"Alright. Enough of this mushy-gushy stuff. Can we get out of here now?" asked Alba.

"Yeah. After you, girls."

17

*B*efore leaving Habernackle's, I texted Libby and Cinder and told them we were on our way. The night before, Alba had texted them a list of ingredients we needed from the potions lab for our little wormhole time travel experiment. Despite the somber reason for our plan, I couldn't help but be a little excited about getting to put our magical skills to use, especially doing it side by side with my brother.

Libby and Cinder were waiting for us in the quad when we got there. "Reign, this is Libby and Cinder." I pointed at the twins.

I knew the girls had seen my brother before. He'd been to campus once or twice, but he hadn't bothered to learn all of my friends' names. "Hello," said the twins in unison.

Reign gave them a *what's up* nod. "Hey." Then he looked around the quad. "So, where are we going to make this wormhole?"

Early-rising students milled around, here and there.

With no classes for the day, it was pretty slow in the quad, but there were a few people around us.

Alba curled her lip. "You think you can say that a little louder, Slick?"

Reign lifted a brow. "I can sure try." He cupped his hands around his mouth and pretended like he was going to yell.

Holly giggled at my brother's lame joke.

I rolled my eyes and tugged on his arms. "Can you quit? Alba's right, this is a super private matter. We can't afford for anyone to find out what we're doing. Why don't we talk about this on the back lawn? It'll be more private back there."

"For sure," agreed Alba. "We're gonna need a lot of space for what I've got planned. Plus, this spell requires running water."

Sweets furrowed her brow. "Like an outdoor spigot?"

"No, like a river. I know exactly where we're going," said Alba. "Follow me."

I buried my hands in the front pocket of the new Halestorm hoodie I'd found at the secondhand store downtown and followed the group past the low retaining wall that enclosed the quad and down the cobblestone sidewalk. Even though the sun was out already, the temperature hadn't gotten very high yet, and it was still chilly. I glanced over at Holly in her sleeveless shirt, skirt, and heels. "Aren't you cold, Holly? I'm freezing."

"Yeah, it's kind of cool. I suppose I should've brought a jacket. I wasn't thinking we'd be outside all morning."

I knew what she *was* thinking. Impress my brother. It's what she was *always* thinking. Comfort came second to showing off her assets to boys.

Reign pulled off the Sherpa-lined flannel jacket he wore and put it over Holly's shoulders.

Holly's eyes lit up. "Reign, that's so sweet of you. But I can't take your jacket."

Reign winked at her. "Don't worry about it. I'm wearing a long-sleeve shirt and jeans. You're wearing a mini-dress *thing*. I think you need it more than I do." He rubbed his hands together and then, with laced fingers, he extended his arms in front of him, cracking his knuckles. "Besides, we'll be firing up some magic soon. That'll surely warm us up."

Holly grinned and settled into the jacket. "You know, I don't think I know much about the kind of magic you do."

"Yeah," I agreed. "I don't either. Spill, big bro."

Reign lifted his chin to smile at both of us coyly. "Wouldn't *you* like to know!"

"We would, actually."

Reign wiggled his fingers. "Let's just say I've got more than one trick up my sleeve."

I could tell Holly wanted to cling to his arm, but she resisted. She was trying to play it cool. "Are you going to show us sometime?"

"Maybe. I definitely don't like using my powers for no reason, but if something ever comes up, I won't hesitate to use them."

Cinder looked around. "Alright, I'm bored already. So, what's the plan?"

Alba pointed ahead at the big empty field just behind the Institute's buildings. The grass had finally greened up, and Seymour Hartford, the school's custodian and maintenance man, had mowed it just the day before. The scent of freshly cut grass hung in the air. "There's a small river that runs through campus. It's that way. We'll do the spell there."

Following Alba's lead, I took a step off the cobblestone sidewalk and onto the lush green carpet. Small pieces of dewy grass clung to my Converse sneakers. "Eww, it's all wet," I complained, holding my feet up. At this rate, they would be soaked by the time we got all the way to the brook on the other side of the field.

Holly stopped on the path and looked down at her sandaled feet. She wrinkled her nose. "It is?"

Alba looked back at her. "See, what'd I tell you? You shoulda worn your sneakers."

Holly rolled her eyes. Then she reached down to take off her shoes. "It's no big deal. I'll just go barefoot."

Reign looked at down at her feet. "Don't do that. How about a piggyback ride instead?"

None of us could believe our ears. My *brother* was offering *Holly* a ride? On his back?! I mean, I understood, she was wearing sandals and he was wearing army boots, but *still*. Weird.

Holly smiled excitedly. "Yeah, Reign. That would be great."

Reign unloaded the backpack he'd been carrying and handed it to me. "Carry the food?"

I sighed but took it from him and slung it over my shoulders. Reign squatted slightly and Holly climbed aboard. "Jeez, Holly, you're light as a feather," said Reign, standing back up again.

She squeezed her arms around his neck. "Am I?"

"Yeah, do you ever eat?"

Holly giggled. "Of course I do. You're just super strong, that's all."

Alba and I rolled our eyes. The flirting made me want to vomit, I could only imagine it was doing the same to Alba and the rest of the girls. But we had to ignore it and press on, there was work that needed to be done. Our large group tromped across the damp grass, and when we got to the graveyard in the center of the field, Alba hooked a left. We kept going until finally, we came to a narrow river that ran all the way from our campus straight through the heart of Aspen Falls. The spot Alba picked was a wide-open flat plain where the river had narrowed. The sound of rushing water and birds chirping in the branches of nearby trees filled the air. "This'll do."

Libby and Cinder looked surprised. "I had no idea there was a river back here," said Cinder.

Libby looked around in awe. "Me either."

Alba nodded. "We saw it when we took flying lessons last fall. I think it's gonna work perfectly."

Cinder handed Alba the backpack of supplies she'd brought from the potions lab. "So now what?"

"Now, we make a wormhole."

"Are you sure you know what you're doing, Alba?" asked Holly, still clinging to Reign's back.

"Yeah, of course I know what I'm doing, Cosmo. Why?"

"Well, if it's so easy to do that a couple of relatively inexperienced witches can do it, then why isn't time travel a big thing?"

Alba looked at Holly blankly. I could tell it was something she'd never considered. "I don't know. I guess because not everyone in the world has powers. Maybe more people are doing it than we realize. I really don't know," she admitted.

"Maybe people don't do it because it's morally wrong or something," suggested Sweets.

"Morally wrong?" I asked. "How's it morally wrong?"

Sweets shrugged. "I don't know. Churches and other religious organizations probably disagree with time travel for some reason. Maybe that's why more people don't do it."

Alba squinched her eyes like we were giving her a headache and shook her head. "No. More people don't do it because it's hidden in some obscure magical book on the third floor of the Great Witch's Library, and it's protected by a ghost. That's why more people don't do it. It worked just fine for Davis Krasnikov. At least in the parts that I read." She mumbled that last part. "Listen, are we gonna sit around debating the moral and ethical implications of this, or are we just gonna do it?"

"Wait a minute. You didn't even finish reading the book?" asked Holly.

"I got through the important parts! I can't believe you guys are questioning me right now. I didn't see any of you staying up late to read with me."

Reign stood up straighter and helped Holly down off his back. "I think we should just get started. This could turn out to be a very long day if you all keep arguing with one another."

I stifled a laugh. Reign didn't even know the half of it. This was like the tip of the iceberg with their arguing.

"Alright, alright, let's get started." Alba navigated down closer to the edge of the creek and opened up the bag of ingredients. She pulled out a small knapsack and handed it to Libby. "Here, you and your sister take this and sprinkle it in a circle over there where it's flat."

Libby looked around. "How big of a circle?"

Alba pulled the book out of her bag and flipped through the pages of the book until she found the passage she was looking for. "Krasnikov made his circle six meters in diameter."

"How many feet is that?" asked Sweets.

"About twenty," said Libby, pouring out a portion of the contents of the bag into her hand.

"I'll walk it off for you," said Cinder, counting out the measurements by walking.

"What is that?" I asked, pointing at the dark granules that Libby poured on the ground in a circle.

"It's finely ground magnetic powder," said Alba.

"Magnetic powder," said Reign with surprise. "Whoa, I had no idea that's how you made a wormhole."

"Well, hang on to your boxers, because there's more." Alba walked over to Libby and held out her hand. "Pour out what you need to finish the circle. I need the bag for the other side of the river."

Cinder poured a handful into her sister's hand and handed Alba the bag. "Here you go."

Alba handed it to Sweets. "I need another circle on the other side of the river. It needs to be the same size as this one."

Sweets took the bag as Alba pulled a long, pointed chef's knife from the bag.

Sweets' eyes widened. "Holy macaroni! What's that for?"

Alba dropped the knife onto the ground. "It's for slicing open a new time window."

I wasn't sure if I understood what she meant. "A new time window?"

Alba nodded. "It's like cutting a door out of a wall." She walked to the edge of the small river and tossed a second knife to the other side. "I need you on that side, Sweets. Take Cosmo, she can help you."

Sweets locked arms with Holly, and together the two of them walked to the creek's bank and looked to the other side. It was too wide for them to jump across, and I knew neither of them wanted to wade through the water. "A little help here?" said Sweets.

"Ohhh, let me," I begged, wiggling my fingers. "I need the practice."

Holly lifted one carefully sculpted brow. "We should trust you?"

"Yeah, Mercy, you better not drop us," agreed Sweets.

"I'll try not to." Even though I didn't feel confident, I was badly in need of practice if I was going to pass my kinetic energy final. I smiled as I concentrated on collecting the needed energy from things around me.

Alba eyed me wearily. "You sure about this, Red?"

"Yeah, yeah. Don't worry. I can do it. One at a time, though. Sweets, you're first."

Everyone stopped what they were doing to watch as I gathered energy from the river, the plants and the trees around me. *All eyes on you, Merc. No pressure*, I thought. With one mighty thrust of energy, I proudly managed to get Sweets several feet off the ground. She wobbled in the air for a moment.

"You sure about this, Mercy?" she asked.

"Shhh," I hissed. "Don't talk to me. I need to concentrate."

"You have to be able to do it even with distractions, Red."

"Shhh!" My powers felt like they were wavering. Sweets was heavier than I'd thought she was. It felt as if I hadn't collected enough energy before launching her into the air. Maybe I'd rushed the lift, but I'd felt under pressure with all those eyes on me. If I did that during a final, I'd surely fail. One of the first rules of thumb before lifting a human or an animal was to make sure you had enough energy to see the lift through. I was trying to simultaneously gather more energy while holding Sweets up, but the girls' voices were a distraction. I couldn't concentrate. Sweets dipped. I was sure I was going to drop her.

"Ahhh!" Sweets screamed as she dropped.

My heart lurched as I realized I didn't have the lift under control. *Crap.* There was no way I was going to get her over the river, let alone set her down gently. *Prepare for a bumpy landing, Sweets.*

And then, she was out of my control. Sweets floated up into the air and landed gently on the other side of the river. I stared at my fingers and then turned to stare at Alba.

"Alba! What'd you do that for? I had her!" It was a lie, but I felt like I had to save face. It would have been embarrassing to admit that I would've dropped her without Alba's help.

Alba shook her head. "I didn't do that."

"But…"

"Sorry, sis," said Reign, dusting off his hands. "It looked like you got in over your head a little."

18

"*Y*ou did that?!" I stared at him in disbelief. I couldn't recall a time that I'd seen my brother lift a single magical finger since I'd met him. I'd begun to think that he hadn't really been born with powers after all!

"Thank you, Reign!" said Sweets, shooting me the evil eye as she straightened her top and dusted off her pants. "She scared me there for a second."

"Reign! I had it under control!"

He patted the top of my head as if I were a cute little puppy. "Sure ya did, kid."

I ducked out of his reach and frowned at him. "I did! And don't call me kid."

"Uh-huh."

Steaming mad that Reign had felt the need to step in, I felt the need to prove myself to everyone. I wiggled my fingers in Holly's direction.

"Oh, no, you don't!" she shouted before I could even

lift her an inch off the ground. "I really don't trust you now. I think I'll let Reign lift me over if you don't mind."

"I do mind!"

Holly gave a nod to Reign and I watched in shock as my brother telekinetically lifted her across the river like she was light as a feather.

"Impressive," said Alba with a smirk.

When Holly was safely on the other side of the river, he wiped his hands on his pants. "You're not the only one with talent around here."

"Apparently not."

I fumed at him. "I could have done it, Reign. I needed the practice."

"I know you could have if you had a little more time to collect energy. You'll get faster the more often you do it. I just didn't think now was the best time to practice."

Alba didn't give me any time to respond to him. She shouted across the river. "Now make the same size circle over there."

Sweets nodded and poured some of the contents in the bag into Holly's hand. "I'll step off the measurements. Holly, you do the sprinkling."

As the two of them worked, Libby and Cinder rejoined us. "We finished our circle, now what?"

"Now comes the tricky part. We need to set a bonfire under the river and between the two circles."

My jaw dropped. "A bonfire *under* the river? Alba, are you crazy?"

"No. I know it sounds crazy, but it's how you make the portal."

We all stared at the river. I wasn't sure how she thought we were going to get a fire started beneath it.

Cinder shook her head. "There is no way to set a fire *under* the water, Alba. It is not possible."

Alba waved a hand. "Yes, it is. This is how it's going to work. We're going to *lift* the river so you can start the fire below it. Then once the fire is going, it'll heat the water. Once the water is boiling, it'll create steam, which will rise into the air. Libby will cool down the steam, which will result in precipitation. We'll have to blow the precipitation towards the two circles. The magnetic powder will act as a drawing agent, to pull the water down. The combination of the heat, the smoke, and the cooling will seal the water into a tunnel. Once we've created the tunnel, it's up to us to use our powers to open the tunnel up to time travel. It's really pretty simple."

I glanced at the confused faces around me. "I don't know, Alba. Sounds hard to me."

Alba curled her lip. "How's it hard? We make a tunnel and then do a spell on it to time travel."

"How do we get back?"

"We return to the doorway in whatever time period we've gone back to. We do our tweaks and we come back to the present day. When we're done, we extinguish the fire, lower the river, and close the portal. Easy peasy."

When Sweets and Holly finished creating the circle on their side of the river, they walked back down to the bank. "A lift?" asked Holly.

With one finger, Alba lifted Holly over. "Sweets, I need you to stay on that side. Get in the circle you just made and take the knife."

"Yes, ma'am."

Alba nodded. "I think we're ready for the fire. Are you ready, Cin?"

Cinder held her hands at the ready, just waiting for a signal. "Ready."

Alba looked around, ensuring that everybody was where she needed them to be before we began. "Wait. Cosmo, I need you to get in this circle and take the knife." Then she pointed at my brother. "Slick, I'm gonna need you and Red to help me lift the river."

Reign nodded. "No problem."

"Libby, as soon as we get the water heated to boiling, I need you to cool it at the top. Don't freeze it, alright? Just cool it down. Understand?"

Libby lifted a shoulder. "I think so."

Then she looked at Reign and me again. "Now, once Libby's cooling the water, I have to let go, so I'm gonna need you and Red to hold the river up as high as you can for me. You can't let it extinguish the fire. Think you two can handle it?"

Reign lifted his brows. "Yeah, I assume I can. So let me get this straight. You thought you were going to do all of this without my help?"

"I would've figured out a way," said Alba.

"What do you want Holly and me to do with our knives?" asked Sweets.

Alba held a hand out. "Just stay in the circle. Don't move. Once we've got everything going, then I'll give you instructions. Okay?"

Holly and Sweets looked at each other and nodded.

"I think we're ready, then. We start by lifting the river. I'll stand here. Red, you stand with me. Slick, you get over there." She pointed upriver. "Just a couple yards oughta do it."

When Reign was in his place, she looked at Cinder and Libby. They both gave a nod.

"Okay. Here we go!"

My heart pounded wildly in my chest as I closed my eyes and began to absorb the necessary energy from everything around me. The magnitude of the lift we were about to perform astounded me. I'd barely been able to lift a person into the air, but to think of lifting an entire section of the river?! The idea blew my mind.

With my eyes still closed, a deafening sound blasted my ears. That was when I knew Alba and Reign had already fired their energies towards the river. I tried not to let that distract me. I had to gather enough energy. So I focused on the task at hand, and when I thought I was ready, I opened my eyes. Alba and Reign had already lifted a section of the river several feet into the air. It poured down like a mighty waterfall.

"It's heavy," Alba shouted at me over the pounding. "Red, save your energy for when I have to let go. Just absorb as much as you can now! Cinder, go!"

Cinder was stationed along the bank between Alba and Reign, her eyes glowing a fiery red. She threw her head back and held her arms out on either side of herself. Then, in one mighty burst, she threw a fire bolt at the riverbed. As soon as that one launched, she hurled a second bolt with her other arm. Bolt after bolt she threw until a fire raged beneath the water. The flames shot higher and higher, spewing clouds of smoky black air into the sky.

It took little time for the water to heat. Steam began to rise off the river.

"Now?" screamed Libby.

"Not until it boils!" Alba grunted through her gritted teeth. She strained to keep the water lifted.

As I continued to gather energy, I glanced over at my brother. His face was blood red and his hands and arms shook as he held them up in front of him. "Hurry! I can't hold this forever."

I swiveled my head up and trained my eyes on the steaming water. *Boil. Come on, boil!* I silently begged. Then I heard my mother's voice in my head. *A watched pot never boils, Mercy.* I looked away. Libby stood behind Alba and me, just waiting for her signal to blow and cool the water. Sweets and Holly were each inside a circle, holding butcher knives and awaiting further instructions. Sweat poured down Alba's face like she'd just finished a marathon as she struggled to keep the river up.

"It's boiling!" shouted Holly, pointing to the water.

Sure enough, I saw bubbles at the very peak of the raised river. "Go, Libby!" I shouted.

Libby wasted no time in cooling the bubbling water. As soon as the frosty air hit the boiling water, waves of steam rolled off.

"You're on, Red," she shouted.

Immediately, I unleashed the energy I'd gathered and aimed it at the river. Surprisingly, the river didn't feel that heavy.

"I'm letting go now, Red. You got it?"

I nodded. "Yeah. Let go."

Alba stared at me as she slowly released her power. The weight of the water fell heavily onto me then. It was heavier than anything I'd ever tried to lift before. I struggled to keep it up high enough not to put out the water. "It's heavy!"

"You can do it, Red. You only need to keep it up for a minute," Alba shouted and then used her powers to separate the steam into two separate puffs of moisture, aiming one over Sweets' head and the other over Holly's. As soon as enough steam had accumulated, the magnetic powder took over. It sucked the steam down like a vacuum, hiding Sweets and Holly inside the steaming tunnel.

"I can't see anything!" Holly shouted, her voice muffled by the pouring water, the fire, and Libby and Alba's magic.

"It's time!" Alba shouted. "Cosmo, Sweets, on my count, use your knife to pierce a doorway through the steam. Start up high, over your head, and pull it down to your feet. You have to do it at the exact same time. Understand?"

"I understand," shouted Sweets.

"Got it, Cosmo?"

"I think so." Holly didn't sound very confident.

"On three. One, two, *three!*"

Knives punctured the outer ring of the steam tunnel. Holding my breath, I continued to hold the river but watched as the knives slid down to the ground.

"Now open up the doorway!" Alba shouted.

Sweets and Holly each pulled the steam apart as if they were separating a set of hanging curtains. Sweets stuck her head out. Her face was beet red. "Oh my gosh, it's hot in there! Now what do you want me to do?"

"Now I need you on this side." Alba pointed at me and then at my brother. "I think you can let go now. The tunnel should be suctioning the water up on its own."

"Let go?" Reign called out over the roaring noise.

"Yeah, let go!"

Simultaneously, my brother and I let go of the river. I half-expected it to drop back down into the riverbed and extinguish the fire, but as Alba had predicted, it stayed up.

We all stood back and admired our handiwork. We'd done it! We'd created a time machine! *If only Jax could see this!* I felt guilty for leaving her behind, but I told myself it had to be done.

"Whoa!" hollered Sweets from the other side of the river. "This is so cool!"

"Very cool," agreed Reign.

Alba smiled. I could tell by the look on her face she was just as excited as we were, but she was trying to play it cool. There was still a lot more to be done. We had to do a spell to connect our time machine to a time traveling wormhole, and then we had to figure out how to send ourselves to the right place back in time. "Sweets, we need you over here now. Bring the knife."

Sweets nodded and closed her eyes as Alba lifted her back over and set her down next to me on the grass.

"Now, everyone inside Holly's circle."

Alba took the knife from Sweets and slipped it inside her backpack along with Davis Krasnikov's autobiography. Tying the knapsack of magnetic powder shut, she added it and the rest of the ingredients Cinder and Libby had brought with them. Reign scooped up his own backpack of food and supplies, and one by one, the group all ducked through the doorway and into the twenty-foot circle of steam that Holly stood waiting for us in.

The inside of the steam tunnel was hollow. The steam had only been sucked down around the perimeter of the circle where the magnetic powder had been applied, and aside from the doorway Holly had cut open, you couldn't see any sunshine through the steam, making it dark, gray, and very humid. It felt like we were in the eye of a hurricane.

"This is super creepy," hollered Libby over the roar of the water.

"I second that," agreed Sweets.

Standing in the center of the circle, Alba took the knife from Holly. "Okay. I'm gonna cut open the portal door. Everyone get behind me, it's gonna get a little windy in here!"

We all stood behind Alba and watched as she reached up as high as she could and pierced the air with her knife. It was as if she'd just punctured an oversized balloon as a gust of wind poured through the invisible cut. She tugged the knife down towards the ground and stopped when the blade of the knife was about a foot off the grass. By now, the air blowing on us was stronger, and it was cool, like an Arctic breeze. It sent our hair skittering around us in waves.

After she'd put the knife back in her backpack, Alba motioned to us. "Okay, so, here we go. Time to do the spell. Get around the portal opening, palm to palm. We have to connect our energies."

The seven of us touched hands as Alba began to chant the spells she'd memorized.

Beyond this world, the current time and space,
Exist the past and a previous place.
Take us there to find the answers we all seek,
We must go back and have a peek.

We must right the wrongs and fix the crimes,
So open this portal and take us back in time.

The wind that poured out of the cut stopped blowing. Alba reached her hands in and pulled the sides apart. I was shocked to see that we'd actually opened a doorway.

"Wow, Alba!" gushed Sweets. "That's amazing!"

I nodded and once again wished that Jax had been here to witness this amazing thing that we'd done. She would've loved to have seen it. "Yeah, Alba. I'm impressed. This is awesome!"

"Ditto, Alba," agreed my brother. "Very nice. Now what do we do?"

"It's time to decide where we wanna go first."

We all exchanged nervous looks. No one knew where we should start. There were so many things on our list to do. We had to save Sorceress Stone. We had to reverse the curse on Jax. And we had to catch a murderer.

"As much as I don't want to say this, I think reversing the curse and getting Jax's powers are at the bottom of our priority list, don't you think?" asked Reign. "I want my cousin to become a witch, but I think she'd rather have a mother that was alive."

"Reign's right," said Alba. "Priority one is to catch the murderer in the act and if possible stop the murder from happening at all. Then we can try and figure out how to reverse the curse on Jax," said Alba. "We all okay with that?"

All of our heads bobbed in agreement.

Alba nodded and began to chant.

SaraLynn Stone was the victim of a horrendous crime,

So take us back to that place and time.
We ask to see when she fell to her death,
We must see when SaraLynn Stone took her very last breath.

We all heard a whooshing noise from inside the doorway Alba had just opened. She pulled it open and stepped inside. "Everybody in! It's time to go!"

19

*C*autiously, each of us followed Alba through the opening that hung in the air. Inside, we found ourselves at the mouth of a long tunnel of spinning air. This new tunnel was cooler and brighter than the dismal sauna we'd just come through and smelled fresh like springtime. Standing in the tunnel felt as if we were standing outside amongst the vibrant outdoor colors. The green grass and trees, the blue-and-gray rocky river, the bright azure-blue sky, and the puffy white clouds all smeared together into a blurry Monet painting that spun around us in a burst of light.

Alba's eyes were wide and her jaw hung slack. "This is…"

"Amazing," I finished.

She nodded. "It's beautiful."

"Where do you think it leads?" asked Libby, looking ahead through the long tunnel.

"If the spell worked like Davis Krasnikov said it would, we just created a wormhole. We're literally walking through the very fabric of time and into the past. I'm hoping that it's gonna lead us back to yesterday so we can stop the murder from happening in the first place. Once that's done, then we'll get to work on reversing the curse."

With her brows scrunched up high on her forehead, Holly's fingernails made their way to her mouth. "You really think it's safe to go through there? I mean, if there's a murderer at the end of this tunnel…"

Reign pushed past all of us so he was at the head of the pack. "Maybe I ought to go first, just in case."

Holly nodded in agreement. "Maybe that's not a bad idea."

Reign took several steps with Holly clinging to his shirttails. He threw a backwards glance over his shoulder at Libby, Cinder, Sweets, and me, who had yet to move. "Come on, ladies. No lollygagging today. We have work that needs to be done."

"Who's lollygagging?" asked Alba, pushing past Reign so she was back at the head of the line.

Sweets huddled behind me as we walked. "This is amazing," she breathed, her voice muted by the swirling tunnel around us. "I really wish Jax was here to see this."

"Me too," I whispered back.

Not only did the lights spin around us, the tunnel also curved as we walked, making us feel like we were moving in a circle, but before we knew it, the tunnel ended and we found ourselves back in the steam sauna. One by one, Alba led us out of the circle of steam and into the bright daylight.

As the last to exit, I looked around to find that we were

on a green patch of grass next to the same river we'd put the spell on. The sun shone brightly, and I could smell freshly cut grass, just as I'd smelled when we'd entered the tunnel minutes before. "Nothing's changed!" I said in surprise. Had we even left the present? Or had we gone through all that trouble just to get ourselves back to where we'd started?

"Did we even leave?" asked Cinder.

Holly shook her head. "It doesn't look like it!"

Alba frowned. "There's no way that wormhole brought us back to where we started. We went back in time. I know it. Come on. We're gonna find out." Alba tromped off, leading the way back towards campus, leaving the steaming time portal behind us.

Cinder and Libby exchanged skeptical glances but took off following Alba nonetheless. When Reign and Holly followed, I grudgingly fell in line behind them.

As we closed in on our campus, Sweets caught up to me. "Mercy, do you really think we went back in time to yesterday?" She kept her voice down so Alba, who was several paces ahead, wouldn't hear her.

"I don't know, Sweets. I feel like Alba's right. We had to have done *something*. I guess we'll find out."

Then my brother's deep voice carried back to me. "What if we're walking into some kind of a trap?"

Unable to tear her fingernails away from her mouth now, Holly stopped walking and looked up at my brother, wide-eyed. "A trap? What kind of trap?"

Looking pensive, my brother stopped next to Holly and shrugged. "I have no idea. Maybe the killer set some kind of trap for us to fall into."

I wrinkled my nose. "Conspiracy theory much? If we

went back in time, the killer doesn't even know we're onto them."

"Are you kidding? They might. We're dealing with paranormals here, not regular humans."

I linked my arm through Holly's and tugged her past Reign. "Don't listen to my brother, Holl. We're not walking into a trap." I glanced back at him. "I had no idea you were going to be such a downer, bro. If I'd known you were going to be like this, I would have left you back at the B&B."

Reign caught up to me. "A downer?! How am I being a downer? Because I'm cautious?"

"That's not called being cautious. That's called paranoia, and I'm not gonna lie. You sound like a delusional whackjob."

"A delusional whackjob?" He chuckled. "Where'd you get your extensive vocabulary, sis? Urban Dictionary?"

"Can you two quit?" asked Alba, still paces ahead of us. "I can hear you, you know."

"I didn't know we were in class," Reign snapped back.

I giggled.

"We're not in class, but we also don't know what we're walking into. Wasn't it you that just said that? If we're walking into a trap, don't you think we should be a little quieter about it instead of announcing to the murderer that we're on our way?"

Reign groaned and rolled his eyes. Holly and I exchanged looks and fought back giggles.

As we neared the Canterbury Building, Alba pulled us off to the side. "Okay, we're here. I think we have to assume we've gone back in time a day and the Council is meeting in that second-floor room this very second. Any ideas on how we're gonna pull this off? We gotta be inside that room to stop the murder before it happens, but obviously we can't let the Council or Stone know we're watching."

"Well," I said, tugging on my ear, "I feel like we need eyes and ears both inside *and* outside the room. We need to make sure no one else came in or out."

Alba nodded. "That's a valid point. Any volunteers for staking out the hallway outside the lounge?"

Cinder raised her hand. "Yes. My sister and I will volunteer."

"Good. Now we gotta get eyes *inside* that room. How are we gonna do that without the Council seeing us?"

Suddenly an idea hit me. "What if we could have eyes on the room without actually being *inside* the room?"

Alba lifted a shoulder, her brows knitted together. "Yeah? How we gonna manage that?"

I wiggled my fingers in front of her face. "Simple. How about a little magic?"

*M*inutes later, all of us except Libby and Cinder, who had decided to hide themselves in an empty classroom next door to the teachers' lounge, stood on the lawn outside the Canterbury Building. All of our heads were cranked back, looking up at the second-floor window.

Alba nodded. "Yeah, I think this is gonna work. Good thinking, Red."

I smiled excitedly. "So I'll lift you up and Reign can lift Holly up."

Alba shook her head. "Oh no, no, no. Reign can lift Cosmo, but I'm lifting *you* up."

"Alba! This was my idea. I'll lift you up. Come on, I need the practice! Finals are in a couple of days."

"It ain't happening, Red. You can practice on someone else in your free time. Right now, there's too much at stake for any mistakes."

I glanced over at Reign and the girls. Sweets and Holly both avoided making eye contact with me.

Reign sucked in a deep breath, flaring his nostrils and raising his brows. "I'm going to have to agree with Alba, sis. I'm sorry. I agree that you need more practice before your finals, but this isn't the time. I'll work with you when we get home."

I knew I wasn't that great at lifts, but I wouldn't have suggested it if I didn't think I could do it. I'd only almost dropped Sweets because they'd all broken my concentration and I hadn't absorbed enough energy prior to the lift. I crossed my arms across my chest and turned my back to Alba so that I was looking at the brick building. "Whatever."

"Sweets, it's your job to keep watch down here. We can't have anyone seeing what we're doing or interrupting, alright? Signal if you see someone."

"I'll do my best."

Holly stood next to me, just a short arm's length away. She turned her head to look at me as she bounced nervously. "So, what do we do if we get up there and see the murder happening in front of us?"

I had no idea what to tell her. I was just as clueless as she was, but I didn't want to come off as being nervous. "We'll play it by ear."

That seemed to placate her enough to turn around and nod to Reign. "I'm ready whenever you are."

I sucked in a deep breath and, closing my eyes, let it out slowly, trying to ease the nerves that had seemingly worked their way up into my throat. "Yeah, me too," I croaked over my shoulder.

"On three," said Alba. "One, two…"

The word three was replaced by Holly's squeal as we suddenly shot up into the air. The energy Alba fired at me tingled my backside. It felt like tiny bits of electrically charged atoms were crawling around in the pockets of my jeans. The ends of my hair suddenly became unrestricted by gravity and my hair fuzzed up around my face, a side effect of using kinetic energy that I hadn't known about.

As we hovered at the base of the second-floor windowsill, I looked down at the grass below. My heart thundered in my chest. I'd flown on broomsticks before, but at least then I'd felt somewhat safe. Not only had I had something under me, but I was also controlling my movement. Now I had no control and nothing solid beneath me. I peered at the white windowsill again. I couldn't see a single thing. I was too low. I gave Alba and Reign a signal to lift us higher.

A second later, Holly and I were nose to windowpane. My eyes widened as I saw Sorceress Stone standing erect, pacing in front of the table that we'd found her lying dead on a day ago. Just as shocked, Holly glanced over at me. We'd actually done it! We'd *actually* gone back in time. I glanced down at Alba and Reign and gave them a thumb's-up. Then Holly and I concentrated on our mission. Spying.

I took note of the Council members. Poppy, Gemma,

and Elodie sat side by side on the small sofa that was positioned just beneath our noses. Stella and Daphne sat beside them on a pair of folding chairs. Several of the women had pads of paper in front of them, taking notes as Sorceress Stone spoke.

I tried to hear what she was saying through the closed window, but only the dull murmur of her voice was audible. I watched her mouth move though. I saw the words *graduation project* spill from her lips, but as she paced, her head turned slightly and I lost sight of her lips.

"See anything?" hissed a voice from below.

Looking down, I merely gave another thumbs-up. I couldn't risk being heard. I'd share the minute amount of details with them later. I turned my attention back to the room while my pulse pounded in my ears. I felt like at any second I was going to see someone get up and put a spell on the room. I couldn't peel my eyes away.

Gemma uncrossed her legs and then crossed them again. Elodie cleared her throat and shuffled in her seat. Stella leaned back in her seat and readjusted her cane. Daphne doodled on her notepad, and Poppy scratched an itch behind her ear. Was it just me or did they all look guilty? I glanced up at Sorceress Stone as she stopped pacing. Now she faced the women with her mouth closed. It was as if she'd just asked a question.

Just a few short inches away from me, Gemma flinched, and in that very next second, I blinked.

It happened so quickly that I didn't even realize I'd blinked. But when I opened my eyes from that split-second movement, Sorceress Stone was lying on the table just like each of the Council members had told us had happened!

A collective gasp escaped the glass pane and made it to my ears. "SaraLynn!" breathed Gemma.

Daphne was the first to her feet, with Elodie following close behind. Stella lifted her cane and dragged herself to her feet. Wide-eyed, Poppy covered her open mouth with her hand as she sat stunned in her seat.

I turned to look at Holly, who was also staring wide-eyed. "I blinked," she whispered.

"Me too," I mouthed back. We'd missed it! We'd missed the moment that Sorceress Stone had been killed! Had it been Gemma? I'd seen her flinch last! Had it been one of the other women in the room? Had it been someone new from the hallway? I couldn't wait to talk to Libby and Cinder and find out if they'd seen anything.

As all hell broke loose inside the teachers' lounge, the only cool-headed one seemed to be Daphne as she took Sorceress Stone's vitals and then attempted CPR on her. I motioned to Alba and Reign. There wasn't anything else to see. The deed was done, and we'd missed it!

20

*D*espite Alba's annoyance, Holly and I refused to speak a word about what we'd seen inside the teachers' lounge until we reunited with Libby and Cinder back at the time portal. Seeing Sorceress Stone go from alive to dead right in front of my very eyes and knowing that there was a murderer in that room made me nervous, and all I'd wanted to do in that moment was to high-tail it back to safety before even breathing a word of what we'd seen.

So when we were finally back to safety, Alba turned to face Holly and me with her hand on her hip. "Well? Are you gonna tell us what happened?"

Holly's eyes flicked over to look at me encouragingly. She wanted me to speak first.

Leaned over slightly, trying to catch my breath from the brisk jog, I shook my head sadly. "We couldn't save her."

"You saw Stone?! And she was alive?" breathed Alba. "So the time machine *did* work!"

Holly held her stomach. "It worked alright, but there wasn't anything we could do."

Reign grimaced. "Yeah, I figured as much. It didn't look like much happened from where we stood."

Alba's arms flailed out in front of her. "Cripes, Red. You had *one job!*"

I shook my head. "You don't understand," I said through shallow breaths. "We saw her alive, and then we saw her dead."

Alba looked unimpressed. "Yeah, well, that's generally how death works. First they're alive and then they're dead. At least tell us who did it, and how!"

"I know that's how death works, Alba. But I'm not kidding. It happened just like the Council said it happened. She was pacing the room, telling them all about the graduation project. I couldn't really hear what she was saying, actually," I admitted. "But I saw her mouth moving a little and I definitely heard her talking about graduation."

Holly's head bobbed in agreement. "Yeah, I saw that too."

Alba rolled her hand along in the air as if to prod our story along. "And then?"

"And then I looked at all the witches in the room. Everyone was chill. You know, minding their own business. Scratching their itches, shifting in their seats, nothing out of the ordinary. And then all of a sudden, I literally *blinked* and she was lying on the table."

"You *blinked?!*" Alba hissed as if I'd just committed the most atrocious crime.

I stared back at her. "I was supposed to not blink?! It's not really something I can control, Alba."

"Yeah, what did you expect?" asked my brother.

Alba ignored my brother and looked at Holly. "Cosmo. Tell me you saw something that this moronic *blinker* missed."

Holly swallowed hard and then shifted in her wedge sandals. "Well, Alba, I sort of blinked too, I guess. I mean, one second she was alive and in the next split second she was dead. I didn't see anything either."

Alba threw her hands up in the air. "Oh, for crying out loud! This is what happens when you send idiots to do a job you shoulda done yourself. Just like my father always said, if you want something done right, you should just do it yourself."

I understood Alba's frustration, but I didn't appreciate the attitude. I frowned at her. "Look, Alba. I offered to lift you up. This is *not* Holly's fault, and it's *not* my fault."

"Yeah, chill, Alba. That's hardly fair," snapped Reign. "Whoever did this must have put a spell on both of them too."

Holly sucked in her breath and her head snapped up to look at my brother. "Put a spell on us too? You think they saw us?"

I shrugged. "I didn't see anyone notice us, but it totally wouldn't shock me if whatever spell the murderer did on the rest of the Council, they also did on us." I looked at Libby and Cinder. "Did anyone go in or out of the room?"

Cinder shook her head. "Not a single soul."

"So now what?" asked Sweets expectantly.

Alba dropped her head. She thought about things for a long minute and then slowly lifted her head. "We have no other choice. I think we have to move on to Plan B."

"What's Plan B?"

"Well, it's obvious these witches aren't telling us the whole story. Someone in that room is lying to us about their relationship with Stone. So, I say, we go back in time and learn more about each of their relationships with Stone."

My mouth gaped. "Uh! But that's going to take forever! We don't have that kind of time! Plus it might be dangerous!"

Alba shook her head. "We have no other choice. If there was another way, we would've done it. Come on." She led the group back into the steaming sauna, where we surrounded the tear in time that she'd made.

"If you had to pick one of the women right now, based on our interrogation alone, who would your number one suspect be?" asked Alba, looking at Libby, Cinder, Holly, and me.

We all answered in unison. "Gemma."

"For sure," added Holly.

Alba nodded. "She'd be my number one suspect too. We'll start with her."

When we were all linked once again, Alba began the chant.

Relationships formed in the very distant past,
Don't always work and don't always last.
Arguments happen and conflicts arise,
Take us to when Gemma and SaraLynn had drama for the very first time.

I heard a whooshing noise as the wormhole began to spin again. Alba held open the slice in time, exposing the tunnel once again. We watched as it picked up speed, spinning, then it quickly reversed course and now pointed several feet in a different direction.

Our eyes all widened. To see a giant magic wormhole was one thing, but to see it shift directions was a whole other ballgame.

"Amazing," said Sweets, wide-eyed.

Alba was less impressed. "This is it, guys. We're gonna find out who told the truth in their interviews and who lied to us. We're finally gonna get some real answers." She pointed at the tunnel. "Come on. Let's go."

The group of us rushed through the tunnel, less cautiously than we had earlier. This time when we reemerged, I was once again surprised to see us back on the same grassy spot next to the river.

Holly looked bummed. "Back in the same spot *again*?!"

Alba shook her head. "We have a lot of ground to cover, there's no time for sight-seeing. Come on." She took off on a jog across the field headed towards campus. There we discovered that once again, nothing seemed to have changed. The buildings were all just as they had been when we'd left them.

I shook my head. "I don't understand, Alba. Where are we going? I don't think we went anywhere."

"Or maybe Gemma and Sorceress Stone didn't have any drama," suggested Sweets.

Holly wrinkled her nose. "No, I definitely sensed drama when Gemma was talking about Sorceress Stone."

I shrugged. "Maybe we did the spell wrong. Maybe we should go back to the time rip and try the spell again."

Alba looked over her shoulder as she walked. "There's

no way we did the spell wrong. The tunnel changed direction. Maybe their drama didn't start until a few days ago. Maybe they got in a fight or something. If I had to guess, I'd guess that we went back in time to Monday. I'll bet if we go into the gym right now, we'll find everyone assembled, just like they were the other day. Come on, let's go check it out."

We made a beeline towards the Clara Mason auditorium, where all our assemblies were held. But since we were trying to keep our time-traveling presence on the down-low, we avoided the busy main entrance and opted to go in through the rarely used back door instead. Inside the small vestibule just outside the gym, we hid behind a set of doors, peering out at the gym carefully.

Sure enough, we found the place packed, just like it had been on Monday. Handfuls of students milled around the gym floor while others were seated in the bleachers and many climbed the steps trying to locate their friends. A stage was set up on the gym floor, just as it had been two days prior. I didn't give the students much attention, because once I saw the podium and the stage, I knew that Alba had been right.

"See," hissed Alba. "I told you we went back to Monday."

No one responded, but instead we watched as a woman with blond hair piled high on top of her head approached the stage from the other end of the gym. She was average height, thin, and wore a pink short-sleeved sweater tucked into a gray pencil skirt that stopped just below the knee. Her gray high heels clicked on the gym floor and her hips swiveled slightly as she walked. I stared at her, puzzled. I'd never seen her before.

My eyes swung up to take in the students in the bleachers. No one seemed to pay the woman any attention as she got up on the stage and tapped the microphone before adjusting the height of the microphone stand.

"Who is that?" I hissed.

Alba shook her head in bewilderment. "I have no idea."

Holly scooted closer, leaning her head on the side of my arm. "What's going on?"

With my mouth gaping slightly, we continued to watch as a woman in a big black cape came out next, followed by five old women, none of whom I recognized.

The scene played out almost identically to the assembly we'd had on Monday, except the players in this scene were different. There was no Sorceress Stone, no Brittany Hobbs, and the members of the Great Witches Council appeared to have been swapped out by an older, more crippled version.

"Good morning, students," sang the middle-aged woman in the black cape.

"Good morning, Sorceress Livingston," the crowd cheered back.

Our jaws dropped. *Sorceress Livingston*?! *Who in the heck was Sorceress Livingston?* What was going on?

"Today is a very special day for the Paranormal Institute. Today we discuss graduation requirements!"

The crowd cheered. Were we in a parallel universe? One that didn't contain Sorceress Stone anymore? My eyes flicked up towards the bleachers and scanned the faces of the girls staring at the stage. That was when I realized I didn't recognize a single face in the crowd. I certainly didn't consider myself friends with all of the girls at the Paranormal Institute for Witches, but it was a small enough school that I knew most of their faces, if not their names. But as I looked out at the crowd now, it suddenly became completely apparent that I knew *none* of the girls' faces!

My eyes swung up towards the seat I'd sat in two days before, where Alba, Holly, Jax, Libby, and Cinder had been too. We'd all been in a little group towards the top of the bleachers, all the way to one side. My heart began to beat wildly when I realized I didn't see myself up there. What was going on?

"Alba," I hissed.

"Shh!"

"And I'm so excited to get to introduce to you this year's Great Witches Council!" said Sorceress Livingston. "But before we get to that, I have an exciting announcement. Today I have the honor of announcing this year's graduation speaker! As you all know, I select our speaker from the top of our graduating class. This year, it was not an easy decision to make. We had two students who, for the last two years, have been neck and neck and are now tied for valedictorian of the graduating class." The crowd cheered.

"Those ladies up there don't look like the Great Witches Council," whispered Holly.

Libby scrunched her nose. "What is going on?"

"Shhh," hissed Alba. "I'm trying to hear her."

I shook my head. None of this was making any sense at all. "Alba, there's something you need to know."

Alba waved her hand backwards at me. "Tell me later, Red."

I looked up at Reign.

"What?" he mouthed.

I shook my head, mashing my lips together as the applause died down and Sorceress Livingston began to speak again. "So, this year we've decided on *two* graduation speakers, but the official class valedictorian will be announced on graduation day!"

My eyes scanned the crowd again, hoping I'd recognize *someone*, and I'd realize that all of this was silly. It *had* to be the scene from two days before. Suddenly, my eyes stopped on one face in particular. Something about that face looked eerily familiar. I sucked in my breath as Sorceress Livingston continued.

"And this year's first graduation speaker will be none other than Gemma Overbrook!"

The crowd clapped as the face I'd been staring at smiled and stood up to wave at the crowd from her spot on the bleachers. A couple girls shouted. "Go, Gemma!"

"Gemma Overbrook!" breathed Holly. "But that's—"

"Yup." I couldn't believe it. We'd truly gone back in time!

"And the second graduation speaker will be...," she began slowly.

My eyes swept the crowd now as I had a feeling I knew who else I'd find if I kept looking. There was one girl who sat off to the side by herself. She looked familiar as well. She had straight white hair that fell just below her shoulders and a long thin nose. I'd recognize that nose anywhere! I sucked in my breath.

Sorceress Livingston's voice boomed out of the speaker. "SaraLynn Stone!"

The applause wasn't as strong or impressive, but the

crowd clapped politely as the girl stood up. She was hardly any bigger than Jax was now. Maybe she was taller, though it was hard to tell from so far away, but she was certainly as petite. Her posture was just as it was now. With her shoulders pulled back regally, she looked down her nose at the crowd that clapped pathetically for her.

Everyone hiding behind me sucked in their breath.

"Sorceress Stone!" whispered Libby.

"She looks so young!" hissed Sweets.

My mind reeled at the realization that not only were we looking at Sorceress Stone in her youth, but once again, she was *alive*!

Before they could even finish the assembly, Alba tapped me on the shoulder and jerked her head towards the back door. I nodded before turning to beckon Reign. We were leaving. The group of us left, regrouping on the back lawn behind the gymnasium.

"Oh my goodness," breathed Sweets, her brown eyes wide. "It worked, Alba. It really worked! We went back in time! And not just a day—we went back *years*!"

"Gotta say, I'm impressed," said my brother, leaning an elbow on Alba's shoulder.

Alba shoved his arm off her. "That doesn't mean you can touch me. Got it, Slick?" She circled the air around her body with her hands. "This is a strict no-touching zone."

Reign straightened, crossing his arms in front of him. "No-touching zone, got it."

Alba leaned into our circle. "Listen, we don't have a lot of time here. That assembly is gonna let out and then we gotta be on Gemma Overbrook like the stripes on Jax's tights. Got it? She's a major person of interest as far as I'm concerned, and we need to find out more about the relationship between her and Stone."

"But, Alba, this scene happened decades ago," said Holly. "You really think we're going to find a clue as to their current relationship?"

Alba shrugged. "I have no idea, but we gotta start somewhere, right?"

"Well, how do we find out more about their relationship?" asked Libby.

"If a visitor from the future came back in time to find out more about *our* relationships, where would they go?" I asked the girls.

Holly and Sweets smiled as they said in unison. "The quad!"

*D*uring the first four months of school, the quad was the place us girls had spent almost every meal. After Christmas, the weather had gotten too cold to sit outside, but now that it was springtime, we'd gotten back into the habit of eating our lunches outside again. With the sun shining and the temperature warm, we all believed it was incredibly likely that even the witches of the past had enjoyed sitting outside for lunch. We'd brought along such a large group that we had to spread out to hide. My brother, Holly, and Sweets hid behind a big bush on the wizards' lawn that faced the quad. Libby and Cinder hid behind a stand of scarlet oak trees, and Alba and I hid behind the low retaining wall that circled the quad. I could only hope that someone wouldn't see us and that Sorceress Overbrook or Sorceress Stone would take a seat near us.

We'd hung out for all of twenty minutes before the quad doors burst open and the first group of girls came out carrying lunch trays. While their clothes and hairstyles were different, it was just like a normal day when we had lunch. Everyone spoke excitedly, likely over the announcements of the graduation projects and the speakers.

We watched as a group of girls sat at the table directly in front of us. We didn't recognize any of the witches but, unable to move from our spots without being seen, we listened to them anyway.

"Hey, Kelly, what are you going to do for your project?"

A girl in a yellow shift dress smiled. "Are you kidding? I haven't given it any thought yet. After lunch I'm gonna go to the Great Witch's Library to get started. You're all welcome to join me and help if you like."

"I can't," said another one of the girls. "I need to study for finals or I'm going to flunk out for sure. You're so lucky you're graduating this year. I'm so tired of homework it's not even funny."

"Yeah, me too," said another.

The dorm doors opened again and a diminutive Sorceress Stone appeared, tray in hand. Seeing her up close, I realized she was just as small as Jax was now. The girls quieted down as she made her way over to an empty table and sat down.

Kelly leaned forward and said in a hushed voice, "So —who's shocked that Gemma and Sara got chosen as graduation speakers?" Her tone implied annoyance with the announcement.

"Not me," sighed one of the girls. "They're good at everything."

Kelly lifted a shoulder. "It's got to be *exhausting* being that perfect. I'd rather not be perfect and get to have a life. I couldn't *stand* being the goody two-shoes that those girls are."

We all watched as Sorceress Stone got comfortable in her spot, pulling her napkin from her tray and sprinkling a bit of salt and pepper over her food. She looked like she was used to sitting alone. For a split second, I almost felt bad for her. Then, there was a commotion on the men's side of the quad. A lanky boy appeared, carrying a paper bag and a thermos. He strode over to Sorceress Stone's table and pointed at the empty spot in front of her. She looked up at him and gave him a small smile and a nod. He plopped down in front of her.

"Ugh," said one of the girls. "Elon Ipswich and Sara-Lynn Stone? That's got to be the most awkward couple ever."

Kelly wrinkled her nose. "Ew. Yes! That's perfect! We should nominate them for most awkward couple so it's in the yearbook!"

The girls at the table all laughed.

Then one of the girls at the table put a hand on her hip. "Wait. I thought Elon and Gemma were dating?"

"For like a minute," said Kelly. "Gemma said they only went on a couple of dates. But how embarrassing for Sara to get Gemma's hand-me-downs."

"Speak of the devil!" said the girl next to Kelly, sucking in her breath. "Look who's coming!"

At her prompting, Alba and I looked up to see Gemma Overbrook walking towards Sorceress Stone's table. Gemma had her tray in hand too, but her eyes were focused intently on the boy. When she got to their table, she slammed her tray down, making her silverware rattle and Sorceress Stone's drink tip over.

Sorceress Stone's narrow face went white.

"Hey, man, be cool," we heard Elon say as he stood up to look at Gemma's reddened face.

Gemma said something to him, keeping her voice low so as not to completely make a scene, but Elon simply rolled his eyes at her, making her even more infuriated. He shook his head, snatched his brown paper sack off the table, and stood up. "You're spazzing," he told her before looking down at Sorceress Stone. "I'll talk to ya later, Sara." Then he strutted off, shaking his head in annoyance.

Sorceress Stone looked after him sadly, and then she looked up at Gemma, her face now crimson. From my one-dimensional vantage point, I surmised that Sorceress Stone hadn't invited the male company, but now she had to pay the price with Gemma. Sorceress Stone tried to apologize to her, but Gemma strutted off in a huff and sat down at another table full of girls, leaving Sorceress Stone alone once again.

Despite the fact that after that scene, nothing else happened, we were forced to stay hidden until the bell rang and the girls all left the quad for their classes. When they finally did, the group of us reunited.

"So they knew each other," said Libby. "But they didn't like each other."

"They were fighting over a boy," said Holly.

"And it sounds like they were competing for head of the class too," said Sweets.

"But is that a motive for murder?" asked Reign. "I mean, come on! This was years and years ago."

I shook my head. "I could definitely see Gemma holding a grudge. She seems like that type of woman."

"Plus I think it's sketchy she didn't tell us any of this," said Holly with one crooked brow.

"It's very suspicious. She could have just said, 'I knew her, we were classmates, but we really didn't get along.' Instead, she implied they were old friends."

Alba looked at me incredulously. "Oh, come on, Red! If someone were accusing *you* of murder, you don't think you'd maybe neglect to share that you didn't like the person that got killed?"

I lifted a shoulder. Alba had a point. But it was hard to know exactly *what* I'd do in that situation. "Yeah, maybe."

Alba glanced down at her watch. "Jeez, that took forever. We should probably keep moving. See what else we can find out."

The group of us made our way back to the river where our portal still stood, waiting for us to reenter. Stepping inside the sauna, Holly was just about to lead us back into the blurring tunnel of lights, when Alba put a hand on her arm to stop her.

"Hold up, Cosmo, that tunnel is gonna take us back to where we just came from. We don't wanna go there. Where are we going next?"

I had no idea where else to go, and by the looks on everyone's faces, neither did anyone else. I shrugged. "Can we just roll the dice?"

Alba sighed. "We can try." The group of us got into position and she began to chant.

Relationships formed in the very distant past,
Don't always work and don't always last.
Arguments happen and conflicts arise,

Take us to when another member of the Great Witches Council and SaraLynn had drama for the very first time.

W hen we reemerged to find the same scene as we'd seen before, Cinder curled her lip. "Is this where they all met her?"

"It's definitely the common denominator. Come on," said Alba, once again heading back towards campus. There we headed straight for the auditorium again. But the second we stepped inside, it was obvious we were in the wrong place. The lights were off and the room was empty.

"There's no one here!" breathed Sweets.

"Awww, look at you. You're catchin' on, Sherlock," snapped Alba.

Sweets frowned. "Alba, you sound like you're getting hangry. It *is* almost lunchtime. Need a little pick-me-up? Reign, do you have a Snickers bar in that backpack?"

Reign swung the bag off his shoulder, "No, but I have a—"

"Oh, for crying out loud, Sweets. I don't need a Snickers bar. I need to figure out where we are!"

Holly raised her brows and looked around. "We're at the Institute, Alba, duh?"

Alba's eyes swung up towards the sky. "I know *where* we are, you moron. I *meant* we need to figure out what year it is."

"You don't have to be so mean, Alba," spat Holly. "That wasn't what you *said.*"

Reign threw an arm over Holly's shoulder. "Yeah, how about we knock off the name calling, huh?"

"I wasn't talking to you, Slick."

A vein bulged in the side of my brother's neck. He pursed his lips as if he were trying to restrain himself. "And let's get something straight. My name is Reign. It's not Slick. Her name is Holly. It's not moron. And her name is Sweets, not Sherlock."

"Yeah? Well, maybe if you *knew* what you were talking about, you'd know that her name is actually Mildred, not Sweets. Sweets is a nickname. Everybody's got nicknames. It's a sign of affection."

Reign stifled a smile. "Affection? You think calling Holly a moron is showing affection? Ever heard of a hug?"

"Hugs are for wimps." Alba started towards the quad. "Come on, let's go see where everybody is."

Reign looked at Sweets as the crowd moved away. "Your name is Mildred?"

Sweets nodded and let out a giggle.

The quad was just as empty as the auditorium had been, and we hadn't seen a single student coming or going, making us all even more curious about what time in history we gone back to.

"Maybe we should try Sorceress Stone's office," said Cinder.

"Good idea," said Alba.

Seconds later, we discovered Sorceress Stone's office to be locked. The secretary's door was open, but the lights were off.

"Maybe everyone's in class," I said with a shrug.

Sweets pointed down the hallway towards the kitchen.

"Let's see if the cooks are here. If they're cooking, then we know *someone's* here."

"Yeah, Sweets has a point." I led us down the hallway.

The kitchen door was open. The lights were on, and we could hear the sound of a crackling radio station spilling out. Pots and pans clanged as if someone were cooking.

"Well, at least we know someone's here," whispered Sweets. "I was beginning to think this was a ghost town!"

"Me too," agreed Libby.

"Well, then, where are all the people?" yelled an exasperated Alba. Her voice reverberated down the hallway.

Suddenly, a head popped out of the kitchen. "What are you kids doing here?" said a stout woman with a curly gray mop of hair on top of her head. Her eyes flicked up to look at Reign and her breath caught in her throat. "And men aren't allowed on this side of campus!"

"We're students here," said Libby.

"And he's my brother," I said, pointing at Reign. "He just came to visit."

"Visit?!" breathed the woman, her hand on her chest. "It's summertime! Students aren't allowed on campus during the summer!"

Summertime?

"Oh, yeah," said Alba, nodding her head as if she were playing along. "We know. We just forgot, umm…"

"My bracelet!" chimed in Holly. She showed the woman the gold bracelet on her wrist. "I must have lost it during class. We came back to look for it. Reign gave us a ride. We were just showing him around."

That seemed to relax the woman. "I see. Well, you better go before the Great Witches Council sees you. Men aren't allowed on campus, and neither are students during the summer."

Alba looked around curiously. "The Great Witches Council is here? In the summertime?"

"Yes, they're having a special meeting."

My eyes widened. "A special meeting? About what?"

"Oh, that isn't any of our business, now is it?" The woman winced, like she regretted even mentioning that the Council was on campus.

"Sure, it's none of our business," agreed Alba. Then she glanced towards Sorceress Stone's office and, hooking a thumb over her shoulder, she looked at the cook curiously. "Hey, uh, is Sorceress…"

"Oh, no, she's long gone," said the cook is a hushed voice, before Alba could even finish her sentence.

"Gone?!" said Sweets.

The cook lowered her voice. "But you didn't hear it from me."

"Hear what from you?" I said with a reassuring smile.

The cook pointed at me and smiled. "Exactly! Because the minute it gets around that the Institute is up for sale is the minute that all hell breaks loose."

"For sale!" breathed Holly. "The Institute is for sale?!"

The cook's eyes widened. "Oh, shoot! Do you remember what I said? You didn't hear it from me!"

"Hear what from you?" I repeated.

She nodded and pointed at me again. "Exactly! Now, I need to be going. I have to finish lunch for the Council. They'll be coming out of their executive session anytime now." She shooed us along. "You all better get going before they see you!" After she'd disappeared in the kitchen, she stuck her head out one last time. "And don't forget—you didn't hear any of that from me!"

Alba waved us on. "This way," she whispered, leading us back down the hallway towards the Winston Hall lobby. There, we regrouped by the doors to the quad.

"So the Institute is for sale!" said Cinder.

"Obviously we know who buys it," I said as my brother wandered away. "Sorceress Stone buys it. Why else would time take us back here?"

Alba shook her head. "I don't know. That's what we're here to figure out."

"Hey, girls," said Reign, standing next to the corkboard that held all of the club and extracurricular announcements. "Look at this!" He pointed up at some framed pictures above the corkboard. "It's SaraLynn."

Rushing to his side, I followed his finger to see a professional portrait of a younger Sorceress Stone amongst a row of other portraits. Sorceress Stone wasn't as young as she'd been when we'd seen her as a student, but she was younger than we now knew her to be.

"We had pictures hanging up in our present-day dorms too," said Sweets. "They're of our teachers. I bet these are all teachers here now!"

"You're really on top of your game today, aren't you, Sweets?" said Alba, rolling her eyes.

I gave Alba an elbow to the ribs while Holly pointed at another portrait. "Look! It's Poppy Ellabee!"

My brows lifted. "She looks so young!" Poppy's hair was styled shorter, in a bob cut, and she wore a prim blouse with lace around the collar, but she still had the same friendly smile on her face.

"Poppy told us that she and Sorceress Stone had been colleagues," said Sweets.

Alba's brows lowered. "Did we ask her why she stopped working at the Institute?"

I shook my head. "I don't think we did."

Holly nodded. "Yeah, I'm sure we didn't. That would have been a good question to have asked."

"Well, we'll put that on our list of follow-up questions to ask when we get back to the present," said Alba. "For now, we need to find Sorceress Stone and see what she's up to. There has to be some kind of clue here."

"The Council meeting," said Reign. "Maybe we should see what the special meeting is about. Maybe *that's* the clue."

I lifted my shoulder and looked at Alba. "He could be right. It's worth checking out."

"We don't even know where they're meeting."

"The teachers' lounge seems like a pretty good place to start," said Libby.

"Fine," grumbled Alba. "Maybe we'll bump into Stone along the way."

22

*T*he low hum of voices in the teachers' lounge rolled down the long hallway, hitting our ears before we'd even gotten there. Alba stood with her ear to the door for several long seconds as we all looked at her expectantly.

Finally, I whispered, "Well?"

Alba held a finger to her lips and shushed me, trying harder to hear. Finally, she stepped away, shaking her head. "It's like I'm listening to Charlie Brown's teacher in there. I can't make out anything. Maybe we should go listen outside the window again."

"No. I tried to hear what Sorceress Stone was saying when we were up there, but you can't hear anything through the glass. I mean, obviously we'd be able to *see* what's happening, but we won't have any idea what they're talking about."

Alba ran a hand through her short brown hair, tugging lightly at the roots. "Ugh!"

Cinder frowned too as she stared at the wall that separated us from the Council. On it hung the same bulletin board that had been there the day before, when we'd grilled each of the current Council members. She fingered it lightly and then glanced over at her sister. "Help me out, Lib?"

Libby nodded at her.

Cinder held her arms out on either side of herself while looking at the rest of us. "Stand back."

"What?" Alba lowered her brows. "What are you doing?"

Cinder shooed her back. "Just get back. You'll see."

We all scooted back, except Libby. Instead of scooting back with the rest of us, she took hold of her sister's hand. With their free hands, each of them put a palm on the bulletin board, and then they began to chant.

> *Piece of wood upon the wall,*
> *Show us what's behind.*
> *Let us see, let us hear,*
> *Those that are confined.*

In a low murmur, the duo recited the chant over and over until finally, the bulletin board became a one-way window.

Alba's mouth gaped as she stared at the results of their spell. "Cool! I need to remember that one. Can they see us?"

Cinder quirked a brow. "Would I do it if they could see us?"

Alba smiled. "True."

As we turned our eyes onto the Council inside, it became immediately apparent that once again, they weren't the same members we'd met the day before, nor were they the same Council members that had been on stage when Sorceress Stone was Jax's age. Their ages varied. Two were older ladies, but three of them looked a bit younger.

One of them had short blond hair and wore a dress and heels. She stood at the head of the table. "Is there any discussion on the subject?"

One of the older witches raised a hand. "Sorceress Richardson, if you will, it is my opinion that Sorceress Ellabee has proven to be a commendable teacher and an excellent role model for up-and-coming witches. I have full confidence in her ability to run the Institute fairly and to teach our young witches the morals and ethics necessary to practice magic in today's society. I fully support the Council's acceptance of her bid to purchase the Paranormal Institute."

"Thank you, Sorceress Villanueva. Is there any other discussion?"

Another hand went up. This time it was one of the younger witches, perhaps in her late twenties or early thirties. "I'll be completely honest here. While I appreciate the kind of teacher that Sorceress Ellabee is, I am concerned about the amount of her bid. I feel that it's fairly low in consideration of what the buyout of the previous headmistress amounted to. I feel that we could get a fair amount more if we held out a little longer."

"I understand your concern, Sorceress Hicks," said yet another member, "but we're already in a bind. With Sorceress Klatworthy leaving the Institute in such a rush, she left us little time to do a proper candidate search. I feel that Sorceress Ellabee's offer is low, yes, but as

Sorceress Villanueva mentioned, she's a wonderful candidate and, if given the opportunity, would do great things with the Institute."

Sorceress Hicks spoke again. "I don't disagree with that statement. I readily believe that Sorceress Ellabee would do great things with the Institute. I just feel that if we held out a little longer—"

Sorceress Villanueva clucked her tongue. "Sorceress Hicks, money isn't everything. I'm afraid that by holding out for a higher bid, we'll offend Sorceress Ellabee, and she'll pull her offer. Then the Council will be left holding the bag! I hereby make a motion to vote on Poppy Ellabee's bid to purchase the Paranormal Institute."

Sorceress Richardson, the woman who seemed to be chairing the meeting, lifted her brows. "I see. Do I hear a second on that motion?"

Sorceress Hicks raised a hand before anyone else could speak. "I would appreciate it very much if we could hold off on a second and a vote until after we've had lunch. I'm quite hungry, and I'd like to give this whole thing a little more thought before casting my vote."

Other heads around the table bobbed up and down.

Sorceress Richardson nodded. "Very well, we'll resume this conversation after we've had lunch. Do I hear a motion to recess for lunch?"

Sorceress Hicks raised her hand. "Sorceress Richardson, I move to recess for lunch."

Sorceress Villanueva raised her hand. "I second that motion."

Sorceress Richardson nodded. "Very well, we are hereby recessed for lunch. We will meet again in an hour. Lunch will be served in the cafeteria."

Chairs around the table screeched across the floor as they were scooted back.

"They're coming!" hissed Alba. "We've gotta get outta here before someone sees us!"

Libby and Cinder released their hold on the window, and it immediately reverted back to being a bulletin board. Without another word, the seven of us raced down the hallway to the stairwell as if the devil himself was hot on our tail.

---

*W*hile the Council went to the cafeteria for lunch, the seven of us found a secluded spot beneath a scarlet oak tree in back of the Canterbury Building to hide out until their meeting resumed.

Reign dropped his backpack on the grass and plopped down next to it, leaning his back against a tree trunk. "Well, we've got an hour to kill, we might as well have lunch too."

Sweets nodded and looked at Reign's bag with interest. "Exactly what I was thinking." She rubbed her hands together in front of herself excitedly. "What did you bring?"

"Nothing fancy, just chicken club wraps. It's something new I'm trying." He pulled out little individually wrapped bundles and handed them out. "I brought some chips too if anyone wants some."

Sweets' eyes widened as she pulled the cling wrap off of her tortilla and lifted one of the halves to inspect it. "Wow, this looks amazing! Where did you learn to cook?"

"Funny enough, YouTube and cooking shows. Is it weird that I'm obsessed with Rachael Ray?"

Sweets giggled. "I don't think so. I happen to be a fan of hers too."

Holly wrinkled her nose as she picked at the wrap she'd just opened. "Who's Rachael Ray?"

"You've never heard of Rachel Ray?" breathed Sweets.

Holly wilted slightly. "No, is she like a supermodel or something?"

Reign chuckled. "Not so much. She's got a cooking show."

"Oh," said Holly with a small voice.

Sweets closed her eyes as she savored the taste of her first bite. "Mmm. Is there avocado in this? And bacon?"

"Yeah, I found a really great recipe online. I think we're going to add these to the menu at Habernackle's, but first I thought I'd try them out on you girls. What do you think?"

Alba stuffed her mouth. "It's good."

"Really good, bro," I agreed through a mouthful.

Libby and Cinder both nodded too as they chewed.

"Thank you," said Libby.

Only Holly didn't eat.

"Something wrong, Holly?" asked Reign. "You don't like chicken wraps?"

Holly scrunched up her nose. I knew she was torn. She wanted to eat what Reign had made for her and not look picky in front of her crush, but his wraps had avocado in them, and back in November, we'd discovered that Holly didn't like avocado when our dorm had had guac and chips at our Dia de los Muertes party. "Oh, no. I like chicken wraps."

"Cosmo doesn't like avocado," said Alba while licking sauce off her fingers after having devoured the first half of her wrap.

"Alba!" snapped Holly, her eyes wide and her face flushed. "I do too like avocado."

"Oh yeah? Then what's the problem?"

We all stared at her then. Holly's face burned even redder. "There's no problem. I'm just not really that hungry."

"You don't have to eat it if you're not hungry," said my brother with a shrug. "I can put it back in the bag and you can eat it later if you want."

"I think she should eat it now," taunted Alba. "We won't have time for a break later."

"Alba, leave her alone," I said under my breath.

"I know she's hungry. She barely ate any breakfast."

Holly glanced up at Reign furtively. His hand was extended to take the wrap from her. "No, I'll eat it now," she said in a little voice.

Reign held out the bag of barbecue chips he'd brought along. "Want some chips?"

She shook her head as she stared at the food in her hand. "No, thanks." Finally, Holly put the wrap to her mouth and took a tiny nibble.

Satisfied that she'd tried his wrap, Reign smiled at her. "What do you think?"

Holly nodded, her lips pressed together in a tight smile. "It's good."

"So now that we have a minute to talk about what we just saw, does anyone have a prediction about what's going to happen in there?" I asked in an effort to take all the attention and watchful eyes off of Holly.

"Isn't it obvious?" said Cinder. "Sorceress Stone snuck in somehow with a better bid."

I was fairly confident that Cinder was right. I nodded.

"Unless Poppy bought the place and Stone bought it from her later," said Alba.

Holly cleared her throat.

I shook my head. "I don't think so. When we interviewed Poppy, she said that they were colleagues before Sorceress Stone ran the place. She didn't say anything about her being Sorceress Stone's boss. I think somehow Sorceress Stone came in with a late offer that was better than Poppy's. It's got to be what happened."

Holly let out a funny little cough.

Sweets, who was sitting next to her, leaned over. "You alright, Hol?"

Holly's face was redder than it had been only seconds ago, and her lips looked kind of puffy like she'd gotten a fat lip. "I…" She touched her hand to her throat and let out another wheezy sounding cough.

Sweets scrambled to her knees. "Are you choking?"

Holly shook her head, her mouth opened and closed, but only a weak sound came out as she patted her throat again.

"Oh, jeez, Cosmo. You're laying it on kinda thick, don'tcha think?"

"Alba, I don't think she's faking," said Sweets. "What's the matter, Holly?"

Holly's brows bunched together as her mouth hung open. She looked like she was choking.

"Holly, this isn't funny. You could have just admitted

that you don't like avocados," I said, my heart beating a little faster.

Holly shook her head. Her eyes were wide, and suddenly I could tell she wasn't joking. And then it hit me.

"Omigosh. Holly, are you allergic to avocados?"

Holly's head bobbed up and down as she tried to gasp for air. Her windpipe was closing on her.

My brother jumped to his feet. "She's allergic! Oh no. Alright, think. What do we do?"

"She needs Benadryl or an EpiPen or something. If she doesn't get it in time, she could go into anaphylactic shock!" said Sweets.

I looked around. We were decades into the past! Where were we supposed to go? "But we're back in time!"

"We're still on our campus," said Alba. "Let's get her to the nurse's office. There's got to be an EpiPen or something in there to help her."

That's all it took for Reign to scoop Holly up in his arms. "Mercy, grab my bag," he ordered, his face in a panic. "Just point me in the right direction."

"This way."

———

*B*ursting through the door to the nurse's office with a nearly unconscious Holly in his arms, my brother nodded his head towards the metal medicine cabinet in the corner of the room. "Check in there," he shouted as he gingerly laid Holly down on a small cot. By now, Holly's face was covered in a rash of red hives, and she looked as if she'd been the victim of a Botox injection gone wrong. Her lips were triple their usual size.

"Libby, Cinder, watch the door," shouted Alba.

"Sweets, help me search the medicine cabinet. Red, check the desk."

While Sweets and Alba tore apart the medicine cabinet, I just stared at them blankly. Fear over losing Holly had frozen my brain and made my limbs heavy.

My brother looked up at Alba and Sweets, his brows knitted together and his face covered with fear. "I don't think she's breathing! You need to hurry!" He kneeled next to Holly's cot and patted her face. "Stay with me, Holly."

"I'm not finding anything," shouted Alba.

"Me either," said Sweets in a panic. "What are we going to do?"

"Keep looking. This is a dorm. They're not going to have a nurse's office without some kind of emergency allergy kit," shouted my brother. "Maybe I should give her CPR?"

"Do you know how?" asked Sweets.

"Yeah. I mean, we had to learn in a high school class once. I kind of remember what you're supposed to do." Reign nodded determinedly as he looked down at Holly lying lifelessly on the cot. He tilted her head back and leaned over her.

Oh, Holly! I pleaded in my head. *You need to wake up! You'll want to see this!* But I couldn't seem to get my limbs to move. My eyes widened as Holly's body took on a sort of halo-like glow. I couldn't help but think I was going to see her ghost climb out of her body at any moment.

Reign covered her mouth with his and blew. He did it again and then started doing chest compressions. "Find anything?"

"Not yet." Alba looked over her shoulder at me. "Find anything in the desk?" When I didn't say anything, she hollered at me again. "Red? Did you find anything in the desk?"

I swallowed. My mouth felt dry. It felt like I was in a dream.

"Red! The desk!"

Her last scream seemed to wake me up slightly. I shook my head and pulled out the desk drawers one by one. I shoved aside papers and pens and kept looking until finally I found a small plastic case. I opened it, hoping to find an EpiPen, but discovered it held only Band-Aids and gauze pads. "There's nothing in here!"

Suddenly Libby and Cinder burst inside the nurse's room. "Bad news, girls. Sorceress Stone's coming!"

All eyes fell on Holly. Our time was up. There was no way we were going to save her now.

23

"*We* need a diversion to buy us more time!" I said. "Reign, Alba, can you stop Sorceress Stone from coming in? Throw up some road-blocks, get her to leave so we can get Holly out?"

Reign nodded. "Of course, we'll think of something. What about Holly? She's not breathing."

"I'll take care of her." I shoved my brother towards the door. "There's no time to explain. Go! Meet us at the portal as soon as you can ditch Sorceress Stone."

With that, Alba and Reign disappeared out the door.

Libby, Cinder, and Sweets all stared at me.

"Libby, you've got to freeze Holly. We have to get her to someone that can help her, but we need more time."

"Got it," said Libby. "Give me some room to breathe."

Sweets, Cinder, and I all stepped back while Libby sucked in a deep breath of air. Then, just as she'd done to Sorceress Stone, she began to blow. Her frosty breath surrounded Holly, and within a minute, Holly was completely encased in a block of ice.

"You promise she's going to be okay like this?" asked Sweets as we all stared down at her lifeless frozen body.

"Yes, but the second we thaw her out, she's going to need medical attention."

I nodded. "Yeah, I know."

Sweets lifted her brows. "Now what? How are we supposed to get her to the river? There's no way we can carry a block of ice all that way. It's too cold and too heavy."

I flexed my fingers out in front of myself. "Don't worry. I think I can do it."

"Mercy…," Sweets began nervously.

"Shh, I'm concentrating," I hissed, keeping my eyes closed as I accumulated as much energy as I could. When I felt ready to do the lift, I opened my eyes. "Get the door, Sweets."

I held my hands out in front of myself and felt the energy running through my body. Slowly, I lifted Holly off the cot. But the ice had made her so heavy that I wasn't sure how long I was going to be able to keep her up. We had to go now, before I lost my strength. "Let's go," I muttered through gritted teeth.

"We'll cover you. Don't worry about anything, just worry about Holly," said Cinder, rushing to the door with her sister right by her side.

I let Cinder lead the way. Libby followed behind me, and Sweets stayed right by my side to help me maneuver Holly through doorways. We went out through a back door, and as soon as my feet touched grass, I took off at a slow trot, keeping Holly hovering a few feet above the ground. I didn't want to lift her any higher, just in case my powers gave way. I was afraid if she fell, the ice would break, and with it, Holly's frozen body as well.

It took nearly five minutes to get Holly's frozen body back to our wormhole. I dropped her on the grass in front of the steam sauna as gently as I could, but the second my energy released, I found myself completely spent. I'd never lifted anything that heavy for that long before. I realized then that my magic was a muscle that needed to be developed, and I suddenly understood why my teacher had been so adamant about us doing all the lifts they'd assigned as homework during the semester. I'd thought being able to lift small things once or twice had been enough practice, but now I understood.

Cinder and Libby kept watch. "I can't believe they aren't back yet," said Cinder. "This isn't good."

Libby paced the grass next to her sister. "Should we go after them?"

Cinder shook her head. "Let's give them another minute or two. If they're not back, then we'll have to go find them." She pointed her finger back at Holly. "Get her inside in case we have to leave in a hurry."

I groaned. I wasn't sure if I had enough in me to lift her again.

"Mercy, can you do it?"

"I don't know, Sweets. I'm wiped right now."

"How about I help you?"

"But you don't do telekinesis."

"No, but I have two arms. You get that side, and I'll get this side," she suggested with a shrug.

I sighed. I wasn't even sure if I had the energy for *that*, but I knew I had to try. "Okay, let's try." The two of us squatted down low and got our fingers under the block of ice that encased our friend. The surface was not just cold —it was freezing. It burned our fingers to even touch it. We tried anyway, fighting like hell to get her off the ground, but finally we both stood up without having moved her an inch.

"She's too heavy," said Sweets.

"And too cold. There's no way we're doing this manually. I'll just have to muster up some more magical powers," I said, falling down onto the soft grass. "Give me a second to catch my breath and I'll try again."

Before I'd even had a chance to absorb a single electrical current, voices rang out across the field.

"It's them!" Cinder shouted back at us.

"Why are they yelling?" asked Sweets.

"I don't know," said Libby. "They're too far away to hear."

"Mercy, you need to get Holly into the sauna, now!" shouted Cinder.

"I tried, but my powers are weak," I yelled back.

And then Alba and Reign were only yards away.

"Get in the portal!" shouted Alba. "Now!"

Panicked, I found myself completely unable to summon any energy from the things around me. My heart was in my throat, and I couldn't concentrate.

"Hurry!" shouted Reign. "She's right behind us!"

Alba and Reign raced past Libby and Cinder. Sorceress Stone was hot on their tail but lagged slightly. She'd easily be upon us in seconds, though.

"Alba, I can't get Holly inside," I shouted. "My powers are dead."

Alba and Reign immediately fired at her, lifting her

off the ground, and together they carried her inside the steam sauna. Alba hollered at all of us. "Get in here! Now!"

Sweets and I followed them in, but Libby and Cinder stood several yards away. Libby held her arms out on either side of herself and blew, casting a ten-foot-tall ice wall between Sorceress Stone and our portal. As I peered out the steam curtains, I could see Sorceress Stone firing an electrical current at the wall, trying to use her powers to break it.

Libby and Cinder raced to join us in the portal. "Hurry, that's not going to hold her for long!"

With Holly inside our little circle, the rest of us held hands as Alba chanted.

> *Magic portal, you must know*
> *The three Great Witches left to find.*
> *We're in a rush with an injured friend,*
> *So now we're flying blind.*
> *We seek to find a healing touch,*
> *And don't know what to do.*
> *So take us where we should go,*
> *Because we don't have a clue.*

The tunnel made a whooshing sound the second Alba finished her chant. We worked together to get Holly through the doorway and into the tunnel. Seconds later, we found ourselves on the other side.

We exited the steaming sauna to discover we weren't on the green grass by the river anymore. We'd appeared in the middle of nowhere on a gravel road beside a narrow creek. A small wooden railroad bridge ran across the creek and cut perpendicularly across the gravel road we stood on. Aside from the bridge, the creek, and the gravel road, the only thing we could see for miles was fenced green pastures and cows grazing peacefully.

Sweets looked around. "Where in the heck are we?"

"Heck if I know," muttered Alba. "Looks like we're in the middle of nowhere."

Reign gently lowered Holly's block of ice to the ground. "I don't know, but we've got to get to a town so we can get Holly some medical attention."

Alba let out a puff of air. "You think there's a hospital around here, Slick? We're gonna be lucky if we see another living soul besides a cow for the next sixty miles."

Reign stretched his back and then stood up and put his hands on his hips. "Well, what other choice do we have? We can't let her die."

"We're not gonna let her die," snapped Alba.

"Then we need to start walking." He pointed at the bridge. "I have a strong feeling about that bridge."

"I feel it too," agreed Cinder.

With one swoop of his magical fingers, Reign lifted Holly into the air. "Then we'll head that way. Maybe there's a hospital, or a medical clinic at the very least."

Alba threw her head back and groaned. "You don't

think this medical clinic is gonna have a few questions about administering an EpiPen to a Popsicle?"

Libby shrugged. "Maybe there will be a pharmacy and we can sneak in and steal an EpiPen."

I shook my head. "Alba cast that time travel spell in a hurry. We have no idea where we are in time. Maybe we've gone so far back that EpiPens don't even exist yet! We're wasting time talking about it. Let's just keep moving and see what we find, alright?"

"Fine," grumbled Alba. "Lead the way, Slick."

Reign led us across the railroad bridge. We followed the tracks for the next several miles in silence. I was lost in thought about Holly and what had just happened with Sorceress Stone when Cinder broke the silence.

"So what happened with Stone back there?"

Alba sighed. "What do you think happened? She just about killed us!"

"Did you speak to her before she tried to kill you?"

Alba kicked a rock off the tracks and shrugged. "She told us we weren't supposed to be there."

"What did you say?"

"We said we were meeting some friends, and she told us we'd have to meet them somewhere else."

"And then she just tried killing you? Jeez, that escalated quickly," I said.

"I *might* have told her off," said Alba with a half-smile.

"Alba!" breathed Sweets. "You told off Sorceress Stone?!"

Alba's mouth was in a full smile now. "You don't understand. I've wanted to do that for such a long time. I figured now was as good a time as any. Plus we were stalling. We had to give you guys enough time to get Holly outta there."

"That's still not a very good reason for her to try and kill you!"

"She tried to use force to get us to leave," said Reign from up ahead. "I wasn't about to let her push me around, so I fired back."

"And then she fired back," added Alba.

"And then *I* fired back."

"Next thing we knew, we were running and she was following."

I shook my head. I couldn't believe it. I wondered if, because we were back in time, the present-day Sorceress Stone would remember seeing us. Maybe *that* was why she hated us so much.

We'd only walked about two miles when we came to the edge of a town. We stood beneath a white-and-blue water tower that read Norwalk.

I stopped and stared at the word. "Norwalk. Why does that sound familiar?"

Alba tilted her head slightly as she looked back at Sweets and me. "Yeah, why *does* that sound familiar?"

I put a hand on her hip as I looked down the main drag and into the town. "Didn't one of the Council members say they were from Norwalk? Like Norwalk, Iowa?"

Alba nodded then. "Yup. I feel like it was Elodie Goodwitch."

Cinder curled her lip. "So *this* is Iowa? Not much to the place. I'd put money on there not being a hospital in this town."

As we headed into the downtown area, it quickly

became apparent that Cinder was right. There wasn't much to see. I'd always thought Dubbsburg and Aspen Falls were small towns, but Norwalk had both of them beat.

The main drag was little more than three city blocks of old brick and stone buildings along a pothole-ridden asphalt street. Less than a handful of beat-up cars were parked in front of the few shops along the street. For that I was thankful. A group of strangers carrying a girl encased in a block of ice was likely a strange sight and might be worthy of confrontation. So not to have anyone around was a blessing in disguise. Though I couldn't help but worry about not being able to find Holly the help she needed.

When we hit the second block, one of the buildings caught my attention. It was a narrow two-story brick-fronted building with a red-and-gold awning covering the front window. There was a pickup truck parked in front, and the lights in the shop were on.

"Girls!" I said excitedly, patting Alba's arm. "Look!" I pointed at the painted front window, which read Good-witch Magical Apothecary. My heart raced. "Who needs a hospital when you have a magical apothecary?"

Libby smiled from ear to ear. "It's Elodie Goodwitch's shop! She has *got* to have something that can help Holly. Come on!"

The doorbell jingled as we helped Reign navigate Holly through the narrow glass door. The shop was small, with glass shelving and lots of reflective mirrors, probably to make it appear larger than it was. On the shelves were assortments of crystals and charms, potion bottles and other magical ointments. We'd been in the shop for only a few seconds before a familiar witch with slumped shoulders walked out, carrying a box of merchandise in her arms.

"Hello!" sang Elodie, a broad smile on her face. "May I help you?"

We stared back at her, curious if she'd recognize us.

"Elodie?" I said finally.

She nodded. "Yes. I'm sorry, have we met?"

"Not yet, but we've heard of you. We have a bit of a situation that we're hoping you can help us with."

Elodie's eyes scanned each of us, looking for the problem. Finally, Alba stepped aside and pointed to Holly. "It's sort of an emergency."

Elodie sucked in her breath. "Well! I'd say so!"

24

"*H*ow in the world did she get like this?" asked Elodie, kneeling over Holly's block of ice.

"I froze her," Libby admitted.

"Froze her? Whatever for?"

"She was having an allergic reaction and we didn't have anything to help her."

"And we were running out of time," I added. "We didn't have a choice."

"But you can unfreeze her?" asked Elodie.

Libby nodded. "Whenever we're ready to save her life, I'll unfreeze her, but not until then."

Elodie pushed herself up into a standing position and walked back to her counter. "Do you know what caused the allergic reaction?"

"Avocado," said Reign gruffly. "I didn't know she was allergic to it."

"Neither did we," I said to Reign. "We just thought she didn't like it."

Alba sighed. "It's sorta my fault. I might have harassed her into eating it. I probably shouldn't have done that." For once, Alba actually looked remorseful about giving Holly a bad time.

"No, you shouldn't have," said Reign, his nostrils flared. "You really need to work on your attitude around your so-called *friends*. I mean, if this is how you treat your friends, I'd hate to see how you treat your enemies."

"It's pretty much the same way I treat you," snapped Alba.

Reign's eyes narrowed into slits. "I'm just trying to help clean up the mess that *you* created."

"You're the one that gave her avocado, not me, buddy."

"Alba! You *just* admitted that you harassed her into eating it!"

"Yeah, well, you didn't have to run with it. I already feel guilty. I don't need you making it worse."

I palmed my forehead. This wasn't happening. "Can you two not? Please. We need to help Holly."

Elodie nodded. "Yes, please. Arguing doesn't help. Plus it's giving me a headache, and I need to think."

Reign's lips pressed together tightly, and he clenched his jaw.

Alba crossed her arms over her chest and sealed her mouth as well.

"Thank you," I said before looking at Elodie again. "Can you help us?"

Elodie tapped a finger against her top lip. "Hmmm. Avocado allergy. I'll be right back and see what I have." The small woman disappeared through the doorway she'd just come out of.

When she was gone, Alba let out a breath and strutted away, pretending to inspect the potions on Elodie's shelves.

Sweets gnawed nervously on her bottom lip. "Oh, you guys, what are we going to do with Holly if Elodie can't help her?"

"Sweets, you need to think positively," said Libby. "Elodie will be able to help."

I worried about the same thing. We certainly couldn't go back to Aspen Falls telling Jax that not only hadn't we saved her mother or reversed the curse, but also one of her best friends had died while we'd tried. But I didn't want to contribute to the panic that Sweets was feeling, so I kept my mouth shut and silently hoped that Elodie was going to be able to help.

I glanced up at my brother's face. He looked upset. His face was long and his body looked tense. I'd seen him like that before. It was his worried face. He was worrying just as much as I was. Silently, I sidled up next to him, wrapped my arms around his back and gave him a little squeeze. He looked down at me and slung his arm over my shoulder. "This isn't your fault."

He took a deep breath and then looked away. "Yeah."

"It's not, Reign. You didn't know. None of us knew."

"I know. I'm just worried about her."

"We all are," said Libby.

We were all quiet until Elodie reappeared a few minutes later carrying a small glass beaker filled with a green substance.

We all pounced.

"Is that an antidote to her allergic reaction?" asked Libby.

"What is it?" asked Sweets.

Alba looked at her curiously. "It looks like avocado."

Elodie smiled at us all kindly. "It is avocado peel extract combined with several other ingredients."

My mouth gaped. "But she's allergic!"

"Yes, yes. I know that."

"But won't it kill her?!" I interjected before Elodie had a chance to explain.

"Yes, I understand that's what one would think, but in this particular potion, it will actually save her life. Have you ever heard the expression, 'the hair of the dog that bit you'?"

We all nodded.

Elodie adjusted her glasses. "You see, that expression actually came from a witch. Way back when, there was a witch by the name of Cybil Timberwolf. She discovered that a human that's bitten by a rabid dog could be cured by making a potion that contained hair from the very dog that bit them. It was a revolutionary discovery that has led to many medical cures since then." She tapped the beaker she held in her hand. "This contains avocado, but I can assure you, it's been blended with additional ingredients that will counteract the originally ingested allergen."

I looked down at Holly sadly. We had little other choice. "You're sure?"

"Quite sure." She looked at Libby. "Now, if you're ready? I'll just need you to unthaw her and then I'll have her drink this."

Reign frowned. "Before she was frozen, I think her esophagus was completely constricted. In fact, I'd just begun to attempt CPR on her."

Elodie touched her top lip again. "Oh my. Yes, that

will make this more difficult." She sucked air in quickly and held a finger up. "But I have just the thing!" Before we could ask her anything more, she disappeared into her back room again and then reappeared just as quickly carrying a syringe. "I ordered these when I first opened the shop and have rarely needed to use them, but I'm sure glad I have them for emergencies such as this!"

Libby tilted her head from side to side and then rolled it around on her shoulders. "Stand back."

"Wait," said Elodie, holding a hand out to stop Libby. "Is this going to leave a puddle on my floor? Because if it is, I think I'd like to move her."

Libby smiled. "This is a puddle-free process."

"Good. Okay, go ahead." Elodie turned her back to Libby and began to draw the green liquid into her syringe.

While Elodie prepared the syringe, Libby exhaled as much as she could and then slowly sucked in her breath over the top of Holly's cube of ice. The breath she sucked in gradually became frosty. Breath after frosty breath, Libby sucked in, shrinking Holly's ice cube until the only thing left was Holly, shivering on the floor. A weakened Libby fell back against the counter.

Cinder caught hold of her sister. "Hurry, Elodie, you don't have much time now."

Elodie and Reign squatted next to Holly. Reign took hold of Holly's hand while Elodie injected the magical elixir into her thigh muscle.

We all stared at her lifeless body.

"How long will it take?" he asked, looking up at Elodie with concern.

Elodie shook her head sadly. "I really don't know. I

haven't seen any of these freezing spells firsthand. I've only heard of them. I'm not sure how long that will set back the antidote's effects."

Reign scooped her up in his arms. "Do you have anywhere we could lay her down? Somewhere more comfortable than the floor, until she's woken up?"

Elodie nodded, beckoning Reign to follow her.

*E*lodie reemerged from the back room alone.
"Where's Reign?" I asked.

"He asked to stay with her until she wakes up."

"So," said Elodie, busying herself by wrapping the needle she'd used in some newspaper. "May I ask where you girls are from? Norwalk is a small town, and there aren't many witches nearby. I'm sure I would have heard about you if you lived in town."

Alba and I exchanged uncomfortable glances. We couldn't very well tell her that we'd come through a time-traveling wormhole. We didn't even know what year it was, though I was fairly confident whatever time period we were in was close to present day. Elodie looked exactly the same as she had a day ago.

I smiled at Elodie. "You're right. We're not from here. We were just visiting some family when this happened," I lied.

"Oh, so where are you all from, then?"

"All over the place," said Alba. "But we all attend the Paranormal Institute for Witches in Aspen Falls, Pennsylvania."

I eyed Alba in shock. *Alba! What are you doing?!* I

hollered at her in my mind, hoping that she would read it as she sometimes did.

Elodie's eyes widened. "Oh! You're all students at the Institute?!"

"All of us except Reign," said Alba, pointing at the doorway. "He's her brother."

"I can't believe it! I'm an Institute alum myself and my daughter attended for a short time!" Her tone seemed to change slightly as she mentioned her daughter attending. It was like a dark shadow had passed across her face.

Alba caught it too. "Only for a short time? Why's that?"

Elodie grimaced. "She had some issues there, I'm afraid."

"Really? What kind of issues?"

Elodie sighed, glancing at all of our faces uncomfortably. "Oh, I really shouldn't speak of it. I'm not one for gossiping."

"It wouldn't be gossiping," said Alba. "Think of it as swapping stories. We've had some issues at the Institute ourselves. Maybe if we tell you our story, you'll tell us yours?"

"Maybe," said Elodie with a shrug.

Alba pointed at Libby and Cinder. "Well, I don't know about those two, because they're in the grade above us, but the three of us and Holly, the girl you just helped, we're sort of in Sorceress Stone's LVS club."

"LVS?"

"Least Valuable Students."

Elodie smiled. "Is that right?"

I nodded. "She's one hundred percent right. Ever since we started at the Institute, she's seemed to have a grudge against us. We've been locked in a tower, she's turned her powers on us, yelled at us…" I took a breath and then whisper-hissed, "Once, she even tried to turn us into snakes! But my mom and grandma happened to step in and save us."

Elodie touched her heart, her eyes wide. "You're kidding?"

"Nope, they're not kidding," said Sweets, shaking her head sadly. "Sorceress Stone wasn't very kind to us from the very beginning, and all we've ever done is try to help her. I ended up dropping out early."

"Because of Sorceress Stone? Oh, you poor thing!"

Sweets shrugged. "It's alright. I got a really good job offer that I couldn't pass up anyway. That was the main reason I quit. But Sorceress Stone not being very nice made my decision easier."

"My sister and I have also been locked in the tower many times," said Cinder with a knowing nod. "During our first year on campus, she was especially hostile."

Libby shook her head sadly. "We never understood it. She was never like that with the rest of the students. Mostly just us."

Elodie looked behind her and then lowered her head slightly. "Well," she said in a hush, "since we're swapping stories, my daughter experienced some of those very same things!"

"She did?" I asked.

Elodie nodded. "Yes, and also at the hands of Sorceress Stone. She was cruel to my daughter. She had a horrible time there."

"I'm sorry to hear that."

"So am I. Of course my daughter's father, my ex,

wanted to turn her in to the authorities for kidnapping and get the Institute shut down."

Wow. This was getting interesting. Maybe Elodie Goodwitch had a motive to kill Sorceress Stone after all! "But he didn't call the police?"

Elodie shook her head, her curly brown hair bobbed. "No. I told him that eventually karma would come back around again and she'd pay the price for her actions." Elodie sighed and toyed with the cardboard box in front of her. "Of course, it wasn't just Sorceress Stone's fault that my daughter left that school."

"Oh, did something else happen?" asked Sweets. "Did she not get along with one of the teachers?"

Elodie gave us a tight smile. "No. Actually, there were some students, some of the *other* witches, that gave my little girl a hard time. I wish she would have met some nice girls, like all of you. Then maybe when that nasty group of girls they called the Witch Squad got in her face, she would have had someone else to back her up."

25

*R*eign slid Elodie's office chair over to the small love seat Holly slept quietly on. He'd tucked a plush throw blanket tightly around her shivering body. Her usually glossed lips were dull and pale, as was the rest of her face. Even the blush she wore on her cheekbones only managed to accentuate just how sallow her complexion had truly become.

Reign took hold of one of her icy hands. His head hung low between his shoulder blades with his eyes trained on the blanket that covered her breasts. It wasn't for the reason that Holly would have liked, but simply because he was anxiously watching the methodical rising and falling of her chest. It meant she was still alive and breathing on her own.

Reign scanned the smooth lines of Holly's face for any sign of consciousness and gently pushed back a strand of blond hair that fell across her forehead. He couldn't deny it she *was* a beauty. But despite Holly's silly attempts at impressing him with her killer body or her pretty face, Reign had never bitten. Pretty girls had been a dime a dozen since he'd started attracting them, around the tender age of thirteen. His own good lucks and charming ways had proven to be a hit with the ladies, even back then. But he'd found *those* girls, the ones who knew they were pretty and flaunted it, to be especially unappealing. Those were the ones that Reign kept his guard up around. They moved from man to man like butterflies moved from flower to flower.

Reign was decidedly too somber for a flighty woman like that. While he wasn't necessarily looking for a wife at only twenty-five years of age, he preferred serious relationships to the kind that "those types of girls" offered. Holly had only seemed like one of those busy, beautiful butterflies to him. Bouncing from flower to flower.

So, despite her being one of Mercy's best friends, he'd never *really* taken the time to get to know her. But that didn't mean he didn't *like* her. She seemed like a nice enough girl. He liked the fact that she'd made a fool of herself in an effort to make his cousin feel better. There was no doubt it had put a smile on both his and Jax's faces. He liked the fact that she always went out of her way to greet him with a smile at Habernackle's, and unless she and Alba were clashing, Holly almost *always* was in a good mood. Plus, Holly seemed to be the underdog of the group, always getting picked on by Alba, and after seeing it firsthand, he almost felt bad for her.

So, because he was beginning to see Holly more as a *person* and not just as one of "those types of girls," she'd become more human to him—more *real* and less like the wooden, two-dimensional character she had portrayed herself to be. And now he truly felt horrible about what had happened to her.

"I'm so sorry," he whispered with a bowed head, guilt riddling his voice. "This is all my fault."

"Reign?" breathed a barely-there voice.

Reign's heart lurched. He lifted his head. "Holly?" With her eyes still closed, he searched her face for signs that his name had come from her lips.

"Yeah," she whispered with her eyes still sealed. "I-I'm c-cold."

"I know," he said, tucking the blanket in tighter around her shoulders. "How are you feeling, besides cold?"

"I-I'm okay," she stuttered weakly. "Thirsty."

Reign stood up and rushed over to the small water-cooler in the corner of Elodie's office, grabbing a paper cup and filling it with water. In three long strides he was back at Holly's side, helping her to take a drink.

"Thanks," she whispered. Her eyes fluttered open slightly then. "What happened?"

"You had an allergic reaction to avocado."

"Oh yeah." One of her hands made its way out of the blanket to touch her lips. They'd already lost much of their puffiness. "I remember that. Where are we? Why am I so cold?"

"Well, it's kind of a long story, but we're in Iowa, at Elodie Goodwitch's Magical Apothecary."

"Iowa!" Holly's blue eyes opened wider. She struggled to sit up so she could look around. "How did we get to Iowa?"

After helping her sit upright, Reign tried to explain. "Through the wormhole. We're back in time, but we're not sure how far back. Elodie saved you from your allergic reaction."

"Elodie saved me? Where is she?"

Reign's head bobbed towards the door. "Out there. With the rest of the girls. We were just waiting for you to wake up and feel better before we left."

Holly shook her head as if she were trying to clear the cobwebs. "Oh. What day is it?"

Reign shook his head. "You know, I really don't know. We've been time traveling so much that I'm not sure what day we'll go back to. It was Wednesday when we left."

"It's still Wednesday? Where's Jax?"

"In Aspen Falls with Char. Remember?"

"Oh, yeah." Holly scrunched up her nose and looked up at Reign. "Wait. Why are you sitting over me and not one of the girls?"

Reign let out a heavy sigh. "Well, I sorta feel responsible."

Holly rubbed the pads of her fingers against her temples. She still looked to be a bit dazed and confused. "You feel responsible? For what?"

"For your allergic reaction. I made the wraps that had the avocado in them."

"Oh, yeah," she said quietly. "But I didn't have to eat it. I knew I was allergic. I just thought if I ate around the avocado I'd be alright. I haven't had an allergic reaction since I was a little kid."

"That's probably because you avoid eating it."

Holly grinned sheepishly. "Yeah, probably."

"Why didn't you just *say* you were allergic?"

She shrugged and shifted her eyes off of his. "I just

thought it was nice that you'd made us all lunch, and I didn't want to seem ungrateful by being overly picky."

Reign gave her a half-smile. "By telling me that you were *allergic* to one of the ingredients? I'd hardly view that as being ungrateful."

"Yeah." She smiled at him. "Sorry."

"It's okay. We've all been really worried about you. Even Alba."

Holly let out a snort. "Ha, funny."

"No, I'm serious! She was just as worried as any of us. We were afraid we might lose you." He shook his head. "And then SaraLynn came after us, and we didn't have much time."

"Wait, hold up. Sorceress Stone came after us? When?"

"When you were having your allergic reaction. We'd just taken you to the nurse's office."

"In the past?"

Reign nodded. "Yeah. Don't you remember? We were on the back lawn, waiting for the Council meeting to resume, when you had the allergic reaction. We didn't know what to do, so we took you to the nurse's office. That was when you stopped breathing."

Holly's eyes widened. It was obvious she had no recollection of any of that and was shocked to hear how serious it had become. "I stopped breathing?"

"Yeah. I had to give you CPR."

Her eyes widened even further. "*You* gave me CPR?! You mean you saved my life?"

Reign lifted a shoulder uncomfortably. "Well, yeah. You would have died if I didn't!"

"Wow." Holly sat back against the sofa back, speechless.

"So then, SaraLynn showed up and was all you're not supposed to be here, so Alba and I created a diversion so that Mercy and the girls could get you out of there. Libby froze you to keep you from dying."

Holly's head snapped around to stare at Reign. "Libby froze me?! Is that why I'm so cold?"

Reign hopped up to get the blanket back around her again. "Are you still freezing? Here, let's get this around you."

Holly pushed the blanket away. "No, it's okay, thanks. Now that I'm awake, I'm warming up. I just can't believe Libby *froze* me. Like she did Sorceress Stone?"

Reign shrugged as he stood in front of her. "Not sure. I didn't see her freeze SaraLynn. I assume it was the same."

Holly shook her head as she looked at her arms in awe. "Wow. And I'm still alive. That's amazing."

Reign nodded and sat down next to her on the love seat. "It *is* amazing. I'm thankful you're okay."

"Thanks. And thanks for watching out for me. That was sweet of you."

He grinned at her and threw an arm over her shoulder. "No problem. We're all just thankful you're alive."

Holly leaned her head on Reign's shoulder. "Me too."

Suddenly, the door burst open. "Reign, is Holly oka—" began Sweets breathlessly. Seeing Holly seated and awake on the small sofa caused her to stop in her tracks. She smiled from ear to ear. "Holly! You're awake!"

"Yeah." Holly tried to get to her feet but stumbled backwards slightly.

Reign caught her around the waist. "Whoa. Slow down. I got you."

Holly smiled up at him. "Thanks."

In a panic, Sweets beckoned them forward. The smile had completely disappeared from her face. "Come on. We have to go. Something… umm… *changed*."

"Changed?" asked Reign curiously as he helped Holly to the door. "What's going on?"

"You'll see. Come on, we have to go. Now!"

"*A*re you sure you really have to run off so soon?" asked Elodie. She looked at her watch. "I wish you could stay a little longer and meet my daughter, Victoria. She should be back any minute. I know she'd love to meet you."

When Reign emerged from Elodie's backroom with his arm slung around Holly's waist, but her walking on her own two feet, my heart lifted. I let out a sigh of relief. *Oh, thank God.* We needed to get out of there immediately, before Elodie's daughter showed up, because the second Elodie had mentioned "the nasty Witch Squad," the pieces had begun to fall into place, and I knew *exactly* who her daughter was.

Tori Decker. The girl that Sorceress Stone had expelled because of her lies and manipulations, and her involvement in framing Brittany Hobbs for the murder of our school lunch lady, Denise. Tori had been a horrible girl, causing nothing but trouble. Not only had she made solving Denise's murder harder than it needed to be, but she'd also been the cause of numerous problems in my relationship with Hugh. Ultimately, those problems had resulted in our breakup. It didn't shock me one bit that she'd gone home and blamed all of her problems on us.

I hitched my thumb over my shoulder and edged towards the exit. "Yeah, so sorry, Elodie. We really need to get going. Our friend's little emergency has already derailed our plans for far too long. Come on, girls. Let's get going."

Alba led the pack towards the door. She was as completely aware of the sudden sense of urgency as I was. "Thanks a lot, Mrs. G. We, uh, really appreciate everything."

"Anytime, girls, anytime. Oh, and sweetie, I sure hope you get to feeling better," she said to Holly as Reign helped move her towards the door.

"Thanks, Elodie," said Holly with a smile.

We'd all barely managed to file out the door when a silver car came tearing around the corner and screeched to a halt next to the old pickup. My heart dropped. Before she'd even gotten out of the vehicle, I knew who it was.

"Oh no," breathed Alba.

"What?" asked Libby.

"It's Tori Decker," I said through a clenched jaw and tight lips.

"That girl that got expelled from the Institute at the beginning of the school year?" asked Cinder.

Libby shook her head in confusion. "Wait... is she—"

"Yup. Elodie's daughter. We need to get outta here ASAP."

Single-file, we turned stiffly down the sidewalk to head back in the direction that we'd come, but before we could get far, the car door opened.

"You have *got* to be kidding me!" screeched Tori Decker's familiar voice. "I wouldn't believe it if I hadn't seen it with my own eyes. The Witch Squad is here? In Norwalk? What are *you people* doing in my mother's shop?"

Alba turned around. Her face was beet red already. "You people?" She sneered. "*You people?* How dare you. You insignificant little fly." She flicked her finger towards Tori, and the girl stumbled backwards on the sidewalk.

Enraged, Tori ripped off the black sunglasses she wore and threw them down onto the pavement before charging Alba.

Alba slid out of her thin zip-up windbreaker. She pressed it into my arms. "Hold my jacket!"

"Alba, stop!" screamed Sweets. "Now's not the time for this!"

"Alba don't," barked Reign with one arm still around Holly's back, holding her up against his side.

But Alba and Tori had already closed the distance between themselves. Alba's fist flew towards Tori's face.

But before she could land the punch, Reign threw out his free hand, and a streak of red electrocharged energy flew out and wrapped itself around Alba like a lasso, forcing her arms down next to her sides.

Tori laughed and was just about to land her own punch on a now-defenseless Alba, when Libby threw up a shield of ice between the two women.

"You're coming with us," snapped Reign gruffly, tugging on the red energy lasso. "Come on. We need to get out of here before Libby's ice shield spell wears off."

"Let me out of this," shouted Alba, trying to shrug out of the energy's tight hold. "I can take her!"

"No!" said Cinder. "We do not have time for this. That girl's mother is on the Council. We must go now."

Libby and Cinder took off towards the water tower that we'd seen when we'd first gotten to town. Sweets followed next.

As Alba dug her heels into the ground and fought the lasso, I put my arm around Holly's back. "I'll help Holly. Reign, you keep Alba moving."

I did my best to keep Holly from falling as we sprinted back towards the wormhole we'd left alongside the creek. Reign had to fight Alba tooth and nail not to go back and pound Tori Decker into the ground, but finally the seven of us made it and slipped into the steam sauna vestibule to make our next move.

Alba fumed as she shook off the lingering charges of red static electricity that clung to her clothes. "I could have taken her, you know."

Reign rolled his eyes. "I'm sure you could have."

"No, I'm serious. I've got older brothers. I know how to fight."

"Yeah, well, do you really think getting into it with that girl is a priority for today?"

"No, but it woulda felt good."

"So will a warm bath," said Holly, rubbing her arms. "But we don't have time for that either."

Reign nodded. "See? Even Holly gets it. Now, come on." He spun a finger in the air. "Do your little... thing, and get us out of here."

Feeling a sense of urgency, I looked at Alba curiously. "So, where are we going next?"

"I don't know," she muttered, still salty about her run-in with Tori.

Since she wasn't thinking clearly, I knew I needed to step up. "Okay, well, who have we already visited? We know Elodie had a grudge against Sorceress Stone because she expelled her daughter. Gemma didn't like her because they were in competition for the same grades and the same boy. Poppy's got to be sore because Sorceress Stone bought the Institute essentially out from underneath her. Who's left to investigate?"

"Stella and Daphne," said Sweets.

"Stella and Daphne it is," I said, nodding at Alba. "We need to find out about their past with Sorceress Stone."

"Fine," muttered Alba. "Get into position and let's get this done."

26

"*Y*ou've gotta be kidding me!" I said, my chin jutted out and my eyes wide.

Holly shook her head. "Not again!"

"Well, at least those two were telling the truth. Now we know," said Alba with a sigh.

"Yeah, I guess we do. So now what?" I asked, looking out at the auditorium in front of us. The scene was so familiar that it didn't even warrant watching. Alba's spell and the magical wormhole had brought us back to Monday's graduation meeting in the auditorium. I found it odd to see myself sitting on the bleachers next to Alba and the rest of the girls.

Alba shook her head. She looked like she was at a loss. "I don't know."

Reign peered out into the auditorium and then pulled his head back into our hiding spot. "I think we should talk about this somewhere where we aren't going to be seen or heard." His head bobbed towards the back door.

Minutes later, we sat beneath the very same tree we'd

had lunch under during Holly's allergic reaction. Only now the tree was taller and the branches spanned a wider distance overhead.

"This is getting ridiculous," said Cinder. "It feels like we're walking in circles."

Her sister nodded. "Exactly! I don't think we're going to be able to figure out who killed Sorceress Stone, and obviously we aren't going to be able to bring her back to life. Let's just get back to the present. I have a graduation project to work on."

Cinder's head bobbed in agreement.

"Now wait just a darn minute," said Alba. "We're getting ahead of ourselves here. Now, I know things seem bleak. But we can't just give up!"

"I agree with Alba. We *have* figured out a few things," said Sweets. "Like, Elodie Goodwitch lied to us! She told us her daughter hadn't had any issues with Sorceress Stone. We know firsthand that she did, and she ended up getting expelled over it!"

"She wasn't the only one that lied. Poppy and Gemma weren't honest either," I added.

"But what about Daphne and Stella?" said Alba. "We should keep researching the two of them."

"But where do we go? We asked the time machine to show us their drama, and this is where we were delivered. They were the only ones telling the truth! They'd never met Sorceress Stone before Monday!" I said.

"It could've been Daphne," said Holly. "Remember, Sorceress Stone knew that secret and was threatening to release it to her employer."

"She explained that away," said Alba with a shrug.

"Fine, then what about Stella? Maybe there's something she's not telling us," I said.

Alba sighed. "I don't know. I mean, it's possible she's keeping something from us. But how do we find out? I don't even know where to ask the wormhole to take us."

We all leaned back in the grass, lost in our own thoughts. I racked my brain trying to think of a way to find out if Stella was hiding anything like the rest of the women had been, but nothing came to me. My mind finally wandered, and I began thinking about Jax and the fact that all she wanted for her eighteenth birthday was to finally become a witch. Now it looked like her mother had stolen that from her. If only Sorceress Stone hadn't gone off and died! Then we would've had time to use Alba's magical wormhole to go back to the day Auggie Stone had accidentally killed my granddad! Then none of this would be happening right now! Jax would be a witch. My granddad might still be alive. Heck, Sorceress Stone might even still be alive!

That thought made my breath catch in my throat. A little raspy breath escaped me.

"What?" asked Alba, looking up at me.

I swallowed hard. "I just had a thought."

Alba nodded. "I thought I felt the earth move."

"No, I'm serious, Alba. I think I had a really big thought."

"Like I said, I—"

I cut her off. "This isn't time for snarkiness! I'm serious."

"Then spill already!"

"I was just thinking how it sucks that we haven't had time to work on getting Jax's powers for her—"

Alba sighed. "Because we all agreed that saving her mother was top priority."

"Yeah, I know that. That's not my point. I'm just trying to explain my train of thought. So, I was thinking it sucks that we haven't had time to work on the Stone curse, and then I realized that if that curse had never been placed on Jax, she'd have her powers now and my granddad might be alive."

"Red—"

"Hear me out!" I bellowed.

Everyone's eyes widened as heads began to turn, looking around to see if anyone else on campus had heard my little outburst. But no one said a word.

"As I was saying. My granddad might still be alive if we stopped Auggie Stone from killing him back then. Jax would be a witch. And it occurred to me—Sorceress Stone might still be alive. If we change that one tiny bit of history, it would change so many things for the Stone family, and it might mean that she would still be alive."

"There's no way to know that, Red."

"Of course there's no way to know, but at least Jax would have her powers. And if by changing that one little thing, Sorceress Stone *is* still alive, then it's a win-win. And if my granddad is alive…" A huge smile covered my face. "Then it's a win-win-win."

"And if it's not a win-win?" asked Sweets.

"Then we just wasted a bunch of time that we could have been investigating," said Alba with a frown.

I stood up and brushed little pieces of cut grass off my knees. "Yeah, then we wasted some time, but guess what, Alba? We don't know where to go from here. We're at a standstill. We're stuck. We don't know where else to start investigating. None of these women are from this area. It's not like we can go ask someone in town a bunch of questions. They all showed up for this singular event and now Jax's mom is dead. What if this can fix everything?"

Reign, who had been silent through all of my suggestions, finally leaned forward. "You might be on to something." He raised his hand. "I vote we try."

"Yeah?" said Alba. "And since when do *you* get a vote?"

"Since I kept you from getting your butt handed to you by that scrappy-looking Iowa girl," he said with a cocky smile.

"Are you kidding?" bellowed Alba. "I would've had her on the ground in a second if you'd let me take care of business."

"He gave me CPR," added Holly. "He tried to save my life. He gets my vote."

"Well, there's a shocker," snapped Alba.

"And he carried Holly all the way to Elodie's apothecary," added Sweets. "I agree. Reign definitely gets a vote."

"Big deal. He used his magic to carry her," she scoffed.

"Magic takes a lot out of you. It is a big deal," said Libby. "Trust me, I know. I agree with Mercy and Reign. Let's get this curse lifted. Maybe then Sorceress Stone will be alive and my sister and I can get back to working on our graduation project."

Cinder nodded in agreement. "I'm in favor of that too."

I studied the faces of all of the girls. "Okay, all in favor?"

All hands went up except Alba's.

"It's gonna be a waste of our time," she grumbled. "But if that's what you all want, I guess whatever."

"Good. Alright, let's get to the wormhole!"

A fatal potion was concocted,
And soon thereafter a murder plotted.
Take us back to the place and time
Auggie Stone committed her heinous crime.

After making our way through the spinning tunnel of lights once again, we exited near a small brook situated in a shady spot at the bottom of a hill. The sweet scent of lilacs spiked the warm spring air. At the top of the hill, a split-rail fence surrounded a cottage-style house with a small detached garage. In the backyard, laundry pinned to a clothesline blew in the wind and a little wooden swing set provided entertainment for four small children. It was a picturesque scene, one that I was sure I'd seen in storybooks my mother had read to me as a child.

"I wonder where we are," said Holly, looking around.

"We gotta assume we're exactly where we asked to be," said Alba. "Maybe this is where Auggie Stone killed Red's grandfather."

"No use speculating. There's only one way to find out." My eyes narrowed in on the small house, and I couldn't help but wonder who would be inside. Would my granddad be in there? I'd never met him, and I rarely heard my grandmother or mother speak of him. Of course Mom had been very young when he'd been killed; therefore she didn't even remember her father. Not only had I never met my granddad, but I'd never met my father either. It seemed to be a Habernackle curse, I guessed, to grow up without a father. So to have the opportunity to finally meet one of the men in my family made my hands tremble with nervous anticipation.

No sooner had we taken steps towards the house than a woman emerged from the back door. One of the little girls' voices screeched with excitement. "Momma! Push me!" The young mother busily tended to the children in the yard, giving each of them pushes on the swings and helping one of the smaller girls climb the slide.

Alba beckoned us to follow her. "This way," she whispered. She led us around the back side of a long windbreak of lilac bushes along the length of the hill. When the overgrown shrubs ended abruptly just yards shy of the back corner of the house, we realized we'd have to put in some tummy time in the long grass if we were going to finish our trek unseen. I was thankful I hadn't seen any snakes along the way, or I might have given away our positions with a scream.

When we reached the side of the house, I heard one of the little girls squeal and then the young woman chastising one of the children. "Merrick, stop poking your sister with that stick!"

"Merrick?" whispered my brother, who had flattened himself against the side of the house next to me. "I can't believe it. That little boy is my father?"

We peered around the corner at him again. The little

boy was probably no more than seven years old. He had an olive complexion and dark black hair that hung in his eyes. Armed with the knowledge that the boy was Reign's father, I turned my eyes onto the rest of the children. There were three girls, two of which I realized had to be SaraLynn and BethAnn, but the one that caught my eye had a shock of bright red hair that blew around her shoulders angelically as she climbed the slide. She couldn't have been more than four or five.

"Be careful, Linda," chided the woman. "Your mother will be angry if you come inside with a broken leg."

"It's Auggie," whispered Alba. "Looks just like her daughter does now, except she's thicker."

I nodded wordlessly. I couldn't take my mind off the fact that I was staring at my mother as a little girl! And there she was playing side by side with SaraLynn, Beth-Ann, and Merrick! It was too crazy for words.

With the group of us smashed against the side of the house, Alba silently waved us ahead like a platoon leader signaling his troops. A porch sat at the front elevation of the house and an old pickup truck sat in the dirt driveway, just a yard or two in front of a garage, if you could call it a garage. It looked more like a makeshift barn with a lean-to attached to one side. Several fishing poles leaned against the doorway of the lean-to, a lawn mower rested on its side and a variety of tools were spread out on the ground around it.

Alba cranked her head back to look up at the porch. "We'll have to get up there if we want to see in any of the windows."

"But what if someone sees us?" whispered Sweets. "There're so many of us!"

Alba nodded. "You're right. Seven people standing on a porch is sure to catch some attention. Red, it's your family. You and I should go. You all stay here. The rest of you, why don't you go hide behind those trees over there?" After pointing to a small stand of birch trees, she beckoned me to follow her.

"Whoa, whoa, whoa. This is my family too," said my brother. "And those are *my* parents back there! And my grandmother and my aunts. I have a right to go."

Alba shook her head and whisper-hissed at us, "Three's too many. We'll be spotted for sure."

I put a hand on Alba's shoulder. "You're right."

She sneered at my brother.

"Three *is* too many. Sorry, Alba, but you might have to sit this one out."

"But…" Her mouth hung open, shocked that I'd taken Reign's side. But the fact of the matter was, she was speechless because she knew we were right. This was something that Reign and I had to do for our family. This was about the feud between the Stones and the Haber- nackles. And while I appreciated Alba getting us this far, I knew the rest was up to us to handle.

"Are you ready?" asked Reign, looking down at me.

I took a deep breath and then let it out slowly. Then my eyes swung up to meet his. "As ready as I'll ever be."

27

Squatted down low on the porch, with our noses pressed against the windowpane like puppies begging to be let in, we gazed inside the modest home. Even though the boxy furnishings were simple, the house exuded a feeling of coziness, warmth, and family.

When we were sure the place was empty, Reign tried one of the windows up and, finding it unlocked, slid it all the way open. Seconds later, a door slammed from somewhere inside and then, just like that, I was looking at a young man that I'd only known through pictures.

"Granddad!" I breathed. The man had brown hair that looked as if it had been intentionally parted on one side, but had gotten mussed while working. He was tall, with big beefy arms and legs and thick, muscular hands. I couldn't believe I was seeing him in person.

Reign's brows lifted as he stared at the man. "That's him? That's our grandfather?"

I nodded.

"You're sure?"

"Yeah, I've seen pictures of him. Oh, but he's much more handsome in person." I stared at my granddad, starry-eyed, and then looked up at my brother. "You have his jawline and his mouth."

A slow smile crossed Reign's face as we both turned our attention back to our grandfather, who stood in the middle of the living room. "Phyllis!" he shouted gruffly before pulling a blue shop rag from the back pocket of his grimy-looking pants and cleaning grease from his fingers. "Phyllis!"

A young woman appeared in an interior doorway. "Oh, for heaven's sake, Clark. Must you yell?"

I grinned. My granny looked so different! Of course I'd *seen* pictures of her with my granddad when they were young, but I'd grown up seeing her in a whole different light. She had always been *old* in my memory. She'd always had wrinkles and wiry white hair that she wore pulled back in a bun. Now she had smooth, wrinkle-free skin, and shoulder-length red hair that curled up around her face, and was pinned back at the base of her jaw. It was clear that one thing hadn't changed about my grandmother—her attitude. She sounded just like she had my entire life.

Granddad inhaled deeply as he stared at her.

"What?!" she bellowed. "Why in the world are you looking at me like that?"

"Phyllis, how long are Auggie and her children staying with us?"

Gran looked taken aback. "How long are they staying? Clark, is that why you tromped your greasy shoes all the way from the shed into my clean living room? Hell if I know. Why do you ask?"

My granddad shook his head as if he were worn out. "Phyllis, this house is too small for so many people. We only have two bedrooms. I'm tired of Linda sleeping with us. She needs to get back to having her own bed and her own room."

"Well, that's where Auggie and her kids are staying. Do you expect me to put them on the sofa?"

"No! I expect you to let them be on their way!"

Gran shook her head and wagged her finger at him. "Clark, now you know they have nowhere to go. After Samson left her for that younger witch, Auggie found herself broke and without anywhere else to turn!"

Granddad looked exasperated, like they'd been over this before. "I understand that. And we helped. We gave her a place to stay until she got over the trauma. But she's feeling better now, and that's not our problem, now is it?"

Gran's mouth opened and then snapped shut again just as quickly. She looked back over her shoulder, like she could see Auggie and the kids out a window in the back of the house. "I didn't want to say anything, because I knew you'd get mad," she began uneasily.

"Oh, here we go," he sighed, running a hand through his wavy hair.

Gran held up a flattened palm. "Now just hold your horses." She sucked in a deep breath before continuing. "One of Auggie's friends from back home called her this morning with some news."

"Okay…?"

"There was a wedding announcement in the paper yesterday."

"A wedding announcement?" He looked confused.

"What's that got to do with anything? There are always wedding announcements in the papers."

"Yes, well, this one just happened to be the wedding announcement of Harlow Crandall and Samson Smith."

My granddad threw his head back. "Oh, for Pete's sake."

"Auggie didn't take the news well." Gran admitted while wringing out her hands in front of herself. "Of course she's trying to keep it together for the children."

"I just don't understand this, Phyllis. I thought after what she did to break you and Samson up, you'd never forgive her! I thought you didn't like her anymore."

"Well, she apologized for that," said Gran. "And she was such a good friend to me in college. And now look at where we are in life, and look at where she is! I've got you and Linda, and we've got our home together. My life is great. Auggie didn't make out so well. She's got three little ones and no husband, no job, no money, no place to live. How can I cast more stones at her when she's already down so low?"

Granddad shook his head. "I understand, Phyllis. And your big heart is one of the many reasons that I fell in love with you."

"And your ability to be compassionate is one of the reasons I fell in love with you!" said Gran, her voice softening. She strode over to my granddad and gave him a hug despite his filthy clothing.

When they'd parted, Granddad put a hand on her shoulder. "But that doesn't change the fact that it's time for Auggie and her kids to go."

"But, Clark!" breathed Gran, and then we heard the back door slam shut. Gran looked over her shoulder before turning back to my granddad and whispering to him. "We'll talk about this *later.*"

"Yes, we certainly will," he grumbled under his breath.

Auggie breezed into the living room then and fell onto the sofa dramatically. "My goodness, it's getting hot out there! If this is springtime weather around here, I think we're in for a scorcher of a summer."

Gran nodded uneasily. "Yes, yes, I think you're right," she said stiffly, glancing up at her husband.

Auggie looked from Gran to my granddad and back again. "Oh. I'm sorry. Am I interrupting something?"

Gran shook her head and patted Granddad's arm. "No, no. Not at all. I was just telling Clark I need to run into town. We're out of everything. Would you like to join me? Maybe getting you out of the house would do you some good."

Auggie let out a chortle. "Oh, no. I'm beat. I probably pushed the children a thousand times on those swings. I've had it. I feel like I could sleep for days." She leaned back against the sofa and closed her eyes.

Phyllis lifted her brows. "Well, then, I've got an idea. Why don't I take the children into town with me so you can get some rest?"

Auggie's eyes popped open. "Oh, would you really do that for me, Phil?"

"Of course I would. It's crazy how much small children drain your energy. Especially when you're going through something as you are. I'm so thankful I've got my Clark to help out with Linda when I need a break from time to time."

Auggie's smile disappeared. "Yes, the children are

especially draining right now. Especially after the news this morning." She shook her head sadly. Then she looked up at my granddad, her eyes big and serious. "Phil, you're so lucky. You wound up with the greatest man of all time. I'm jealous, you know."

Gran wrapped an arm around my granddad's thick waist. "Yes, I am a lucky woman. I do love my Clark."

Granddad grunted as if the praise from the two women had embarrassed him. "I have work to do in the shed. I still haven't been able to get the damn lawn mower to start." He turned around and disappeared the same way he'd come in through a side door. From outside, Reign and I heard the door slam and then watched as Granddad shuffled across the dirt driveway to the detached garage.

From inside, Gran spoke again. "Sorry about that. I think he gets a little embarrassed by the praise. Listen, just let me get my purse and my keys and then I'll run out back and get the children. Then you can have the whole house to yourself for a little R&R."

Auggie smiled at her old friend. "Oh, Phil. You're such a sweetheart. I'll just go lie down in the bedroom now. I really do owe you so much, and I'm so thankful that you forgave me for everything that happened all those years ago."

Gran waved a hand as she hugged Auggie. "Water under the bridge, old friend. Water under the bridge."

*O*nce Gran had left to get the children and Auggie disappeared into another room, Reign and I decided to meet up with the girls to give them the scoop on what we'd seen and to regroup.

Alba pounced the second we snuck back around to meet them. "Well, what's going on?"

"We saw our grandfather!" I said excitedly.

"Yeah?" Alba's eyes were wide and her mouth curved into a genuine grin. For once she actually looked hyped about something. "For real?"

"For real," said Reign. "He's tall. And has broad shoulders and dark hair."

"But he's still alive?"

"Yeah, still alive."

Alba nodded. "Alright, well, that means Auggie's gotta be giving him the potion soon."

My head rolled back on my neck. "Oh no."

"What?" asked Sweets.

"Gran just volunteered to take the kids into town so Auggie could get some sleep."

Holly sucked in her breath, covering her mouth with her hand. "You think it's going to happen now?"

"She'll be alone with our grandfather," said Reign. "It makes sense. Especially if the wormhole took us back to the day he dies, this is probably her only shot to get him alone."

My heart raced and my limbs suddenly went shaky again. This was too much. I'd only just laid eyes on the man. I didn't want him to die. "We have to save him."

"Obviously," said Alba. "It's the only way to undo this curse. We have to make it so it never happened. That means doing whatever we have to do to stop Auggie from giving him that potion, because your grandfather cannot die today!"

I threw my arms around Alba. It was something I rarely did—to her or to anybody, but in that second, I felt an onslaught of emotions overwhelm me. "Thanks, Alba. Thank you so much."

Alba pretended to push me away. Hugging wasn't her thing either, but despite her protests, she allowed me to thank her. "Quit, you're making a scene," she grumbled.

Unexpected tears spilled down my cheeks. The idea that everything was about to change overpowered me. I was about to grow up with a grandfather in my life! My mother was going to have grown up with a father! Jax was about to become a witch. It was all finally happening!

"Yeah, thanks, Alba. You made all of this possible," said Reign, throwing his arms around both of us. "Our family owes you a lot."

It took only a second before Sweets threw *her* arms around Reign, Alba, and me. "Oh, you guys! You're making *me* want to cry!"

"See? This is why I don't hug!" barked Alba as she squirmed out of our embrace for real that time. "Everyone gets all mushy and it makes me wanna vomit. Listen, we've got real work to do. As soon as Phil drives away, we gotta be on Auggie like a second skin, got it? We can't let her out of our sight."

"How are we supposed to do that from outside the house?" said Reign. "She could be making the potion anywhere. In her room, in the kitchen, in the cellar…"

Alba nodded. "Fine. Then the second the car leaves,

we spread out. Everyone, find a window and get eyes on her."

We didn't wait long. Less than five minutes later, Gran strode out to the car holding both my mother's and Beth-Ann's hands tightly. As she placed the three little girls in the front seat of the pickup truck, she hollered at my granddad. "Clark! We're leaving! We'll be back in an hour."

Granddad appeared from the shadows in the garage just as Merrick climbed into the bed of the truck. He pointed a calloused finger at Merrick. "You stay seated back there, you hear me, son?"

Merrick's mouth set into a tight line, and his dark eyes blazed. "Don't call me son! You're not my father!"

"No, that's right, I'm not," agreed Granddad patiently, "but if he were here, he'd say the same thing. Now just keep your butt on the bottom of that truck bed, or my wife will make you sit up front with the girls." Then he pointed at his wife as she climbed into the driver's seat and slammed the door shut. "Drive safe, watch that clutch."

She stuck her head and left elbow out the window. "Don't you worry about me, Clark. I know what I'm doing." She waved as her tires sent a puff of dust up into the air.

Once Gran's taillights disappeared and Granddad ducked back into his workshop, the seven of us spread out around the house. Alba and I each took a corner of the back deck, where we quickly discovered a sliding door that led into the kitchen and a window that looked into a small bathroom.

We were silent as we watched, patiently waiting for

anything to happen. Time ticked by slowly, making me begin to wonder if perhaps the wormhole had put us on the scene far too early. Perhaps we'd be waiting for days before Auggie made her move on Granddad. I took the empty minutes to daydream about what it would have been like to have grown up with both my grandparents in my life. They seemed like such a loving, happy couple that I couldn't help but get excited about picturing my childhood with a grandfather that would have taught me how to fish and to tinker with cars and lawn mowers. It would have been great.

A noise inside caught my attention. My daydream faded as Auggie surreptitiously slipped into the kitchen. From the window above the kitchen sink, I watched as her eyes darted towards the sliding door on the back porch, making me sink lower in my position, but her eyes never met mine.

She dropped a cloth bag onto the table and then set about unloading ingredients and candles onto Gran's small wooden table. It was then I knew that we'd been brought back to the right moment in history. This was the very moment that Auggie prepared the potion that would kill my grandfather.

28

*B*iting my lip between my front teeth, I glanced across the deck at Alba, who stared into the bathroom window. Feeling my eyes on her, she turned to look at me. I spoke to her with my eyes. Lifting a brow and cocking my head slightly, I told her that I had eyes on Auggie in the kitchen. She nodded, sank to a crouch, and then duck-walked in my direction, pausing at the threshold of the sliding deck door to peer around the jamb into the kitchen.

We watched silently as Auggie prepared the potion that she intended to use to steal my grandfather away from my grandmother, just as she'd done years before when she'd stolen Samson Smith. Now that Samson had moved on to a newer, younger witch, Auggie was bound and determined to do a repeat performance and attempt to steal my grandmother's man once again. But little did she realize the potion she was concocting would ultimately take Granddad's life. Whether she had done the potion wrong or he had been allergic to the pit viper venom that was in it, Gran had never been sure. The only thing she'd been sure of was that she'd gone out, and when she'd returned, her husband was dead.

As I watched Auggie measuring out ingredients from an assortment of bottles and vials, the only thing I could think was that I wasn't about to let that happen. Not again.

When she'd finished mixing the potion, Auggie snapped her fingers and blew, and all of the candles on the table lit instantly. She placed the bowl in the center of the table, making sure that the candles surrounded it properly. Then she began to chant, holding her arms up to the sky and murmuring the words.

She spoke so quietly and so quickly that I could barely hear or understand her. It sounded as if the chant was in Latin, but I couldn't be sure. When she raised her arms higher into the air, I heard a clap of thunder and saw lightning strike overhead before settling into a hearty, grumbling wave, and then the candles were snuffed out.

As she repacked her bag with the ingredients and the extinguished candles, Auggie grinned to herself. She actually looked *happy* about what she was about to do. I wanted to get up and storm the kitchen. I wanted to scream at her. *How dare you! You miserable, rotten...*

With a heated face, I frowned and glanced over at Alba. I knew she felt the same surge of anger that I felt. But then her lips formed a small circle and her eyebrows lifted. She inhaled slowly. Even though I couldn't hear her, I knew she was telling me to take a few deep breaths and to let them out slowly. It would help to calm me.

I nodded and took her suggestion. It was something my mother would have told me to do too. When I turned my attention back to Auggie, I saw that she'd pulled three vials from her bag and was pouring the contents of the bowl into the vials. Putting the empty bowl in the sink, she went to the refrigerator to pull out a pitcher of lemonade and got two tall glasses out of one of Gran's cupboards.

My hands clenched into tight balls as I watched her set about making two glasses of lemonade, spiking one with one of the vials she'd just prepared and tossing the empty vial into the garbage can. Taking a lemon from the fruit bowl on the kitchen counter, she cut off a wedge and attached it to the edge of the poisoned glass.

Standing back and looking satisfied with her handiwork, Alba and I watched as she fluffed her hair, then took both glasses and headed for the front door. The stage was set. She was going to do it now! Showtime!

"Hurry!" I whispered, taking off like a shot down the back porch steps to run around to the front of the house. We had to alert the rest of the group that she was coming!

The quick sprint and the anticipation of what was about to happen had my pulse racing and my mind spinning. What were we supposed to do to stop Granddad from drinking the poisoned lemonade? And how would we do it without Auggie seeing us?

We passed Libby and Cinder on the side of the house and motioned to them to follow us quietly around to the front. We found Holly and Reign each peeking into windows on the porch, and I knew Sweets was around on the other side of the house.

"She's coming!" hissed Alba, pointing towards the garage. "Come on. We have no choice, we've gotta warn Clark!"

"But what if Auggie sees us?" I asked as we took long strides away from the house. When Sweets saw us heading towards the garage, she met up with the rest of the group.

"Then she sees us. We don't have a lot of time. We have to warn him."

Reign shook his head. "I don't like the fact that we don't have a plan here. This isn't going to go well."

"Listen, Slick. It's easy. We tell Clark that Auggie is about to poison him. He doesn't drink the poison. Easy peasy."

I didn't want to be a naysayer and remind Alba that nothing was ever easy peasy where we were concerned. I had to have hope that we could pull it off without a hitch.

As we crossed the gravel driveway, the sound of a screen door slamming behind us sent shock waves through my system. It was Auggie. She was on the front porch, but I refused to turn around, even after she hollered after us. "Hello. May I help you?" Instead of answering, we picked up our pace and closed the gap between us and the barn, she called out again. "Hello?"

The sound of Auggie yelling brought Granddad out of the garage. Squinting into the midday sun, he wiped his grimy fingers on his shop rag looking at us curiously. "Who are you?"

My mouth went dry. I led the pack, with my brother and Alba flanking me, and my grandfather's green eyes seemed trained on me as if he somehow recognized my face. He tilted his head slightly to the side. I wanted to tell him it was me, Mercy, his granddaughter. But the truth was that I wasn't even a glimmer in my five-year-old mother's eye at this point. He'd never believe me, even if I swore that it was true.

I looked up at Reign. I needed him to do the speaking that I couldn't do.

He held a hand out to our grandfather. "Yes, sir. Hello. My name is Reign, this is my sister, Mercy, and these are a few of our friends."

Granddad nodded at us all but kept mum, waiting for Reign to continue.

"This might sound odd, but—"

Before he could finish his sentence, Auggie was upon us, holding two glasses of lemonade in her hands. "Clark, do you know these people?"

Granddad furrowed his brow and shook his head in confusion. "No, I don't. I assumed that they were friends of yours."

Auggie shook her head. "Not at all. I've never seen them before in my life. I just came out to see if you needed some refreshments. It's so hot out here." She handed him the glass of lemonade with the lemon cocked sideways on the top of the glass, and then tugged at the collar of her shirt with the hand she'd just freed up.

"Oh, uh, thanks," he said, looking at the glass. Then he turned his eyes back on us. "Now, you were saying?"

I couldn't take my eyes off that glass. *Don't drink it, don't drink it!* I squinted my eyes at it, hoping that something in my witchy body would tip the glass over magically, and he'd not drink it. But nothing of the sort happened.

Reign cleared his throat. "Oh, yes, sir. This might sound odd, but we're distant relatives of Phyllis Haber-nackle. You're her husband, Clark, aren't you?"

Granddad nodded. The sparkle in his eyes told us just how much his curiosity had been piqued. "Yes, I am. So you're related to Phyllis. Isn't that interesting? May I ask what the relation is?"

We're just her grandchildren, and yours too, Granddad. No big deal, I thought, wanting to scream it out to him and beg him not to drink the lemonade.

Reign shifted in his army boots. "Umm, it's very distantly. I'm not even sure that I could explain it if I tried."

We all kind of giggled nervously.

Auggie looked at us with suspicion, narrowing her gaze. It was almost as if she'd gotten the distinct feeling that we were there to thwart her plan. "Clark, I really think you ought to drink up. I'd hate for you to get dehydrated out in this heat."

And then, he did the unthinkable. He lifted the glass to his lips. My eyes widened and my heart lurched into the back of my throat.

But before the liquid could touch his lips, Reign flicked a finger and shot an electrical blast at the glass, sending it tumbling out of his hands and onto the ground, where the glass shattered and the parched ground readily welcomed the bitter liquid.

Auggie sucked in her breath and looked up angrily at Reign.

Granddad's brows lowered. "Well, what in tarnation was that about?"

Reign did a good job of ignoring Auggie's hostile stare and instead keeping his eyes on our grandfather. "I'll be honest, sir," he said forcefully. "That was me saving your life."

"Saving my life!" bellowed Granddad, his temper beginning to show. "From choking on a piece of ice?"

"No, from being poisoned," said Alba. "Sir, that glass you were about to drink was laced with a pit viper venom potion that was going to kill you."

Auggie's eyes widened. Her suspicions were confirmed! I could see the wheels turning in her head. She couldn't understand how we'd spoken the truth. How had we known that?!

Alba continued. "Many years ago, Auggie Stone used that same potion to separate her best friend from the arms of Samson Smith. She concocted the potion to separate Phyllis and Samson, and now she's trying to do the same spell on you."

Granddad looked shocked. "On me?! Whatever for?"

I glared angrily at Auggie. I wanted to destroy the woman that had destroyed so many lives. "Isn't it obvious? She's miserable. She's alone with three children to look after. She's got no home, no money, and no husband. She wanted Gr—" I hesitated, forcing myself to swallow down the word *Gran*. "She wanted *Phyllis's* life."

He looked over at Auggie. "Is any of what they say true?"

Auggie shook her head, her face crimson now. "Of course it's not true, Clark! I have no idea what they're talking about! I-I don't even *know* these people!"

But he didn't look convinced. He wagged a thick finger in the air. "Phyllis told me about Samson, and she told me about the pit viper venom potion. I know that much of their story is true."

Auggie's mouth opened, but suddenly she was speechless.

Alba jeered at her. "Sir, we know that she put the very same potion into your drink, just now. We *saw* it with our own eyes. But what she doesn't know is that that very potion will kill you."

"Kill me!" he said with shock.

Auggie wrinkled her nose. "You don't even know what you're talking about. It most certainly would *not* kill him!"

"But you *did* put something in my drink?" asked Granddad, now staring intently at Auggie.

"Well, I—uh…" Wide-eyed and with her mouth gaping open a bit, Auggie looked like a deer caught in the headlights.

"Now how do all of you know all of this? Are you in cahoots with her or something?"

Reign shook his head resolutely. "No, sir. We are one hundred percent *not* aligned with that woman. We really can't explain how we know what we know, but the fact of the matter is, Auggie was about to do to you what she did to Samson. Except for some reason, you die as a result of her selfishness, and we didn't want that to happen. We aren't sure if the potion was made incorrectly or if maybe you're allergic to the venom that's in it, but the fact remains that you will *die* if you drink it."

Granddad looked at Auggie now, his face twisted into an angry snarl. "I can't believe you'd do this to Phyllis. After everything she's done for you and your kids."

"Clark! I most certainly did not—"

"Silence!" he barked. He took a deep breath and tried to get ahold of his rage. "I didn't want you here anyway, you know. I only allowed you in my home because you were an old *friend* of my wife's. I have no idea why she decided to forgive you for ruining her relationship with Samson, but in a strange way, I'm thankful that you did, because that eventually led her to me. But now you're trying to pull the same dirty, underhanded moves on me as you pulled on Samson? Have you learned nothing from your treachery? Haven't you learned that eventually, karma comes back around and gets you in the end?" He shook his head. "I want you out of my house."

"But the children and I have nowhere to—"

"Out of my house!" My grandfather's voice intensified, resounding in anger. "Where you and your children go is not my problem. You are to leave immediately."

Auggie nodded her head gently. "Clark, I beg of you. Please don't tell Phyllis what happened!"

"I wouldn't dream of telling my big-hearted wife what a monster her old friend Auggie truly is. It would break her heart." He shook his head. "No. You will go inside this very minute and gather your things. The second she and the children return, you will load up into the truck, and I will drive you into town and drop you off at the bus station. Where you go from there will be up to you."

"But what will I tell Phyllis?" asked Auggie.

"You'll make up an appropriate story. I don't really care. Tell her that Samson called and wants you back. Tell her that you're moving in with family in another state. I really don't care, but make something up, and make it sound real. And then *never* contact me or my wife again. Do you understand?"

Auggie nodded sadly. "Yes, I understand, Clark. I—I'm so sorry."

"Now go! Get out of my sight," he growled.

When Auggie had gone, climbing the porch steps with her head hanging low, Granddad turned his attention to us. "Now, I want the truth. Who are you really? And how did you know what Auggie was planning?"

"The truth?" asked Reign.

"And nothing less."

Reign's mouth opened to spill the beans on our familial relationship, but Alba beat him to it.

"The truth of the matter is, sir, we're witches, just like your wife is. We read minds, and we know things before they even happen. And we knew what Auggie was up to. We had to stop it before she killed you."

He nodded as if he accepted her answer without question. "Where are you from?"

"We live in Aspen Falls, Pennsylvania, right now."

"Aspen Falls! That's where the Institute is. My wife went to witch school there!"

"We go to witch school there too," I whispered.

His eyes brightened for the first time. "Well, you should all stick around. When I get back from taking Auggie and her children to the bus stop, we'll make you dinner. It's the least I could do after you saved my life. I know Phyllis would love to meet you all. Of course we can't tell her what transpired here today."

I nodded enthusiastically. The idea excited me. Seeing my grandparents together and getting to see and talk to my mother as a child sounded like a great way to spend the evening. I was just about to accept his invitation when Alba beat me to it.

"Thanks, sir. But the clock is ticking, and we have to get going. We're on a tight schedule, and now that we've done what we came to do, we have to get home and see how things have changed while we were gone."

29

Time has been altered,
A change has been made.
Take us back to Aspen Falls,
In the present day.

he whirring of the tunnel as it shifted its positioned filled my heart with anxiety. We were going home! And things were going to be different! I was going to have a grandfather! And Jax was going to have her powers! And if we were lucky, Sorceress Stone would still be alive, and this whole mess would be behind us!

The steam sauna was silent as the tunnel stopped. Our portal home was ready. We just had to step through it. I glanced up at my big brother. He gave me an encouraging wink. I knew he was just as excited as I was.

Alba sucked in a deep breath. "Ready?"

"For sure," said Holly.

"Yes," said Libby and Cinder in unison.

"I can't *wait* to get home," said Sweets. "It's got to be suppertime by now. I'm starving!"

We all laughed and let Alba lead us into the tunnel. When we emerged, we were back in the familiar spot on the back lawn of campus. We were home!

I trembled as I stepped onto the grass. Everything felt surreal. I couldn't believe we'd done it! We'd actually gone back in time and changed history! And we'd done it relatively unscathed. Sure, Holly had given us a scare, but we'd saved her, and we'd made it to the other side. For *once* things were going our way!

"I can't believe this," said Reign, the first to speak as we touched down in present-day Aspen Falls.

"Me either," agreed Holly, her eyes wide. "Alba, I have to admit, your magic skills are… out of this world."

"Very nice," agreed Cinder. "You have second-year witch skills. You should be very proud of the progress you've made this year."

Alba quirked a half-smile. She almost looked as if the praise embarrassed her. "Thanks."

"So, what do we do with this?" asked Reign, pointing at the raised river over the bonfire and the steam saunas.

"Ahh, good question," said Alba, rubbing her temples. "I guess we can shut it down."

Reign squinted one eye shut. "You sure that's such a good idea? Now, I'm not doubting you. Not after everything we've just done courtesy of your machine, but what happens if we get back to campus and discover that Sara-Lynn is still dead? We might need it."

Alba sighed, rolling her head back on her shoulders. "Ugh," she groaned. "You're right. What was I thinking? Of course we have to verify that she's alive before we go shutting down the time portal. Come on, let's get back to campus and catch the scoop."

Excited to see if anything had changed regarding Sorceress Stone's life status, we jogged the short distance back to campus. Everything looked normal. Not a single strand of grass looked different than it had when we'd left earlier in the day.

"So where do we go look first?" asked Sweets. "I mean, should we go hunting for Sorceress Stone, or should we go to the bakery and tell Jax the good news?"

My eyes widened excitedly. I much preferred to tell Jax the good news. "She's got to be off work by now," I said. "I mean, it seems like we've been gone for a while."

Holly nodded and pulled her phone out of her bra. She smiled and showed us the time. "No, it's still only midday. Isn't that crazy we've been gone all that time and it's not much later than when we left!"

Alba's eyes widened as she looked at the phone. "It's not much later? Holly, it's Thursday! We left on Wednesday! A whole day has passed."

Holly flipped the phone around to look at it. "Oh my gosh! I didn't even look at the date. How did a whole day pass?"

Alba shook her head. "I don't know, maybe walking through time took longer than we realized. Ugh, this sucks!"

"Why? If we did everything right, then we shouldn't need more time," I said.

"Yeah, well, until we know that everything is how it should be, losing time is never a good thing."

"And now Libby and I have one day less to put

together a graduation project," said Cinder, her head falling back on her shoulders.

Holly sucked in her breath. "Oh no!"

"What?!" asked Alba.

"I just thought of something. If we've been gone an extra day, Jax has got to be freaking out wondering where we are!"

The thought hadn't occurred to me. "We need to get over to Habernackle's right away and let her know we're okay."

"Maybe she went to work for me," said Sweets with a shrug. "Since we didn't come home."

"She might have," said Alba. "But let's start at the B&B and we'll go from there."

We just begun our walk when a thought hit me. I stopped dead in my tracks as we passed Hallowed Hall. "Alba! It's Thursday!"

Alba looked at me curiously. "Well, that took you a while."

I shook my head. "No, I mean, it's Thursday. Your library book is due."

"Oh man. Good catch, Red," said Alba, pulling her backpack around to her front so she could pull out the autobiography. "I almost forgot I had it!"

"I think that means you owe me one!"

Alba rolled her eyes. "If this all works out and I scored you a grandfather, I think we might call this one even."

*C*rammed in Sweets' small car like clowns in a clown car, we all jabbered a mile a minute on the ride into town. The excitement of seeing Jax in all her glory with her powers made each of us giddy. Even Alba and Cinder, who were both usually pretty straight-faced, wore smiles on their faces. It was like Christmas Eve, and none of us could wait for Jax to unwrap her gift!

Sweets pulled the car to a stop in front of the B&B. None of us paid any attention to the exterior until we had all unloaded and were standing side by side on the sidewalk. Then something caught my eye. The sign that my brother had picked out for Habernackle's Bed, Breakfast, and Beyond was different now. Not only was it a different design, but now it read Smith's Room and Board.

"Smith's!" said Reign, nearly choking on his own spit. "What the hell?!"

I shook my head slowly, my mouth gaping open, staring at the sign in awe. "I don't know."

"I'm so confused," said Holly.

I could tell even Alba had to be confused, because she couldn't even manage to muster up a snappy retort towards Holly.

Reign led the way into the building. The inside was totally different. Gone were many of the changes that my brother had made. It no longer looked like a restaurant, but more like a posh hotel lobby. There were sofas and a television set in one corner. And a small continental breakfast area with a waffle maker, a juicer, a basket of fruit and some cereal dispensers in the other corner. I shook my head. *What in the world?!*

My brother's eyes nearly bugged out of his head. "This isn't happening," he breathed.

"Oh, hello, kids," said a familiar voice from the top of the stairs. We all turned to see my mother smiling down at us. At least I thought it was my mother. She wore a dress and heels and had her hair done up in a professional-looking bun. And she was wearing *makeup*. My mother hardly ever wore makeup. Maybe on a special occasion, but never just to wait tables or spend the day cooking in the kitchen.

"Mom?" I said.

"Yes, dear?"

"Mom, what's going on?" said Reign.

Mom slowly descended the stairs, hanging on to the handrail carefully. "I don't know what you mean, sweetheart."

"You changed the sign out front, and the dining room —it-it's totally different!" said Reign, his voice showing the early stages of a full-on panic.

"We changed the sign?" She frowned slightly. "Hmm. I don't know anything about a sign change."

"Well, what about the dining room? It's different!"

Mom looked around at what had once been Habernackle's dining room. "You mean the lobby? Oh, yes," she said with a nod. "I did switch the sofa and the chair. The balance was off. It's been bothering me since we got this set. I decided this was much more Feng Shui."

"Feng Shui?" I repeated.

She nodded. "You know, the spatial arrangement in relation to the room's energy."

"No, I know what Feng Shui means, Mom. I've just never heard you use that term before."

She smiled calmly. "Oh, Mercy, you're such a doll."

I'm a doll? Since when? "Mom, you're kind of freaking me out." I looked around. "Where's Jax?"

"Jax?" Mom looked surprised. "Your *cousin* Jax?"

"You know any other Jaxs?" asked Alba.

A V formed between my mother's eyes. "Why do you want to know where Jax is?"

"We have to talk to her. It's really important!"

Mom shrugged. "I have no idea where she is."

The bell over the door chimed. We all turned around to see Merrick Stone striding in like he owned the place.

My mother rushed over to him. "Oh, hello, dear. You didn't tell me you were coming home for lunch. I would have whipped you up something special!" I stared in horror as she planted a kiss directly onto the man's mouth!

My mouth dropped open as he wrapped his arms around her waist and kissed her back. I glanced over at the rest of the faces. Reign's eyes bulged, as did the rest of the girls'.

"Mom, what is going on? Why are you kissing *him*?!" I demanded. "What about Detective Whitman!"

Mom looked at me curiously. "Detective Whitman? What about him?"

"What's he got to say about you kissing Merrick?"

"Why in heaven's name would Mark Whitman care what I do?" She took a step towards me and put a hand on my forehead. "Are you feeling alright, sweetheart? You're acting so strangely."

Merrick wagged a finger in my direction. "I know what's going on."

I stared at him uncomfortably. Did he know what

we'd done? Was he going to be upset that our grandfather had kicked his family out all those years ago?

My mother put both hands on her hips and nodded. "Well, good! Maybe you can fill me in!"

"Mercy is worried about her finals, and she's lashing out. I happened to speak to her Advanced Kinetic Energy instructor today and she's not doing so well."

"Mercy!" breathed my mother. "You never told me that!"

"Well, Mom, I—"

"In fact, she's in danger of not passing the course."

"Mercy!"

"Mom, I can explain—"

Merrick ticked his finger at me. "Now, you know how important your education is to me. I expect nothing less than excellence in your magical coursework."

"*You* expect? Why in the world do I care what *you expect?*" I was getting heated now. How *dare* Merrick Stone think he could tell me what kind of grades I should be getting.

"Mercy! How dare you speak to your father like that!"

30

"*My* father?!" I bellowed. My pulse raced. What in the world was she talking about? I mean, for all these years, I'd never been told who my father was, but Merrick Stone most *definitely* could not be my father! He and my mother had been bound apart at the time that I was conceived. I shook my head wildly. The thought made my skin crawl. "Mom! He's *not* my father!"

Merrick didn't look amused. He shook his head. "Is this some kind of teen angst thing? Are you rebelling right now because I grounded you from dating that boy?" He shrugged. "I told you that you can see him again when you get your grades up. Receive high scores on all of your finals, and then we'll talk about you dating again."

My eyes swung up to meet Reign's. I didn't understand what was going on. This wasn't happening!

"I'm sorry. Are you two a thing now?" asked Reign, drawing a line with his finger between our mother and his father.

Merrick lifted a brow. "You're in on this angst thing too? Aren't you a little too old for that, son?"

"Just answer the question, Dad. Are you and Mom back together?"

"Back together?" said Mom. "I have no idea what you're talking about, Reign. We've never broken up. We've been married since the day we eloped twenty-five years ago."

My breath left my body and the world began to spin. The last thing I remembered seeing was Sweets' blurry face before my body hit the floor.

"Mercy?" Sweets' voice grew louder, and then I felt her cold, clammy hands patting my cheeks. "Mercy, wake up!"

My eyelids fluttered open. Sweets' apple-red face was in my direct line of sight. She sucked in her breath and smiled from ear to ear.

"She's waking up!" squealed Sweets excitedly.

I turned my head slightly to my right, and there was my brother. Alba stood behind him. On the other side of me stood Holly, Libby, and Cinder. Everyone stared at me. "What happened?"

"You passed out cold," said Alba with a smirk. "Sunk like a rock. You're gonna have a welt the size of a baseball. You know that, right?"

"I passed out?" I sucked in a big breath of air, and suddenly the memory of what had happened flooded my mind. "Oh no! Reign, please tell me it's not true. Please tell me that Mom is not married to your father."

"Mercy, I wish I could, but——"

I pinched my eyes shut and covered my face with my hands. This was *not* happening. Merrick Stone was *not* my father. My shoulders shook as genuine tears began to pour from my eyes. In getting Jax her powers, somehow we'd inadvertently messed up *my* life.

Alba shoved Sweets out of the way and kneeled down beside the bed. She pulled my hands from my face. "Now's not the time for this, Red. You need to buck up, buttercup."

"How is this happening Alba?" I blubbered through a face full of tears and a runny nose.

"Eww, someone get her a tissue or something. I think she sprung a leak somewhere."

I swatted at Alba. "I mean it, Alba. How is this happening?" Even though I wasn't in the mood for one of her lame jokes, she'd managed to slow my tears. I tried sitting up in bed. Reign and Holly both helped me up. I looked around to see a room I hardly recognized. "Where are we?"

"My room, I guess," said my brother sullenly.

"Your room?!" I looked around. The room looked like a prep school kid lived there, with its navy-and-red striped wallpaper and shelves full of baseball, football, and basketball trophies. Medals hung from almost every trophy, and sports memorabilia decorated every wall. The closet door was wide open and full of suits and dress shirts, and a decorative tie rack hung beside the closet.

He lifted his brows and sighed. "I guess since our parents stayed together, we grew up together, and I had a normal childhood. It seems as if I'm a bit of an all-American guy now."

I shook my head and used the tissue that Holly gave me to wipe my tears. "Don't call them *our* parents. She's *our* mom, but he'll never be my father. This is all just one big mistake."

"Mercy, it's not *so* horrible, is it? That we grew up together and are full brother and sister now? I mean, I'm not in love with the fact that I was some kind of preppy sports star, but it means that I grew up with my biological parents, and you and I grew up together."

"But we don't *remember* any of that!" I bellowed at him. "It doesn't change the fact that you don't remember being that perfect son. It doesn't change the fact that I don't remember a single Christmas with you, or with your father and my mother together. I don't remember any of it, and neither do you." I looked at him curiously. "Wait. Or do you?"

He shook his head. "No, I don't remember any of that either. It's kind of nice knowing you're my full sister, though."

"Reign, it's never mattered to me that we have different fathers. You're my brother and that's all that matters."

He nodded. "Yeah, I know. I feel the same."

I looked around. "Where's Mom?"

"She's making your da… I mean, *Merrick*, lunch," said Sweets.

I glared at her. She'd *almost* said dad. What a creepy, creepy notion, that I somehow had Merrick Stone's blood running through my veins. And then a thought hit me. If Merrick Stone's blood ran through my veins, that meant that so did Jax Stone's. In that singular turn of events, Jax and I had become *real* cousins.

I had to get to Jax. I scampered off the bed.

"Where are you going?" asked Reign. "Mercy, you might have a concussion."

"Yeah, you should be more careful getting up with that knot on your head," said Alba. "Maybe we oughta get you looked at."

Rushing to the door, I stopped and turned around to look at the large group of people in my brother's strange bedroom. "We have to find Jax."

"We will, Mercy," said Sweets. "But Alba's right. Maybe we should stop by the Aspen Falls Medical Center and get you looked at."

I frowned as I fingered the back of my skull and discovered the hard lump that was the source of the throbbing I felt. "We don't have time for that. I'm fine. We need to find Jax, and we need to find her now."

Reign sighed but followed me to the door. "Alright, if you insist. Let's go."

I held a palm up to stop him. "I need you to go downstairs and find out where she is. The girls and I will meet you in the car."

"Whatever you say, sis."

"*I*t never even dawned on me that she'd be in school right now," said Alba as Sweets pulled her car into a spot in the Institute's parking lot. "If classes are back in session, then I have high hopes that Stone's still alive."

I wanted to be excited to see Jax and tell her the good news about her powers, but the fact that we were now officially cousins had me in a funk. It wasn't that I minded that we were actually cousins now. What I minded was having Merrick Stone for a father, and that my mother was now some kind of a Stepford Wife.

"So, where do we start looking?" asked Libby as we all stood in the empty quad minutes later.

Feeling the weight of the situation, I looked down at my Batman watch wearily. "I'm pretty sure Jax is in Advanced Spells class right now."

Holly nodded and pointed to the other side of campus. "Jax and I have Advanced Spells together. It's over in the Broomsgarden Building."

I started towards the cobblestone sidewalk. "Well, then, let's go," I sighed. "We'll wait over there for her to get out of class."

Broomsgarden Building, like all of the other historic buildings on campus, was just your basic, run-of-the-mill multilevel stone building. But this one, located on the northeast end of campus, sat just across from a neatly manicured, flower arboretum. Nestled snugly in the center of the garden, a circular stone water fountain, which had recently been restarted after the long winter season, spewed water into the air at regular intervals. Red columbine, orange azaleas, and pink roses filled the air with the sweet scent of springtime and attracted hummingbirds and butterflies to the garden, making it a popular destination for students eating a sack lunch, or looking for a quiet place to study.

While all beginner broom-riding classes were instructed in wide-open spaces, far away from buildings and other people, the advanced broom-riding classes all took place in the Broomsgarden arboretum. Of course, this was how the garden, and by association, the building, had received their names.

Walking onto the plush carpet of grass in the garden, we all took seats on the knee-high flat seat that surrounded the fountain. With all eyes on the front door of the Broomsgarden Building, we waited for classes to be dismissed.

Excitement radiated off Sweets like warmth from the sun as she clasped her hands together in front of her heart. "Jax is going to flip out when she hears that she got her powers!"

"She's definitely gonna be excited," agreed Alba. "That is, if she doesn't already realize she's got them."

With her butt on the outer edge of the stone fountain and her hands planted firmly behind her, Holly beamed up at the warm spring sun with closed eyes. With her back arched, her wavy blond hair dangled between her shoulder blades, nearly touching the pool of water. "For sure. This is going to be the best birthday present ever! I can't wait to see her expression when we tell her."

Reign smiled softly as he looked down at Holly. "She's definitely going to be blown away. I owe you girls a lot for everything you've done for our family."

I had to bite my tongue to keep from lashing out. Reign didn't seem to mind that I was now officially a Stone. Nor did he seem to care that both our histories had been completely rewritten. While maybe *his* history had changed for the better, mine certainly hadn't. And while I wanted to say all those things—let it out and complain about the new situation I found myself in—I oddly felt like I'd sound ungrateful. No one else seemed to think having Merrick Stone as my father was such a big deal. No one sympathized with my predicament. It made me question whether or not I was making a mountain out of a molehill. Maybe it was a small price to pay for making Jax a real witch finally. I mean, I'd never known my father before. I could certainly pretend I still didn't *know* who my father was. Maybe this didn't have to change anything.

Libby held her hand out for a butterfly to land on. "I'm happy that we got to be a part of it. Thank you for including us."

"Yes, except now we don't have a graduation project to present, and this has taken almost all of our time to prepare," said Cinder with a bit of a pout on her face.

Libby shrugged offhandedly as she stared at the black and yellow winged creature in her hands. "It was worth it."

"Not if we have to repeat second year. I'm not staying here another year."

"Don't worry," said Alba. "We'll help you think of something."

Cinder grimaced. "You mean like you thought of before." She puffed her arms up around her and mockingly repeated Alba's earlier suggestion. "You can make, like, a big bonfire, and there's smoke, and it's on the ground, and you put it out with water. Lame."

Alba rolled her eyes. "Yeah, yeah. Whatever. We'll think of something better than that. I was just thinking out loud. It's called brainstorming."

As the girls talked, I kept my eyes trained on the front doors of the Broomsgarden Building. Class would let out any second, and I didn't want to miss Jax.

"They call it brainstorming, not mouthstorming. That

means you've got to use your brain and not just your mouth," said Cinder.

"Are you kidding me? I was *trying* to help!"

"Didn't your mother ever teach you that if you don't have anything smart to say, don't say anything at all?"

Sweets wrinkled her nose. "I don't think that's how that saying goes. It's if you don't have anything *nice* to say—"

"I *know* how the saying goes," snapped Cinder. "I was making a point."

"Well, maybe next time you try making a point, you should sharpen your pencil," growled Alba.

One of the doors burst open and two students engrossed in conversation appeared. They both had backpacks slung over their shoulders and seemed to be hustling to get out of the building as fast as they could.

"Guys!" I hissed. "Classes are dismissed. Keep your eyes peeled for Jax."

"You know, maybe we shouldn't have taken you along on that life-changing trip," said Alba, ignoring me. "We shoulda just left you here."

Cinder shook her head. "You needed me. Without me, you couldn't have done it."

Students poured down the stairs now. I kept my eyes trained on them, searching for Jax.

"Bah!" spat Alba. "Don't make me laugh! We could have *totally* done it without you *or* your sister."

Holly's head lifted then. She squinted into the sun at Alba, holding a hand up to shield her eyes. "I disagree, Alba. Libby saved my life by freezing me."

"This is true," agreed Reign. "We needed them. Just

be gracious, Alba. Everyone pitched in and made it work. Teamwork makes the dream work."

"There she is!" I said, pointing at the tiny pixie of a girl. Dressed unusually for Jax, in stylish clothing, normal shoes, and nary a pointed witch's hat in sight, my roommate was surrounded by a gaggle of witches.

It was as if someone had pushed the mute button as our group fell silent and all eyes turned to Jax.

After a moment or two, Holly wrinkled her nose. "Who's she talking to?"

Sweets' head tipped sideways as she stared at the group, which paused at the top of the wide stone staircase to whisper in each other's ears. "I'm pretty sure those are the popular witches."

"What are the *popular* witches doing talking to Jax?" I asked. I'd never seen Jax interact with that particular group. With her weird witchy outfits, high screechy voice, and annoying, clingy behavior, those witches had avoided Jax like the plague.

"I have *no* idea," said Holly.

Reign shook his head in confusion. "I don't get it. What's wrong with Jax talking to the popular witches?"

I shrugged. "I mean, I guess there's nothing *wrong* with it. You know, technically. It's just kind of unusual. Jax is sort of a..." The cogs in my mind turned, searching for the most politically correct word that represented Jax.

"Free spirit," said Sweets.

I nodded. "There you go. Free spirit."

"But she can have popular friends."

"Sure she can," said Alba. "She just doesn't."

"Oh, look, they turned around," I hissed. "She's

coming, she's coming." I stood up, ready to rush the side-walk when she got to the bottom of the stairs.

But instead of descending the stairs, she did a strange thing. She and the group of witches she'd been talking to stopped on the top stair. They all seemed to be staring at something on the sidewalk. Following their line of sight, I saw the two girls that had emerged first, paused near a fork in the sidewalk.

"What's she doing?" asked Reign.

No one said a word. We had no idea what she was doing just standing there watching those girls. And then, the two girls stopped talking. One went one way down the fork and the other went the other way. No sooner had they started walking than we clearly watched as Jax flicked fingers on both hands, and instantaneously, each of the girls took a nosedive on the cobblestone sidewalk.

I closed my eyes and shook my head. Had I just seen that? Had Jax just used *magic* to trip those two girls up? My mouth gaped.

Sweets was the first to say something. "Was I the only one that just saw Jax intentionally trip those two girls?"

"Nope," agreed Alba. "I saw it too. Those girls are definitely going away with bruised knees and scraped chins."

"That was so mean!" said Holly, now perched on the edge of the fountain like a bird. "I can't believe she did that!"

I felt dazed and confused. "That had to be a mistake or something. Surely Jax didn't do that on *purpose*."

"It sure looked like she did. And obviously she already knows about getting her powers." Reign pointed at them again. "Look, she and those girls sure are getting a good laugh out of it."

Sure enough, as the two girls on the sidewalk struggled to get back on their feet, Jax sported an evil smirk while the witches around her howled with laughter. It was like mean girls at their finest. I had to find out what was going on. "Come on, guys. We need to talk to Jax and find out what in the world she was thinking."

Before anyone else was on their feet, I was halfway across the garden. Jax and her friends had made it to the bottom of the stairs by the time I got there. "Jax!" I shouted.

With linked arms, Jax let the popular witches flank her on either side and they walked as a unit towards the quad. She didn't acknowledge that she'd heard me.

"Jax!"

By then the rest of our group had caught up to me. When Jax's group of friends stopped walking, I knew she'd finally heard me. Jax turned around slowly. Bracing my footing on the brick sidewalk, I prepared myself for the hug I was about to get as I knew her arms would be around my neck in seconds.

But a strange thing happened. Not only did Jax *not* charge me, but she wrinkled her nose and stared back at me in annoyance. "What do *you* want?"

31

*M*y eyes swung up to meet Reign's. What was happening?

"Jax, we have big news to share with you," said Reign.

Jax lifted a corner of her lip and quirked an eyebrow. "Okay?" she sneered.

Reign looked down at me then. He was confused too. Why was she being so snotty to us all of a sudden. Was she upset that we'd not come home the night before?

"Jax, you're not going to believe it," I said, silently wishing that her new friends would make themselves scarce, so I could share the news in private.

Jax sighed. "Make it quick. I haven't got all day."

Considering everything strange that was happening, and considering the fact that it seemed as if Jax had already discovered that she was *finally* a witch, I had to go with the piece of information that Jax would find the next most exciting. "Jax, it's a really long story, which we'll tell you all about later, but I thought you should know that you and I are *officially cousins*. *Real* cousins. Blood-related ones."

Jax's breath seemed to catch in her throat. She stopped moving and stared at me. It took her a second to snap out of whatever it was that had crossed her mind. She looked at the girls on either side of her. "Girls, I'll meet you in the quad." When the girls didn't move, she glared at them angrily before barking, "Go!"

My eyes widened. Had Jax seriously just barked at the popular girls? I watched in shock as they did as she commanded and took off, hustling towards the quad.

Jax strode over to us and stood directly in front of me. An ugly snarl covered her face. "Do you have to say that so *loud*?!"

I shook my head in confusion. "Say what so loud?"

"That we're *related*. I think I can do damage control, but are you kidding me right now? That was *so* embarrassing!"

"Embarrassing?" I repeated in shock.

"Yes! And why *me*? Why not Calliope?"

"Calliope? Who's Calliope?" asked Reign.

Jax's brow furrowed as she looked up at my brother. "Duh? Your *other* cousin. The one that was standing right next to me? Jeez, what's up with you today? Did you both take a double dose of idiot pills or something?"

Alba cracked a smile. "A double dose of idiot pills." She wagged her finger. "Good one. Mind if steal that?"

Jax looked Alba up and down disdainfully. "I'm sorry, are you actually *speaking* to me?" She shook her head. "This day just keeps getting weirder and weirder."

I didn't have time to think about Jax's dis on Alba. I was too confused about this sudden new revelation that we had another cousin. "Okay, so you're telling me that you have a sister now?"

"Sister? Are you kidding me? Eww. Why would I want a sister? Why would you call her my sister?"

"Then how is Calliope your cousin?" asked Holly.

"Duh, she's Aunt BethAnn's daughter. Are you guys for real?" Jax shook her head. "I don't even know why I'm indulging this ridiculous conversation. Listen. The Stones and the Smiths don't talk. So unless you've got some *real* news, I'm outta here." Jax began to walk away, swinging her purse over her shoulder like the conversation was over.

"Wait!" I said, putting a hand on her shoulder.

Jax turned around and looked down at my hand. "Don't touch me. Eww. Now I have to go take a shower and burn this dress. Thanks."

"That's a little rude, don't you think?" chided Sweets.

"I'm sorry, who are you?"

Sweets looked stunned, like she'd just gotten her finger snapped in a mousetrap. Her eyes began to water as she pointed at herself. "I-I'm Sweets. Are you telling me you don't remember me, Jaxie?"

"Jaxie? Seriously? What am I, five?" She looked at me then. "And quit calling me Jax. No one has called me Jax since elementary school. I don't want that nickname catching on here."

Reign made a face. "Well, then, what are we supposed to call you?"

"How about you don't call me? That would be the easiest."

"But if we're family—"

Jax held up a hand. "I'll stop you right there. We

might share some DNA, but we are most certainly *not* family."

"Not family?" I said in shock. "Why would you say that? Your mom and my"—I had to take a huge gulp before muttering the horribly flavored next word—"my *dad* are siblings."

Jax shook her head. "So? Your *dad* is also the black sheep of the family. He's dead to me, just like he's dead to my grandmother."

"Black sheep? Merrick is the black sheep?" said Reign. "Since when?"

Jax stifled a laugh. "Duh, since he went to live with his father."

"Wait, Merrick went to live with *Samson Smith*?!" I bellowed.

"As if you didn't know that? He's *your* father."

"When did he go to live with Samson?" asked Reign.

"I don't know, it was obviously sometime after what happened between the two families." Jax looked like she was getting more and more annoyed by the second.

My chest felt constricted, like I couldn't catch enough air in my lungs to take a deep breath. Despite that, I managed to whisper, "What happened between the two families?"

Jax shook her head. "Look, I've had enough of these childish games. I have to meet my friends before our next class. Don't talk to me anymore. Got it? Just pretend we aren't related."

"Jax," hollered Reign as she walked away. "What happened between the two families?"

"You should know! Now leave me alone!"

I felt completely bewildered by our meeting with Jax, and now my heart lay firmly ensconced in the pit of my stomach, making me nauseous. The throbbing in the back of my head intensified as my nausea rocked me. I felt unsteady on my feet. This was terrible. What had we done?

"Let's get her to a seat before she passes out again," I heard Sweets say.

I felt Reign's arms scoop me up, felt the bumpy ride of him carrying me, and then I felt the hard, scratchy surface of the fountain's stone ring underneath me once again. The colors of the garden all blended together into a blur, kind of like we were back in the blurry-lighted tunnel.

"It's going to be okay," Reign whispered in my ear. "We'll figure this all out, Mercy."

But the tears were already falling. "How is it ever going to be okay, Reign? We did all of that for Jax. And now Jax isn't even Jax anymore. She's this mean and nasty person now. She doesn't appreciate the fact that we got her the powers that we *thought* she deserved. And now Merrick's my father, and my mother's a zombie and everything's a disaster!"

"Yeah, well, no one ever got anywhere by crying about it," snapped Alba.

"Alba, can't you be a little bit more compassionate about this?" asked Sweets.

"Don't get me wrong," said Alba. "I feel bad for everyone involved. This whole thing sucks. And I feel partially responsible. We went through everything so fast that we didn't stop to take into consideration that reversing the curse meant that it reversed the *whole* curse. Not just the curse on Sorceress Stone, but also the curse on Merrick and the Black Witch."

Reign nodded. "Yeah, that's probably something that should have been considered."

"That's definitely a rookie mistake," said Cinder, nodding.

Alba's head reared back. "A rookie mistake? I didn't hear any warnings coming out of *your* mouth."

"I didn't know what all the curse entailed," said Cinder. "If I'd have known that there was more to it, I would have brought that up. But I assumed you'd done your due diligence." She shrugged. "But this is something you'll learn in your second year. Like I said, a rookie mistake. Soon you'll learn more about the ethical and moral considerations about performing witchcraft."

"This isn't about ethics or morals, Hot Stuff. This is about reversing a curse that plagued an entire family for decades!"

Cinder shrugged. "It's all interrelated."

"Can we *not* argue right now?" said Reign, his tone somber. "I've got a splitting headache, and all this hollering is making it worse."

"I just don't understand," I said quietly. "How did reversing the curse change Jax into... into someone completely different?"

Libby sat down next to me. "Mercy, admittedly I don't know Jax as well as the rest of you, but from an outsider's perspective, it's pretty obvious."

"It is?"

She put her arm around my shoulder. "The old Jax,

the one we knew and loved, grew up all those years around other witches. Her aunt and uncle, her mother, her mother's students. But she could never *be* one of them. Because of that, I think it humbled her."

Alba nodded. "That makes a lot of sense. She grew up as an outcast in that family. They sent her off to boarding school, and her mother has never treated her right. So when we changed history and the curse didn't happen, Jax probably grew up as a full-blooded witch with all of her powers. *And* it would be my guess that she grew up in the Stone family, no longer as an outcast. Her powers made her cocky."

"I liked the old Jax better. The *real* Jax. Not *JaclynRose*," I said staunchly.

Reign grimaced. "I think we *all* liked the old Jax, sis. Now, I know this sucks, but we've been through worse in our lives. We'll get through this."

"Worse? I don't think I've been through anything worse than this," I muttered.

"Okay, well, *I* have been through much worse, and I can assure you, if I got through all of that, we can get through this together."

I wiped my face with the sleeve of my hoodie, sniffed back my runny nose, and stood up. "I need to see Gran, and I need to see my grandfather," I announced. "I need to know that all of this happened for a reason. I need to see my grandfather's face and know that at the very least, my mother grew up with her father. Maybe then I'll see that this was all worth it."

Reign stood up next to me, slinging his arm around my shoulder. "Say no more. Let's go meet our grandfather for the second time in our lives."

"*H*ey, Mom, it's Mercy," I said into my phone as Sweets drove us away from the Institute.

"Mercy! I can't believe you left without checking in with me. You hit your head *so hard*. I wanted to make sure you were alright."

I sighed. I hadn't called to talk about that. "Yeah, I know, Mom. I'm sorry. We were in a hurry."

"In a hurry for what?"

"Class," I lied. "Hey, Mom. I just need to know something. Tell me your dad is still alive."

"What?" she breathed into the phone.

"Please, just tell me that Grandpa Clark is alive and he's okay."

"Mercy!" She kind of sounded panicked now. "What happened?! Was he in an accident or something?"

"So he *is* alive?"

"I don't know why he wouldn't be. I hadn't heard anything. What's going on? You're scaring me."

I shook my head, thankful to hear that he was alive. "I'm sorry. I just had a really bad dream about him last night, and I was worried that maybe it was real."

"Is that why you're acting so strangely today?"

"Probably. Hey, I'd like to go see him and Gran, Mom. You know, make sure he's alright."

There was a pause on the other end of the phone. "Boy, that dream must have really shaken you up. You've never had a relationship with your grandfather."

I glanced over at Holly, who sat smushed in the car

next to me. "I've never had a relationship with him? Why's that?"

"Mercy, I think that fall has really messed with your memories. Maybe we should run you into the Aspen Falls Medical Center for a quick evaluation."

"No, Mom, I'm fine, I swear. I just want to go see Granddad. Where does he live again?"

"As far as I'm aware, the same place he's lived for years."

"And where's that?"

"Mercy, please may I take you to the hospital?"

"Mom, just Granddad's address. That's all I need."

She sighed on the other end of the phone. "He lives at the Institute. In the Stone family's home."

32

"*A*nd she didn't say *why* he's living with the Stones?" asked Alba as we climbed out of the car and onto the gravel driveway in front of Sorceress Stone's home.

"Nope." I frowned. Since I'd hung up the phone with my mother, thoughts of why my grandparents now lived with Sorceress Stone wouldn't stop spiraling through my head, yet none of them seemed to make any sense. Granddad hadn't died all those years ago, so we'd done what we'd intended to do when we'd gone back in time and stopped Auggie Stone from killing him. And in turn, we'd obviously stopped Gran from putting the curse on the Stone family. And now the two of them were living in Sorceress Stone's home? It just didn't make any sense.

The outside of the gray stone home was stark and somber and more than a bit intimidating as we all stood in front of the oversized wooden door, feeling like unwanted intruders.

I held up a fist to knock, but my hand paused in midair. "Alba, you knock. I can't," I whispered.

"Fine, I will." She shoved me out of the way, moving me from center stage to stage right and positioning herself directly in front of the door. There wasn't even a hint of hesitation as she reached up to give the heavy door knocker a steady *thud, thud, thud*.

We waited in silence, with my breath dammed up in my lungs. When no one answered, Alba reached up to knock again, but before her hand could touch the knocker, the door opened with a loud squeak. A weasel of a man with only a layer of thinning black hair on his otherwise bald head stood just inside. "Yes?"

"We're here to see Clark," said Alba.

"Is he expecting you?"

"Probably not."

"Then I shall have to announce you. Whom shall I say is calling?"

"We're not calling," said Alba with a curled lip. "We're here to see him."

"Yes, ma'am, I understand that," said the small man. "But whom shall I say is here to see him?"

That was when Reign stepped forward from the back. "Tell him it's his grandchildren. Reign and Mercy."

The butler bowed. "Very well. It will just be a moment." He shut the door, leaving us to wait on the front step.

"This is so weird," whispered Alba. "Where I'm from, if someone comes to your house to visit, you don't just leave 'em hanging on the front doorstep."

I didn't say anything, but I thought it was strange as well. Gran had never been a very formal person. In fact,

Gran *preferred* to keep things casual. I found it hard to believe that she'd want to live in a place that was as big as this one, so big that it had to have its own butler.

"It's very rude," agreed Sweets with a frown.

Two minutes later, the weasel was back. "Please come in," he said with a slight bow. When all seven of us filed in, he closed the door behind us. Alba, Holly, Sweets, and I had all been in the Stone family home once before, when Jax had given us the unofficial and highly unapproved tour. We'd come in through a basement tunnel that connected the Institute and the Stones' castle. Because of that, I wasn't surprised to see the oversized ornate furnishings and the grand rugs and curved staircase. "Which of you are the grandchildren?"

Reign pointed at me. "That's my sister, Mercy. I'm Reign."

The butler nodded. "Only you two. The rest of you may wait here." He gestured towards a high-backed wooden bench that reminded me of a church pew. "This way, please."

Alba's shoulders crumpled inward. She was disappointed she didn't get to come along to meet my grandparents. I didn't blame her. To come all this way and not get to find out what was going on would be irritating.

"We'll tell you what happens," I whispered to her as we passed by.

She grimaced. "Don't forget a single detail."

I waved goodbye to my friends before allowing the butler to lead us down a series of hallways. Finally we stopped at a pair of carved, sliding wood doors. He pushed one of the doors open and stepped inside. "Your guests, sir."

"Thank you, Wallace." I glanced around the room, searching for the face to go with the voice. We were in an enormous office library with dark cherry bookshelves lining every wall, except the one straight ahead of us, which was covered in windows overlooking the backyard, lending warmth to an otherwise stuffy room. Off in a corner, further back in the room sat a dark cherry desk with a high-backed black leather chair behind it, facing the backyard.

"Yes, sir." Wallace slipped out the door, sliding it shut behind us, leaving us alone in a room with my grandfather.

And then the office chair behind the cherry desk swiveled around, and an older version of the grandfather we'd met earlier in the day was right there in front of us. His face displayed more age lines, and his hair had grayed, but it was definitely Granddad. I wondered if he would remember meeting us. To us it was only a few hours ago. To him, it was decades ago.

"So you're Reign and Mercy," he said, placing both hands on his desk and pushing himself up into a standing position. "Finally, I get to meet you!"

Finally he gets to meet us? What's he talking about?!

Smiling broadly, he gestured us forward as he came around the desk. "Come, come. I've waited years to meet my grandchildren. I was beginning to think I might go to my grave without ever getting to lay eyes on the two of you!"

Reign glanced down at me as we slowly walked towards our grandfather. He was just as shocked to hear Granddad's words as I was. "You mean we've never met before?"

Standing directly in front of Granddad now, we watched as his smile disappeared completely. He tipped his head sideways. "No, of course not. You thought we had? What has your mother told you?"

"Honestly, not much," I said quietly. It was the truth. She hadn't told us hardly anything about our grandfather, mostly because he'd died before she was old enough to remember much about him.

Grandfather stared at me then, extending his arms to put a hand on either of my shoulders. "So you're Mercy." He smiled wistfully. "You look like your mother."

"That's what I've been told."

"How's she doing?" he asked in little more than a whisper.

I shrugged. "She's alright, I guess."

Then Granddad moved on to Reign. "And you're Reign. My first-born grandchild. A grand*son*." Our grandfather blotted away the dampness in his green eyes. "I really thought this day might never come. I'm so sorry you didn't grow up with me in your life."

I swallowed back the lump that had begun to form in my throat. This was a lot for me to handle. I was sorry that I had grown up without him in my life too, and having him alive now was something I never would have dreamed of in a million years. I had so many questions to ask him, and things I wanted to do with my grandfather, but for now, we had a lot of ground to cover. I knew I had to start there. "Granddad, we came to see you to find out what happened. Why haven't we been in your life all these years?"

He inhaled a deep breath through his nose and then

let it out slowly. "It's a very long story. I assumed your mother would have told you all of this."

I shook my head.

Granddad hung his head and sighed. Then he looked up at us and nodded. "Okay. I understand. Then it's time we had a talk. Let's sit down and hash this all out. Is that alright with the two of you? Do you have time?"

Reign and I nodded. It's why we'd come. We had to find out the truth in this new reality that seemed to be getting odder and odder by the moment.

"Very good," he said, then walked us over to a little sitting area. There were two sofas and a chair. The set was worn and didn't quite match the rest of the room. "You'll have to excuse the furnishings. My wife has been pestering me for years to replace this set, but it's one of the few sofas in this whole house that I can sit comfortably on while reading the paper, and at my age that's a blessing and worth its weight in gold."

I looked around. "Where is Gran? I'd like to see her."

He looked confused. "Auggie? She's around here somewhere." His chin jutted back slightly as if to show surprise. "You want to see her?"

"No, not Auggie," I said, lifting a brow. "I want to see Gran. You know, Phyllis, our grandmother."

"You want to see Phyllis?" Granddad's face went ashen. "But, sweetheart, Phyllis is dead!"

"Dead?!" Reign and I shouted in unison.

My eyes were wide. Surely, I hadn't heard him correctly. Surely my grandmother wasn't dead?! "That's not possible," I breathed as my heart rate sped up.

Reign put a hand on either of my shoulders to steady me. "When did she die?"

Granddad's eyebrows rose high on his forehead as he sucked in another deep breath. "Oh, years and years ago. I believe Linda was only about five years old when her mother passed."

"But you mentioned your wife," said Reign.

"Oh, yes, Auggie. Surely you've heard your paternal grandmother and I married? Of course, Auggie and her girls went back to her maiden name after her first marriage to the children's father ended badly. She decided not to change it when we married."

I had been so shocked to hear that Gran was now dead that I couldn't have possibly heard what he just said correctly. I shook my head. "Wait. You're not telling us that you actually *married* Auggie Stone, are you?" After everything we'd done. I still only had one grandparent, and now *Auggie Stone* was Granddad's *wife*?

Granddad nodded. "Yes." He shook his head. "I can't believe your mother didn't tell you any of this. I mean I assumed, but…"

"How long have you been married?" asked Reign.

"For a very long time. You see, when your grand-mother died, Auggie and her children were staying with us. She'd just found out her first husband, your paternal grandfather, had left her for another woman, and she'd needed a place to stay. Of course, Phyllis, your grand-mother, being the sweet, big-hearted woman that she was, allowed her old friend to stay with us until she got back on her feet. But then, Phyllis passed." His voice softened and he took on a faraway look. After a few moments of silence, he seemed to remember that he had been telling a story. He glanced up at Reign and me, cleared his throat, and continued. "Auggie offered to stay through the funeral, to help us with the arrangements and to help me with little Linda while I grieved the loss of my dear, sweet Phyllis."

As he explained, I felt Reign's grip on my shoulder tighten. Gran had died after we'd left. Grandfather had never taken her and the kids to the bus stop! We'd left too soon! My eyes welled up with tears. Gran was really gone? We'd had our differences over the years, but I loved my grandmother. I didn't want to see her dead!

He continued. "Once the funeral was over, I asked Auggie where she'd go, and she didn't have a clue. She had no family to help her, and now her best friend was gone. She was grieving just as I was. So I told her she could stay awhile longer. And as things sometimes happen, we bonded over our mutual loss, and eventually we discovered that we'd fallen in love."

"Grandfather, didn't anyone ever warn you about Auggie Stone?" asked Reign.

"Warn me about her? What do you mean?"

I balked. "Didn't anyone ever warn you that she liked to steal her men from Gran?"

"Steal her men from Gr—are you talking about Auggie's first husband, Samson?"

"And you, obviously!" I said, louder than I intended.

"Well, I hardly think she *stole* me from Phyllis." He chuckled. "Phyllis was gone before Auggie and I fell in love. But, yes, Phyllis did tell me about her college rela-tionship with Samson. But she'd buried the hatchet, and because my wife was able to forgive and forget, I could hardly hold that against Auggie."

I didn't understand. How did he not remember us coming and spilling the lemonade and saving his life?

That singular incident had become a major turning point in all of our lives! Tears began to run down my face.

"Granddad, how did Gran die?" I asked through the tightness I felt in my chest.

He shook his head sadly. "We're really not sure. I was outside, working in my shop one day. Your grandmother had taken Auggie's children and your mother into town to do some grocery shopping. They'd only just come home and unloaded the truck when Auggie spotted your grandmother outside in the backyard dead. She'd gone out to take the clothing off the line. We're really not sure what happened. The doctor thought she'd had a heart attack. Though she was so young that I've always had a hard time believing it was her heart."

"Did it ever occur to you that Auggie poisoned her?" I asked through a face of messy tears.

"Mercy," whispered Reign. "Now's not the time. You have to hold it together. We need answers right now, not accusations."

"Auggie?! Poison my wife?!" Granddad shook his head. "No, she'd never! She loved Phyllis as much as I did. They were dear friends." He looked at me sadly. "Is that what your mother told you happened?"

I ignored his question. "They weren't dear friends," I muttered. "Auggie was an evil, evil witch!" And I wanted to wring that evil witch's neck for murdering my grandmother! Somehow, she must have erased Granddad's memory of our little intrusion, and instead of lacing *his* drink with her potion, she'd gone after my grandmother.

"Mercy, I know your mother feels a certain way about her stepmother, and that's partially my fault. Auggie didn't treat her as well as I would have liked over the years. I get that. I should have been more assertive in putting your mother's needs over the needs of my wife and *her* girls. Maybe then I would have gotten an opportunity to be in my grandchildren's lives over the years."

Reign shook his head. "I don't understand. What happened? Why weren't you in our lives?"

Granddad shrugged lightly. "When your mother became a teenager, she'd had enough of Auggie treating her poorly. She asked to be sent away to a boarding school. I suppose if that had never happened, she would have never met your father."

"She would have never met Merrick?!" I said, in shock. "But Merrick lived with you, didn't he? She would have already met him."

He smiled. "Merrick lived with us for a very short time. But he was always very resistant to me. He didn't want to be my son. He was Samson Smith's son, and no matter what I tried, he disliked me immensely. When he turned eight, he asked to go live with his father and his new wife and their new child. Linda was only five or six when Merrick left. Auggie was so disappointed in Merrick's decision to leave her that she never spoke of him in front of Linda or her girls. The girls stopped speaking of their brother as well. It was as if Merrick didn't exist anymore. So when she went away to boarding school, Merrick was only a vague memory, just a little boy she played with on the swings in her backyard. Then, when Linda was sixteen years old, she met him at her boarding school. Merrick was returning his stepsister to the very same boarding school, and the two of them just happened to meet again. From what I understand, it was love at first sight. The next thing I knew, she was pregnant with you, Reign."

I looked up at my brother. He couldn't tear his eyes off my grandfather. The story seemed to have him mesmerized. While I was over here mourning the loss of our beloved grandmother, he was there feeling feels over the meet-cute scene between our parents. It made me want to slap some sense into him.

"When Linda came home and told us that she was pregnant, we were understandably shocked and upset. She was so young, after all. But when Auggie discovered that her *son* was Linda's beau and had fathered the baby, she became enraged. She demanded that I force Linda to leave our home, and because Merrick wanted nothing to do with his mother or me, he picked Linda up and we never saw or heard from her again. Years went by and I had no knowledge of anything about my daughter's life. It was heartbreaking. I didn't know if I had a grand-daughter or a grandson. I didn't know if my daughter was alright. I didn't know where they lived or what they did for a living. It wasn't until SaraLynn bought the Para-normal Institute for Witches that we discovered that Merrick already owned the Paranormal Institute for Wizards next door."

"Granddad!" I exclaimed. "How could you let Auggie Stone kick our mother out of your house? How could you let her treat your own daughter like that?!"

Our grandfather's mouth opened, and then promptly shut again. He scooted forward on his easy chair and leaned his elbows on his knees. "Look, you have to under-stand. Auggie, is a very... opinionated woman. After your grandmother died, Auggie did a lot to hold me together.

She was strong when I was weak. I guess I let her get out of control, and by the time I realized how she really was with Linda, I'd lost my voice where my daughter was concerned."

Reign and I both stared at him. I certainly couldn't read my brother's thoughts, but it didn't sound like he'd tried very hard to be a father to my mother. Especially after she'd lost her own mother.

He hung his head. "I know. It's not a very good excuse. I can promise you, I've kicked myself for the way things went down for years. Had I known what the future would hold, I certainly would have done things with Auggie and your mother differently."

"Did I hear my name?" said a voice from the doorway.

33

*G*randdad boxed at his eyes while Reign and I bounced off the sofa and onto our feet. Quickly we spun around to face the door.

"Auggie, dear," said Granddad, shoving his glasses back onto his face in a hurry. He walked towards her, his outstretched arm trembling. "You'll never guess who's come to visit me."

Auggie raised a brow as she gave Reign and me a once over. "I imagine it's quite obvious. She's the spitting image of her mother, and he looks like my s—like his father." Her tone was harsh and biting. As Merrick's mother, and now my *grandmother*, she certainly didn't seem excited to see her grandchildren.

Granddad beamed at his wife. "After all these years, isn't it wonderful to get to see Linda and Merrick's children?"

She pursed her lips. "Mmmm," she groaned. "It's something alright."

"Mother, what did you want to see me about?" said another familiar voice from the hallway.

And then, just over Auggie's shoulder, I saw Sorceress Stone's head poke into Granddad's den. She was alive! While we'd guessed that she might be, since classes were now in session, to see her alive and in the flesh was a shock to the system.

So we'd indeed done everything we'd set out to do. We'd helped Jax become a witch. We'd brought Sorceress Stone back to life, and now there was no need to search for her murderer.

It seemed we'd done everything we'd set out to do. All was well with everyone. Except…

My grandmother was dead. My mother had grown up without her mother, but instead with a wicked witch as a stepmother. Merrick Stone—er, Smith—was my father. Auggie Stone was my grandmother. And Jax was a mean girl. My heart felt like it had shattered into a million pieces inside my chest. I didn't think I could handle Sorceress Stone being my aunt right now.

"Reign, I think we should leave," I whispered as Auggie welcomed Sorceress Stone into the den.

"Yes, SaraLynn, I thought it important for you to know that Merrick's children have finally decided to pay Clark and me a visit. I believe one of them is a student of yours, is she not?"

Sorceress Stone's ice-blue eyes turned on me then. Ignoring my brother completely, she glared down at me. "Yes. I am quite aware that Merrick's progeny attends my institution. It is what it is. We've made it work."

I bit the inside of my lip, fighting the tears that threatened to fall. I wouldn't give Auggie and Sorceress Stone the satisfaction of seeing me so vulnerable. Without moving my lips, I growled under my breath at my brother. "Reign, I want to go. Now."

He squeezed my arm and then pretended to glance down at the nonexistent watch on his wrist. "Granddad, it seems we've run out of time to visit. Perhaps we'll stop back again sometime when there isn't such a crowd."

"Oh, no! You don't have to run off. Maybe Auggie can give us a few minutes to visit alone?" He looked to his wife hopefully, but when he saw her face screwed up into a scowl, he knew he wouldn't be granted any alone time from the evil witch. "Right. Well, at least let me walk you out."

"No need," snapped Auggie. "Wallace! Our guests are ready to be shown to the door!"

Seconds later, the butler appeared in the doorway. He bowed deeply. "Right this way."

Granddad stared after us as we left, and for a split second, I stopped in the doorway and looked back at him. Just like that, my relationship with the grandfather that I'd wanted had blown up in my face. Now, not only didn't I have a grandmother, but I didn't have a grandfather either.

I clung to Reign's arm as we walked down the long hallway towards the foyer. "I wanna go home, Reign."

He patted my hand. "I know. I'm taking you home."

"No, Reign. I don't want to go to Smith's Room and Board. I want to go to Habernackle's Bed, Breakfast, and Beyond. Please?"

He looked at me sadly. "I don't think I can do that, Mercy. I'm so sorry."

*L*ater that evening, after dropping Libby and Cinder off at their dorm rooms for the evening, I lay motionless in my frilly pink-canopied bed. Staring at the pop music posters on my walls, I wished I could just crawl into a hole and never wake up. I felt worse than I'd felt since I'd seen my mother's face when I was arrested for shoplifting on Christmas Eve. And I'd thought *that* had been an all-time low.

Sweets, Holly, Alba and my brother all stared down at me, waiting for me to say something, but I couldn't speak.

"Come on, Red, you gotta say *something*," begged Alba, poking me with a finger.

I mashed my lips together. How could I tell them how brokenhearted I was? Mercy Habernackle was supposed to be one of the strong members of the Witch Squad. Jax, Sweets, and Holly were the sensitive, emotional ones in touch with their feelings and all that. I was more like Alba. I was tough and strong. I knew how to keep my guard up. I didn't cry all the time. I didn't wear my heart on my sleeve. But today, I felt like I'd snapped. Things were so messed up that I didn't even know how to begin talking about it.

Sweets looked at me with concern-filled eyes. "Yeah, Mercy, you can't keep it all bottled up inside of you. It's not good for you."

Reign sat down at the foot of the bed. "Leave her alone. She'll talk when she's ready to talk."

Holly put a hand on Reign's shoulder. "Well, just know that we're all here for you, Merc. Anything you need, okay?"

Reign nodded. "Yeah, just like Holly said. We're here for you. I'll do anything you want me to do to make you feel better."

I looked up at Reign then, and I realized the answer couldn't be any clearer. What good had come of everything we'd done? My grandfather was alive, but he hadn't gotten to be my grandfather. Jax had her powers, but she used them for evil, not good. Sorceress Stone was alive, but she hated me. What was the point in what we'd done?

I looked up at all of the faces staring at me and inhaled a deep breath. "I want it all put back."

"You what?" asked Alba, staring at me incredulously.

"I want it all put back. I want my Gran brought back to life. I want my mother to have grown up without her father, but with a loving mother instead. I want Jax never to have gotten her powers. I want Sorceress Stone to be dead again. I want everything put back the way it was before we stuck our noses into it!"

Alba sucked in her breath, her eyes wild. "But then your grandfather will be dead!"

"Yes, I know," I whispered, hanging my head sadly. "But Gran will be alive."

"But we went to all that trouble!"

I leaned forward in bed. "So what?! It was *one* day of our lives wasted. Big deal! Look at all the damage that we caused! *Nothing* good came out of it."

"We're full siblings," said my brother. "That's not good?"

"Reign, I *told* you that I don't care about that. You're my brother whether we have the same father or not."

"But then Sorceress Stone will be dead!" said Sweets. "It can't be right to undo what we've already undone."

"So what? Either we'll figure something else out or…" I threw my hands up into the air. "Or, it'll just be the way that it is. The universe put it that way in the first place. *We* didn't kill her."

"But even if we could figure out a way to redo the curse, I think it would be like killing Sorceress Stone ourselves, even if *we* weren't the ones that did it," said Sweets.

"If you look at it like that, then we have to feel responsible for killing my grandmother! Because she was alive yesterday and now she's not. *We* are responsible for that, then!" I argued emphatically. I had it in my mind now, and it was clear as a bell. We had to undo all this. I wasn't about to take no for an answer.

"Listen, Red, I get what you're saying, but isn't undoing everything again begging for more trouble?"

"How? How could things *possibly* be worse than they are now?"

"Well, in that scenario, Stone's still dead. So now we have to tell Jax that not only is she's not getting her powers, but her mother's dead too. That's pretty bad."

"So? What's the alternative? Jax gets her powers *and* her mother, but both of them are epic a-holes?"

Alba nodded. "I see your point."

"Thank you!"

"I just don't know how to do it."

"Are you kidding?" I bellowed. "The answer is simple. We left the time machine running. It's out there in the field, remember? We kept it going just in case Sorceress Stone was dead when we got back. Let's get back over there and go back in time again. We'll tell ourselves to abort mission!"

"Can we *do* that?" asked Holly, looking at Alba curiously.

Alba made a face. "I mean, I don't know. I didn't see anything about it in that book, but then again, I didn't read the whole thing. It sounds like it could work."

I looked in the mirror, pulled off my glasses and wiped away my smudged eyeliner. I readjusted my braid and then stood up. "What are we waiting for? This needs to be done, and it needs to be done *now.*"

My brother touched my shoulder. "Mercy, it's almost dark out."

"Yeah, Red. We can't do this in the dark."

"Then we're doing it first thing tomorrow morning. I don't want to be Merrick Smith's daughter a single moment longer than I have to be!"

"Fine," said Alba. "If that's what you want."

"It's what I want!"

Alba pulled her phone out of her back pocket. "Alright. I'll text the twins and tell them to meet us at the time portal at the crack of dawn." When she'd fired off a message, she peeled off her jacket. "We should get some sleep."

"Good idea," said Reign.

Alba looked around. "What room am I sleeping in tonight? Because I'm certainly not sleeping in this ridiculous froufy bed of yours. You know, Red, full disclosure, this is the real reason I'm okay with putting things back to normal. I can't handle having you as a friend if you're into this froufy crap. You know that, right?"

I grinned. "Alba, whatever reason makes you sleep at night is reason enough for me."

34

*T*he sun had barely broken the surface of the horizon as we stood looking at the time portal we'd constructed.

Holly stretched her arms up over her head and yawned. "I can't believe we're up this early. I don't think I've been up this early on a Friday since the last Black Friday before online shopping was a thing."

"Lucky. I'm up before the sun comes up *every* morning. A baker's life," Sweets said with a shrug. "But you know what they say, the early bird gets the worm!"

Holly rolled her eyes. "Eww. Worms are gross. The early bird can have the worm. Mornings are dumb."

Reign chuckled. "I must say I have to agree with Holly. Mornings definitely aren't my thing either."

Holly looked surprised. "But you get up early to make breakfast at the B&B every morning!"

"Yeah. I mean, it's my job. I have to. But in real life, I'm a night owl through and through."

She nodded her head emphatically. "Me too."

"Alright, can we focus now? We have a lot to accomplish today," said Alba. Shaking her head, she stared at the portal. "I can't believe we're gonna go back there again."

My heart felt like it stopped beating for a second. "You're not changing your mind about helping me do this, are you?"

Alba swatted the air and adjusted the straps of her backpack. "Nah, I'm not changing my mind. I just can't believe we wasted all that time."

"How were we supposed to know the chain reaction that was going to happen?" asked Sweets.

"There's no way we could've known," said Reign. "But now we do, and we just have to fix it. That's all."

I nodded, thankful for my brother and my friends. I didn't know what I'd do without them. Despite my exhaustion, I rubbed my hands together in front of myself. "So, let's get going."

We all entered the steam sauna once again. By now we'd done it so many times that we knew the drill well, and we all took our spots, shoulder to shoulder.

A fatal potion was concocted,
And soon thereafter a murder plotted.
Take us back to the place and time
Auggie Stone committed her heinous crime.

We waited for the wormhole to change directions, then stepped through the slit in time and walked single-file through the tunnel of lights. In under a minute, we found ourselves exiting near the same little brook at the bottom of the grassy hill. My grandparents' small house sat just as it had the day before. The laundry on the clothesline blew in the lilac-scented air. Everything was just as it had been when we'd been there earlier. We'd made it back!

As I trained my eyes on the house, I noticed something different. The playground sat empty. There were no children playing on the swings, and no one on the slide. "Guys!" I breathed, pointing towards the empty backyard. "Look! Mom, and Merrick, and the rest of the kids aren't there anymore."

Alba's face went white. "Oh no! Maybe the portal sent us to the wrong time!"

"We better get up there. Come on." Reign led the way. This time, we weren't as careful about staying hidden as we had been the first time we'd been there.

My pulse raced as I followed my brother, hoping that we'd find out we weren't too late. But when we approached the house, we saw them. They were peering in the windows, watching as Auggie prepared the potion. I saw Alba duck walk across the back deck. I saw another version of myself glancing down at her. It was a surreal feeling looking at myself in the past, but I didn't have time to dwell on it. Things were going to move fast from here on out, and if I hesitated at all, I might miss the opportunity to stop things.

From the outer perimeter of the yard, I crouched down in the tall grass and hissed at the girls on the deck. "Mercy!"

The back-in-time me looked down at Alba and then held a finger up to her mouth to shush her. She thought it had come from her.

"Alba!" I hissed.

Back-in-time Alba looked at back-in-time me.

"Alba!" I hissed again.

This time, it was obvious the voice hadn't come from the deck. She looked around. Immediately, our whole group waved our hands in the air at her.

Alba's eyes nearly bugged out of her head when she saw all the doppelgangers crouched down in the tall grass. She made a startled noise, and back-in-time me looked down at her. Alba nodded her head towards all of us in the grass. I watched myself turn and look at the group of us waving. My eyes bugged out just as Alba's had done.

Together, we all beckoned the old Alba and Mercy to come to us. They looked around in confusion but slipped down the deck, careful not to be seen, and came to us. Back-in-time Libby and Cinder, who had been peering in the side windows, heard us hissing and came too.

"What in the world is going on?" breathed the old Alba. "Why are we seeing duplicates of ourselves right now?"

The old me nodded, staring directly into my matching green eyes. "Yeah, my mind is blown right now."

"We're here to tell you to scrap the plans," I said.

"Scrap the plans?" said my duplicate. "What do you mean?"

Alba shook her head. "We don't have a lot of time to explain, because in a few minutes you're gonna stop Clark from drinking that lemonade."

"You know about the lemonade?" old me asked in shock.

"Of course we do. Why do you think we're here? We're coming from the present."

"No, no, no, *we're* coming from the present," argued the old Alba.

"Yeah, well, we're a day older than you are," said Cinder.

Alba nodded. "Listen, just do as we say. Don't stop Auggie from giving Clark the lemonade."

The old me widened her eyes. "We can't do that! If we let her give it to him, Granddad will die!"

I sighed. "If Granddad doesn't die, then Gran dies instead."

"Gran!" the old me screamed. "How?"

Without having seen it with my own two eyes, I'm not sure that I would have believed it either, and we didn't have much time to explain. "We're not sure of the exact details. All we know is that if Auggie finds out that Granddad will die if he drinks the potion, she decides to kill Gran instead."

"Well, then, we'll warn Gran instead of Granddad!"

I shook my head. "If you alert Auggie to any of this, she'll just do some kind of brainwashing spell. Listen, we know what we're talking about. We saw firsthand the damage that was done by reversing this curse." I looked the old me dead in the eye. "Mercy, if you reverse the curse, Merrick becomes your father. Jax gets her powers, but she's a mean girl and you two can't stand each other. Reign is this weird preppy kid. And Gran is dead. It's a horrible reality that we came back to stop from happening."

Alba nodded. "And you sleep in a froufrou bed with a pink frilly bedskirt and a sheet over the top. *And* you have a poster of Carly Rae Jepsen on your wall. It's ridiculous. Save yourself the embarrassment and just leave things alone. Don't tell Clark about Auggie. Just let things happen as they happened before we messed with anything."

"But—" began the old Alba.

The new Alba looked at her day-younger self sternly. "Listen, who's got two thumbs and is the only person in the world that knows you better than you know yourself?" She pointed at herself with both thumbs. "This girl. I'm a day older and a day wiser, and I'm tellin' you, you don't wanna reverse this curse. Got it?"

The old Alba didn't seem to like taking orders from her older self, but she seemed resigned to it. "Fine," she grumbled. "So do we just go home?"

"Yup. Gather the troops and hit the road. We gotta head back first, we're pressed for time, but then you guys go before anyone can see you."

The old Mercy looked at me with a down-turned face. "And then everything goes back to normal?"

I nodded. "Yup. Let's hope so."

"But what about Jax and her mom?" asked the other Libby.

"We don't know yet," I admitted. "One thing at a time. We had to fix this huge mess we made first. When we get back, we'll put our brains to work on that."

"But it's Friday, Mercy!" said Sweets. "Jax's birthday and graduation are on *Sunday*! How are we supposed to figure something out by Sunday?"

I shook my head. "My brain can only handle one thing at a time, Sweets. Let's get home and make sure we put everything back the way it should be and then we'll talk."

Alba nodded. "Then what are we waiting for? We have a lot to do when we get back. Let's go!"

———————————

I held my breath as Sweets rounded the corner towards the B&B. Would the sign say Smith's Room and Board or Habernackle's Bed, Breakfast, and Beyond?

"I can't look," I whispered, closing my eyes as Sweets pulled into a parking spot. "What's it say, Reign?"

"It says…" He paused and took a deep breath, making me wait to find out. Finally he exhaled as he said the words I'd hoped to hear. "It's Habernackle's!"

"Oh, thank God," said Alba, crumpling against my shoulder.

I opened my eyes and looked around my brother to stare at the sign. It was just as it had been. I could only hope that everything else was as it had been as well. "Come on. I need to see Jax, and I need to see my mother!"

Inside, I found Mom pouring a cup of coffee at the bar.

"Mom!" I screeched the second I saw her.

She looked up at me. Her face looked pinched with worry. The second she made eye contact with me, she put the coffee down and rushed around the counter to throw her arms around me. "Mercy! Oh, thank God you're alright!"

"Yeah, I'm fine, Mom, why?"

"Is your brother with you?" she asked, her eyes filled with tears.

I nodded and turned to see him coming through the doorway behind Sweets. "Yeah, he's right there…"

But she was off and hugging him. "Oh, my kids are safe! I was so worried!"

"I was worried too," agreed Detective Whitman. I hadn't noticed him sitting at the bar when I'd come in, but now he had come over to join our group. "Where have you all been?"

"It's a really long story," said Alba. "Witch stuff."

Sweets nodded. "Yeah, witch stuff."

My mother clucked her tongue at us. "Witch stuff! You could have *told* someone that you were going to be gone for two days!"

I shrugged. "Sorry. We didn't know it was going to take us so long."

Reign threw his arms around my mother again. "I'm sorry, Mom. We shouldn't have done that to you. Especially me. I know we're in this business together and you need to be able to count on me. But Mercy was right, we had no idea we'd be gone so long."

"Well, you could have called! I gave you all the benefit of the doubt the first night you didn't come home, but when you were gone a second night, I had to tell Mark."

"I understand," I said quietly. "Mom, can I speak to you privately for just a moment?"

Mom's face went from relieved to pensive. "Privately? Of course. Let's go in the kitchen. Mark, will you excuse me for a minute?"

Detective Whitman shooed us away. "Yeah, of course, go, go! I have tons of questions to ask the rest of these guys. You go. Have a mother-daughter talk."

When the double swinging doors shut behind us,

Mom looked at me sternly. "Are you going to tell me what's happened now?"

"Mom, I can't."

"Mercy! You were gone for two days!"

"I know, Mom. And like I said, I'm so sorry. I learned my lesson for sure. We all did. We were trying to fix something, and we made it worse and then we had to fix it again. It just got out of hand. But we're back now and we're still running against a really tight deadline."

"Does this have anything to do with Jax's eighteenth birthday?"

"Yes! It has *everything* to do with that."

Mom nodded. "I figured as much. That's why I didn't call Mark right away. I assumed you and your brother were up to something. Well, is she a witch? Will she get her powers by her birthday?"

I let out a heavy sigh. I wished so much she would, but it wasn't looking like that was going to happen now. "Unfortunately, she won't. It's a really long story, but we're running out of time, and I need to go see Jax. But I wanted to ask you a question in private before we left."

"Okay? Ask away."

"Is Merrick Stone my father?"

My mom's eyes widened with shock. "Is Merrick your father? Mercy! You know that your grandmother bound us apart. I wasn't anywhere *near* Merrick when you were conceived!"

I let out a huge sigh of relief. "Oh thank God!" My heart instantly felt a million times lighter.

"Why would you even *think* that?"

I shrugged. "I don't know. You've never told me who

my father was, so I just thought maybe there was a chance and you were just scared to tell me."

"I can't believe that would even cross your mind."

"I just had to ask." I threw my arms around her and gave her a huge squeeze. "Mom, I'm really sorry for what we put you through, but I need to go find Jax. Where is she? Is she in our room?"

"No, she's been helping Char all week. With Sweets gone, Char's just been beside herself with worry. Jax has been too, but I think helping Char has taken her mind off of worrying about all of you."

"So she's at the bakery?"

Mom nodded. "She should be."

I kissed my mother's cheeks. "Thanks, Mom, I gotta go. Love you!"

"I love you too, Mercy Bear."

35

Sweets wrung out her hands in front of her as we walked the few blocks to Bailey's Bakery and Sweets. "Jax must have been worried sick. I feel so bad for everything we put her through."

"We all feel bad about everything," I agreed.

"So are we going to tell Jax about her mother? Or just that we weren't able to get her powers for her?" asked Cinder.

"She's definitely going to want to know what we've been up to for the last two days," said Reign. "I don't think we should lie to her."

"But then she's going to get all sad," said Holly. "I hate seeing Jax sad."

"We all hate seeing Shorty sad. She turns into this high-pitched, squeaky water fountain, but we have no choice. She has to know the truth."

Opening the door to Bailey's, my hand trembled. The thought of telling Jax that her mother was gone ate away at my insides. I wasn't sure if I had the stomach to do it.

The doorbell chimed, and Char's muffled voice rang out from the kitchen. "Be right there!"

"Is anyone else nervous?" asked Holly.

Sweets nodded uncomfortably. "I feel like my insides may become my outsides."

"Eww, Sweets."

"Sorry."

Then a puffy white head of hair came wheeling around the corner. "Well, hello, girls! *Finally* you're back!" Char threw her arms out with emphasis. "You know, the group of you got Jax worked up in a tizzy. She had no idea where you'd gone!"

"Yeah, we assumed." I nodded uneasily as I looked over her shoulder. "That's why we're here. We came to apologize. Can we talk to her?"

Char swatted a hand at us. "Oh, she's not here. I got tired of her moaning and groaning about you not showing up again last night, so I sent her to the store."

"Char, I am *so, so* sorry about not showing up for work for the last few days," said Sweets. "I had *no* idea that it was going to take us so long to get Jax's powers for her."

Char lifted her brows is surprise. "You mean it worked? You actually reversed the curse on Jax?"

I frowned. "Nope. It didn't work. That's what we came to talk to Jax about."

"Well, that and to tell her her mo—" began Holly.

"Cosmo!" shouted Alba, swatting Holly across the shoulder.

Holly grabbed her arm. "Alba! You didn't have to hit me."

"What'd you expect me to do? You were gonna tell her something you weren't allowed to tell!"

"But we're gonna tell Jax. Why can't Char know?" asked Holly, her forehead wrinkled.

"Because Shorty should get to know first. It's only right."

Char leaned forward on the counter. Taking in each of our long faces, she shook our head. "Okay. What's going on?" When no one volunteered any information, she looked directly at Sweets. "Sweets?"

Sweets swallowed hard. "Going on?"

"Yeah. It's not like you not to show up for work with no phone call, no explanation, no nothing. Usually you tell me everything."

Sweets' eyes darted around the room from person to person. We all knew Sweets couldn't lie. It wasn't in her nature. "Well, Char, you see…"

I didn't want Sweets to lie to her boss, and I'd had enough of beating around the bush. I turned to face my friends, holding my hands out on either side of me. "Listen, guys. Char's a veteran witch."

Char bobbed her head as she cut in, "Ooh, *veteran* witch. I like that. It's got a much better ring to it than *old* witch."

I stared over my shoulder at her.

She mashed her lips together. "Oh. Sorry. Proceed."

I faced the group again. "She's got connections. She knows things we don't. Maybe if we tell her what's going on, she can help us with our problem."

Char shook her head. "I'll stop you right there, Little Linda. I'm not reversing Phyllis's curse. I told you. I'm staying out of it."

"No, not help reversing the curse. We have another

343

problem. A big problem, and when Jax finds out, it's going to crush her."

"Red! You really think we should be sharing this with Char? She's one of the busiest busybodies in town. Word will spread like wildfire once we put this bug in her ear. No offense, Char."

Char shot Alba an annoyed glance but grumbled at her, "None taken." Then she looked at me with one eyebrow up. "This… problem you speak of. Is it going to crush Jax more than finding out that she still isn't a witch?"

Biting the inside of my lip firmly, I nodded.

She sighed. "Oh, that's just great. What did the lot of ya do now?"

"We didn't do anything," said Alba. "It was the Council."

Char quirked a brow. "The Council? What Council?"

"The Great Witches Council. The one in charge of the Institute."

"Oh. What did they do?"

Everyone was quiet for a really long time. No one had the nerve to say out loud what had happened.

Char's eyes moved from person to person, waiting for someone to speak. "Well, don't all speak at once."

"It's just that we're all still in shock," said Sweets.

"Still in shock?" She waved a hand in our direction dismissively. "You kids with your dramatics. Everything's always gloom and doom with you people. It's not like they killed someone or something."

My eyes widened. I glanced over at Alba. She'd swished her lips to one side and her eyes concentrated on the wood floor.

Char frowned. "Alright, what's with all the long faces?"

"Char, someone on the Council actually did *kill* some-one," my brother finally said.

Char's frown lines deepened. "You can't be serious."

"We're dead serious."

"They actually *killed someone*? Why would they do that?"

I shrugged.

"Well, who was it?"

Reign glanced over at me and then back at Char. "They killed SaraLynn."

Char's eyes opened wide as she stood up straight. "Stone?"

We all nodded sadly.

She put a hand to her mouth. "Auggie's SaraLynn?"

"Yup," I said. "And Jax's mom."

Char's mouth gaped. She cupped her forehead and turned around to face the kitchen, trying to make sense of what we'd told her. Finally, she turned around to face us again. "Which of the Council members killed her?"

"We don't know," I said. "That was part of the reason we were gone so long. We were trying to figure out who killed her so we could then figure out how to bring her back to life."

"Girls, if she died on Wednesday—"

"Tuesday," Sweets corrected.

"Fine. If she died on Tuesday, I hate to break it to you, but you're not bringing her back to life now. It's been far too long!"

"Actually, it's not. We froze the body," said Libby.

"Froze the… you froze SaraLynn?"

Libby nodded. "To preserve her. It's my major at the Institute. When she's unthawed, she will be just as she was when I froze her. Only an hour or so past her death."

"Still, even then it's going to be next to impossible to bring her back! I'm not sure it can be done."

"Yeah," I said, nodding.

"But you've been trying anyway?"

"We had to," said Sweets. "Jax won't be able to handle it."

Char shook her head. "I don't understand. Why has this not made the town paper yet? I assume Detective Whitman is on the case?"

Alba shook her head. "Nah. We haven't told him. We're handling the case ourselves."

"Yourselves?! Girls! This is a really big deal! I'm sorry, I know you've solved quite a few murders since you've been residents of Aspen Falls, but that hardly makes you professional detectives. Why would you not tell the authorities?!"

"Because it's a paranormal death. He's not going to be able to figure it out any more than we can. Plus, we wanted to tell Jax first."

"Well, then, why haven't you told her?"

"We thought we could fix it," I said sadly, shaking my head. "And we thought we could figure out who did it."

"So let me get this straight. You think it was a Council member that did it?" she asked.

All of our heads bobbed.

"How do you know?"

"Oh, we know alright," said Alba. "We just don't know which one of 'em did it."

"Who's on the Council?"

346

Alba held up a finger and began to recite the names from memory. "Poppy Ellabee, Daphne Fletcher, Stella Blackwood, Gemma Overbrook, and Elodie Goodwitch."

Char curled her lip. "Well, I've heard of Poppy and Gemma. Poppy used to teach at the Institute, and Gemma runs an online witch school. But can't say I've heard of any of the rest."

"Yeah, they aren't very well known," I agreed.

Char shook her head. "Well, there's a clue right there. That's pretty strange. Who appointed them to the Council?"

I shrugged. "I have no idea, why?"

"Well, members of the previous Council appoint the new members, and it's tradition to select members that are well known in the witch community or in the media."

I hadn't realized that. If I had, I would have asked each of the members who had appointed them.

"Well, Daphne Fletcher works for the Texas Army National Guard preventing natural disasters and helping with emergency situations," said Holly. "That's pretty impressive."

Char nodded. "Well, it's commendable and all, but hardly worthy of being put on the Council. You don't understand. Usually they appoint judges and governors or celebrities. Once they even had a vice-presidential nominee on the Council, but we won't speak of her. She was a bit of a nut." Char nodded. "So for example, this Elodie Goodwitch. You said she's on the Council? What does she do?"

"She owns a magical apothecary in a small town in Iowa," said Reign.

Char twirled a finger in the air. "Well, whoopty-do.

My husband and I own a magical bakery. Does that make *me* worthy of being on the Council? What's Stella's claim to fame?"

I thought about it. "She researches plant-based potion ingredients, and she's worked with some major pharmaceutical companies."

"So essentially what you're saying here is that you've got a botanist, a witch who runs a store, an Army witch, and two teaching witches? That's hardly an impressive Council. In fact, that's got to be the *least* impressive Council I've ever heard of."

"Huh," said Alba. "I didn't know the Council had to be so well known. That piece of information might have been good to know when we questioned them."

"So you have questioned them all?"

Cinder nodded. "Yes, and we've done our best to research their history with Sorceress Stone. Unfortunately, we could point fingers at each of them. They all seemed to have grudges against the headmistress."

Char wagged her finger at us. "I'm telling you, there's where you should be looking. *Someone* was responsible for assembling that cast of misfits. What you need to find out is who put a council together that all carried grudges against SaraLynn and why. I have a very strong feeling *that* will lead you to your killer."

I shook my head. Why hadn't we thought to ask Char for help sooner? I needed to start remembering that sometimes it was okay to ask for help. Without warning, the front door lurched open, setting off the door chime. I turned to face the door.

Jax stood in the doorway, carrying plastic grocery bags on each arm. Her eyes were wide as silver dollars, and her mouth gaped open. Dropping the bags to the ground, she sucked in her breath before launching herself at me while squealing like a stuck pig. "Omigosh, Mercy! I was so worried about you!"

"Hey, Jax," I said, grinning as she hugged me. It felt good to have the old Jax back. The one we knew and loved and not the mean witch that would use her powers for evil instead of good. "Miss me?"

"Miss you? Of course I do! I was going *crazy!* I thought maybe something happened to all of you!"

"Now I know how I rate," said Reign. "Don't I get any hugs?" He held his arms out.

Jax peeled herself off me and flung her tiny frame into Reign's arms. He swept her off her feet and spun her around. "Reign! I missed you too!"

"Uh-hum," coughed Holly.

Jax smiled and threw her arms around Holly's neck, then took turns giving each of the group hugs. She came to a screeching halt in front of Alba. "Fist bump?"

Alba held up her balled hand and tapped Jax's hand. "Glad to see you, Shorty. You doin' alright?"

"Now I am! Omigosh, where have you been?!"

"It's a long story."

"Tell me, tell me, tell me!" she pleaded, bouncing up and down on the balls of her feet anxiously.

"We will," I promised. "Just not right this second, okay? We have some things that we need to go take care of. When we come back, we'll tell you what's going on."

Jax's face screwed up into a pout. She stomped her foot on the floor. "No! I'm not letting a single one of you out of my sight! I've been sitting around here for three days. *Three days!* Char's great and all, but I need to be with my witches! Wherever you're going and whatever you're doing, I'm going with."

"Shorty, I don't think that's such a good idea…"

Jax closed her eyes and held up a flattened palm in Alba's face. "No, no, no. You are *not* getting rid of me. You know when you're doing a craft project and you get glue all over your fingers and it dries and it's like you have a second layer of invisible skin? Yeah, that's gonna be me. I'm gonna be the glue you get all over your fingers. I'm gonna be stuck to you so tight that you won't even know I'm there. And whatever you do, you won't be able to peel me off." She stood proudly with her hands propped up on both hips in a superhero pose. "I'm part of this team, and whatever the team has cooking, I'm gonna be right there in the kitchen too, cooking up a—"

"We get it," said Alba rolling her eyes. "You're coming with."

Jax squealed. "Char, I hope you don't mind, but I have to go with my friends. We've got some serious witch business to attend to."

Char nodded. "Yes, that's what I hear. Well, good luck. Sweets, when will I see you back at work?"

"Can I still have tomorrow off for Jax's birthday and graduation?"

"Of course!"

"Then I'll be in on Monday."

Char nodded. "Monday it is." She waved at us as we moved towards the doorway. "Good luck with your project. I hope it all works out."

As the last to leave, I stuck my head back inside. "We do too, Char. We do too."

36

"So are you gonna tell me what you've been up to now?" asked Jax, bouncing up and down on her toes.

Alba scowled at her. "No."

"Oh, come on, Alba, don't you think it's time we told her everything?" said Sweets.

Jax cuddled up next to Alba's side and looked up at her, doe-eyed. "It's okay, Sweets. I think I know what you've been up to anyway," she sang.

Sweets looked shocked. "You do?"

Jax's head bobbed up and down assuredly. "Of course! You've been working on getting my powers for me for my birthday, haven't you?"

"Jax," I began hesitantly. While that was definitely part of it, it wasn't all of it, and by now I was tired of hiding the truth from her. I was starting to think we weren't going to be able to fix anything, and Jax had a right to know what had happened.

Jax shot forward and clapped a hand over my mouth.

"You don't have to say another word, Mercy. I'm just so thankful that I have such great friends, and such a great cousin! I don't need to know *how* you're doing it, I'm just thankful that you are!"

"Shorty, listen," said Alba, slowly. "There's something you need to know."

Jax hung her head. When she looked back up again, her eyes were filled with tears. She swallowed hard. "Alba, please don't say it. I already know what you're going to say. I know that it might not happen for me. I know that the reason that you've been gone for so long is because it's been harder than you thought it would be to reverse the curse. I might be a little naive, but I'm not stupid. Here's the thing. I know that if I don't become a witch by tomorrow, I'll never be one. Time's running out. And then you and Holly are going home for the summer. Libby and Cinder, you're both graduating. And next year I'll be going away to nursing school, or maybe a performing arts school. That might be fun." She smiled through a face full of tears.

Reign threw an arm over Jax's shoulder and squeezed her head under his arm. "Don't cry. I hate it when you cry."

Jax pushed herself upright. "It's okay, Reign. I'm okay. While you've been gone, I've finally had a chance to make peace with who I am and who I'm not. I'm not a witch," she said with a half-smile. "I'm just a girl. In a day and a half, I'll be eighteen, and I'll have to start adulting. I'll have to learn how to lead a nonparanormal life with normal people at a normal school." Her voice quivered as she spoke, but she fought hard to keep it together. "But *today*, I'm still a witch in training. *Today* I'm still a member of the Witch Squad. So, whatever you're working on, whatever you have to do—whether it's still trying to get my powers for me, or whether it's working on graduation projects—I just want to be a part of it, because it's probably going to be the last time that I ever get to be a part of the paranormal world and hang out with all of you."

"Aww, Jaxie," cooed Sweets, reaching out to grab her hand. "We love you. Of course you can be a part of what we're doing today."

"Thanks, Sweets," said Jax, wiping her tears with the back of her hand.

Holly and Libby took turns giving Jax a hug.

Then I walked over and put a hand on either of Jax's shoulders and looked her in the eye. "You know, Jax, it doesn't matter if you are or aren't a witch. No matter what, we're still cousins, and you and I will always hang out."

"I know, Mercy." She nodded and gave me a tight smile.

"So, can we quit all this moping around and just go do whatever it is that you're doing? You don't have to tell me anything. Just let me come along for the ride. Okay?"

Alba was the last to toss an arm around Jax's shoulder. "You're a cool kid, Shorty. You know that? I'm gonna miss you this summer."

Jax leaned her head on Alba's shoulder. "Aww, thanks, Alba. I love you."

Alba shoved her away, reaching up to swipe at her own eyes. "Eh, I love you too, kid."

*S*tanding in the middle of the Winston Hall dormitory less than thirty minutes later, I pointed at the little couch and chairs in the downstairs lobby area. "Okay, I think you guys should stay out here."

Holly wrinkled her nose. "Why?"

"Because I think Brittany will tell us what we want to know if she's not surrounded by this flash mob of people," I explained. Our group was up to eight now. And while there was logic to my explanation, I'd neglected to add the real reason I wanted the whole group to stay in the lobby. If Jax came with us, Brittany might do something stupid, like tell Jax sorry for her loss or offer up one of those other generic bereavement greetings. No, Jax had said that she didn't need to know what was going on, she just wanted to go along for the ride. That meant we had her permission to keep her in the dark about her mother until we had finished our investigation.

Holly looked confused but nodded like she wasn't. "Oh."

Reign nodded too. "You know what? I think us not going in is a great idea. How about we all go get a cup of coffee and a bagel or something? I don't know about you guys, but I'm positively starving."

Sweets nodded emphatically. "I'm starving too, and they make the best chocolate chip bagels here."

"Oooh, Sweets, grab me a double caramel macchiato and one of those bagels, would ya?"

Sweets smiled. "Of course."

"I'm going with you, Red. Just in case Hobbs doesn't wanna give out the information we need. I might need to lean on her a little."

I rolled my eyes. "Oh, jeez. As tough as you think you are, Alba, you're not a member of the mob."

"Shut up. Come on."

We entered Brittany's office, her eyes widening when she saw us. "There you are! Finally!"

I quirked a brow. "You've been waiting for us?"

"Well, not me! The Council! From what I understand, you were supposed to be investigating Sorceress Stone's death and then you just disappeared!"

"Yeah," I said with a sigh and a nod. "Sorry about that. We have been investigating, but the trail finally went cold."

"Well, you just left the entire Council hanging. They aren't very happy about that. You're lucky they were here all week anyway to judge the graduation projects. But after that, they're leaving."

"Then whoever did it will get away!" I said.

Alba held a hand out to settle me down. "Don't worry. We're trying not to let that happen." She looked at Brittany. "We're gonna need a little information from you."

"I'm not sure what information I can give out that would help."

"We need to know who sat on last year's Council."

"Oh," said Brittany with a surprised face. "Yeah, I have that list somewhere. I think I actually have it saved on my computer." She studied her monitor carefully as she clicked through a bunch of different screens, until finally, we heard the printer behind her sputter to life. She reached around behind her and grabbed the sheet of paper. "Here you go."

I was shocked at how easy that had been.

"Thanks," said Alba with a little salute.

"No problem. So what should I tell the Council if they ask about the investigation?"

"Tell them we're really close to solving it and just to stay put for another day," said Alba.

I looked at Alba with surprise. We were hardly close to solving the murder, but I wasn't going to counter her.

Brittany nodded. "Okay. Will do."

We met the rest of the group inside Paranormally Delicious. The group had taken up residence inside the little coffee shop by pushing together two tables and collecting all the chairs.

Cinder was the first to pounce the second we walked in the door. "Well? What did you find out?"

Alba held up the sheet of paper and waved it in the air proudly. "We got the list!"

"Yay!" said Holly, grabbing at the sheet. "Lemme see!"

Alba tore the paper away from Holly's greedy hands. "Hold your horses. I haven't even looked yet!"

"Why do you get to look first?"

Alba sneered at Holly. "Because *I'm* the one holding the paper."

I plucked it out of Alba's hands when her eyes were turned. "Now I get to look first," I said with a small laugh. I slid into the chair between Jax and Reign. "Okay, let's have a look, shall we?"

Jax rubbed her hands together excitedly. "What are we looking at?"

"It's a list of last year's Council members," explained Reign.

"Oooh. And why are we looking at it?"

"I thought you were just along for the ride," said Reign. "You said you wouldn't ask any questions."

Jax bit her lip and pretended to zip her mouth shut.

I scanned the list, shocked to see some of the names as people that I actually recognized. "Avery Brooks, she's the lady that does all those infomercials."

Sweets nodded. "I've seen them! Yeah, I know who she is too. Cool."

Reign pointed at another name. "Sally Murtaugh, she's a retired senator."

Suddenly, Holly, who was sitting across from me, sucked in her breath. She'd been staring at the list too. She pulled the list over to her and spun it around. "Oh. My. God. You guys! Dixie Carlton is on this list!"

"Dixie Carlton the actress?" asked Jax with shock.

"Yes!" breathed Holly. "I can't believe this! I didn't think she was actually a real witch. I thought it was just a rumor! But it's true! And she was on the Council."

"Wow," said Alba. "I guess Char was right, they were big names up until this year. That's so strange."

Holly put her hands flat on the table and pushed herself up. "Guys. We *have* to go interview Dixie Carlton. We just have to! I want to meet her so bad!"

"Sorry, I guess I'm a bit celebrity challenged. Who's Dixie Carlton again?" asked Reign.

Holly turned to face my brother. "Oh my gosh, Dixie has been in a *ton* of movies. She actually started out as a country music singer in Nashville, but now she has her own clothing line and she's all over social media. I'm a huge fan of hers."

"I can tell."

Holly faced Alba. "Oh, come on, Alba. Let's go see

her. Maybe she can tell us how last year's Council appointed this year's Council!"

Alba shrugged. "I don't have a problem with it. We need to talk to *someone* on the Council. According to the list, her home address is still Nashville."

Jax crinkled her forehead. "Nashville! The eight of us are going to go to Nashville and be back in time for graduation Sunday? That just doesn't sound realistic."

I beamed at her. "Don't worry, Jax. We have a new, high-tech ride. And lemme tell you, you are going to *love it*!"

"*W*hat is *this*?!" asked Jax as the eight of us stared at the raging bonfire beneath the raised river and the two spinning steam saunas.

"It's a time portal," said Alba proudly as she stood back to admire her handiwork. "We made it."

"You guys *made* this? No way!" breathed Jax. She stared at it in awe, as did the rest of us. It *was* a pretty cool sight to behold, and it was still shocking to me that we'd pulled it off.

"Way," said Alba with a nod. "It's gotten quite a workout. We've been going back in time trying to stop the curse from ever being placed."

Jax's eyes widened. "You went back in time?!"

"Yeah, but it didn't work out so well," I admitted. "It started this whole chain reaction." I stopped talking. I couldn't bring myself to tell Jax about everything that had changed as a result.

Jax looked sad only for a split second. "Oh well, it's

still really cool that you went back in time. I just wish I'd gotten to go with you."

"Well, hold on to your panties, cuz we're going for a ride now," said Alba, stepping into the steam sauna. "Come on!"

Inside, we took our positions. This time, Jax stood between Holly and Sweets and straight across from me. She wore her excitement on her face the same way she wore her heart on her sleeve.

"Now what?" she asked, looking around at the inside of the steam room.

"Now Alba chants," whispered Holly. "Hang on. It won't be long."

Dixie Carlton is a well-known witch,
She's an actress, a singer, and she's really rich.
She lives in Nashville and is a superstar,
We need to see her, but it's too far.
So take us to the place and day,
Where we can see her right away.

When the tunnel of lights changed directions, Jax's ears perked up. She looked around curiously. "What's that noise?"

"That's the sound of our ride." Alba grinned. "Right this way."

37

"That. Was. *Amazing!*" screeched Jax as we exited the spinning tunnel of lights onto a super plush lawn next to a lazy river. The sun blazed down on us, making us all squint and cover our eyes with our hands.

"Yeah, it was cool." Alba dropped her backpack onto the ground and arched her back while looking around. "Unfortunately, it doesn't come with any directions. I have no idea where exactly we are."

Only a wide expanse of the same plush green grass seemed to surround us in every direction. But Reign pointed towards the horizon. "I'm pretty sure I see something up there. Come on."

Sure enough, after walking for several minutes, we came to a tennis court. Then we passed a basketball court, then a pool with a pool house bigger than my house in Dubbsburg. Then, finally, we came to the mansion. It was a sprawling house, with numerous patios and nooks, and doors all over the place. We tried the first five doors we saw but found them all locked.

"Well, how do we get in?" asked Sweets.

Libby pointed towards another, smaller pool closer to the house. It was just off a side patio that had sliding glass doors leading to the house. One of the pool chairs had a towel strewn across it, and a fruity beverage sat on a side table with a bottle of sunscreen lying next to it. "That one."

"Looks like a safe bet," I agreed. "Come on."

Keeping low so we wouldn't be spotted, we tried the sliding door, and sure enough, it slid right open. The door led to an oversized living area with high ceilings and big bright windows that overlooked the pool. The furnishings were all beige and white and looked like something that had been ripped right out of a home furnishings magazine.

"Oh my gosh, I can't believe we're in Dixie Carlton's house right now!" squealed Holly.

Sweets nodded, equally starstruck. "This *is* pretty exciting! Just think, we might even get to meet her!"

Alba lightly fingered a platinum record plaque hanging on the wall. "That's the plan."

Suddenly a scream tore through the quiet of the living room, followed by the sound of glass shattering. The group of us turned to find a blonde bombshell in a barely-there black bikini and a filmy kimono-style cover-up standing in front of broken glass with a puddle of pink slush at her feet. Painted with a distinct Southern twang, Dixie's fierce voice filled every corner of the room as she shouted out, "Don't move! I'm calling security!"

Holly's hands shot up in the air defensively. "Please!

Ms. Carlton! You don't need to call security. We're totally not here to hurt you!"

She struggled to keep her eyes glued to us while also dialing her phone. "How'd you get in here?"

"Through the back. The sliding door was unlocked," I said, pointing over our shoulder.

"Goran, get in here now! There's been a security breach," she yelled into her phone. Hanging up, she stared at the group of us. "My security team will be here any second, so don't try anything! I don't understand how you managed to get past them. You must have climbed the fence or something."

My brother stepped forward holding his hands out to show that he was unarmed, "Ms. Carlton, we're so sorry for breaking in. But there's an urgent situation that we needed to speak to you about immediately."

Dixie looked my brother up and down. The look in her eyes suggested she liked the look of him but was too upset over our intrusion to respond.

"Listen, Dixie," said Alba, creeping forward slowly, her hands out in front of her. "I know you're freaked out, and we don't blame you at all. But we've come a long way to speak to you, and this'll only take a minute."

"Stop right there!" Dixie bellowed as a team of security guards in brown uniforms flooded into the room.

One of the security guards grabbed Holly's arm. "Please, Ms. Carlton," begged Holly as he began to pull her towards the exit. "We swear we won't hurt you."

An oversized man with bulging arms and a mullet grabbed my arm and pulled it behind my back roughly. "Ouch!" I couldn't help but squeal as the security guard jacked my arm up into a hammerlock behind my back, sending a searing stab of pain through my shoulder. "Easy!"

"Dixie, please!" begged Holly. "We're students at your old school."

"Take them away," she hollered to the guards.

"We go to the Institute. We have important Council business to discuss with you!" I hollered just as the guard had me to the doorway.

Dixie's head whipped around. "Wait! Andre, wait!" She looked at me. "Did you just say the Institute?"

I nodded. "Yes. You were a member of the Council last year. We have some very important questions to ask you. It'll only take a second."

She looked all of us up and down. "So, you're all…" She glanced up at her security guards as her sentence trailed off.

We all nodded.

"Yes!" said Holly.

She cleared her throat and straightened her posture. Once composed, she gave a slight head tilt towards her apparent head of security. "Goran, thank you. But I'll handle this. Please ask the rest of your team to let us be."

"But, Ms. Carlton, I highly recommend—"

Dixie shook her blond head. "No recommendations needed. I'll be fine. You may go." She extended her arm and her fingers fluttered towards the door. "Oh! And, Goran, please send someone in to clean up this mess." She glanced down at the glass and the spilled drink.

Goran didn't look pleased, but he snapped his fingers and pointed to the hallway anyway. Andre and the rest of the security staff let all of us go and filed out the door like puppies with their tails between their legs.

"Thank you!" I said with a flourish, dusting off my shirt.

Holly rushed back inside the living room. "Oh, Ms. Carlton, you have *no idea* how thankful we are that you'll see us! And we're so sorry for breaking into your beautiful home and scaring you."

Alba shot Holly a look that plainly read *kiss-ass*.

I nodded and walked towards her calmly. "Yes. Thank you, Dixie. Now, down to business. We've got an important Council matter to discuss with you."

She held a finger up to her lips to silence me and pointed at the glass sliding doors. "Outside," she mouthed before leading the way onto the patio. When we'd all filed outside, she shut the glass door behind us and then strode over to her lounge chair and sat down.

As I stared down at Dixie Carlton, in her strappy black two-piece that barely served to cover her important parts, it finally hit me that *this* was the woman I'd watched in movies and had seen gracing the cover of countless magazines. Dixie Carlton was a major celebrity and fashion icon, and it was no wonder. Even without makeup on, she was gorgeous. She was curvy, but toned. She had bleached blond hair, a deep golden tan, and a splay of freckles across the bridge of her nose that gave her a down-to-earth look, making her seem approachable and real. Her Instagram feed portrayed her to be the girl-next-door type. Always in plaid shirts tied high at the waist or off-the-shoulder crop tops, Dixie seemed to like her tall cowboy boots and her cutoff denim shorts.

The young woman, now reclining comfortably, pulled her sunglasses off her head and pulled them on over her eyes before exhaling a big puff of air. "There, that's better." She looked up at the group of us, all staring back at her. "Alright. Let's start over, shall we? Exactly who are you, and what do you want?"

Jax, who had kept fairly quiet thus far, rushed forward with an extended hand. "Ms. Carlton, it's so nice to meet you. I'm such a big fan of yours. I'm Jax. These are my friends. We're all students at the Institute. Well, except Reign. He's my cousin and her brother." She pointed at me.

Dixie lightly shook Jax's hand but dropped it the second she mentioned Reign. She quirked a brow and lowered her glasses so she could peer over them at him. "Reign, is it? Do you attend the wizard school next door?"

Reign shook his head. "Nah, I've never gone there. But my father runs the place."

Dixie looked stunned as she bolted upright and peeled off her glasses. "Shut up! Merrick Stone is your father?!"

"You know him?"

"Well, of course I know him!" she said excitedly. "I went to the Institute, you know. That was many years ago, though. Back before, all of *this*…" She lifted her arms up to show she meant the big house and pool and whatnot. She shook her head. "I should have known you were related. You look just like him."

"I'm his niece," said Jax, her eyes wide. "Sorceress Stone is my mother."

That seemed to shock Dixie. Her eyes widened. "Sorceress Stone had kids? I had no idea!"

Jax lifted a shoulder. "Well, just one kid. Me."

Holly rushed forward next to shake Dixie's hand. "Ms. Carlton, I would just like to say what a fan I am of your work," she gushed. "And I had no idea that you were actually a witch. I mean, I'd heard the rumors, but I didn't believe them."

Dixie nodded. "Yes, that little nugget of information got released by a salty ex. After the breakup, he tried like hell to ruin my career. Thankfully none of my fans bought it. The public all saw him as being petty and flocked to support me. It was a win-win. Little did they know it was the truth. But I do like to keep that part of my life under wraps, so if you don't mind keeping this to yourselves? People can be so judgmental."

"Oh, of course! Of course!" said Holly.

Dixie pointed at her then. "Wait, are you wearing one of my shirts?"

Holly looked down at her top. It was a navy-and-white polka dot tube top that cinched her breasts together with a giant matching bow. "Yes! I ordered a few of your spring pieces, and they just came in the mail the other day! I think this one might be my favorite!"

Dixie nodded at her in approval. "It looks good on you. Very flattering."

Holly's eyes widened. She'd just gotten a compliment from one of her favorite celebrities. Knowing Holly, I was sure she was bursting with excitement. It was more than likely we'd hear about that compliment for the rest of our lives. "Thank you! Thank you so much!"

"Now, tell me—what kind of Council business is so pressing that you had to come all the way to Nashville to break into my house just to talk to me?"

"Well, Dixie," began Alba, "we're having this issue with the new Council."

Dixie's brows furrowed. "An issue? What kind of issue?"

Alba glanced over at Jax, then back to Dixie. "Someone on the Council did something, umm, bad."

"Bad? Like what?"

"I'm actually not at liberty to say right now. But here's the situation. We just came to learn that all of the Council members are usually... well, they're usually..." She paused as she tried to come up with the right word.

"Big names," I supplied. "Like you. And the retired senator lady."

"And the infomercial girl," added Sweets.

"Ahh, yes, Avery Brooks. Her and I became good friends during our time on the Council together. She's going to be in one of my new music videos."

Jax smiled from ear to ear. "That's so cool!"

"So, anyway," said Alba, "we happened to notice that this *new* Council that was appointed by you guys isn't exactly as big of a deal as most of the other Councils have been."

"Yes, that's true," agreed Dixie. "Some of the Council members were concerned about that. I, personally, didn't see the big deal."

"So we were wondering if you could tell us who appointed all of the new members?" said Reign.

Dixie adjusted herself on her chair. "Well, I know that I appointed Daphne Fletcher. I know she's not nationally famous or anything, but she's very well known in Texas. She's a member of the Texas Army National Guard, and it just so happened that she single-handedly saved the house I grew up in from a particularly bad hurricane. To this day, my parents still live in that house, and we've all got Daphne to thank for it. So when I found out that old Council members get to appoint new Council members, I was adamant that she be my appointee, especially after she got sick this past year. I thought it would do her some good to get out after she'd holed herself up for so long."

Alba nodded. "What about the rest of the Council? Who appointed them?"

"Umm, I'm pretty sure Harlow appointed the rest of them."

I pulled the folded-up list out of my back pocket and scanned the list of names. There was Dixie Carlton, Avery Brooks, Sally Murtaugh, Jill Dennisen, and Harlow Smith. *Harlow Smith*. Where had I heard that name before?

Dixie drummed the fingers of one hand on her temple. "If I recall correctly, the rest of the Council was super hesitant to appoint some of the lesser-known names. They thought doing so undermined the role we played in the paranormal community. Like the club they were in would become less exclusive if just *anybody* could get appointed. Harlow told us that we all sounded like a bunch of snobs. She said that was an outdated tradition, and that we needed to put together a Council that was more relatable. Of course the Council balked at the idea, but Harlow suggested they could compromise by appointing more local celebrity types. Like Poppy Ellabee was one we all knew well. She'd been a teacher at the Institute for years, and everyone knew and loved her."

"So then the Council just let Harlow finish appointing the rest of the members?" asked Alba.

Dixie nodded. "Pretty much. I mean, she had a list of ideas and they were all pretty good ones. No one had a reason to reject any of them, so with my one appointee, and her four appointees, it made quick work of the selection process. Which was fine with me. I had a movie shoot to get to that day, so leaving early really helped me out a lot."

Libby shook her head. "I'm sorry. My sister and I aren't from America, so maybe this is a stupid question, but who is Harlow Smith? I've never heard of her."

Jax nodded too. "It's not just you, Libby. I've never heard of her either."

I was glad that Libby had asked, because I'd been wondering the exact same thing.

"Harlow is the daughter of Wade and Delores Crandall," said Dixie as if that explained why she was considered a "big name."

Libby wrinkled her nose. "Who are Wade and Delores Crandall?"

"Yeah, I've never heard of them either," said Alba.

"I'm sure you've heard of the Crandall Hotel Group?" asked Dixie.

Several of us nodded, myself included. "They own lots of big-name luxury hotels and resorts, don't they?"

Dixie nodded. "Yes. They're huge. They've slowly been buying out other hotel brands and adding them to their extensive list of properties. Anyway, Wade and his brother Ernest own the company. So Harlow is—"

"An heiress to millions," breathed Holly.

"Yes. And when she was younger, she came out as a paranormal in the media. She kind of went through this wild and crazy phase, like so many children in the public eye do. Her parents sent her away to the Institute to take care of their *problem* child, and she ended up refining her skills and making something of herself." Dixie shrugged. "She's been working for her father's company ever since."

Reign pinched the back of my arm discreetly. "Hey, sis, can I talk to you privately for a second?"

Dixie pointed at me. "This is your sister? And that's your cousin?"

Reign nodded.

"Wow, this really is a family affair."

"Yeah. I just need to talk to my sister privately for a moment, if you'll all excuse us?"

While Reign pulled me aside, Holly, Jax, Sweets, and Libby took the opportunity to ask Dixie for autographs. Alba and Cinder didn't like being out of the loop, so they followed us over to the other side of the pool.

"What's going on?" asked Alba.

Reign looked down at me. "Do you recognize that name?"

I shook my head in confusion. "Which name?"

"Harlow Crandall?"

"I mean, I thought the name Harlow sounded familiar, but I couldn't remember where I'd heard it before."

"Yeah, it took me a minute, but I finally remembered where I'd heard it. Remember when we went back in time and you and I were hiding on the front porch of our grandparents' house and listening to their conversation? They were talking about a Harlow Crandall then."

I could picture Reign and me looking in the window, but I had to squeeze my eyes shut to recall what they'd been talking about. That was when it hit me. "Harlow Crandall! That was the name of the woman that Samson Smith left Auggie Stone for!"

Reign nodded and pointed at me. "Bingo."

38

"*I* can't believe this," breathed Jax as we rushed back to the time machine. "So my grandfather remarried Harlow Crandall after divorcing my grandmother? I have a step-grandmother I've never met before?!"

I looked at Jax in surprise. "You mean you've met your grandfather before?"

Jax's eyes widened. "No. Why? Have you met him?"

"No, I haven't met him! Just the way you said you have a step-grandmother you've never met before made it sound like she was the only one you'd never met."

"Oh, no. I haven't met either one of them. I don't know anything about my grandfather. Or really my grandmother, for that matter. My family is so tight-lipped about everything."

"So, Harlow Smith is Sorceress Stone's stepmother," said Alba. "This is an interesting development in our case."

"Interesting development in your case?" Jax looked around curiously. "What case?"

I stared at Alba. I couldn't believe she'd practically spilled the beans.

Alba looked like a deer caught in the headlights. "Oh. Nothing, just this Council case we're helping out with. It's no big deal. Really."

"Plus, Jax, you weren't going to ask any questions," chided Sweets.

"Darn it!" said Jax. "I keep forgetting. I'll try and keep my mouth closed from here on out, I promise!"

"I think our next stop should be getting to know Harlow Smith, don't you?" Cinder asked Alba.

Alba nodded. "I was just thinking that. Okay, everyone in the sauna. We're headed to Samson and Harlow Smith's home!"

The crickets chirped with reckless abandon as we stood on the sidewalk across the street from Harlow and Samson Smith's home in the early hours of the evening. When we'd arrived in the quaint hillside village, it had only taken us stops in three different shops before we'd found someone who recognized the name and was able to point us to the right home. Though we'd neglected to ask for the current date, we were able to judge by the cars and the clothing styles and predicted with confidence that we weren't in the current decade. It was more than likely that we'd landed ourselves several decades in the past, only how far in the past, we weren't sure.

I was thankful that darkness had already started to fall around us. This gave us an opportunity to snoop without it being obvious. The house we stared at was a two-story Tudor with an attached carport on one side, fronted by a wooden trellis covered in climbing red roses. Parked beneath the carport was a light blue hatchback that looked straight out of an old movie. Between the parked car and the lights in the house being on, we felt confident that someone in the Smith family was home.

"I can't believe this is my grandfather's house!" said Jax, sucking in her breath excitedly. She looked up at Reign. His face was solemn, showing us all just how indifferent he felt. "He's your grandfather too, Reign. Aren't you excited?"

Reign lifted a shoulder. "I don't think *excited* is the word. He left our grandmother and our parents when they were little kids, Jax. I guess that's not something I condone."

Jax lowered her head. "Yeah, I guess," she whispered.

Reign put a hand on her shoulder and gave her a little squeeze. "But I'll admit, I *am* curious."

She smiled lightly. "Yeah, me too."

Alba turned her eyes towards the lit-up house. "So, are we just gonna be Peeping Toms again? Or are we gonna try to get inside the house this time."

"Alba!" said Sweets in surprise. "You don't seriously want to break into their house. We'll get in trouble!"

"Yeah, but only if we get caught," said Alba. She pointed at the carport. "There's gotta be an entrance on that side. Back in the day, people in these little communities never locked their doors. I'm willing to bet that one's unlocked."

One by one we snuck across the street and up the Smiths' driveway until all eight of us were pressed up against the side of their house. Alba tried the door handle.

"Dang it," she whispered. "It's locked. I was sure it'd be open."

Libby rolled her eyes and pointed her finger at the lock, freezing it instantaneously. Once it was frozen, she hit the door handle with the heel of her hand. The knob shattered into pieces and the door fell open.

"Nice," said Alba with a smile.

Libby and Alba slid into the house first, followed by Cinder and Sweets, then Holly and Jax, then me, and finally, Reign brought up the rear. Inside, we found the group had reassembled inside a small bathroom at the end of a long hallway. We almost didn't all fit inside the bathroom. Sweets, Holly, and Reign had to stand in the tub while the rest of us crowded the floor. A set of voices from down the hallway poured out.

"I don't know what we're going to do with her," a low male voice said clearly.

A woman's voice chimed in immediately. "You're too hard on her. Give it a little time."

"Too hard on her? I'm not too hard on her."

"Yes, you are, Samson. You expect too much. You've always expected too much."

"I don't expect enough," snapped the male voice, whom we now knew was none other than Reign and Jax's grandfather, Samson Smith.

Crouched in the doorway of the bathroom, Jax looked up at me, her eyes lighting up. "I wanna see my grandfather!" Without another word, she duck-walked out of the bathroom before I could stop her.

Alba lurched around my shoulder. "Jax! Get back here."

But Jax kept going, out of the bathroom and down the small hallway that appeared to lead into the kitchen. My heart sank. What if she was caught? She had no powers to defend herself.

"I'll go with her," I whispered, taking off next.

Alba reached out to try and stop me from following, but I kept going. Jax couldn't go alone. It wasn't safe.

As I got into a crouched position up against the wall next to Jax, the voices continued. "I think we should send her to boarding school," said Samson. "She'll learn more there than what we could ever teach her here."

Jax and I peeked our heads around the corner.

"She doesn't want to go to boarding school," said the woman's voice. We had to assume it was Harlow Smith. "She likes her school here. The children there don't know her. She'll be made fun of, Samson. I don't want to do that to my daughter. I can't, and I won't." From where we crouched, we could barely see Harlow leaned up against the kitchen counter. She didn't look very tall. In fact, she wasn't what I'd pictured some rich hotel heiress looking like at all. I'd pictured a tall brunette with an exotic tan and supermodel good looks. This woman was almost the opposite. She was stocky, with sandy blond hair and pasty white skin.

"Harlow, let me be clear. This isn't up to you. She's *my* daughter too, and I'm putting my foot down," Samson growled.

Jax and I stared at each other in shock. Samson and Harlow had a daughter together?! Jax had another aunt?!

"You don't think I have a say in this?!" Harlow strode across the kitchen, moving out of my line of sight.

"We did it your way long enough. I'm enrolling her in boarding school. I know of one not far away. She'll start at the beginning of next month."

"Next month? School here doesn't start again until the fall! You're being unreasonable!"

The voices continued, but then we heard a door slam at the front of the house. Jax looked up at me as I mashed my lips between my teeth. My heart pumped faster. I prayed there was another entrance to the kitchen from the front of the house and that whoever had just come in wouldn't be coming down our hallway.

"She's home," hissed Harlow. "Not a word about boarding school. It's her last day of school, and I want her to enjoy her break before you force her to spend her entire summer vacation away from home."

"No, we'll tell her today. She'll thank us for it some-day," said Samson coarsely.

"Samson, don't you dare." Suddenly Harlow's voice went from a threatening snarl to a sugary-sweet liquid. "Hi, honey! How was your last day of school?"

Jax and I craned our necks trying to catch a glimpse of Samson and Harlow's daughter, but the cabinets obscured our view.

"Eh, it was okay. We didn't do much," said a young-sounding girl's voice. I wondered how old she was. She couldn't have been more than ten or twelve. "We had to wipe down our desks, and we helped our teacher clean out her room. We had a picnic on the playground for lunch, and then we watched a video for the rest of the day."

"And you had fun at Heather's house after school?"

"Yeah."

"Did a lot of girls show up for the party?"

"Most of our class."

Then Samson's voice sounded again. "Well, I'm glad you're home. There's something your mother and I need to speak to you about."

"Can I have a snack first? Lunch was a bologna sandwich, and I hate bologna sandwiches."

"Didn't Heather's mother have snacks at the party?"

"She did, but I'm still hungry."

"Okay, well, I bought some of those really good apples. Can I slice you one of those?"

"Do we have any cupcakes left?"

"You don't need any more sweets. You should have an apple," snapped her father.

"Samson!" chastised Harlow. "She'd like a cupcake. It's her last day of school. She's allowed to have a treat to celebrate."

"Thanks, Mom," said the girl.

We could hear feet shuffling around the counter, and the next thing I knew, the girl stood in plain sight with her back to us. She had the same body type as her mother, short and fairly thick. She had short blond hair and seemed to walk with a limp. Something about that limp seemed very familiar.

"Now that you've gotten your snack, there's something we need to get out on the table."

The little girl noshed on her cupcake. "Get what out on the table, Daddy?"

"Your summer plans."

"I'm going to spend my summer reading," said the girl excitedly. "I've already got a stack of books waiting for me. I can't wait!"

"Spend the summer reading? How about you spend the summer practicing your craft?"

"Practicing my craft? You mean magic? Daddy, you know I really don't do magic very well."

"If you tried harder and practiced more, you'd get it. All of your older siblings know magic quite well, and they knew it before they were even your age. You're almost twelve years old, Stella. You should be much further along then you are."

My eyes widened. *Stella?* I knew Jax wouldn't get the reference, but if the rest of the group had heard it, they certainly would. I glanced down the hallway. Alba had her head stuck out of the bathroom and was just as dumbstruck as I was. *It couldn't be?*

"But, Daddy, I don't like doing magic. I'd rather read a book." The girl leaned on the counter, and from that angle, I could finally see her face. Though she was considerably younger, I could definitely see the outline of Stella Blackwood's face. Finally! We'd tied Stella Blackwood to Sorceress Stone!

"You're going to learn how to do magic whether you like it or not. Your big sister SaraLynn is amazing at doing magic. In fact, I hear that she's already at the top of her class. She'll likely go on to do amazing things and have an amazing life."

"Samson, you know I hate it when you compare Stella to Auggie's children," snapped Harlow.

"Why doesn't SaraLynn ever come here to visit?"

asked Stella. "Or BethAnn or Merrick? Don't they want to meet me?"

"Stella, don't you understand? Your brother and sisters are just so busy doing amazing things that they don't have the time to come and see you. Maybe if you'd do amazing things, they'd want to meet you."

From somewhere in the kitchen, Harlow sucked in her breath. "Samson!"

Little Stella didn't seem to notice her father's mean words. "But I don't know how to do amazing things. I just want to read. I like reading, Daddy."

"Well, there are a lot of things you can do in the paranormal world that require reading."

"Like what?"

"I don't know. Like research. And potions."

"Research and potions? Ugh, that doesn't sound fun."

"Regardless, Stella, you're going to boarding school. So enjoy the rest of this month. Next month, you start at your new school."

"New school? But, Daddy, I don't want to go to a new school!"

"No buts, Stella. It's final. Now I'm going up to my room. I've had a long day, and I'm exhausted. Oh, and Harlow, please stop feeding this child sweets. Look at her. She's much too big for a child of this age. I've seen pictures, and SaraLynn was half this size when she was her age."

"Samson! How dare you compare the children! It's not right."

When Samson didn't answer, we realized he'd already left the room through another door. We could hear the girl crying as her mother comforted her from across the room. "Oh, Stella, sweetheart. He doesn't mean it. He's just had a hard day."

"Daddy doesn't love me as much as he loves the other kids," whispered Stella through sobs. "I know it."

"Oh, he does too. He just has a poor way of showing it. I'll talk to him."

"Thanks, Mommy."

"Now, finish up your snack and run upstairs and take a bath while I finish cleaning the kitchen."

Before they could say their goodbyes, I tugged on Jax and led her down the hallway. Passing the bathroom, I waved at the group inside. "Let's go," I mouthed to Alba.

Seconds later, the group of us stood outside the home of young Stella Blackwood, feeling like we'd all just received the shock of a lifetime.

39

*I*t might have been dark when we left Stella's small hillside village, but we found the sun peeking up above the eastern horizon when we arrived back in present-day Aspen Falls. Our short walk through time had been both dark and quiet, as no one spoke a word until we'd emerged from the steam sauna into the light, feeling both stunned and curious.

"I can't believe how mean my grandfather was to the aunt I never knew I had," said Jax, her voice filled with both shock and sorrow.

Alba put both hands on her hips. "Listen, Shorty. The least of our problems right now is that your grandfather was mean." She looked at all of us seriously then. "Alright. I don't think we can keep this secret from her any longer. I think it's time the kid knows what happened to her mother."

Jax's eyes widened as her head whipped around to stare at Alba. "My mother?! What happened to my mother?"

"Alba, are you sure this is such a good idea?" asked Holly.

"We have no choice. We have a lot of things we need to figure out, and I think now that we have all of the pieces of the puzzle, I think it's time we went to the Council with everything we know."

Jax wrinkled her nose. "What are you guys talking about? Does this have something to do with you trying to make me a witch?"

I shook my head. "I wish it did, Jax. We tried to make you a witch, we really tried. But this is about something else. Something that took precedence over us trying to get your powers for you. For the most part, it's what we've been working on since we've been gone."

"Ohhhkay?" said Jax, looking at each of us curiously. Her eyes narrowed in on Reign, who couldn't look her in the eye. "Reign, why don't *you* tell me what's going on?"

"Me?" he asked, pointing at himself.

Her head bobbed up and down.

"Well, Nugget. You see…" Reign rubbed a hand across the back of his neck. "It's about SaraLynn and the Council."

"Oh no. Did she do something to make the Council mad at her?"

Reign nodded. "They certainly are mad at her. At least they were…"

"Were? They aren't mad at her anymore?" Jax looked around, confused.

I shoved my brother out of the way so I could look Jax directly in the face. This information needed to come from me. "Jax, you remember the day you were home sick?"

"Yeah?"

"Well, while you were gone, Brittany called us all into an assembly, and she delayed finals week until next week."

Jax looked shock. "She did? Why?"

"Well, because something happened to your mom during a Council meeting."

"What happened?" Suddenly Jax sucked in her breath and her eyes widened. "Omigosh. Did my mom get fired?! Is that what all this is about?"

"I wish it were that easy, Jax. No, Sorceress Stone didn't get fired." I took both of her hands. "Jax, she got killed."

Jax pulled her head back. She furrowed her brows. "Killed? What do you mean?"

"Killed Jax. Like dead. Sorceress Stone is dead," I squeaked, my heart lodged squarely in the back of my throat.

"Dead? No way. My mom's not dead."

"Jax, she is dead," said Sweets with a nod. "I'm so sorry, sweetie."

"Yeah, Jax," agreed Holly. "I'm sorry too."

"We're sorry too," whispered Libby.

"Shorty, we tried lots of things. We went back in time to stop the murder from happening, but it didn't work. It happened in literally the blink of an eye."

Jax, whose jaw had yet to shut, blinked several times. Finally, she closed her mouth and looked at Reign curiously. "Is it true, Reign? Is my mom dead?"

Reign swallowed hard. He had to force his eyes to look up at her. "Yeah, Jax. It's true."

Jax's knees looked like they might give out as she stumbled backwards.

"Catch her!" hollered Sweets.

Alba and Reign both shot out their magic to catch her midfall. Slowly, they lowered her to the ground until Jax was seated on the soft grass.

"Is this a dream?" Jax whispered.

I crawled onto the grass in front of her. "Jax, it's not a dream. I'm so sorry."

She looked up at all of us with tears beginning to cloud her eyes. "But you're all witches. Why didn't you bring her back to life?!"

"It's still possible," said Libby, sitting down on the grass in front of me. "I froze her. She's stowed away safely in the tower. I'll unthaw her, and maybe we can come up with a way to bring her back."

"But why didn't you do it already?!" sobbed Jax.

"Because we needed to figure out who murdered her first. Otherwise we were afraid whoever it was would just kill her all over again. We had to solve the mystery first, and we haven't been able to do it yet."

"I don't understand how this happened. She was murdered? Why?"

"We're not really sure," said Alba. "We have a lot of suspects, and we're trying to narrow it down."

Jax ground at her eyes. "Who are the suspects?"

"The Council," I said sadly.

Jax's eyes popped open wide. "The Council? The Great Witches Council?"

"Yeah."

"The *whole* Council?"

I nodded. "They all had motive, means, and opportunity. One of them did it. We just have to figure out which one."

"They all had motives to kill my mom? What were their motives?"

Alba shook her head. "I know you want answers to all these questions, Shorty, but I'm gonna be honest with you. Going into that time portal makes time out here move at different speeds. Time's running out. By the look of that sun, it's not Friday anymore. If I had to bet, I'd bet it's Saturday already."

"Saturday?!" bellowed Jax. "My birthday is tomorrow?"

Cinder shook her head. "And graduation is tomorrow too. We haven't even begun to work on our project."

"Don't worry," said Libby. "Tonight. We still have tonight, Cinder. We'll get it figured out."

"Tomorrow's Mother's Day," whispered Jax as sobs began to rack her body. "Now I don't have a mother anymore?"

Reign got down on his knees and put his arms around Jax. "I'm so sorry. We're still working. Maybe there's more we can do."

"Like what?" bawled Jax.

"For starters, we have to solve her murder," said Alba, taking charge once again. "Shorty, I know you're grieving, but we have to keep moving. After discovering that Stella Blackwood is Stone's half-sister, we have to ask ourselves why she didn't mention that when we interviewed her."

I nodded. "I was thinking the same thing. She lied to us!"

Holly shook her head. "Technically it wouldn't be a lie. We asked her when she first met Sorceress Stone. Maybe they never met until this week."

"Well, then, she withheld important information," I said.

"She could have told us," said Holly, nodding. "But Elodie didn't mention that her daughter had had serious problems with Sorceress Stone and that she'd been expelled."

"And Poppy didn't mention that Stone had bought the Institute out from underneath her," agreed Libby.

"And Gemma Overbrook made it sound like she and Stone were old buddies," added Alba. "She never mentioned that they'd fought over a boy and over class rank."

"And then there's Daphne," I added. "She had that secret that Sorceress Stone was threatening to divulge."

"But I find it really suspicious that Harlow Smith added her daughter and three other witches that all had grudges against Stone to the Council." Alba shook her head. "That's what's standing out to me."

"But she didn't add Daphne," said Holly. "Dixie did."

"And yet somehow Daphne still wound up with a motive to kill Stone," said Alba.

"Somewhat of a motive. Sorceress Stone knew about her secret, but Daphne said herself that she was getting her powers back. It wasn't exactly as big of a bombshell as people might have wanted us to believe," I said.

Alba wagged a finger in the air. "Okay, so let's just say that Stella was the one behind this. So her mother adds all of these people with motives to the Council so the finger isn't pointed at her. Except one of the members doesn't have a motive, Daphne. Now, Stella has to come up with a motive for her."

"But how would she know Daphne's secret?" asked Holly, confused.

I shook my head. I wasn't sure how she'd have figured that out either. "I don't know, but we need to find out if Gemma was the one that told Sorceress Stone Daphne's secret. Because if she wasn't, I think we need to find out who did."

Alba nodded. "I think you're right. We need to talk to the Council."

I looked over at Jax. Her head was on Reign's shoulder as she sobbed. He was doing his best to comfort her. "Jax, we have to go. We need to talk to the Council. We're going to get to the bottom of this, I promise!"

Reign smoothed back Jax's hair. "It's okay. You guys go on ahead, I'll carry Jax. She's not in any condition to walk right now."

I nodded and the group of us took off towards campus.

"*H*obbs, we need to see the Council. ASAP," said Alba as we rushed into Brittany's office, where we found her seated at her desk in a very formal pale pink suit. Alba wrinkled her nose. "Why are you dressed like that?"

Brittany looked down at her outfit. "I like to dress up for graduation." Then she glanced over at us. "Tell me you girls are sprucing up a little. You look like you've been through the grinder."

"Graduation!" gasped Libby. "But graduation is on Sunday."

Brittany nodded. "Yes. Today's Sunday. I hope you've all remembered to call your mothers and wish them a happy Mother's Day."

All eyes widened in shock. "Mother's Day? It's Sunday?" I gasped.

"Yes, and let me tell you girls, the Council is so upset with all of you. After everything you've put them through, they've all agreed that if you don't end this investigation by the time the graduation ceremony is complete, they're informing Detective Whitman about Sorceress Stone's death, and then they're all going back to where they came from."

"But they can't do that!" said Jax as she and Reign came around the corner.

Brittany's face fell. "Oh! Jax!" She rushed around the desk and threw her arms around the girl. "I'm so sorry for your loss. I really liked your mom. She was a misunderstood woman, but deep down, she wanted what was best for this school and all of the students."

Tears sprang loose from Jax's eyes. "I know she did," she squealed before breaking into a full-out sob again.

"It's still raw," I said to Brittany.

She nodded and squeezed Jax one more time. "And I know it's your birthday, sweetheart. Happy birthday. Your mom would have loved to be here for your big day."

"Happy birthday?" whispered Jax. "It's Sunday? I thought it was Saturday."

Brittany looked at us with confusion. "You're all a day behind?"

Alba waved a hand dismissively at the school's secretary. "We just need to get in touch with the Council. Are they in their rooms?"

Brittany pointed. "No, they're in the teachers' lounge, preparing for graduation."

"Thanks, Hobbs," said Alba as she took off for the door.

Brittany looked down at her watch. "Graduation is in two hours!" she hollered as we all ran out of the room. "You should be getting ready!"

40

"*N*ow we will never graduate," Cinder muttered under her breath as we waited in front of the teachers' lounge for someone on the Council to open the door.

Reign had decided that Jax wasn't ready to face the Council and her mother's killer yet, so they stayed behind in the dorm lobby.

"We will graduate, Cinder," Libby assured her. "We will do Alba's suggestion of the bonfire. Everything will turn out alright."

Alba nodded. "See? My idea came in handy after all. You're welcome."

"Your idea did not come in handy. Your idea wouldn't get us graduated from junior kindergarten, let alone from a witch's institute of higher learning."

"You don't know that," grumbled Alba as Gemma Overbrook opened the door.

The woman's green eyes narrowed on us. "There you are! Finally! After all this time you've returned." She opened the door, allowing us in, and turned to stare at the rest of the Council. "Look! They've finally returned."

Elodie shook her head. "Gemma's right. You girls have been gone for far too long. We should have notified the local authorities by now."

"We already agreed. We're notifying them the minute the ceremony is complete," snapped Gemma.

Alba nodded. "We know, we know. We heard. Listen, we're making some serious headway into the case."

Gemma's eyes widened. "And how are you doing that if you're not even on campus? You've been MIA for days now!"

"We have spent the week doing research on each of you," explained Cinder. "We have deduced that each of you had a motive to kill Sorceress Stone."

Stella's eyes widened as she gasped. "I certainly didn't have a motive to kill her! I didn't even know her!"

Daphne nodded in agreement. "I didn't have a motive either!"

"Oh, but you both did," said Alba. "Just like the other three did."

"And you all withheld information or flat out lied to us," said Holly.

"I did no such thing," said Poppy.

"Oh, but you did, Poppy. You neglected to tell us that you'd been the front-runner to purchase the Institute before Sorceress Stone slid in at the last moment and bought it out from underneath you," said Alba.

"That was years ago. I've gotten over that."

"Are you sure? Because I feel like you're still salty about it."

"I'm completely sure."

"And, Elodie, you told us that your daughter went to the Institute. You neglected to tell us that your daughter was Tori Decker and that she'd been reprimanded harshly by Sorceress Stone and finally expelled from the Institute."

Poppy's head snapped sideways to look at Elodie in surprise. "SaraLynn expelled Victoria? I had no idea. Why didn't you mention it when we were in executive session and speaking about—"

"I didn't want my business made public. We had enough other claims. We didn't need mine."

"Why didn't you tell us that you'd wanted to purchase the Institute when we were discussing everything?"

Poppy raised an eyebrow. "That was in the past."

Gemma shook her head. "So there are two pieces of information you dug up. Is that all?"

"Hardly," said Cinder.

Alba waved a finger in the air. "Nah. We're just gettin' started." She pointed at Gemma. "Why didn't *you* mention the truth about your relationship with Stone when you were in school together?"

Gemma's face flushed. "I told you we were old schoolmates."

"Yes, but you didn't mention that you not only fought over a boy, but you also fought over your class standing."

"I wouldn't say that we fought—"

Alba crossed her arms over her chest. "There was definitely contention between the two of you."

Gemma narrowed her eyes. "Where are you getting all this information?"

"We have our ways," I said.

"And then there's Stella," said Alba. "Stella Black-wood. Or should I say, Stella Crandall-Smith."

"Crandall-Smith?" said Gemma, shaking her head in confusion. "What does that mean?"

I glanced over at Stella. Her face was white as a sheet.

"Oh, didn't Stella tell you who her family was?" asked Libby.

"No, we've never gotten that personal. I'm not sure that her family matters," said Gemma.

"No, it doesn't matter much—unless it means that you're *related* to the victim," said Alba.

All eyes turned to Stella. Her mouth opened and then immediately snapped shut as color began to flood her face.

"Related to the victim? How?" asked Gemma.

"Stella is Sorceress Stone's sister, as a matter of fact."

"Her parents are Samson and Harlow Smith," I explained.

Daphne looked around, confused. "But I thought Auggie Stone was SaraLynn's mother."

"She is, but Samson Smith is her father, just as he's Stella's father. Isn't that right, Stella?"

Stella looked at me then, daggers nearly shooting out of her eyes. "Well, yes, of course Samson Smith is my father. And yes, it's true, SaraLynn was indeed my half-sister."

"Your half-sister?! Stella, you don't think you should have shared that piece of information with us?" asked Elodie.

"Let me finish," breathed Stella. "She was my half-sister, but in all honesty, she and I had never met! She was estranged from our father. I never even knew her."

Alba wagged a finger in the air. "Oh yeah, you're right. But we also found it interesting that *Harlow Smith* was your mother. Does anyone here recognize that name?"

Stella mashed her lips between her teeth as she stared hatefully at Alba.

Elodie tipped her head sideways. "Wait a second. Harlow Smith was the one that nominated me to the Council."

Gemma's head bobbed up and down. "She nominated me as well."

Poppy grimaced. "I was surprised when she'd nominated me, too. It didn't make any sense at the time. But now I'm wondering if this wasn't all one big conspiracy."

Stella shook her head. "You're all reading way too much into this. I have no idea why my mother nominated all of you. She never said a word to me about it." Then she pointed at Daphne. "Did my mother nominate you too?"

Daphne shook her head. "No, actually Dixie Carlton did."

"See!" shouted Stella. "This isn't a conspiracy. None of this makes any sense."

"You know, I'm glad you brought up Daphne," said Alba. "We have a few questions about her motive."

"From the very beginning when we did our interviews, we discovered that Sorceress Fletcher's motive was never very strong," I explained.

Poppy shook her head. "What was her motive?"

I glanced over at Daphne.

She gave a slight nod and then began to speak. "About a year ago I got influenza, followed by a horrible case of pneumonia. While I was sick, I discovered that my powers had begun to wane."

Elodie's eyes widened. "That's only what happens when a witch gets sick!"

Daphne nodded at her. "Yes, I know that. And because of my age and my illness, my magic was very weak. I took a few classes at Gemma's online school. I was using it as a way to regain lost strength. Anyway, somehow SaraLynn found out and threatened to tell the people who I provide contractual services to."

"She was threatening you?" gasped Stella.

Daphne lifted a shoulder. "To be truthful, it wasn't that much of a threat. I'm old. I knew I was getting to retirement age sooner or later. I didn't think it was that big of a deal. My powers have gradually started to return, but I don't think they'll ever be what they were."

I leaned back against the table that sat in the middle of the teachers' lounge. "One of our burning questions is how Sorceress Stone found out your secret." I looked at Gemma. "One would think that was classified information."

Gemma's eyes widened as she touched her fingers to her chest. "You think *I* told SaraLynn?"

"Someone told her," shrugged Alba. "We're curious who it was."

Gemma shook her head. "I admit that I knew what was going on, but do you really think I'd ruin my school's reputation by releasing information like that? Never. I didn't tell her."

"Well, someone told her." I looked around the room.

All heads shook. No one wanted to take responsibility for having told Sorceress Stone Daphne's secret.

Alba bounced forward then. "That's what we figured. Well, alright, then. We have a way to find out the truth. It's the same way that we've found out all these little secrets you've all kept from us."

Gemma put a hand on her hip. "If you have a way to get to the truth, then let's hear it! I'd love to have my name crossed off your short list of suspects, because I wasn't the one that told SaraLynn."

"I was hoping you'd say that." Alba strode to the door and opened it. With a sweeping gesture, she invited everyone to leave the room. "Right this way, ladies. I think you'll want to see what we have to show you."

"What in the world is this?!" bellowed Gemma Overbrook as we all stood proudly in front of the time machine, which continued to steam over the small river that ran across the back lawn of our campus.

"It's a time machine," said Alba proudly. "We made it."

"*You* made a time machine?" said Elodie. The shock in her voice told us how impressive that statement was.

Cinder nodded. "We did."

"Does it work?"

"Of course it works," snapped Alba. "We used it to go back in time so we could find out the type of relationship all of you had with Sorceress Stone."

Poppy Ellabee shook her head. "I don't understand. If you made a time machine, then why didn't you just go back in time and stop the murder from happening?"

"We tried," I said sadly. "We went back to Tuesday morning. We saw all of you gathered in the teachers' lounge. We saw Sorceress Stone pacing the floor in front of you. But then, it was as if we blinked, and we missed it. She was dead on the table."

Holly nodded. "It's hard to stop what you can't see happening."

Poppy lifted her brows. "You're absolutely correct. So if you couldn't save SaraLynn with your time machine, then why did you bring us here? We've got a graduation to get to in a couple hours."

"Because we have to solve her murder!" said Alba. "Before you all go back to where you came from! The girls and I are convinced that whoever told Sorceress Stone about Daphne Fletcher's secret was trying to make it look like Daphne had a reason to want Stone dead."

"Maybe she *did* want her dead! Did anyone think of that? Maybe *Daphne* is the murderer!" barked Stella.

Daphne eyed Stella angrily. "I did no such thing, and I certainly didn't *want* SaraLynn dead." She looked at us. "So how is this contraption going to help us find out the truth?"

"Easy," said Alba. "Girls, get everyone inside. Let's show them what we've got!"

The steam sauna was packed, but we managed to get the five Council members, Libby and Cinder, and Alba, Sweets, Holly, and myself into the ring.

"It's hot in here!" said Elodie, tugging at the collar of her shirt.

"Well, it's a steam sauna," agreed Sweets, wiping the perspiration from her own brow. "It's bound to be hot."

"Are we all ready?" asked Alba.

"Ready as we'll ever be," said Poppy. "Let's get this show on the road."

Alba nodded and began to chant.

> *Spirits, spirits, hear us now.*
> *A witch has spilled the beans.*
> *Daphne's secret was revealed.*
> *Was it an accident or just them being mean?*
> *So take us to the day, the month, and hour,*
> *Someone told about Daphne's waning powers.*

We heard the familiar whirling of the wormhole.

All of the members of the Great Witches Council looked around curiously.

"What's that sound?" Elodie asked, her eyes wide.

"It's just the wormhole shifting directions," said Alba, holding open the nearly invisible slit in time. "After you."

One by one, we all crawled through the slit and made our way down the tunnel. I knew we didn't have much time, so I pushed my way to the front of the line and rushed everyone along. At the end of the tunnel, I climbed out into the waiting steam sauna, and then into the light of day. What I saw next took my breath away.

41

*W*hen Holly, the last to emerge, stepped out of the tunnel, she immediately hollered, "Dixie's place? Why are we back at Dixie's place?"

Sure enough, we'd landed squarely in the middle of Dixie Carlton's sprawling, well-manicured lawn, next to her lazy river once again. I shook my head. "I have no idea."

"*Dixie* spilled the beans?" said Sweets, her brows lifted in surprise. "Did she even know about Daphne's secret?"

Daphne slowly raised her hand. "I think I can answer that. When Dixie called me to let me know that she'd decided she wanted to appoint *me* to the Council, I felt that I needed to be completely honest about my situation. I told her the truth, that my powers weren't what they had once been. She told me that was even more of a reason for me to be on the Council. She thought it would help me get my groove back."

"So Dixie knew," I whispered to myself, trying to

piece it all together. "She had to have told Sorceress Stone, then, right?"

"Why would Dixie have told Sorceress Stone? It doesn't make any sense," said Holly.

All of a sudden Daphne made a noise. I turned to see her palming her forehead. "Oh my goodness. I can't believe I didn't think of this sooner. I know exactly what happened."

We all stared at her.

"I told Dixie because I thought it was important that she know the truth. Even though Dixie thought it was no big deal, she did tell me that she'd need to run it past the Council before they voted to approve my appointment. She told me it would be strictly confidential, and though no one ever mentioned it to me, I'm fairly confident the whole sitting Council knew."

"Which means that Harlow knew," said Alba, her brown eyes brightening.

"And since Harlow is Stella's mother, there's a very good chance that Stella knew Daphne's secret too," I said. I couldn't believe it. There it was. Once again, all roads led to Stella Blackwood!

I turned to look at Stella. I wanted to know what she had to say for herself—find out what her defense would be. But when I turned around, she wasn't standing next to me anymore. "Stella?"

As I further turned, I caught sight of her, sneaking into the steam sauna. "Stella's going for the portal. Stop her!"

Alba was the first to dash forward, firing off a green bolt of energy at the sauna. Unsure if she'd succeeded in stopping Stella, Alba poked her head into the steamy ring. A split second later, we heard a scream ring out, and Alba fell to the grass in a big lump, her backpack falling by her side.

"Alba!" I screamed, falling to my knees to find Alba unconscious, but breathing. A red lump had already started to form on the front of her skull.

Before we knew what was happening, we heard the familiar whirling noise of the wormhole moving. Stella had activated the portal!

"Oh no! She's trying to take off in the time machine!" bellowed Sweets.

I leapt to my feet, leaving Alba in a lump on the ground, and tried to push my way into the steamy ring, but found the walls to be impenetrable now. "It's, like, locked or something."

"Locked? It's steam!" cried Cinder. She rushed to stand next to me and pressed against the steam walls too, but her hands couldn't break the barrier either.

"What's going on?" asked Poppy. "Why won't it let you in?"

"I guess because Stella's using it," I said, unsure. Alba was the one who had done all the reading about creating the time machine and time traveling with it. I could only make a simple uneducated guess.

"Using it?! Where's she going?"

Cinder and I shook our heads. Their guesses were as good as ours.

"Back to present-day Aspen Falls, I assume. Does she really think we won't hunt her down once we get back?" I asked.

Poppy's head rolled back on her shoulders. "I don't know, but this is as good of a guilty plea as I've ever seen."

Elodie wrung out her hands in front of herself. "I can't believe Stella would do such a thing! She seemed like such a nice lady."

"I don't know about that. It takes a pretty disturbed individual to commit murder. I mean, who kills their own sister?" asked Daphne, shaking her head. "Something had to have gone wrong in their relationship that we're unaware of."

"When we went back in time, we *saw* Stella's father berating her. He basically made fun of his ten-year-old daughter because she wasn't as good at magic as her sister SaraLynn," I explained to the Council.

"And he was also pretty mean to her about her weight," said Sweets. "I'm sure that hurt her too."

"He kept comparing her to SaraLynn and his other children," added Holly.

I shook my head. "If that's the kind of emotional abuse she dealt with her entire life, she must have finally snapped."

"So what do we do now?" asked Poppy, staring at the walls of the impenetrable steam sauna.

"I guess we wait until Stella's done using the time machine and then we get in there and get ourselves back to present day," I said, wishing Alba would wake up. "How's she doing, Sweets?"

Sweets, who was kneeling next to Alba, grimaced. "She's breathing, but she hasn't woken up yet."

I'd turned my head for only a moment to look down at Alba, when I heard Holly suddenly gasp. "Oh no!"

My head whipped around to face her. "What happened?!"

She pointed towards the time machine behind me.

I turned around again to look at it and, shockingly, found it nowhere to be seen! My eyes widened and my heart dropped. "What just happened?"

"Everything just disappeared!" shouted Holly.

"Disappeared?" asked Elodie. "How did it disappear?"

Cinder threw her head back and groaned. "She put out the fire."

"What?!" breathed several of us in unison.

"Stella Blackwood. She must have gone back to present day and put out the fire, closing the portal."

"She can do that?!" gasped Elodie.

Cinder tossed her arms out on either side of herself. "I think she just did."

"But she's going to get away now!" said Gemma.

"We've got a bigger problem than that," said Daphne. "We've got no way to get home now!"

I rested my head in my hands. This was quite possibly the worst thing that could have happened. We were already almost out of time. Now Stella was going to get away scot-free. Graduation was in a few short hours. It was Jax's birthday, and now there would be no way we could spend the day with her. And on top of everything, it was Mother's Day, and if I wasn't home to wish my mother a happy Mother's Day by the end of the day, she'd never let me live it down.

Cinder glanced over at her sister. "No. There's a way to get home. We must recreate the time machine."

My mouth gaped. "But Alba's out cold and Reign's

not here! We can't do the spell without them. How will we lift the river?!"

Cinder looked me squarely in the eye. "You'll have to do it."

"Lift the river?! I can't lift the river by myself! Alba and Reign could barely do it together. Even if I was as strong as either one of them, it took *two* of them to do it."

Gemma stepped forward. "I can help. My magic isn't as strong as it was when I was in my twenties, but I can still certainly do my best."

Daphne frowned. "My magic is a fraction of what it used to be too, but maybe between Gemma and myself, we can at least equal a whole person."

"But I don't know if I can even do my part," I protested. The thought scared me. It felt like all of our futures were resting on me being able to be as strong as Alba. "Sweets, try and wake Alba up again. Please! I can't do this."

Sweets shook Alba's shoulders. "I've been trying, Mercy. She won't wake up. We need to get her to a hospital. You need to hurry."

Cinder put a hand on my shoulder. "You can do this, Mercy. You just need to focus and gather your energy. Libby and I are ready whenever you are."

"But we need the magnetic powder and the knife!" I said.

Sweets reached across Alba's limp body and grabbed her backpack. She handed it up to Holly. "All of those things are still in Alba's bag. Holly and I'll get it all set up. You just worry about lifting the river."

I kneeled down in front of Alba. "But what about Alba? Someone's got to keep an eye on her."

Elodie waved me away. "You worry about getting us home. I'll take care of your friend."

I swallowed hard. The pressure was on. If I wanted to get back to Aspen Falls to see Stella Blackwood behind bars and figure out how to bring Sorceress Stone back to life, I had to do this. There were no other options. The clock was ticking.

Inhaling a deep breath, I closed my eyes and focused all of my nervous energy and everything inside of me on gathering enough pure energy from the things around me. My arms and legs began to tingle, and slowly, I could feel the energy building in my body. But instead of rushing it this time and risking burning out early, I kept collecting. When I heard Sweets and Holly holler, "Ready!" at me, I knew it was time. I felt a sudden burst of strength and adrenaline powering my body. I opened my eyes. Daphne and Gemma both stood down river, directly across from me, both of them at the ready.

"Now!" I yelled and launched everything I had at the river. At first it seemed as if the river barely moved. But I didn't waver and instead continued to fire everything I had.

"It's moving!" hollered a voice. I wasn't sure who it was.

"You're doing it, Mercy," shouted another.

But I refused to let the voices distract me. I kept lifting, until finally, I could hear the water rushing down and hitting the earth like a pounding waterfall.

As soon as I had it up high enough, Cinder launched fire bolt after fire bolt at the river basin until finally a fire began to burn beneath the waterfall.

"It's working," shouted a voice. "See the steam?"

But I couldn't look. I could only hold. The river was so heavy and my arms felt so weak that my powers seemed depleted, as if I could drop it at any second.

"Just a little bit longer, Mercy."

Every muscle in my body burned hot. My face felt like an inferno as I gritted my teeth.

"It's boiling, Libby," shouted Cinder.

But her sister was already on top of it. Libby blew a gust of frosty air to cool the boiling river. Steam rolled off it like a dense fog.

"Quick! Someone needs to part the steam!" I hollered. There was no way I could do it. I could barely hang on to the river as it was. I had no powers to spare.

And then, miraculously, the steam separated into two distinct directions. Half of it hovered over one side of the river and half of it hovered over the other side. Holly and Sweets stood in the centers of their rings with their knives held at the ready. Then the magnetic powder did its job, sucking the steam down to the ground around them, creating the steam sauna once again.

With Sweets and Holly now hidden from our view, they counted in unison. "One, two, three!" On three, both of their knives sliced through the steam, creating a pair of doorways. Both girls pulled the slit they'd just cut apart and stepped back out onto the grass.

"We did it!" said Sweets excitedly.

Holly leapt across the narrow river and high-fived Sweets.

"Can I let go now?!" I shouted.

"Yeah, Red, let go! It worked!"

I released my hold on the river and spun around

immediately to see Alba on her knees in the grass. "Alba! You're awake!"

"Something told me you might need my help!"

"You're the one that split the steam?"

Alba gave me a crooked smile. "Yeah, but you had things under control. Red, you lifted the river!"

"Daphne and Gemma helped."

"But still! You got it up there and held it there! I'm impressed! If you can lift a river, I definitely don't think you're gonna have any issues passing your Advanced Kinetics final."

Gemma and Daphne walked back over to rejoin the group.

Gemma shook her head in disbelief. "I can't believe what we just did. That was…"

"Impressive," said Daphne. "Beyond impressive."

"And to think a group of junior witches did this," added Poppy. She smiled wildly. "You girls are nothing short of amazing."

Elodie helped Alba climb to her feet and steadied her when she stumbled backwards slightly.

"Alba, you alright?" asked Sweets.

Alba nodded. "Yeah, I'm fine. Just have a bit of headache. That's all. What happened?"

"Stella knocked you out before stealing the time machine. When she got back to the present, she must have extinguished the fire," explained Cinder. "If we want to catch up to her, we've got to get going. Can you walk?"

Alba took a couple of uneasy steps forward with Elodie and Sweets flanking either side of her. "Yeah,

yeah. I'm good. Come on. We have a murderer to catch! And a sorceress to bring back to life!"

42

*B*ursting through the time portal back into present-day Aspen Falls, the Council paused before we headed back towards campus.

"Wait. What about this time portal? It shouldn't be left open like this. Someone else could come along and use it for nefarious purposes," said Poppy.

Alba and I looked at each other. We still had two big issues to resolve: helping Jax get her powers, and bringing Sorceress Stone back to life. Closing the portal meant neither of those things could be accomplished by going back in time.

"But there were things we wanted to fix before we closed it," said Alba with a hint of a whine sounding in her usually authoritative voice.

Poppy looked over at Alba disapprovingly and wagged her finger. "Learn it now. Nothing good comes from rewriting history, dear."

"Poppy's right," agreed Gemma. "Granted, we're witches and have the power to do so, but I live by the mantra: *Fixing past problems only creates future problems.* Just because we're witches and have the power to change things in our lives doesn't mean it's wise to do so."

"So true," said Daphne with a nod. "Now, we can discuss the things you wish to fix once we get things with Stella sorted out. But unfortunately, she's got a head start on us. We need to find her and deal with her before we can discuss any other issues. So let's get this beast shut down before she can use it against us in some way."

Alba hung her head. "Fine," she grumbled. She rolled a finger in the air at the twins. "Do your thing."

Libby and Cinder both stood back. Holding their arms out on either side of themselves, they fired at the river. Libby aimed at the fire, fighting to put it out with her icy blasts. Cinder fired heat at the uppermost point of the waterfall, where Libby had cooled it earlier. The combination of the two sent the water crashing back down into its carved course, completely dousing the fire, extinguishing it into a huge smoky burst of air.

"Wow," said Holly. "Just. Wow."

Sweets stared, wide-eyed. "That was amazing!"

Daphne patted Cinder and Libby each on the back. "Very impressive indeed! If you two ever need a job, I'm pretty sure I can get you hooked up helping with disaster relief efforts anywhere around the globe."

Libby and Cinder both smiled. "We will go home to Sweden first to see our family. Then maybe we will take you up on your very kind offer," said Cinder.

"Okay, enough playing around," said Gemma. "Let's get back to campus and see if we can't find miss Stella Blackwood and make her pay for her sins."

*W*e saw the flashing lights and heard the sirens before we'd even reached campus. We followed the sounds of commotion, which led us directly to the quad. There we found Detective Whitman slapping handcuffs on Stella Blackwood's wrists. Off to the side, Reign held a sobbing Jax in his arms while Detective Whitman finished reading Stella her rights.

"There you are!" shouted Reign. "Oh, thank God!"

"Mercy!" squealed Jax when she caught sight of me leading the pack. Through a messy face full of tears, her eyes brightened when she saw the rest of the pack behind me. "Oh! It's all of you! You're here!"

"How in the world…?" breathed Stella.

"But we saw the portal close with our own eyes!" said Reign in shock.

Cinder lifted a brow. "We reopened it."

"You were there when she closed it?" asked Alba.

Reign nodded. "Jax decided she wanted to be there when you got back. We were on our way to the time portal when all of a sudden, we saw Stella emerge. Of course I knew she was our prime suspect, so when I saw her extinguish the fire and close the portal, I had to stop her."

"Oh, Mercy, you should have seen him!" gushed Jax. "He was so brave! He got ahold of her and wouldn't let her go! And then I called Detective Whitman and told him everything."

"You did all of that in the few minutes that we were gone?" asked Holly.

"Few minutes?" said Reign. "It's been over an hour."

"Over an hour?!" cried Gemma, looking at her watch. She looked up anxiously. "Witches, we must don our robes. The ceremony starts shortly."

Poppy looked down at Alba and me. "You'll finish up here?"

"Yeah, no problem," said Alba.

I shooed them all on their way. "Of course. Go get ready. We'll see you all at the ceremony."

Holly turned to look at Libby and Cinder then. "Oh no! We're so late that you two didn't get to work on your graduation project."

Cinder waved a hand. "It is okay. We will make a big bonfire and put it out with water and air." She smiled at Alba.

Alba pointed at her and grinned back. "You're welcome."

Libby waved her sister on. "Come on, Cin. Let's go get our caps and gowns on and freshen up before the ceremony."

"We'll see you there," I hollered as the two of them rushed away, leaving the Witch Squad and my brother alone with the growing police presence on campus.

"Has she told you why she did it?" Alba asked Detective Whitman.

"No. I haven't heard a motive." He looked at Stella. "Care to tell them why you did this before I have my officers take you away?"

Stella lifted her chin up into the air and turned her head away obstinately.

"Oh, please, Aunt Stella. I need to know why you would have done this. Why did you take my mother away

416

from me?" begged Jax, her face wet, red, and swollen from crying all day.

Stella turned to look at Jax then. Her face softened slightly. "Aunt Stella?"

Jax nodded, her face filled with tears. "I don't understand. Why did you do it?"

Stella sighed, slumping forward as Detective Whitman held her cuffed hands behind her back. "I was so tired of hearing about her," she admitted. "Year after year after year, my father told me how worthless I was and how magnificent his daughter SaraLynn was. My entire life, it was always SaraLynn this and SaraLynn that. It didn't matter that I convinced one of the biggest pharmaceutical companies in the world to carry my medicines, SaraLynn was always better than me." She sniffed as her own eyes filled with tears. "I guess I'd just had enough. When my mother mentioned that her term on the Council was expiring, she asked if I'd like to take her seat." Stella shook her head. "This—this *plan* to eliminate the competition just began to take shape."

Jax sobbed on my shoulder through Stella's entire story. When she was done, Jax wiped her eyes on her shirt and looked up at the woman. "Thank you for telling me," she whispered.

Jax's words seemed to pierce Stella's heart. She hung her head. "I'm sorry I took her from you. I was so consumed with my own grudge that I didn't think of the children that she would leave behind. I only wanted to hurt my father."

I patted Jax on the back. "Take her away, Detective. Please? Jax shouldn't have to see her anymore."

We watched as Detective Whitman handed Stella off

to one of his officers. While we waited, we quietly explained to Jax and Reign what had happened on our last little adventure. Finally, when Stella was led away, Detective Whitman approached us. His face was somber. "Reign, Mercy, girls, do you mind telling me *why* I wasn't informed about all of this when it happened? Though she caused some problems in my relationship with Linda, SaraLynn was an old friend of mine, and I would have liked to have been involved in catching her murderer."

"We knew you'd want to be involved, but there was no way you'd have solved this one with forensics and normal detective work," I said. "It literally took us going back in time to solve this case."

"Regardless, we should have had SaraLynn seen by the medical examiner by now. This isn't the right way to conduct an investigation. This will really muddy the case against Ms. Blackwood. And then there's her funeral arrangements. Have her brother or sister been notified yet?"

Jax shook her head sadly. "No, I haven't told my aunt or uncle. Unless you guys did?"

Reign frowned. "No, we were holding off."

Detective Whitman stuck his hands in his jeans pockets and rocked backwards on the heels of his shoes. "Mind explaining why?"

I shrugged. "Sure. We were holding out hope that maybe we'd be able to bring Sorceress Stone back to life."

"Bring SaraLynn back to life?" breathed a voice behind us.

We all turned to find the Great Witches Council dressed all in black robes behind us.

"Is that why you wanted to keep the portal open?" asked Gemma.

"Well, yeah. I mean, that's part of the reason. Sorceress Stone was our friend's mother. We couldn't let Jax lose her mom, no matter how terrible Sorceress Stone has been to us this past year," I admitted. "But, honestly, we also wanted to get Jax her powers. Today's her eighteenth birthday. Before she was born, a curse was put on her family. We tried reversing time, but…"

"But you discovered that reversing past problems created future problems?" asked Gemma.

We all nodded quietly. I prayed they wouldn't ask what had happened. I really didn't want to get into all that. It was too humiliating.

Thankfully they didn't. Instead Poppy looked over at Jax fondly. "You're SaraLynn's daughter?"

Jax nodded.

Poppy put an arm over her shoulder. "We're so sorry for your loss, sweetheart."

Jax's bottom lip quivered. "Thank you."

"Listen, girls, and, uh… fellow," said Daphne, pointing at Reign. "We don't have a lot of time right now, but we did want to take a minute to thank you for all the trouble you went to to solve SaraLynn's murder. Not only did you put a deeply disturbed woman in police custody, but you also proved our innocence. And for that we're eternally grateful."

"Not only that, but you did all that just to help your friend," added Elodie. "That's a pretty special thing."

"Especially for a witch," added Poppy.

Daphne nodded in agreement. "A witch's coven is everything to a witch. And to know that you were all willing to go to the ends of the earth to help a witch in your coven, it... it's simply a beautiful thing." Daphne batted at a stray tear that trickled down her cheek.

Jax shook her head as her own tears began to course down her cheeks. "But don't you understand? I'm not a witch! I can never be part of their coven! And now my mother is dead, so I can't even be part of a family!"

Reign pulled a distraught Jax in against his chest. Her shoulders shook as she sobbed.

The Council all eyed each other. "Witches, a moment?" asked Poppy, beckoning the rest of the Council to speak privately.

When they stepped away, Detective Whitman patted my shoulder. "It looks like you have a lot going on right now. I need to get Ms. Blackwood booked down at the station. If you could all just stop down after the gradua-tion ceremony to give statements, that would be great."

We all nodded.

"Thank you, girls." Detective Whitman and the rest of his men left the quad as the Council reunited in front of us.

Gemma pursed her lips and stepped forward. "Per-haps I was the biggest naysayer in the group. I didn't believe that a couple handfuls of inexperienced witches could solve a mystery that I didn't even think that I myself could solve. But you did it. And you did it for your friend. We discussed this in private and have agreed that we'd like to do something to not only thank you for your commitment to solving SaraLynn's murder, but also to make amends for not believing in you as we should have."

Jax's shoulders stopped shaking as she pulled herself

away from Reign's chest hopefully. She wiped her eyes with the hem of her shirt, sopping up her tears.

"And I think we've just been inspired as to what we can to do thank all of you. The four of us, with the help of the group of you, should be able to summon enough powers to offer Jax the opportunity to finally become a witch." Gemma said it proudly and then looked back at all the other witches, who smiled happily as well.

"What?!" breathed Alba. "You can do that?! That… that… that's amazing!"

"Jax! Omigosh!" squealed Holly. "You're going to get your powers! Finally!"

"This is incredible," added Sweets, her face shining as bright as the sun.

But as I watched Jax's face crumple, I could tell that she didn't think it was incredible news. Tears filled her eyes once again as she turned back into Reign's arms.

The Council all frowned, surprised that Jax wasn't leaping with excitement. But Reign and I knew what was wrong. She wanted her mother to be alive.

"You don't want to be a witch anymore?" asked Poppy.

Jax lifted her head. "No, I *want* to be a witch. But I want my mother to be alive more than anything. If there's something you can do to thank my friends, it's to bring my mother back to life. That's the only thing I want. Please! Can you do that? Can you bring my mom back to life?"

Poppy turned to face her peers. Gemma curled her finger, bringing the four of them into a huddle. They spoke in hushed whispers for a long minute, and then returned to the group.

Poppy narrowed her eyes as she looked at Jax. "Sweetheart, are you *sure* that's what you want? You'd rather have your mother's death reversed than to finally become the witch you were destined to become?"

Jax's head bobbed up and down. "I'm one hundred percent positive!"

"Very well," said Poppy. She looked around. "Well, we'll need her body."

Alba and Reign jumped to attention. "Got it! We'll have her here in a jiffy!"

They disappeared into Winston Hall to retrieve Sorceress Stone's frozen body from the tower.

"We'll go gather our needed items," said Poppy, leading the Council back into the dorm and towards Sorceress Stone's office.

While they were gone, Holly, Sweets, and I surrounded Jax.

"Jaxie, you sure about this?" asked Holly. "Today's your eighteenth birthday. If you don't take their offer, you're never going to be a witch."

"Yeah, Jax. *Never,*" echoed Sweets. "Maybe you should take a minute to think about this."

Jax looked at me, her face red and puffy from crying. She swiped her hand across her nose. "You think I'm doing the right thing, don't you, Mercy?"

"I'm not the person to say whether or not you're doing the right thing, Jax. *You're* the only person who can say that. You have to be the one to accept the fact that you'll never be a witch if you do this. And you'll have to go to normal college next year."

Jax's bottom lip began to quiver. "I don't want to go to normal college next year," she bawled.

I wrapped my arms around her shoulders. "I know, Jax. But it's your mom. I know you. And I know how much your mother means to you. You have to do what you think is best."

"Saving my mom is best," Jax whispered, choking back a sob. "I know you guys don't get why I love her. I know she's kind of mean, but she's *my mom*. You'd all do whatever it took to save your mothers. Even it if meant not being a witch."

Sweets nodded. "I'd do anything for my mom, for sure."

"Me too," whispered Holly.

"So would I." I looked Jax right in the eyes. "So let them bring her back to life. It's the right thing to do, Jax."

Jax smiled at me. "I know it is. I just wanted to hear you say it."

The four of us hugged it out and the next thing I knew, I could hear Alba and Reign's voices. I rushed to open the door for them, and they carefully placed Sorceress Stone's frozen body down on one of the tables in the quad. Libby and Cinder, now dressed in their graduation caps and gowns, followed them into the courtyard, followed by the Council members.

"Let's get her unthawed!" Libby rubbed her hands together and blew into them. Then she began to suck in the air around Sorceress Stone, just as she'd done to Holly only a few days before. Little by little, Sorceress Stone defrosted, until finally, she wasn't a witch pop anymore, but a soft, fleshy dead witch. Libby stood back and gestured towards her. "There! She's done. Ready to be brought back to life!"

We all inadvertently took a step back, casting a wide

circle around Sorceress Stone. Gemma took charge then. "We'll need everyone's help. Bringing a witch back to life requires more energy than one would imagine. Not only must we restart her life core, but we must call her soul back to her body. It'll take a team of us to do it."

I looked around the quad. The rest of the members of the Witch Squad, not including Jax, my brother, Libby and Cinder, and the four members of the Great Witches Council. Altogether, there were eleven of us. That had to be enough. I'd never done a spell with so many witches. Especially so many senior witches.

She pointed across the circle at Holly. "You. Here take this piece of chalk and draw out a proper casting circle." Then she passed a basket of white candles to me. "Take one and pass it down. Everyone should have a candle."

I took a short, stubby piece of white wax into my hands and passed the basket to Reign. The basket continued around the circle until it got back to where it had started. Gemma took an extra candle and handed it to Holly once she was done drawing the casting circle.

"Now, get in a circle. Spread out. Close enough that you can hold hands, but far enough away to give us some room to work," she instructed. When we'd gotten into the proper arrangement, she took a deep cleansing breath and then said calmly, "Light your candles."

> *SaraLynn Stone slumbers in wakeless sleep.*
> *We ask to bring her back from the deep.*
> *Walk her through the spiritual door,*
> *Assemble flesh and soul, let her walk once more.*

Thunder grumbled overhead and the wind whipped

up behind us, sending our hair up in rollercoaster waves around our shoulders. And then a single white bolt of lightning struck Sorceress Stone as she lay peacefully in the epicenter of our casting circle. Her body lashed against the table like a limp rag doll as electrical sparks crackled off of her fingers and toes.

Jax screamed, "Mom!"

43

*W*hen the wind finally subsided and the sound of the grumbling thunder lessened to little more than a distant murmur, all eyes turned to Sorceress Stone. And just like a scene ripped right out of a Frankenstein movie, Sorceress Stone's hand began to tremble ever so slightly. Eyes widened and jaws dropped as her chest faintly began to rise and fall.

"Oh my God," whispered Jax as she began to sob once again. When Sorceress Stone's eyelids fluttered open, Jax rushed to be by her mother's side. "Mom!"

"There we are," said Gemma, dusting off her gown. "Per your request. Now, I think our debts have been settled. We must get to the ceremony. We'll see you there."

The Great Witches Council left the quad in a hurry, leaving the rest of us behind to stare at Jax, who was now sobbing over her mother.

"Oh, Mom!" she sobbed. "You're alive!"

"JaclynRose," whispered a hoarse Sorceress Stone.

"What are you doing? Why am I on a table? And why is it so cold?"

Through her tears, Jax blubbered incoherently. "You were dead, Mom. Dead! Stella murdered you and I didn't know what I'd do without you!"

"JaclynRose, you're not making any sense. I can hardly understand a word that's come out of your mouth. Why are you blubbering so?"

Alba stepped forward then. "She's upset. You've been incapacitated for a few days."

"Incapacitated for a few days? What do you mean?"

"It's a long story," I promised. "But we'll tell you after the ceremony."

"Ceremony? What ceremony?"

"The graduation ceremony. It's probably already started," said Libby. She bobbed her head towards the Broomsgarden arboretum, where the ceremony was to be held. "We should probably get going Cinder."

Alba nodded. "Go ahead. We'll catch up in a minute."

Sorceress Stone struggled to sit up.

Reign pointed a finger at her and magically raised her to her feet.

Sorceress Stone lifted a brow as she considered him for a brief moment. "Thank you," she said curtly. "Now what are you all talking about? Graduation is on Sunday."

"Today is Sunday, Mom," said Jax through a sniff. Her sobs had finally subsided, but her face was a slobbery mess of tears and nasal fluid.

"No, it's not. It's Tuesday." She looked around at all of our faces. "It's Tuesday, isn't it?" she asked Holly.

Holly shook her head. "No. It's Sunday, Sorceress Stone. You've been out for about a week."

"Out? As in unconscious?" asked Sorceress Stone, looking more confused than I'd ever see her before.

Alba shook her head. "No. More like out as in dead."

Our headmistress pulled her head back. "Dead?!"

"I told you it's a long story," I said. "But right now, we have to get to graduation."

---

*P*oppy Ellabee stood center stage at the podium and read the next name on her list with a deliberate slowness. "Adele Catherine Lowenstein."

The audience clapped for a slender girl with limp, wavy brown hair as she slid across the stage and took a spot next to Poppy. Poppy stepped sideways and let Adele have the microphone.

"I presented my project on Thursday. I did a simple energy transference spell. Using only my mind, I was able to convert water into air, air into fire, and fire into rock. I didn't use any spells or potions, simply the power of thought."

Poppy nodded and shot Adele a megawatt smile before taking the microphone. "Adele did very well with her project and has received a passing score. Therefore, Adele Catherine Lowenstein, you have met the necessary graduation requirements, and on behalf of the Para-normal Institute for Witches and the Great Witches Council, we hereby present to you your Powers Unleashed certificate!"

As Poppy handed a certificate to Adele, the audience

clapped. Several members of Adele's family stood up to cheer and fist-pumped the air. Someone even let an airhorn blare, making the audience laugh.

"And our final two candidates for graduation are Libby Anne Hafström and Cinder Ray Hafström," said Poppy before stepping back and clapping with the rest of the audience.

Holly, Jax, Alba, and I, all seated in a cluster in the back of the student section of the audience, hooted and hollered for them as the twins stood and plodded towards the stage. One look at their long faces told me that they weren't looking forward to presenting Alba's lame idea to the audience. Not only was the project late, but they were completely unprepared. We all worried the lack of preparation might very well cost them their Powers Unleashed certificates.

When the applause died down, Libby was handed the microphone. She looked at it uneasily before handing it to her sister.

Cinder's eyes widened. She cleared her throat. "We were unable to present our graduation project during the week, so we will present it for you now."

Standing in the wings, Poppy furrowed her brow. She scurried forward, covered the microphone with her hands, and whispered something to Cinder and Libby. They both looked shocked but nodded. Poppy stepped back into the wings of the stage.

Cinder looked out into the crowd again. "I take that back. My sister and I presented our graduation project to the Council earlier today. Utilizing magnetic powder, the energy of a slow-moving river, and our powers of both fire control and water temperature control…"

Cinder handed Libby the microphone and Libby continued Cinder's sentence. "We were able to create a time portal. This morning, we transported the members of the Great Witches Council to a different time and location and returned them in time for the ceremony."

Before Poppy could even respond to that, gasps, followed promptly by applause, thundered around us. Libby and Cinder both smiled out at the crowd, pleased with the response their inadvertent project had garnered.

When the applause died down, Poppy spoke. "These girls did absolutely *amazing* with their project. I've never seen such a big project come from a pair of second-year students, and as a former teacher at the Institute, I've seen *many* a graduation project. This one was by far the best I've ever seen. So, I'm very honored to present to both of you, on behalf of the Paranormal Institute for Witches and the Great Witches Council, your Powers Unleashed certificates!"

"Woooo!" I screamed, clapping wildly, a huge smile across my face.

Alba cheered next to me as she pounded the air with her fist. "Yeah!"

The combination of the audience's applause and cheers were deafening, filling my ears. I couldn't believe it. Libby and Cinder had done it! They'd graduated from the Institute! It was a surreal moment, and for the first time since the ceremony had begun, it hit me that Libby and Cinder would be moving away and wouldn't be returning in the fall. It was more than likely that this might be the last day I ever saw the Fire and Ice twins, and it made me feel a way that I'd never felt before. I couldn't quite put my finger on the feeling, but I felt a lump in the back of my throat as I watched them holding their certificates high in the air before walking back to their seats.

After the dust settled, Poppy took the microphone once again. "Now that we've presented all of the Powers Unleashed certificates for the graduating class, it is time to address the upcoming second-year students. Typically this is the part of the ceremony where first-year students are told whether they've been approved to move into their second year. If so, they are asked to declare a major. Unfortunately, this week we've had some, umm..." She glanced over at the Council and Sorceress Stone, who sat in Poppy's seat. After being brought back to life, Sorceress Stone had been too weak to conduct the graduation ceremony, and therefore Poppy had taken her place. "Technical glitches. So the last few days of finals were postponed, and the exams will be held tomorrow and Tuesday. This means that while witches may declare their intended majors, report cards and pass/fail status will be handed out next week."

Groans went up around the student section from everyone, including Holly and Alba. Jax looked at me sadly. I knew that, though she was happy her mother was now alive, she was also sad that she wouldn't be declaring a major. I felt horrible that we hadn't been able to get her the one thing she'd wanted more than anything for her birthday.

Then, one by one, Poppy Ellabee called each of the first-year students up to the podium. Late to arrive to the ceremony, the Witch Squad occupied the very last row of student chairs and had to wait for Poppy to call every single other witch's name before she finally got to ours.

"Alba Suzanne Sanchez," said Poppy in a slow deliberate tone.

After walking up to the stage, Alba stepped up to the podium and looked out into the audience. "I declare that I will major in mind control and minor in kinetic energy."

The audience applauded before she pivoted and walked down the other side of the stage.

"Holly Elizabeth Rockwell."

Holly followed Alba to the podium. "I declare that I will major in clairvoyance and minor in aesthetics."

When her applause died down, Sorceress Stone called my name out. "Mercy Mae Habernackle."

My brother gave out a hoot and a holler from the crowd, making my face immediately heated.

As I took the microphone, I looked out over the crowd. It was filled with lots of familiar faces. Mostly students. But I also saw my teachers listening intently, excited to hear what all of us first-year witches would be majoring in next year. And then, of course, there were the families of the second-year students. Towards the back row, I saw my brother sitting next to Sweets, who gave me a little excited wave. Brittany Hobbs, who had nearly fainted when she'd seen Sorceress Stone follow us to the ceremony, was seated primly in the front row, dotting her eyes with a handkerchief. And then I noticed the one face I hadn't expected to see.

Houston Brooks.

He looked at me intently, like I was the only person in the room. My heart raced and I felt blood rushing to my face. Suddenly, my brain turned to mush and the words I'd been practicing in my mind seemed to disappear. "Umm. Yeah," I said awkwardly into the microphone. I cleared my throat. *Think, Mercy, think. Your major declaration. Oh yeah...* "I declare that I will major in ghost studies and minor in kinetic energy."

The audience applauded, and I let out the breath I'd been holding. As I made my way off stage, I heard Poppy call the next name.

"JaclynRose Stone."

Jax and I passed each other in the aisle, and any lingering questions about why Hugh was in the crowd disappeared completely. Instead, Jax's long face and tear-filled eyes nearly broke my heart. I'd failed her. What kind of a witch was I that I couldn't even help my friend?

Jax tromped up to center stage with a wrinkled nose and a face that was all mushed together as if she were fighting a sneeze. I knew Jax well enough to know that was the face she made when trying to keep from bawling. Her squeaky voice was shaky as she began. "I declare that if I pass my finals, I will major in animal spirits." Her head bobbed as if that were that. Then it tipped sideways. "Or maybe invisibility studies." She thought about it for another second and smiled. "Actually, maybe I might want to be a medium, or even major in atmokinesis because it would be *really* cool if I could control the weather." She paused again. "But you know, now that I think about it, I've always wanted to learn to animate inanimate objects, so maybe I should major in that, and then maybe I'd minor in potions. Oh! Or flying. I think I could be a really good flier, even though heights kind of scare me."

Poppy cleared her throat.

Jax looked over at her and smiled shyly. "Oh, sorry. I can't really pick just one thing. I want to do it all."

I glanced over at Sorceress Stone, whose eyes were cast downwards, concentrating on her hands in her lap.

Poppy gave Jax a slight nod and then stepped towards her and whispered something in her ear.

Jax grinned from ear to ear, nodded her head eagerly, and then looked out at the crowd. This time when she spoke, her voice was much more buoyant. "I declare that if I pass my finals, I will major in general magic studies."

The crowd let out a collective laugh. Jax's broad smile and unwavering optimism lightened the sadness I'd felt only minutes before. However, knowing that I had no way of making her dreams a reality, even Jax's smile of acceptance couldn't remove the heaviness I felt on my heart.

44

*A*fter the ceremony was over and all the students and their families had gone their own way, all that remained was the Great Witches Council, Sorceress Stone, the members of the Witch Squad, my brother, Libby and Cinder, and Brittany Hobbs.

Sorceress Stone pushed herself up off her chair and looked down her nose at Poppy Ellabee. "Poppy, I appreciate you conducting the ceremony for me. After everything that happened, I-I just wasn't up to it, but I'm pleased that we were able to see the graduation through. I am, however, disappointed that finals were delayed until next week. It's unfortunate that all that time was wasted while I was unconscious."

Poppy gave Sorceress Stone a tight smile. "SaraLynn, I do think it's time we discussed the events of the week with you. Perhaps you don't understand the severity of what happened. You weren't unconscious. You were dead."

Sorceress Stone's brows knitted together. Her hand went to her heart. "Surely you don't actually mean…"

Poppy shook her head resolutely. "No, I actually mean *dead*. You were gone."

"But…how in the—"

"Stella Blackwood," cut in Alba. "Recognize the name?"

"Yes. Of course I do. Stella was on the Council. I met her just the other day."

"And that was the first time you'd ever met her?" I asked.

"Yes, it was the first time I'd met a few of the Council members. Why?" She was starting to look annoyed.

"Stella's maiden name was Stella Smith, Mom," whispered Jax.

"Smith?"

Jax nodded. "She's Grandpa Samson's daughter."

"Grandpa Sam—JaclynRose, Samson Smith is not your grandfather. He's just an old man that contributed to your DNA. Please do not refer to him as your grandfather."

"His title doesn't matter," said Alba. "Samson Smith and Harlow Crandall married. Did you know that?"

The look on Sorceress Stone's face told us that the marriage didn't come as a surprise. "Perhaps I'd heard that once or twice as a child."

"And they had a kid together," added Alba.

Sorceress Stone looked appalled. "They did no such thing!"

Alba's shoulders and eyebrows lifted simultaneously. "I don't know what to tell you, but they did."

"Surely I'd have *known* if my biological father had had another child."

"How would you have known?" asked Reign. "If Auggie didn't want you to have anything to do with your father after their divorce, do you really think she'd want her children interacting with Harlow's?"

Sorceress Stone had to chew on that for a moment. "What of all of this, anyway? Is there a point here somewhere?"

Gemma Overbrook strode over to the fountain. "Stella Blackwood took your life, SaraLynn. That's the point in all of this."

"You'd all have me believe that some sister that I've never met came all the way here from Alaska just to kill me?" She shook her head. "That's preposterous!"

I shrugged. "It might be far-fetched, but believe us, it's the truth. We've got no reason to lie."

Daphne Fletcher nodded from her chair on the stage. "It *is* true, SaraLynn. And what's more, these girls and that young man over there went to a great deal of trouble to solve the mystery surrounding your murder."

"But why would she do such a horrible thing?" asked Sorceress Stone.

"She was jealous of you," explained Holly.

"Jealous? How could she have been jealous? I'd never met the woman!"

"Using the time machine we made, we went back in time and saw your father and Harlow together," said Reign. "Samson constantly compared Stella to you. It was like he had you up on a pedestal and Stella could never measure up. The way he spoke to her was terrible. It seems she endured that type of mental and verbal abuse

439

for years. She finally snapped. She wanted to hurt your father."

"Were you aware that Harlow was on the previous Council?" I asked, suddenly curious if Sorceress Stone realized she'd met her stepmother.

Sorceress Stone lifted a brow. "Yes, Harlow and I were aware of each other's presence. We never spoke of our personal connection."

"Stella got her mother to load the Council with people that aren't your biggest fans, so everyone else would look guilty," explained Cinder.

Sorceress Stone's icy-blue eyes flicked up to look at the rest of the Council.

None of the older witches were able to meet her scornful gaze.

"I see," snapped Sorceress Stone. With her lips pursed together tightly, she glanced over at Jax. "And if my half-sister did as is charged, how is it that I stand before you today?"

"I can answer that," said Elodie, standing up from her seat. "When we discovered that you were dead, we knew that it was someone on the Council who had committed the horrendous act. Fingers immediately began being pointed in all directions, and then these girls showed up. Once they understood what had happened, they demanded to be in charge of the investigation, and because none of us knew who did it and therefore who was to be trusted, we felt obligated to let them take over. They spent their entire week using their powers and their wit to hunt down the answers needed to solve the case. Because of them, the police were not only able to apprehend the murderer, but also to clear all of our good names."

Sorceress Stone cast a small glance in our direction.

Elodie continued. "And when we tried to understand *why* these girls would have gone to all that trouble, we discovered it was because of their friendship with your daughter. They didn't want her to lose her mother, and from what we understood, part of their mission had been to reverse a curse that has plagued your family for decades."

Sorceress Stone looked down at her hands again. "Yes, that curse has been an unfortunate burr in my saddle, and it's been my daughter who's paid the price for sins of the past."

Daphne nodded. "We decided that we owed these girls and this young man *something* for their trouble. We settled on rewarding your daughter by making her a witch finally."

Sorceress Stone's chin lifted and her head snapped over to stare at Jax. "JaclynRose! You're finally a witch?!" Hope filled Sorceress Stone's eyes.

Sitting cross-legged on the lush carpet of grass, Jax swallowed hard and looked away. It was obvious she didn't have the heart to disappoint her mother.

"No, as a matter of fact, she isn't," said Alba bitterly. "She gave up her one and only chance to be a witch."

Sorceress Stone sucked in her breath. "JaclynRose! Why on Earth would you do such a thing? You've wanted to be a witch for as long as I can remember!"

Jax's mouth opened, but no words came out. She snapped her mouth shut and lowered her head again as tears fell to the grass.

"She gave up her chance to be a witch for you," I said.

"For me?!"

"She asked that instead of them granting her the chance to finally be a witch, that they'd use her any wish fulfillment that she had coming to her to bring you back to life," said Reign. "She gave up her chance to be a witch for you."

Sorceress Stone's eyes flicked over to her daughter. "JaclynRose... I-I'm stunned. I don't know what to say."

Jax stood up from the grass she sat on and walked over to her mother. She threw her arms around her mother's waist. "I wasn't ready to have a Mother's Day without you in my life. I'd do anything for you, Mom. I love you. Happy Mother's Day."

Sorceress Stone's mouth gaped as she looked down at her daughter, clinging to her midsection with Jax's head buried in her chest. Sorceress Stone's usually cold and rigid demeanor relaxed slightly, and for the first time since I'd met her, I saw her eyes glisten with dampness. She put her arms around Jax and hugged her back, quietly whispering into Jax's ear, "I love you too, JaclynRose."

A lump in the back of my throat made it hard to swallow. Behind me I heard sniffles and turned to see Sweets and Holly clinging to one another and bawling like babies. Reign had a dumb smile on his face, and even Alba and the twins looked like their eyes had unshed tears in them.

"I—I don't know what to say," said Sorceress Stone finally. "I guess I owe you all a thank-you." She looked over at the Council. "Thank you for granting my daughter's request and for bringing me back to life." She looked over at the Witch Squad. "And thank you all for doing what it took to find out the truth about Stella. I know I probably didn't deserve your efforts. I haven't been the kindest to you all."

"That's the understatement of the year," said Alba.

Sorceress Stone nodded. "I know. I know. And I promise I'll do better in the future."

Gemma Overbrook cleared her throat. "SaraLynn, surely you haven't forgotten what we'd spoken about in private before your untimely *event*."

Sorceress Stone's brow furrowed. She looked more than slightly stunned. "You mean those are still your wishes? I thought that after everything that happened…"

Gemma glanced over at the rest of the Council.

Elodie Goodwitch nodded her head.

Poppy pursed her lips and nodded as well.

Daphne cleared her throat. "Yes, SaraLynn. Our feelings haven't changed."

Sorceress Stone looked defeated. "Oh. I see."

Alba stepped forward, holding her hands up on either side of herself. "Whoa, whoa, whoa. What are we missing here? What's going on?"

The Council all exchanged uncomfortable glances while Sorceress Stone sucked in a deep breath.

"I've been asked to leave the Institute," admitted Sorceress Stone. "Apparently there have been complaints about my leadership style. Perhaps my discipline style is unorthodox."

"Perhaps? Puh!" breathed Alba. "Ya think?"

Sweets elbowed her in the ribs. "Alba! Now's not the time."

As the news sank into Jax's head, she let go of her

mother's waist and looked up into her eyes. "Wait, Mom? You're leaving the Institute?"

Sorceress Stone nodded. "Unfortunately, I have no choice. The Council has offered me a suitable buyout. I was asked to leave after graduation, but since finals aren't completed yet, maybe I'll be here for another week?" She glanced up at the Council.

"We'll handle finals week," said Gemma curtly. "There are only a few days of school left. It shouldn't be a problem for a few of us to stick around to handle Institute business until we can find a suitable replacement."

Sorceress Stone glanced down at Jax. "Then we'll be leaving as soon as I can get our belongings packed."

Jax looked like she might cry even more now. "We?! I have to go with you? But, Mom! Without powers, I can't go to the Institute in the fall, and it's summertime. I don't wanna leave my friends yet!"

"We can discuss it at another time, JaclynRose."

"Discuss it? But today's my birthday! I'm eighteen now. When do I get to start making my own decisions?"

"Today's your…" Sorceress Stone seemed to run out of words. She shook her head sadly. "I'd almost forgotten it's your birthday," she murmured under her breath.

"Well, it is!" said Jax. "And I don't want to leave my friends. I wanna stay in Aspen Falls! I know I'm not a witch, and I know I won't pass my finals, but I wanna stay. At least for the summer."

"JaclynRose, it's Mother's Day…"

Jax pounded her fists down on either side of herself. "I know it's Mother's Day, Mom, but—"

Sorceress Stone held up a hand in front of her. "Let me finish. Please?"

Jax gave her a tiny nod and mashed her lips between her teeth.

"As I was saying, it's Mother's Day, and I'm finally realizing that I don't deserve to be your mother. I'm not cut out to be a mother. Maybe this all goes back to the curse and the fact that you never became a witch. But despite the fact that I've treated you poorly your whole life, you continue to amaze me, JaclynRose. You've got a big heart. I know all you've ever wanted in life was to be a witch, and when you were finally given the opportunity, you decided to save *me* instead of getting what you always wanted." Tears trickled down Sorceress Stone's face as she spoke now. "I don't deserve that kind of unconditional love. I've been unkind to you. I've been unkind to your friends. And it's all caught up to me. Karma has come back around to me."

Jax took her mother's hands. "Mom…"

Sorceress Stone shook her head as if she'd made up her mind and then looked over at the Council. "I want to exercise my right as a witch to invoke a legacy power transfer ceremony immediately."

I glanced over at Alba. I'd never heard of a legacy power transfer ceremony before. Alba shook her head as if to say she'd never heard of it either.

The Great Witches Council members all gasped.

"A power transfer ceremony? But, SaraLynn, that's unheard of!" cried Poppy.

"Yes, I know," snapped Sorceress Stone as she wiped away her tears and tried to regain her composure. "But it's what I want to do. I have the right. She's my legacy. Now, the ceremony requires ten witches. We have ten witches present. And it requires the power transfer to happen before the end of her eighteenth birthday. We've still got a few hours left."

Jax looked around, confused. "What's a power transfer ceremony, Mom?"

Poppy put a hand on Jax's shoulder. "She wants to give you her powers, sweetie."

"Give me her…" Jax's eyes widened. "Mom!" Jax's head shook wildly. "No! You don't have to do that!"

"JaclynRose, I know I don't have to, but I want to."

"But, Mom…" Jax cried.

Sorceress Stone let go of Jax's hands and straightened her shoulders. "You know how I feel about 'but Moms,' JaclynRose. Now, I want to do this. Being a witch hasn't fulfilled me as I would've liked. I have been unable to find happiness in my own life. And now I've lost my position here at the Institute. I've lived a full life as a witch, but I'll learn to live a full life as just a woman. I know the one thing you've ever wanted is to be a witch. I haven't been able to give you much during your life, but I can give you this. You gave up something meaningful for me, and now it is my desire to return the favor. My wish for you is that you fulfill your destiny."

Jax's shoulders shook as she bawled.

Sorceress Stone put a hand on either side of her daughter's shoulders. "You are destined for great things, JaclynRose Stone. I know it. I can feel it in my bones. So please, don't take your powers for granted. Make the most out of your life."

"Mom, I…"

Sorceress Stone pushed her away then and strode over to the Council. "I'm ready. Let's begin."

45

*a*s Holly and I each held one of Jax's hands, she nibbled on the side of her lip. "Oh, girls. Is this really happening right now? Am I really about to become a witch?"

"It's happening, Jax. It's really happening," said Sweets, hugging herself excitedly.

Jax fell backwards slightly, making Holly and me tighten our grips on her. "But I feel so terrible about taking my mom's powers. I shouldn't let her do this. Really, I can't."

Alba wagged a finger in the air and looked Jax directly in the eye. "Oh no, you don't, Shorty. She *owes* you this. And besides, she *wants* to do it. For the first time in her life, she's putting your needs before her own."

Holly nodded. "Yeah, Jaxie. You have to let her do this for you."

"But what if I'm not a good witch? What if I get my powers and I don't know how to make them work, or what if I do something wrong?"

I squeezed Jax's hand. "Jax, we've all made mistakes as witches. We're entitled to make mistakes. And as far as not knowing how to use your powers, don't worry about it. You go to the Paranormal Institute for Witches. It's the perfect place to learn how to use your powers."

Jax smiled at me and leaned her head on my shoulders. "You're right. Oh, my gosh. I'm totally freaking out right now."

"Really? We couldn't tell," said Alba, rolling her eyes. "You just need to take it down a notch."

"Yeah, Jaxie. Relax," said Holly.

"Relax?" breathed Jax. "How can I relax? I'm about to become a *witch*! It's only all I've ever wanted for my entire life!"

"Breathe in, Jax," I commanded, sucking in a deep breath with her. "Now close your eyes and let it out slowly as you count to ten."

Jax nodded and did as I'd suggested. When she was done, her eyes popped open and she looked at me anxiously. "Nope. Still freaking out."

From across the arboretum, my brother strode towards us, calling out to Jax. "They're ready for you, Nugget."

Jax sucked in a deep breath and then let it all out excitedly. "Eeeee," she squealed, squeezing our hands tightly to her chest. "Omigosh, omigosh, omigosh."

"Breathe, Jax."

"I *am* breathing!" she cried as her chest rose and fell rapidly.

"Yeah, you're gonna hyperventilate," I said, changing my mind. "Maybe you should *stop* breathing."

Jax's head bobbed up and down and her eyes bugged

out as she sucked in a big puff of air and kept it dammed up in her chest.

Frowning, Holly grabbed Jax's face. "Jax. Today's your birthday. You are *eighteen* years old, but you're acting like a little kid. It's time to put your big girl panties on and do the damn thing."

Jax let out the breath she'd been holding. "Do the damn thing?"

Sweets giggled.

"Yes. You can do this. You were *born* to be a witch."

"I was?"

Holly nodded. "Yes. You were. Repeat after me. 'I was *born* to be a witch.'"

Jax giggled. "I was born to be a witch."

"Say it louder. Like you mean it."

"I was born to be a witch," she said, a little more seriously this time.

"Now say it like you *believe* it. Louder!"

"I was born to be a witch!" she hollered. With that, Jax bounded forward, seemingly more confident and determined.

"Attagirl!" cheered Holly.

Reign squeezed Holly's shoulder. "Wow! Go Holly. A clairvoyant *and* a life coach. Who knew?"

Holly giggled and linked arms with Reign. The two of them walked up the aisle towards the stage. Libby and Cinder followed next. Sweets, Alba, and I brought up the rear.

"This is so exciting," gushed Sweets, clinging to my arm.

"I gotta admit, I'm pretty excited too," said Alba. "I was beginning to think this day might never come."

"Same," I agreed. It was still a bit surreal to think that it was actually going to happen for Jax. But there they were on the stage, the four members of the Great Witches Council, holding hands in a semicircle, waiting for all of us to join in. Libby, Cinder, and Holly took their places first. Alba, Sweets, and I filled in the remaining three holes. In the center of the circle stood Sorceress Stone and Jax. Reign and Brittany Hobbs took front-row seats in the audience.

As Jax stood in the center of the circle, shoulder to shoulder with her mother, her eyes were on me. I did my best to calm her with my mind. I sucked a breath in through my nose and let it out slowly. Jax did as I did and nodded confidently.

"Now, JaclynRose. Face me. Put your hands to mine," said Sorceress Stone, turning to face Jax. "Our fingertips must be touching at all times during the ceremony."

Jax looked up at her mother in awe and did as she instructed. I couldn't help but wonder what was going through her mind in that moment. Was it gratitude? Sadness? Excitement? Fear? I couldn't tell. Jax's face wore a mask of somberness that I rarely saw on her. She'd done as Holly had asked and put on her big girl panties. I felt a surge of pride.

On stage, white candles flickered in each corner and along the outer perimeter of the covered wooden rectangle. And with ten sets of linked hands, Gemma Overbrook began the ceremony reverently. "We are gathered here today to call upon the divine spirits to request a legacy power transfer. Spirits of the North and the elemental earth, we call to you. Guide us with your wisdom and noble ways. We invoke you, show us that you are upon us."

A grumble could be heard around us, and then the earth shook beneath our feet, rattling the stage and making the candles flicker wildly.

Poppy spoke next. "Spirits of the East and elemental air, we call to you. You are the breath of life and new beginnings. We call to you to provide clarity and mindfulness to the participants before you. We invoke you, show us that you are upon us."

The wind crept up around us, whipping at the black gowns the Great Witches Council wore and twisting our hair up around our faces. The candles threatened to go out as they danced in the fast-moving air.

"Spirits of the South and elemental fire, we call to you. You are the guardians of the spiritual realm. We ask for your courage and protection as we complete this transfer of power. We invoke you, show us that you are upon us," called out Elodie.

Lightning flickered in the sky around us. The flames on the candles suddenly grew, doubling in size.

"Spirits of the West and elemental water, you are the key to transformations and rebirth. We call upon you for your gifts of change and transition of power. We invoke you, show us that you are upon us!" called out Daphne.

Rain began to fall, soaking the grass and the flowers around the perimeter of the stage, soaking Reign and Brittany and the empty seats, but refusing to touch the stage.

"Spirit keepers, we welcome your presence and ask that you look upon this legacy power transfer ceremony with kindness and grace as it is presented to you with goodwill and love," said Gemma.

Poppy closed her eyes. "O great spirit keepers, please know that ten witches sit before you. Ten witches who can vouch for the legitimacy of the claim of legacy status. Ten witches who attest that each of the participants in the power transfer is willing. One to give and one to receive." Poppy then opened her eyes and looked around the circle. "Witches of the circle, is this true and accurate?"

"It is," we all answered in unison.

"Great spirit keepers, we further attest that the witch to receive the powers has yet to see sunset on her eighteenth birthday and has yet to possess her own witchly powers through no fault of her own," said Daphne. She looked at Jax. "Is this true?"

"It is," said Jax.

"Through the divine witch's prophecy, it is so requested that SaraLynn Stone pass along her magical witchly powers to her heir, JaclynRose Stone," added Elodie Goodwitch.

Gemma opened her eyes and looked at Sorceress Stone. "SaraLynn Stone, we ask that you answer the call of the spirit keepers. Is it your will that your daughter JaclynRose Stone is to receive your powers, magical abilities, and witchly prowess?"

Sorceress Stone bowed her head. "It is."

"JaclynRose Stone, we ask that you answer the call of the spirit keepers. Is it your will to receive the powers, magical abilities, and witchly prowess currently possessed by your mother, SaraLynn Stone?"

Jax did as her mother had done and bowed her head. "It is."

Then, in unison, the four Great Witch's chanted, "Spirit keepers, we ask that you release the witchly powers possessed by SaraLynn Stone and pass them to her heir, JaclynRose Stone. Let the binding transfer of power be irrevocable and unbreakable by the will of any outside magical force."

The members of the Council then closed their eyes, and we listened to the wind blowing around us. It was as if the spirit keepers were speaking to them through nature. After what seemed like an unending silence, they all opened their eyes in unison and stared at Sorceress Stone and Jax.

"By the powers vested in each of us by both the great spirit keepers and our own divine energy, we hereby grant your legacy power transfer request. By the will of you, the spirits, and the good faith of each of the witches before us today, *so mote it be!*"

A flash of lightning ripped through the sky, tearing the air apart in a blinding flash of light. It struck the stage between the two women, sending electrically charged currents into each of them. Sparks flew where Jax and her mother were connected at the fingertips. Jax's spiky green hair discharged sparks of electricity, as did Sorceress Stone's hair. Jax's body took on a faintly glowing aura. Sorceress Stone seemed to visibly wilt in size and stature.

And then, as if it had never been there, the lightning and the wind disappeared, and all that was left in the middle of the circle was SaraLynn Stone and her daughter.

"Jax?" I said, cautiously breaking the silence. "Are you alright?"

Jax pulled her fingertips away from her mother's and looked down at them in awe. "They tingle," she whispered.

I couldn't stop the smile from spreading across my face. "Jax, that's what magic feels like."

"It is?" she asked, looking up at me hopefully.

Her mother nodded. "It is. Happy eighteenth birthday, JaclynRose. I love you."

Jax threw her arms around her mother and squeezed. "Thanks, Mom. I love you too. Happy Mother's Day!"

a huge bonfire crackled brightly, illuminating the night sky. Lanterns and white Christmas lights were strung from trees, and picnic tables dotted the grassy landscape. Graduates, first-year students, whiz kids, and a few handfuls of family members littered the area, clinging to red Solo cups and laughing away the last few hours of graduation day.

I'd been to a few other parties while attending the Institute, but this was the biggest. I wasn't sure if it was the warmth of the party atmosphere, or knowing that I was only two days away from completing my first year of witch school, or knowing that I knew I wouldn't have to deal with Sorceress Stone anymore next year, *or* if it was simply the realization that my best friend was now officially a witch, but something had me feeling more relaxed and at ease than I'd felt in probably a few years.

A warm breeze caressed my cheeks as Alba and I leaned against the trunk of an old oak tree, watching Holly, Sweets, and Reign trying to teach Jax how to use her magic. While she knew it was there, she hadn't quite figured out how to make it work for her yet. Only her hands, arms, and fingers tingled with unspent electricity. Her mother had walked away powerless and happy for her daughter. It had been a bittersweet ending, but for once, I felt like SaraLynn Stone might truly become the mother that Jax had always wanted her to be. And maybe it wasn't an ending after all. Maybe it was just the beginning of their new mother-daughter relationship.

With her back and one foot against the tree trunk, Alba shook her head. "No, no, no. Don't teach her to do it like that. Ugh," she groaned as she shoved herself forward. "Don't listen to these fools, Shorty. I'll show you how to do it."

I laughed as I watched them all having fun together, and a sentimental feeling washed over me. I didn't want the night to end. I didn't want our time together to end. I wanted to be this happy and contented forever.

"Hey, Mercy Mae," said a low rumble of a voice behind me.

My breathing stopped for a split second, and then my heart rate picked up in double time. *Hugh.*

"Hey." Trying to appear calm, I looked over my shoulder at him.

"Mind if I join you for a minute?"

"Of course I don't mind. How've you been?"

Hugh took Alba's spot next to me. His woodsy scent was comforting and familiar—like the way the air smelled after rain. Leaning back against the trunk of the tree, he pulled his cowboy hat off and held it down by his side, revealing a tousled mess of sandy blond curls. It looked like he hadn't had a haircut in a while. I kinda liked it.

"I've been alright. Busy with finals."

I lifted my brow. "Finals? Finals don't start until tomorrow."

"I might have schmoozed a few of my teachers into giving them to me early," he admitted with a half-smile. "I got a summer job lined up, and I promised I'd start beginning of the week. I couldn't stick around any longer even if I wanted to."

"Wow, don't tell Alba and Holly that. They both had plane tickets. Alba would flip if she knew you managed to get your finals done."

Hugh pretended to zip his mouth shut. "I won't tell a soul."

I smiled at him. He sure was cute. "Thanks."

"So what are your summer plans?"

I shrugged. "I really don't have any plans. I figured I'd work at the B&B, help Mom and Reign out. You know, earn my keep a little."

"Attagirl," he said, leaning into me to give me a gentle bump with his shoulder.

"How about you? What summer job did you get?"

"Ranch hand. A friend of the family back home had an accident and is laid up for the next six months or so. I said I'd be happy to step in and help the family out."

I lifted my brows. "Six months?! Hugh! What about school in the fall?"

He shrugged. "To be honest, I don't know if school is my thing. I miss Sonny and my family. And really, there's not much here for me."

I looked down at my Converse sneakers. After all the tromping around on grass over the past week, they were now tinted green. I swallowed hard. "You've got me."

Still leaning against the tree trunk, Hugh rolled sideways so he was resting on one shoulder. He looked directly into my eyes. "Except I don't have you anymore, now do I?"

My heart stopped beating for a split second. My mouth went dry. I swallowed hard and had to blink a few times to catch myself. "I mean, we'll always be friends. Won't we?"

"I have a lot of friends, Mercy Mae."

My heart dropped into the pit of my stomach. "So you're saying you don't need another one?"

He stood up straight then and swatted the air beside him with his hat. "Dammit, Mercy Mae, I don't need another *friend*. I need my best girl! I need *you!*" He dropped his cowboy hat on the ground then, and before I knew what was happening, his calloused hands clamped around my jaw and drew me in so he could plant a mammoth-sized kiss on my lips.

Feeling the familiar warm tenderness of his lips against mine, I slumped into him. The kiss felt good. It felt *right*. I kissed him back, matching his passion and wishing that the liplock would never end.

"Oh, gross, get a room," snapped Alba.

Alba's voice tore us from our little bubble. Hugh and I parted. He looked down at me with a million unsaid words glistening in his eyes, and I suddenly felt like I could read each and every one of them.

"Is it alright if I write you letters this summer?" he asked, ignoring Alba.

And suddenly, I felt this need to be connected to him more than just through an occasional letter. "Or you could text me," I suggested with a shrug.

"I'm not much of a texter. You know me. I've got sausage-finger syndrome," he chuckled. "But I'd like to write you."

I nodded at him. "You can write me."

"Will you write me back?"

"I'll try. My handwriting kind of sucks."

"I'm sure mine is worse, darlin'."

I grinned. "Probably not, but I'd love to keep in touch."

"You would?" Hope filled his eyes.

"I mean, yeah. I wanna know you're doing alright."

Hugh wrapped his arms around my shoulders. With my head pressed against his chest, I heard his heart beating. "I'm gonna miss you this summer."

"I'll miss you too, Hugh." And somehow I knew I meant it.

He kissed my forehead and took a step back. "I gotta go," he whispered. "My truck's all packed up and ready. I'm gonna drive through the night. I just couldn't leave without saying goodbye."

"But it's not forever, right? Promise me I'll see you again."

"If it's meant to be, you'll see me again, I promise you that. Bye, Mercy Mae."

I waved at him as he walked away. "Bye, Hugh. Drive safe! Text me when you get there, at least. So I know you made it alright." As he disappeared into the darkness, I suddenly felt alone. I wondered if I'd ever see him again.

Holly threw an arm around me then. "It'll be alright, Mercy."

I leaned my head on her shoulder. "Why do I have this feeling I'll never see him again?"

"You'll see him again," she said confidently.

"You think?"

She nodded. "I don't think. I know." She tapped her finger against her temples. "I'm clairvoyant, remember? Come on. Libby and Cinder are taking off. Their flight leaves first thing in the morning, so they're going to get a hotel next to the airport tonight."

Holly led me to the crowd of people gathered around the Fire and Ice twins. They were hugging and saying goodbye to all their friends. I used my magic to push people aside so I could get through the crowd faster.

"Libby," I said, "I'm sure going to miss you and your icy ways."

Libby smiled at me. "I'll miss you too, Mercy. You've got a tough year ahead of you. I wish you the best of luck."

"Me? My last year of witch college can't compare with your year. You have to find a job! And become an *adult*. That sounds way harder."

Libby laughed and gave me a hug. Then I turned to her sister.

"Cin, thanks for everything. You're an awesome chick."

Cinder lifted an eyebrow. "You're an awesome chick too," she said in her cute little accent. "Thank you for including my sister and me in everything this week. It was a great way to end our time here."

"Yeah, it was," I said, nodding. I gave her a hug.

"Now, keep that one in line," she said, pointing at Alba. "She can be a little mouthy."

"Don't we know it," I said with a laugh. "Don't worry.

We all keep her in line. Our friendship is all about checks and balances."

"Good."

"Come on, Cin," said Libby. "We better get going."

"Bye, girls," said Sweets, giving them a wave as they pushed through the crowd.

When they were gone, the five of us and Reign found ourselves seated at a picnic table away from the crazy chaos and noise of the party.

"Can you believe Libby and Cinder are *done* with school?" said Holly, leaning her chin onto her hand dreamily. "I'm so jealous."

With her hands clamped together in front of her, Jax squeezed her shoulders forward. "Eee, not me! I can't wait to start school in the fall! I am *dying* to learn to use my magic!"

Alba shook her head. "Why do I have a sneaking suspicion that you're gonna be even more annoying next year than you already are?"

"Alba!" said Sweets. "Don't say things like that! And it's Jax's birthday on top of it. You have to be extra nice on someone's birthday."

Alba grimaced. "Eh. Sorry, Shorty. I was only joking. You'll be alright."

"Thanks, Alba," said Jax with a sheepish grin.

"Hey, speaking of birthdays," I said, glancing over at Alba and Holly. "I'm pretty sure we've got something special for you."

Jax sucked in her breath and lifted her brows. "You do?! I already got the best two presents I could ever ask for! My mother is alive and I have magic!"

"Yeah, this is on a *slightly* smaller scale," I said, pinching my fingers together. I nodded at Alba and Holly.

The two of them snapped their fingers, and out of nowhere appeared a pink-and-purple unicorn birthday cake. The gold spiral unicorn horn was a candle, and after conjuring the cake, Alba snapped her fingers again and magically lit the horn.

"Omigosh!" squealed Jax. "A unicorn birthday cake! I can't handle the cuteness!"

We laughed.

Reign started us out by singing the first words of the birthday song, and we all joined in.

When it was over, Jax closed her eyes to make a wish and then promptly reopened them. "I don't even know what to wish for now. The only wish I've ever made on a birthday candle was to be a witch." Her eyes grew damp again. "Thank you all for making my eighteenth birthday so special. I'm never going to forget everything you've done for me." She threw her arms around Reign and Holly and squeezed. "Bring it in, girls."

"Group hug!" said Sweets, joining in on the hug.

Feeling sentimental and centered, I joined in too. I looked over at Alba, who sat staring at us uncomfortably. "Oh, come on, Alba. You can make an exception to the no-hugging rule just this once. You have to admit, this is a pretty big day."

Alba rolled her head back on her shoulders and groaned. "Ugh! Oh, fine! But I can promise you, I'm not gonna like it!"

I welcomed her into the huddle. "After all, days like this don't happen every day. Jax finally became a witch!"

*J*ax, Alba, Holly, and I piled out of my little beater car and into Habernackle's B&B late Thursday afternoon. We'd stuck around just until Brittany Hobbs finally posted the pass/fail lists on the bulletin board outside her office.

"Finally," grumbled Alba. "Now I can *finally* pack up my stuff and go home!"

"You were worried or something?" asked Holly.

"No, I wasn't worried. I knew I was gonna pass. I just didn't wanna leave until I saw it with my own eyes. There'd be nothing worse than telling Pops I passed, only to get my report card in the mail and find out I didn't."

I plopped down on one of the barstools and let my head drop onto my crossed arms. "I don't know about you guys, but I think I'm going to sleep hard for the next two days. This has been *such* a stressful year, and I'm exhausted."

Holly nodded. "I agree. I'm even thinking about waiting a day or two before getting my plane tickets home. I could use the break."

I looked over at Jax. She was sitting with her palms resting calmly on the countertop. She'd hardly said a word after seeing the final results posted. "Jax. You okay?"

"Yeah, I'm okay," she said.

"What's the matter with her? She in shock or something?" asked Alba.

"Must be," said Holly. She put both hands to her stomach as a loud gurgling noise let out. "Oh my gosh, can we make something to eat? I'm starving."

"Yeah, me too," I agreed, just as my mom, Reign, and Sweets pushed through the swinging kitchen doors.

"Hi, girls," said my mom brightly.

"You're back! Finally! I never beat you home," said Sweets, a big smile on her face.

"Yeah, what's up?" asked Reign, looking at his watch. "We thought you would've been here hours ago."

"It took Hobbs forever to post the results. There was no way I was leaving until we got 'em, though," said Alba.

With her hands clasped by her chest expectantly, Sweets looked from face to face. "Well? How'd everyone do?"

"Pass," said Alba. "Easy peasy. I wasn't worried."

Holly rolled her eyes. "Sure, you weren't. I passed too."

I nodded and looked at Mom across the bar. "Me too. Thank God. I really didn't want to have to retake first year."

Mom rushed around the counter to hug me. "Oh! Mercy Bear! I'm so proud of you!" She patted Holly's shoulder. "I'm proud of all of you girls."

Everyone looked at Jax.

"Well?" said Reign. "What about you, Nugget? You pass too?"

Hearing Reign address her seemed to tear Jax out of her daze. "Oh. No. I didn't pass."

Reign looked stunned. "Get out of here. Even with your new powers you didn't pass?"

"Oh, Jax," breathed my mom, putting her arm around Jax's shoulders.

Jax bit her lips together. "I couldn't make my powers work."

Alba patted Jax on the back. "Meh. Don't get your panties in a knot. Sometimes it takes a little time, that's all. I'm not surprised you're having problems, to tell you the truth. It took me years to figure out how to make mine work like I wanted 'em to."

Jax looked up at Alba hopefully. "It did?"

Alba nodded. "Are you kidding me? Absolutely. Using magic is like riding a bike. Once you get it, you get it, but it takes a while to get your bearings straight, and sometimes you gotta use kid wheels to get started. Ya know?"

"Alba's right," agreed Reign. "Mine took a while too. So what if you have to retake your first year?"

"Yeah, Jaxie. It'll be okay. At least you've got your powers now, and we're all together. That's all that matters anyway," said Sweets. "Right?"

Jax smiled. "Right."

The doorbell behind us chimed. When we turned, I think all of us were shocked to see Merrick Stone stride in.

"Dad, what are you doing here?"

"I need to speak with you and your mother for a moment. It's somewhat urgent." Merrick looked over at the group of us seated at the bar. "Is there somewhere we can go to speak privately?"

Mom nodded and gestured towards the kitchen. "Of course. Girls, can you please keep an eye on the dining room? Merrick…right this way."

47

"So, what's going on?" Reign asked his father as he jumped up to sit on the stainless-steel countertop in the kitchen.

Linda nodded. "Yes, Merrick. You're worrying me. Has something happened?"

Merrick propped himself up against the commercial refrigerator with one hand. "I assume you've heard about everything that happened with my sister?"

Reign lowered his head. Even though he'd had a firsthand account of everything that had happened to Sara-Lynn, he hadn't thought it right to share *every* detail with his mother. If Mercy wanted to, that was her prerogative, but Reign wasn't one to spread information like that.

Linda frowned. "I mean, I heard she'd given her powers to Jax. Mercy said you and your sisters have a half-sister you didn't know about. Stella Blackwood?"

Merrick sighed. "Yes, I guess so. I had no idea. Samson wasn't in our lives after my parents separated, so there would've been no way for us children to know."

Linda sighed and reached a hand out to touch Merrick's forearm. "I also know that Stella tried to kill SaraLynn. I understand it was the Great Witches Council that brought her back to life. I'm so sorry, Merrick."

"Yes. That's all true. Is it safe to assume you've heard the rest?"

Linda shook her head. "The rest? The part about SaraLynn leaving the Institute?" Linda looked down at her hands. "Yes, I heard that part as well."

Reign wasn't surprised that Mercy had told their mother everything. It was obvious they had a pretty close relationship. He could only hope that he and his father and mother could have that kind of relationship one day. His relationship with Linda was progressing along nicely, but his relationship with Merrick wasn't as fluid as he would have liked.

Merrick sighed. "Yes. It's unfortunate. I know the Institute was SaraLynn's life. Mine as well."

"Surely that's not true…"

"It is, Linda. SaraLynn and I have put everything we've had into our magic careers. Neither of us have been very good parents. Of course I didn't know about Reign until recently, but perhaps even if I'd been in his life, I might not have made a very good father anyway."

"Merrick, you can't know that!" breathed Linda. "I'm sure you would've made an excellent father. Luckily you still have that opportunity."

Merrick looked across the room at Reign. Something in his father's face told Reign that the news he was about to hear would challenge that statement. "Maybe. Unfortunately, I've made a very difficult decision, which will make fatherhood that much more difficult. Linda, Reign, I've decided to leave town with my sister."

"Leave town?!" said Reign, jumping off the counter. "You can't be serious!"

"I'm very sorry, son. I know we were only starting to get to know one another, but I admit that it's a selfish reason I have for wanting to go."

"Selfish?" asked Linda.

He nodded. "I don't think you understand how difficult it's been for me to know you're here, but also know that you're with someone else. I thought I could handle it, but knowing that you're so close and yet we can't be together... well, it's become my own private hell on earth."

Linda's brows knitted together. "Oh, Merrick..."

"And I know I can't move on with my life until I get far enough away that I can't feel your energy every waking moment. Because I can feel it now. You know? Even as far away as our houses are, I can feel it." He looked over at Reign then. "And I know that's not fair to you, son. I want nothing more than for us to form a bond, but I can't do it this close to your mother. There's too much history there, and too much regret."

Reign sighed. He understood history and regret as much as anyone. But he had a hard time understanding how his father could voluntarily leave after finally finding his son. "I wish you'd reconsider."

"I'm sorry," whispered Merrick. "The movers have already packed our things. SaraLynn, BethAnn, and I are all leaving together."

"Where will you go?" asked Linda.

"We're not sure yet. Hopefully the spirits will guide us to our destined direction."

"I'm sorry things didn't work out between us, Merrick."

"I know. I'm sorry, too, Linda. Believe me. It haunts me to this day."

Linda walked around the counter and gave Merrick a hug.

Reign watched his mother and father hug one last time and wondered if he'd ever see his parents unified like that again. The feeling raked across his heart.

Merrick walked over to Reign who couldn't seem to get his legs to work. "Goodbye, son. I hope once I get settled, you'll come visit me."

Reign began to speak but found a hoarseness there that hadn't been there only moments ago. He cleared his throat. "I'm sure I will."

"Good." Merrick clapped Reign on the back and then stood back. He gave a little wave, leaving an awkward silence between the three of them.

Finally, Linda stepped forward. "Can I walk you out, Merrick?"

"Of course."

Linda shot Reign a tight smile as she led Merrick out of the kitchen, but Reign couldn't quite manage a smile. While he was old enough to know that his parents would never be together, he'd enjoyed having them both in the same town as he was. That way, he could get to know them both over time and let their relationships unfold naturally. Now he'd have to schedule awkward trips to see his father and aunts. Things would be stiff and uncomfortable, and he wouldn't be able to just head home for a break when those times happened.

As he sank to the kitchen's tile floor, his jaw clenched tighter. A piece of the anger that he'd had all through his childhood seemed to rear its ugly head again. It had been a while.

He heard the swinging doors make their familiar swooshing sound, and his head snapped sideways to see Holly bursting through them with a rush of bright-lighted energy. She walked around the counter and looked down at Reign just in time to catch the set jawline and seething red glow of anger covering his face.

"Reign," she said with surprise. "I'm sorry if I interrupted something. I thought you guys were done in here. I was just going to get something to eat. I'm starving."

"It's fine," he growled through gritted teeth.

Holly walked over to him, her head cocked sideways. "Is everything alright?"

"Yeah."

She frowned. "Everything doesn't look alright. What's wrong?"

He was quiet for a moment. He hadn't let the anger he'd grown up with rise to the surface very often since he'd come to Aspen Falls. He'd put too much effort into connecting with his family and building his business to let that happen. Anytime he'd felt that anger bubble up, he was quick to squash it back down again. He tried once again to push that anger down. "I'm fine," he said, this time a little more calmly.

"What happened with your dad?"

Reign looked up at Holly. She wore a crinkly white blouse that laced up the front. Her bright blue eyes looked down at him intently, and the fluorescent light of the kitchen illuminated her blond hair, giving her an almost angelic glow. And in that moment, the vixen of his sister's friend group looked sweet and innocent. He knew she wanted to look sexy, but all he could see was a sweet and innocent angel sent to him at exactly the right moment. The moment he needed someone.

Reign reached up and grabbed hold of her wrist as he climbed to his knees on the floor. Hugging himself to her chest, he squeezed her tightly as if he were being pulled down by quicksand and she was his only savior.

Holly seemed to be caught off guard at first, but slowly, she put her hands over his head. Gently, she stroked his hair and allowed him to just hold her. "It's going to be okay," she crooned. "I promise, Reign. I can sense it. Everything is going to be okay."

Something about her touch seemed to calm him. He felt his heart rate returning to normal. His breathing began to regulate back to normal. Slowly, he looked up at her. She looked down at him so lovingly that he was drawn to her. Still on his knees, he reached a hand up and snaked it through the back of her hair. His eyes were transfixed on the soft curves of her pillowy lips. He couldn't tear his eyes away from them.

He began to pull her head down towards him, but the sound of the swinging kitchen doors let out their familiar squeak again. "Reign, are you alright?"

Reign's eyes popped open and his hand reeled back. Holly's eyes interlocked with his for a split second before Reign leapt to his feet. "Mom! Yeah, I—I'm fine." He swallowed hard, looking over at Holly.

Holly's eyes were wide and filled with shock and

surprise. He could only imagine what she was thinking. Holly gave Linda a tight smile. "I was just looking for something to eat. We didn't eat all day."

"Oh, I have dinner in the oven. If you want to go help the girls set the table, I'll bring it right out."

Holly nodded. She glanced at Reign for only a brief moment before making a beeline for the dining room.

When she was gone, Linda looked over at Reign. "You sure you're alright?"

Reign's heart raced in his chest. He wasn't sure if it was because he was about to lose his father again or if it was the moment that he'd just had with Holly. "I don't know, Mom. To be honest, I'm kinda feeling shook right now."

Linda put her arms around Reign, engulfing him in a hug. "Don't worry, sweetie. It'll all work out in the end. I promise."

---

*A*fter dinner, the five members of the Witch Squad looked at each other.

I shook my head. "I don't know, you guys. This school year started out with so many uncertainties. I can't believe that we're finally where we are today."

"In the B&B?" asked Jax, quirking her head to the side.

"No! In life! I mean, for starters, who knew we'd all still be friends?"

Probably the most surprised out of all of us, Alba nodded. "Yeah, no kidding. There's no way I would've guessed that the five of us would still be hanging out together. You're not exactly the normal kind of people I'd hang out with back home."

Holly snuffed air out her nose. "You can say that again!"

"And who would've thought that *Sweets* would've dropped out of witch college!" I said.

Sweets raised her brows. "I certainly didn't think that was going to happen when I started."

"None of us did!"

"And when I think back to my witchy little room-mate," I continued, shaking my head, "there's no way I would have ever guessed that *she* wasn't a witch. But now look at her, she's a real witch. Granted, she didn't pass her first year of witch school…"

"Hey!" screeched Jax.

"Kidding," I said with a smile.

Jax giggled. "Yeah, me too."

"But the fact of the matter is, we made it to the other side together. We're still friends!"

"Yeah, we did," agreed Alba. "I guess that's cool."

"You guess? I hardly had any friends in my whole life, and to walk away from the first year of witch school with *four* friends? I'm in awe."

"Hey, guys, we should do something to celebrate," said Holly with a huge smile on her face.

"Celebrate what? We haven't graduated yet," said Alba.

"Not celebrate school. Celebrate our friendship."

"Oooh, that sounds fun! What should we do?" asked Jax.

Holly shrugged. "I don't know. Like go on a trip together or something."

Alba shook her head. "Nah. I don't have the money for a trip. I lost out on the airline tickets I'd booked for this week. Of course they were nonrefundable, so now I gotta shell out another couple hundred bucks to rebook. Plus my brother's getting married in a week and a half, so I really gotta get back to Jersey for the wedding."

"Yeah, and I just took off a *ton* of days at the bakery," said Sweets. "I don't think I can go anywhere either."

"Oh, come on, girls. I'm not talking about going far." Holly's eyes lit up excitedly. "Hey, I've got the *perfect* idea. Oh man, you girls are going to love this. What if we drove Alba home."

"What?" asked Alba curling her lip. "All the way to Jersey?"

"Yeah!" said Holly. "We're in Pennsylvania. It can't be that far. We'll take you home, and then we'll drive back. I bet we could do it in a three-day weekend. Sweets, you could get at least *one* more day off from the bakery, can't you?"

Sweets lifted a shoulder. "I mean, I don't know. Actually... now that I think about it, Char did say we were going to be closed for Memorial weekend. I think that included Monday."

Holly smiled. "Perfect!"

Alba shook her head. "Naw, I gotta be back by Memorial Day. That's Vinnie's wedding day."

"Well, duh. We'd have you back by then. We could leave when Sweets gets off work on Friday night. Shoot, we'd probably be in New Jersey by Friday or Saturday. You'd have plenty of time to get to the wedding."

Jax's eyes lit up. "Are you serious right now? A girls' road trip?"

Holly shook her head. "No, I mean a *witches'* road trip."

Jax nearly couldn't contain herself. "Ahhh!" she squealed, leaping up off her chair. "*Even better*! I am so totally in!"

Sweets giggled. "Yeah, I'm sure I can make it work. I'm in."

Holly looked at Alba. "Alba, come on. Think of all the money you'd be saving. You wouldn't have to buy new airline tickets now. And no sitting on a stuffy plane with a bunch of sweaty men."

Alba lifted a brow. She seemed to like the sound of that. "Yeah. I guess I could handle that. As long as we make it there in time for me to go to the wedding."

Everyone looked at me then. Jax pleaded silently with her eyes. Holly blinked up at me expectantly. Sweets looked excited by the idea, and Alba looked like she was ready to save a few hundred dollars.

"Well, what do you think, Mercy?" asked Holly.

I didn't even have to think about it. I smiled at my friends. "Are you kidding? A road trip with my witches? Yeah, I'm in. I'm definitely in!"

ALSO BY M.Z. ANDREWS

Have you read all the books in the Witch Squad series?

Book 1: The Witch Squad

Book 2: Son of a Witch

Book 3: Witch Degrees of Separation

Book 4: Witch Pie

Book 5: A Very Mercy Christmas

Book 6: Where Witches Lie

Book 7: Witch School Dropout

Book 7.5: Witch, Please!

Book 8: The Witch Within

Have you read my Spin-Off Series also set in Aspen Falls, PA?

Book 1: That Old Witch!

Book 1.5: Hazel Raises the Stakes

Book 2: That Crazy Witch!

Mystic Snow Globe Romantic Mystery Series:

Prequel: Deal or Snow Deal

Book 1: Snow Cold Case

ABOUT THE AUTHOR

I am a lifelong writer of words. I have a wonderful husband, whom I adore, and we have four daughters and two sons. Four of our children are grown or in college and two still live at home. Our family resides in the midwest United States.

Aside from writing, I'm especially fond of gardening and canning salsa and other things from our homegrown produce. I adore Pinterest, and our family loves fall and KC Chiefs football games.

If you enjoyed the book, the best compliment is to leave a review - even if it's as simple as a few words - I tremendously value your feedback!

Also, please consider joining my newsletter. I don't send one out often - only when there's a new book coming out or a sale of some type that I think you might enjoy.

All the best,
M.Z.

Follow me at:
www.mzandrews.com

13054756R00288

Made in the USA
Middletown, DE
16 November 2018